ASSISTING FATE

autolemy®

A True-to-Life Musical Fiction

First published in Great Britain in 2025 by AU Recordings & Publishing Limited.

First impression

A CIP catalogue record is available from the British Library

ISBN (Hardback) 978-1-7399618-1-7

ISBN (e-Book) 978-1-7399618-3-1

ASSISTING FATE ALBUM

01 LET ME GO (Ft. Drew Tyler)
02 BE SOMEONE (Ft. Deza)
03 TELL THE WORLD ABOUT YOU (Ft. Teerare/Drew Tyler)
04 I'M A PSYCHO NOW (Ft. Hamza Zalach)
05 AND I WONDER (Ft. Cass Beg)
06 5:50 AM
07 ANOTHER LIGHT (Ft. Kris Lindstrom)
08 GIVEN UP (Ft. Drew Tyler)
09 IN FRONT OF ME (Ft. Trippz Michaud)

BONUS TRACKS
10 TELL THE WORLD ABOUT YOU (Instrumental)
11 AND I WONDER (Instrumental)
12 ANOTHER LIGHT (Instrumental)
13 GIVEN UP (Instrumental)
14 IN FRONT OF ME (Instrumental)

I would also like to thank the following people who contributed to this album: Arman Petrosyan, Morgane Matteuzzi, Paola Barba, Martin D'Alesio, Steve Turner, Harken Audio, Antonio D'Amato & Jonah Krull.

All songs written & arranged by autolemy® - Produced by autolemy® & Jedidiah Allcock
Mixed & mastered by Matt Bishop.
Recordings licenced to AU Recordings & Publishing Limited 2025 - www.aurecordings.co.uk
Published by AU Recordings & Publishing Limited 2025 - www.aupublishing.co.uk

For more information and licensing opportunities, please contact -
email: info@aurecordings.com
Telephone: +44 (0) 7761 760419

"Never interrupt your enemy when they are making a mistake."

- Napoléon Bonaparte

RECAP

Dear Reader,

In my first book, *Say Goodbye*, Lee Walker's family life had deteriorated to the point where he'd been completely abandoned, thanks mostly to the scheming of his mother and sister. But Lee felt that his father hadn't done enough to keep him either, so he ran away from his dire situation at the age of seven.

In the first story, I also highlighted how technology had yet to really permeate people's everyday lives. Tills in shops were mechanical, there were no cash machines to withdraw money from, letters had to be physically posted, and pretty much everything needed to be done in person or by appointment. Telephone calls outside of the home needed to be paid for there and then, and reverse charges were horrendously expensive... a far cry from today's world.

This is the second book in the Walker-Powell series, beginning exactly where *Say Goodbye* left off, with Lee sat in a plush restaurant in West London between his nan and the chief of MI6.

In line with my signature approach, every installment in this trilogy is accompanied by a new album featuring original, multi-genre compositions that delve deep into the thematic essence of pivotal chapters. More information about each song can be found at the end of the story.

I hope you enjoy the continuation of sound and thought.

autolemy

PART 4

(February 1978 – March 1978)

CHAPTER 25

IDENTITY

Lee sat quietly between Nancy and The Chief, weighing up the choice he was about to make. He thought back to the decision to run away last year, breaking and entering into shops, escaping the French police cell, stealing the gun, nearly killing himself as he jumped from the bridge in Ancenis and shooting two people in Paris. He no longer felt like a seven-year-old having made huge life-changing decisions by himself. He thought about what life would be like if he went back to live with his dad. He loved his father immensely and any good memories of the family always included him. But Lee also knew that he could be weak. In his opinion, David should never have left home and instead should've kicked out that no-good wife who'd ruined all of their lives. He'd also spent most of his time at work to get the management promotion and Lee wondered if this would ever change. As he weighed up the choice, he realised that his dad probably couldn't be counted on when he needed him. Lee also figured that he could always contact or see David at a later time without anyone knowing. The new life he was being offered would open doors he could never have imagined possible six minutes ago, let alone six months ago. As he caught a glimpse of his reflection in the glass partition behind The Chief, Lee scratched his thick blond hair – a reminder of how different he was to the rest of the family. He had one more question to ask his nan before making his final decision.

"Who am I, Nan?"

Nancy gave a questioning look at Lee. So far, she felt that she'd been the only person left in his life who could be trusted. There was nothing to be gained by lying to him now, and she certainly didn't want to betray his trust at this crucial time. *How did he find out?* she thought. "What makes you ask?"

"Before I was sent to the home, Mum told me I wasn't her child. And besides – I look different from everyone else in the family."

Nancy sighed and asked The Chief if he wouldn't mind giving them both some time by themselves. He looked at Nancy and happily obliged – leaving the restaurant table to stand outside for a short while. Once alone, Nancy chose her words carefully.

"Before I tell you what I'm going to tell you, please don't judge anyone too harshly, we just tried to do the best we could – especially for you." Lee nodded and ate a spoonful of ice cream from his pudding. "David had been driving home from the pub one afternoon a little too fast and collided head on with another car along a country lane. There was a woman and a small child in the other car. That was you and your real mother." Nancy paused. "I'm sorry, Lee, but your mother died there and then at the scene of the accident. Miraculously, you survived with minor injuries." Nancy gently caressed her finger along a small scar on Lee's forehead. "You were about ten months old at the time." Nancy held on to Lee's hand. "There was no-one on the road at the time and David panicked. He knew that if he went to the police he'd be arrested and probably put in prison for drunk-driving, but he couldn't bear to just leave you there. You could've died if there was a fire or something, so, he pulled you from the wreckage and brought you home." Lee gave a questioning frown. "I know it was stupid," she said with a raised eyebrow. "Anyway, David and Louvaine had been trying for another baby and wanted a baby boy, as they already had Laura. With the best intentions they agreed to take you in, but really hadn't thought about the consequences. Try to remember that your dad was only about twenty-seven. His career was just beginning to show prospects at the time and he really didn't want to go to prison. As you can imagine, I was pretty furious with him for putting the whole family into a precarious position. If you think about it, David and Louvaine could've been sent to prison which would've resulted in Laura being put up for adoption."

"I wish she had been," Lee scoffed quietly.

"I know she's not been the nicest sister to you, but you'll have to trust me when I say that we really did just want the best for you at the time. There's more to the story so I want you to be fully informed before making any decision. There was a huge police appeal for witnesses to the accident. The paper mentioned the woman's parents and where they lived, but strangely, there was no mention of a child at all. When David and Louvaine came to their senses, they went round to your real mother's parents to say that they'd found you abandoned. The whole thing was very odd. The grandparents didn't ask any questions and initially denied your existence. They just didn't want you."

Lee sighed. *More people that didn't want me.*

"From what we could gather," Nancy continued, "the daughter had been stigmatised by having a child out of wedlock which was against her family's strict religious values. They'd actually declared their own daughter an outcast. With some significant help from a friendly chief inspector and the family's agreement, David and Louvaine took you in as their own. Within a few weeks the adoption papers were signed and you were given a new Birth Certificate." Nancy paused to let Lee take it all in. "In answer to what I expect is your next question, your original name was Joseph Merry. But I think Lee's much more butch, don't you?" she said with a smile. Lee smiled back... *She's right!* "And that, my 'not so little' detective, is how you became part of the Walker family. If it's any consolation to you, I know that your dad still has problems with it to this day."

Nancy looked at Lee as he relaxed his shoulders, trying to gauge his reaction, but he remained stoic. She motioned subtly for The Chief to come back to the table.

Lee thought about his father again and decided not to think too harshly of him – the man had saved his life, after all.

"So, do you feel that you're able to make a decision, Lee?" The Chief said, as he sat back down and looked at them both individually.

"Yes, I'll do it," he said enthusiastically. The Chief looked at Nancy and smiled, as she put a reassuring arm around Lee whilst he finished his pudding. He paid the bill and ordered a taxi to take them all to Century House.

* * *

The Chief had a big office on the 11th floor. His assistant greeted him and Nancy as they walked through the outer office, but looked surprised when she saw the young boy. She immediately knew who it was from the photographs Nancy had given her during the search in France.

"So this is the crafty little warrior we were after?" she said, praising the young boy. "Glad you're back home and safe." She smiled as she spoke. Lee gave a half-embarrassed smile back as the three entered the inner office and The Chief closed the door.

The Chief began to write an itemised list of things on a large whiteboard with a black pen, the complete opposite to the blackboards Lee was used to at school.

"I think that about covers the first stages. Is there anything I've missed?" he said, turning to Nancy.

"No, that's what I had in mind too."

The Chief then turned his attention to Lee. "So, Lee, I'm going to walk you through the initial stages of what my proposal entails. Once we've talked it through, I will ask you again if you want to go ahead with this – it's a life-changing decision you're making, after all. Does that seem fair?"

"Sure." Lee had already read through the man's list as he was writing it down.

"OK, let's start at the beginning. Firstly, we're going to have to change your name. I'm sure you'll understand why Lee Walker can no longer exist?" Lee nodded. "I have a family in mind for you who will act as your guardians. Their surnames are Powell, how does Lee Powell sound to you?" The Chief looked at Nancy. "I don't see any reason to change his first name, do you?"

"No, not unless Lee wants to?" she said, looking at her grandson.

Lee thought for a while. He quite liked Robert Powell from the *Jesus of Nazareth* series, so why not.

"Sounds fine with me," Lee said. The Chief wrote 'Lee Powell' on the whiteboard in red as Lee began repeating *Powell... Powell... Powell* over in his head.

"OK, so back to family and accommodation. I'm not expecting this to be easy for you but the couple I have spoken with have said they'd be prepared to give things a go if you are. My suggestion would be that we treat this as temporary to see how you all get on with each other and go from there. The cover will be that they've taken you into foster care for now. Would that work for you?"

Lee frowned. He knew from experience that being a foster child was not exactly going to be easy to live with – especially in school. "Do they have other children?" he asked.

"That's the good thing, Lee – you'd be their only child. Unfortunately they're unable to have children, so they were looking to foster anyway."

Lee felt a little relieved, and smiled. But inside he felt a little out of control. All these decisions about his life and future were being made so quickly.

"I will just say that this will not be an excuse to try and manipulate them or behave badly. We don't have an endless supply of parents and if this didn't work out, there's no guarantee where you'd be housed next – if at all!" The Chief wanted to draw an authority line for Lee early on. "It's going to need some give and take from everyone. Do you think you could go along with that?"

It seemed to Lee that the art of being in control as an adult was the ability to make decisions quickly. He wanted to be decisive, just as like his Nan and The Chief. The four clocks mounted on the office wall that read New York, London, Moscow and Tokyo all ticked synchronously, seemingly counting down to the biggest choice of his life. "Yes," he responded again.

"Excellent. So the next thing to cover would be your education. At the moment you're very young – too young to be in with the seniors at Harrow. There's a big difference between a seven-year-old compared to the teens; so we've got a place for you at a boarding school called Caldicot – I think it will be good for you. Everything else on this list we can work out along the way. Would you agree Nancy – no need to go overboard right now?" Nancy agreed. "So, Mr. Powell, I shall repeat the question I asked in the restaurant and ask if you'd like to come and be one of us? If you still decide yes, there's no going back!"

Lee observed how similarly The Chief and his nan had both spoken to him. Did all agents speak this way? Is this the way agents need to act? It began to dawn on Lee how serious this now was. A new family, new identity and a new place to live... but was it really that different to what he'd become used to? He'd already made the decision before and saw no reason to go back on it now. But this wasn't going to be a one-way street and he needed some assurances.

"If I say yes, there are some things I want in return."

The Chief raised an eyebrow but was quietly impressed. *Kids are such natural negotiators!* he thought. "No guarantees but we'll do our best to meet your terms."

Lee recalled how people negotiated on television and showed one finger on his left hand saying, "Firstly, I want to see my Nan regularly, please."

"I wouldn't have it any other way, Lee," she replied softly.

With his attention still on Nancy, he said, "Secondly..." His bottom lip quivered. "Please don't let Dad forget me?"

Nancy felt the sudden painful jab to the heart and eyes too, but they both tried hard to hold it together. "Of course not."

After taking a deep breath, Lee put up a third finger. "Lastly, that family must be made to suffer for what they did!" he said in a hard angry tone that Nancy had never heard from him before.

Lee looked at The Chief and back at his Nan. The Chief gave no indication so the answer was left squarely upon her shoulders.

"If you mean Louvaine, Jon and Laura, then you have my word that they will be made to suffer," she finally agreed.

The Chief took the pause as time to close the deal. "Are we all in agreement, then?" he asked. Lee nodded his head and The Chief put out his hand. "Welcome to your apprenticeship, Trainee Agent Powell!" he said, shaking the boy's hand vigorously. "Do you mind waiting outside for a bit whilst I go through the finer details with your Nan?"

"Is it alright if I say I'd like to start learning straight away?" he asked in response.

The Chief looked at Nancy and smiled. "Why not? No time like the present to learn the trade!"

The Chief called his assistant in to take notes and after thirty minutes, he and Nancy had set out a clear near-term plan of action. Once finalised, the assistant excused herself to begin executing her tasks, whilst Nancy took Lee to another empty office. She gestured for Lee to sit and sat down in a chair opposite.

"It's going to be a little while before I see you again, Lee. I need you to tell me everything that happened to you with Louvaine, Jon and Laura."

Lee wasn't sure and hesitated; it had become second nature for him to clam up when this subject arose.

"The more you give to me, the more I can make them suffer for you," she coaxed.

This was just the motivation Lee needed. He gave detailed accounts of the lies, the beatings and general unfair abuse he'd been on the receiving end of. "I tried to do as they asked, but every time, Laura found a way to get me in trouble again."

Nancy knew that he and Laura rubbed each other up the wrong way on many an occasion, and so probed him a few times to test the validity of each story. When Lee talked her through the final episode, she could barely hide her shock. Everything the boy said sounded so fantastical that a person on the outside would have trouble believing any of it. But Lee had provided such detail that tying everything in to what she already knew meant the jigsaw puzzle was complete. She had interrogated people before and Lee had presented no signs of inconsistency or delusion that she could detect.

The information he provided also left Nancy with a sharp stab of guilt. She could have helped Lee more than once and she had failed him each time. Her mind raced back to the occasion in the café when he had given her a clear message: *Help, Danger, Fear* and *Anger*. She got up and walked over, put her arms out and hugged him tightly. Nancy was close to breaking down as Lee finally released all of the pent-up anguish and pain he'd kept inside for a quarter of his life, and sobbed his heart out until it had nothing left to give.

Eventually, she asked one last time: "Are you sure about your decision, Lee?"

Lee nodded. His throat hurt too much to talk. Besides, what other choices did he really have?

Nancy stiffened up and looked Lee in the eye. "They will suffer... that's a promise."

* * *

CHAPTER 26

IDENTIFY

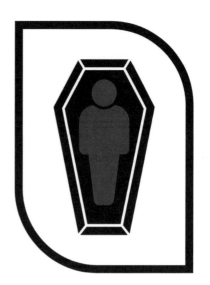

That afternoon, The Chief's assistant made a number of calls. One of the calls was to Kim Montrall on instruction from Nancy.

Kim had been busy all day typing up her notes and putting her invoice together from the case to find Lee in France. Compared to the run-of-the-mill titbits she had been getting by on before, the earnings from this case alone would keep her going for three months at least. She knew that Nancy and David would have a hard time swallowing the full extent of the costs, so she made sure to leave some wiggle room in the price, in case they wanted to negotiate it downwards. Even though she wasn't expecting to see Nancy for a week, it was always good practice to get everything written down whilst the memories were still fresh. She picked up the phone on the third ring.

"Montrall Investigations," she answered.

"Miss Montrall. This is HQ. I have a message from The Chief. Are you able to speak?" the woman asked.

"Go ahead," Kim said. It was the first call she'd had in ages from HQ and the first time directly from The Chief's office.

"It is unfortunate that Lee Walker died after jumping from a bridge a few days ago. You are to go back to the location and speak to the Commandant to ensure that all loose ends are tied up and all papers, certificates and ashes are collected. He will guide you through the process. He will be expecting you at 9 o'clock sharp tomorrow morning – local time. You are to deliver the ashes and paperwork directly to your client. Is there any other information you need?"

Kim was shocked and said nothing. *What's going on? Why do they need a cover-up?*

"Miss Montrall?" the assistant said in a clipped voice.

"I understand what you've said… but why?" she enquired. It was a big mistake to ask questions and Kim realised the moment she'd said it.

"Do you understand what is required, Miss Montrall?" the assistant said.

"Yes, I understand," she replied.

"Please ensure that your client report reflects what we have discussed. You are to dispose of anything non-essential in the usual manner. And one other thing – you are to ensure that the story is picked up by a French newspaper."

The phone clicked off before Kim could say anything else. Her mind was nothing but questions. She could never have seen that call coming. She looked at her watch. It was just after 4 o'clock in the afternoon; just enough time to call Dover port for the ferry times back to Calais – there was no way The Office would stump up for flights. She put her report and invoice in the safe, but kept the photo of Lee and packed some things for the long overnight journey to Nantes. It was going to be another all-nighter and she hadn't fully recovered from the previous expedition.

* * *

Nancy left Century House alone that afternoon and hailed a taxi to Charing Cross train station. She used the travel time home to prepare for what she was going to have to tell her son. She contemplated different ways of putting it, but it didn't matter – David would be crushed no matter how she gave the news. Instead of driving home from Sevenoaks, Nancy drove round to David's apartment.

He'd been home less than forty-five minutes when the doorbell rang. He opened the door, half surprised and half eager to see his mother standing there. "Come in Mum, I've been trying to get hold of you all day! Do you have any news?"

Nancy walked in to David's living room before she said anything. She sat down and motioned for David to do the same. As she looked at David, she sighed.

David sensed that something bad had happened but didn't want to recognise the feeling until his mother spoke.

"I'm sorry, son, but I'm afraid Lee has died." David stood straight back up again and began pacing around the room nervously as his mother continued. "I didn't think it would be fair for you to hear it over the phone, but I just found out from Kim earlier this afternoon."

As soon as Kim's name was mentioned, David went berserk. "How did this happen? What did she do?" he said furiously, tears welling up in his eyes.

Nancy was annoyed at this reaction, but tempered her response. "David, you can't keep blaming Kim for these issues. If anything, it's you and me that are to blame and no-one else. We both had the chance to get him away from Louvaine, and neither of us did." The last part of her sentence softened, as she bowed her head and took a handkerchief from her handbag.

David stopped pacing when he saw his mother upset. He hadn't seen her tears since the death of his father thirteen years ago. "I'm sorry Mum, but I can't believe it; after all this." Nancy and David hugged for a while until David broke the silence. "I don't know if I want to know this, but how did it happen? Please tell me it wasn't bad, Mum – please?"

Nancy spent some time appearing to regain her composure for David's benefit.

"Well, as you know, he'd escaped a police cell in France. What I didn't know was that he'd managed to take a gun with him from an officer who was asleep on duty."

David's face was a picture of astonishment. "A gun?"

Nancy continued. "Kim was on his trail and nearly had him in custody, but as you can imagine, the French police were pretty serious about finding him... I don't think they would've been that bothered otherwise. After another day or so on the run, the police found him whilst he was walking along a bridge." Nancy paused briefly, dabbing the tears from her eyes before returning to the story. "He'd managed to raise himself onto the edge of a beam, and when they tried to recapture him, he shot himself with the gun and fell to his death. I guess he just couldn't think of any other way out of the situation," she said, slowly shaking her head.

David was stunned; his eyes began to water.

Nancy pre-empted his next question. "Kim's currently over there now trying to sort everything out for us, but I may need to go there if they need a member of the family – I don't know what their rules are like about foreign deaths."

"I should come over there with you, Mum – you shouldn't have to do this alone!"

Nancy cursed herself for answering a question David hadn't asked. She quickly played to her knowledge of his frailties. "Well... there's no guarantee that they need us there, but if they did, it would probably be to identify the dead body," she said solemnly.

David's stomach tightened involuntarily as he pictured Lee with his head blown to bits. He jumped up, rushed over to the kitchen sink and retched four or five times before the nausea subsided.

Nancy walked over to him and ran a tea-towel under the cold tap – giving it to David to wipe his mouth with as she put her arm upon his shoulder. "You don't have to go if it will be too upsetting for you," she said.

"Thanks, Mum, you're too good for me sometimes."

Nancy felt relieved that she'd managed to reign in David's involvement. The last thing she needed was create more of a cover-up than was strictly necessary. She stayed with David for a few more hours reminiscing about some of the good times they'd experienced with the boy. From the time they'd introduced him into the family, Lee had always had his own distinct personality, from the obsession with football and Kevin Keegan, to the funny ways in which he'd mimic the adverts on television.

David knew that Nancy was trying to help him cope with the loss and he loved her for it. But when she left later that evening, all he had left were thoughts of how he'd failed Lee swirling inside his mind. "Can I go with you?" Lee had asked when he'd confronted his whore wife with the damning evidence of her treachery. Instead of listening to the boy, the boy who'd been loyal enough to alert him to the problem in the first place, he'd been selfish and left him alone to face the wrath of that disgusting woman.

The self-recrimination continued as his mind wandered to the drink-driving accident he'd caused, killing the boy's real mother. Everything was his fault and he knew it. David had never really been a big drinker since the accident, but that night he reached for whatever he could find in the kitchen cupboard.

* * *

Kim managed to board the 20:05 ferry from Dover and went to one of the lounges. She bought herself a couple of snacks and a can of drink to pass the time, and sat as far away from everyone else as she could. The hour-and-a-half duration of the ferry trip was the only time she was going to get any sleep that night. The way she saw it, she had over three hundred miles to cover in about nine hours once she got through French immigration. Kim had pulled all-nighters before, but usually with a little more preparation and notice than what she'd been given today. She tried to fall asleep, but as her mind kept wandering, the more intense her thoughts became. *Why did Nancy want Lee to appear dead? Was David in on this too? No, you silly cow, they wanted your report to reflect the death! But this has gone to the very top – why was the call was placed by The Chief's assistant?* Kim couldn't figure it out. The best she could come up with was that Nancy wanted to give Lee a new start in some way without the family knowing. But that didn't completely make sense if David wasn't in on the plan. No, something else was going on here and Kim wanted an explanation when she saw Nancy next. She also wondered who would be picking up the bill for this little jaunt. She hoped it wouldn't be HQ, but she had a suspicion it would be… she was already on a retainer, so there'd be no extra payments coming her way.

Once through French border control, Kim took the most direct route she possibly could. The one advantage to overnight driving was that the autoroutes were relatively empty of traffic. She decided to play the journey as safe as possible and stopped every couple of hours for a toilet break, refreshment and an ice-cold face wash. It worked for the most part, except for the time she nearly veered off the road just on the outskirts of Le Mans. It had scared her enough to stay awake for another thirty minutes or so, before she pulled over for a quick rest. She'd been asleep for about half an hour when she was rudely awoken by the loud honking of a French lorry horn – the driver seemingly just wanting to have some fun. Still, it was just as well, because she only made it to Nantes with a half-hour to spare.

After arriving at the central police station, Kim had no idea what to expect. She did as she was instructed and asked for Commandant Marchand.

"*Bonjour, Mademoiselle Montrall, comment allez-vous?*" he began. (Good morning Miss Montrall, how are you?) "I am so sorry that we meet under these circumstances. Please, come and talk with me in my office." He let her through the secure side-door and took her up to his own office on the first floor. Always polite, he directed her to be seated and closed the door behind them.

"After the debacle in Ancenis, I did not expect to see you again."

"Neither did I," she replied.

"The Inspecteur Général has asked me to handle this unusual request on behalf of our governments, so I shall do as I've been asked."

"I... We appreciate your efforts in this matter," Kim said diplomatically.

"So, I just want to be clear what my orders are to ensure this aligns with your expectations. You will require a Medical Certification of Death and you will also require the deceased to be cremated so that you can take possession of the ashes, yes?"

"Yes, that sounds about right," she replied.

"Good, we are in agreement then. Now come with me please." Marchand escorted Kim through a labyrinth of corridors down to the station basement and walked towards the big sign green sign that read 'Morgue'. The Commandant called out for the morgue assistant and within thirty seconds a man dressed in a white hospital coat entered the room.

"Inconnu six, s'il vous plaît," Marchand asked him.

"Inconnu?" Kim whispered. She'd never heard that term before.

"Unidentified male," he explained. The assistant opened the sliding drawer out to its full extent and pulled down the shroud covering the body to expose the head and upper half of the chest. Kim instantly drew back at the sight and smell of the dead man.

"I am sorry, Miss, but can you confirm that this person as Lee Walker?" Kim was about to say no, when she realised what Marchand was doing... discretion was the most important thing here.

"Yes," she said, wiping her eye as if a tear had appeared.

"Thank you, Miss Montrall. Please can you write down the date of birth here for me?" He passed her a pen and pad. Kim said nothing and wrote down Lee's date of birth as instructed. "Please, be seated outside in the hall, I will be with you momentarily."

Kim did as she was told whilst the Commandant spoke with the morgue attendant. After about ten minutes, Marchand appeared outside with the freshly inked copy of Medical Certificate in hand. She followed him back up to his office where he explained what would happen next. He would be calling *Pompes Funèbres et Marbrerie*

Gonard (*Gonard Undertakers and Marble*) in Ancenis who would collect the body from the morgue. They would arrange for the death to be registered at the Ancenis Town Hall, and cremation of the body. They would also provide her with a properly sealed urn as required by law. "This process may take about three to four days. If you keep in touch with me, I can instruct you on when to go and collect the ashes." He passed Kim his direct number again along with a copy of the death certificate. "One piece of advice," he said sagely. "Whilst we will sort out payment at this end, I would advise you to give the owner of the Undertakers an additional cash payment of 800 Francs."

Kim cursed internally. She knew that her own funds were running low. "I cannot thank you enough for your help Commandant Marchand," Kim said with a genuine appreciation of the man. *I guess not all French police are idiots*, she thought, her mind turning back to her chaperone at La Chapelle-Basse-Mer. "I have a question. If I needed a friendly reporter, who should I speak to?"

Marchand wrote down the details of Claude Lebesque, a man he knew at *Ouest-France* – one of the two main newspapers in Nantes.

"Please be careful what you say. I will call ahead to make sure he is receptive to your needs."

Kim thanked the man again as he escorted her out of the front security door of the station.

Kim had been fighting her tiredness for the last two hours. She was shot and her energy levels were at an all-time low. She decided that rather than call Nancy now, she would call later when she'd had a chance to eat and properly rest. She went back to the boutique hotel she'd stayed at the last time she'd been in Nantes and, once checked into her room, lay down on her bed – passing out through sheer exhaustion.

The next morning when she woke up, Kim instantly hated what she saw in the mirror. She'd barely moved the whole time and had only removed her shoes before getting into bed. Her clothes and hair were a mess, and she'd neglected to cleanse her face of make-up the night before. After bathing and arranging her things in the room, she rang reception for the laundry service – the clothes she'd slept in were too creased to be worn again. She then arranged for an international call to Nancy from her room.

Nancy was pleasant to Kim, something that had not come across from the assistant's tone the day before. She updated Nancy on how helpful the Commandant had been and that it would be a few days before everything could be fully wrapped up. In the meantime, she'd contact a reporter from *Ouest-France* about the story.

"There's a few things I need to understand. What information would you like the paper to report on?" Kim asked, ready to make notes on some hotel stationery.

Nancy thought about this question for a few moments. "I don't think the reporter needs to know exactly why a seven-year-old would run away to France, but they may want to give an opinion. They will need to cover how long Lee was on the run for and maybe throw a few 'eye-witness' accounts on the final incident whilst you're at it. Be sure to include the names of the parents. As far as the actual death, it is thought that the young boy was knocked unconscious when he hit the water and subsequently drowned." Kim made her own notes as Nancy spoke. *Don't mention the gun then!* "You can give the location of death, but make sure to be vague about where he was found and the various forces involved – we don't want to stir a hornet's nest here. The most important thing is that Lee's picture must be in the story. I think that should cover it," she said.

"OK, I understand." Kim replied. "If I can't get the story out before I have to leave, I'll make sure I get a copy of the paper sent to me – would that be OK with you?"

"It may be best to wait until the story breaks first – let's see how cooperative they are? I'm sure you've got questions, Kim, so we'll catch up when you get back with your report and invoice. Oh, by-the-way, this particular jaunt is on the company – I'm sure you'll understand," Nancy said dryly.

"Understood," Kim replied as they ended the call. It was always good to know who to invoice her expenses to. After making one last call to the number Marchand had given her, she left the room and headed downstairs for some much-needed breakfast.

At 1 o'clock Kim met up with Claude Lebesque at a pre-arranged small café on La Place Catinat – a small roundabout that had no less than six exits. She arrived a little early and really wasn't happy with the location, as it potentially left her extremely exposed to covert photography from every direction. They'd each given a description of themselves on the phone, and Lebesque had suggested they could sit outside as the weather was good, but Kim found a table inside. When he arrived, a waitress escorted him to her table, and Kim introduced herself, saying that she had a headache and needed to stay out of the sun.

"*Parlez-vous anglais*?" Kim asked. She was still tired from the day before and knew they'd be less likely to be understood in the café if they spoke English.

"Oui... yes, of course," he replied. Kim gave him a business card and they ordered some coffees, and lunch for Lebesque. Kim had barely finished breakfast and just ordered a croissant to be polite.

"Did Marchand brief you about why I need to talk with you?"

"He said it was about the death of an English runaway in Ancenis?" he replied, leading her to provide more information.

"Well, it's quite a story really," Kim began. "A couple of months ago, a seven-year-old boy ran away from an orphanage in England. He stowed away inside a lorry and made it all the way to France. In fact, he first found his way to La Grassinière – just south of here, I believe."

"Why did the boy run away?" he asked. "I know orphanages aren't always a nice place to be, but it seems a little... er... drastic for someone so young to run away."

"You're right, Claude," Kim replied, "and although I don't fully know the answer to this, my opinion is that he may have been mistreated at home by his mother and stepfather – which is why he ended up in the orphanage in the first place. For reference, their names are Louvaine and Jon King. Unfortunately, I can't give you more on the specifics because I wasn't brought in to help until after the boy had absconded. I'm a Private Investigator and the real father paid me to try and find him after the police in England ran out of leads." Lebesque finally took a small pad from his pocket and began making notes with a pencil. "Anyway, I managed to track the boy, whose name was Lee King, to Nantes. He had been living rough for a while and had begun to move eastwards."

"How long was he in Nantes for and how did he survive?" Lebesque asked.

The waitress brought over their food, so Kim waited for her to finish before answering the man's question. "Maybe about five days or so? He slept outside at different locations, with a preference for the riverside. I don't know how he got by for food – maybe scraps here and there; I'm really not sure. I tracked him as he moved through Saint-Julien-de-Concelles to Ancenis. A very kind lady had helped him in Saint-Julien-de-Concelles, but after leaving that town, his luck began to run out. He'd been caught taking food from a small shop and attracted the attention of the police. Of course, the police here were more efficient than the ones we have at home and they also tracked him all the way to Ancenis. They eventually trapped him along the suspension bridge. According to eyewitness accounts, when Lee saw the police, he climbed up on to the side rail. They tried to talk him down but the poor boy jumped before they could help him. I can't imagine how bad he must've felt to have resorted to such an act." Kim shook and bowed her head slightly. "Unfortunately it's believed that Lee must have hit his head on the way down or been knocked unconscious on impact... he was found drowned further down river."

"Do you have a picture of this... (he looked at his pad) Lee King?" Kim went into her handbag and pulled out a copy of Lee's picture she'd been given by Nancy. Lebesque still seemed to be pondering. "I'm surprised I didn't hear about this before, how long ago did this happen?"

"He died on 25th January, so just over a week ago. I'm staying here to help with the repatriation of his ashes back to England."

"So what is it you want from me, Miss... Montrall?" he asked, looking over her business card.

"I think it's a story that attests to the bravery of such a young boy. I mean, how many seven-year-olds have you heard of that would kill themselves in such a drastic way?"

Lebesque nodded thoughtfully – knowing this might sell a few papers.

"When do you think you'd be able to publish?" she asked.

"I'm not sure, something like this, maybe 3...4...5 days?"

"Well, I expect to be in town for another two to three days. It would be really helpful if you were able to print the story before I leave to take the boy's urn back to England?"

"Let me see what I can do," Lebesque said. "It's not always in my control."

"Well, I would definitely appreciate any assistance you can provide in speeding up the process." Kim wrote her hotel details on the back of the card she'd given him. "If you can't get a copy to me at the hotel, can you send one to my office in England, please?"

"Of course, I will do my best." Lebesque was still eating his lunch when Kim put 20 francs on the table and stood up.

"Please don't stand, Claude, I have so much to do before I go back. Please enjoy your lunch – I'm sure we'll speak soon."

* * *

CHAPTER 27

SIX OF ONE?

In the four months since receiving the local authority grant, Laura King began her first year of senior school. The leap from a primary to a Grammar school was a significant and cruel one. To begin with, none of the very few friends she had transferred with her, which left her feeling alone. It also determined her exclusion from the top set, and she was put in the third set of six. After being the big fish in her previous life, academically, her stature was now that of a minnow or even algae in the rankings. Girls will be girls, and when they found out that Laura's parents had to rely on a grant for her education and clothing, her fate as an outsider was sealed. Wealth was how the ranking system worked amongst the girls, not just intelligence. Some were fortunate to have both. Her dream of being the top girl in a Grammar school was so far from reality that it took a toll on her confidence. In the beginning she retreated to her room most evenings to complete her homework. She would come out for dinner, but just head back upstairs again saying that she still had homework to complete.

Although her mother's attention was mostly spent with the new baby, her new dad would often pop his head around the door to see how she was. He knew she was unhappy, and because their friendship had blossomed, Laura was open about not being liked and not being as elevated as she would have expected. Like any father, real or otherwise, he'd try to offer solutions – one being that they could remove her from the school if she wanted; but that just upset her more. Jon sometimes gave her a reassuring hug or stroked her long hair, which comforted her greatly. The only thing he could suggest academically was that maybe she could talk to the head of her year. If she was top of the third set, then maybe they might promote her up at the end of term? Laura loved the idea and it actually worked when the year head promised to look into it. The second thing Jon suggested was that maybe she could look at what made the popular girls... well... popular, and try to copy them.

He'd clearly been on fire with the suggestions that day because it really gave her something to think about. Over a few days a plan a formed in her head, but the execution would require time and sacrifice. Instead of worrying about the girls in her own year, Laura had noticed that the 13-14-year-olds seemed far more confident in comparison. Over the following three months she managed to ingratiate herself with a group of three girls. By chance, Laura's luck was in when they needed a fourth body to meet up with a group of boys from nearby school one afternoon. She knew that the girls were using her, but she was using them just the same, which had the effect of relieving her tension and inflating her confidence a little. Laura was free to just enjoy the times and actually have fun... with the whole group.

The biggest disadvantage Laura had was clothing. She really didn't have much in the way of 'going out' clothes – even if it was just down the high street or cinema on a Saturday. But she turned this into her advantage one weekend when she borrowed one of her mother's tight-fitting tops. Louvaine had never been a proponent of wearing a bra and Laura had decided to follow suit, by going out just like her mother would – *au naturel*. Her breasts had developed enough to show her slight curves and the semi-sheer top teased just enough for everyone to look twice. The exhilarating feeling of freedom and the attention she received seemed to flick a switch within her. When the group met in town, the four boys were transfixed and fell over themselves to find a reason to talk to her. Instead of acting embarrassed, Laura pushed against her insecurities by deciding to be even more overt. This *new* Laura resulted in a slight shift in the dynamic between the girls. They'd noticed, and rather than be carefree themselves, had chosen to try to stop 'their' boys from interacting with Laura. The power surge was euphoric and it marked a significant turning point in Laura's life.

When the girls decided to stop talking to her at school, the boys found other ways to get word to her to meet with them separately. They would come to meet near her school, sometimes bringing other friends with them. Laura now realised that a new advantage lay with the boys and not the girls. Rumours began to circulate between the other first year girls that Laura King was hanging around with boys two years her senior – which meant that other girls now wanted to talk to her. Not only was Laura selective with who she invited into her 'exclusive club', but she'd also been promoted to the top set... her confidence was sky high.

At home, the family had somehow settled into two distinct sides. Louvaine had distanced herself, taking care of the baby – although Jon tried to play his part, Lou didn't really seem to need his help with anything. After a long day at work it was easier for him to spend more time with Laura. He liked how she had bloomed and was pleased with himself that he'd been partly responsible for her transformation. Like she did with the boys, Laura would sometimes tease her dad when she felt inclined. She'd sometimes bend over provocatively in front of the television whilst he was watching, or sometimes sit on his lap. If she was feeling really brave, she'd do it in the presence of her mother. Louvaine would chastise Laura, telling her to pull her skirt down or to keep her legs closer together, but Laura was having fun... and Jon never complained. The more attention she got, the more she wanted.

One evening Laura was feeling more daring than usual. She'd got changed after school into a skirt and top and decided she wanted to be completely free of any underwear. In the evening when her mother was putting Jon Jr. to bed, Laura asked her dad to watch as she began doing handstands up against the wall in the living room. Jon watched on, chuckling and salivating, as each time she leapt up against the wall, Laura's skirt would fall with gravity's assistance. As taboo as it was, Jon found it hard to restrain himself. He hadn't been intimate with Louvaine since the baby was born and desperately needed to ease his pent-up frustration. He walked out to the back room which initially disappointed Laura, who thought he wasn't interested. But Jon was soon back with his Polaroid camera in hand. Laura's heart raced with exhilaration when he asked her to do the handstand again. She became more daring this time by opening her legs into a sideways split – sensing the merest air movement across her skin as her skirt once again dropped down past her waist. Jon just managed to take a picture before they both heard Lou coming downstairs. Guiltily, Laura immediately stood down and Jon rushed back to the sofa, hiding the camera and picture on the way – both giggling like five-year-olds. Just to be annoying, Laura sat between her mum and dad for the rest of the evening until it was time to go to bed.

At bedtime, she gave her mum a hug and kiss goodnight, and did the same with Jon – the only difference being that she ground her pubic bone against Jon's knee at the same time. He wanted to follow her upstairs – there were so many things he wanted to do to her, but knew he shouldn't. His frustrations remained as he and Louvaine sat alone downstairs. He put his arm around his wife as they watched television, but it wasn't the same. She wasn't unkind to him, she just seemed so unreceptive to his needs; the total opposite of what she was like when they first met. That night before going to bed, Jon hid the picture in his tool box and put the camera back where he'd found it.

A few evenings later Laura walked into the bathroom whilst Jon was taking a bath. She knew he was bathing alone and used the pretence of needing to 'desperately' go to the toilet as an excuse to barge in unannounced. Jon's initial protestations were silenced as, from the side, he watched Laura lift her skirt and squat over the toilet bowl. His breathing intensified as the blood pumped faster around his body. Although it was risky, he took the chance and stood up and faced Laura... proudly. Laura was transfixed, having never seen a fully grown man naked before. She felt the same pulses throughout her body that she'd felt before when she'd posed for the photograph. She flushed the toilet and slowly walked towards the bath.

"What do you think?" he asked.

Laura's heart continued to race. Unable to control the hormones that raced around her body, her ability to make clear decisions became blurred. Fundamentally she knew that the situation they'd both brought about was wrong, but another part of her was nervously excited. "It's... massive. Is that what happens to it?"

Jon smiled – she was so innocent. "You can touch it if you like." Laura slowly reached out and put her slender fingers around his shaft.

Jon twitched and she felt his pulse from within her grasp. "Why don't you come in with me?"

Laura wasn't sure. The bravado she'd shown by bursting in on her stepfather was slowly ebbing away now that he'd called her bluff. But to keep up with her new persona, she slowly removed her clothing and stepped naked into the bath.

Jon watched eagerly. She'd developed like her mother with the shapeliness of her breasts and the beginnings of her dark bush. He could barely contain himself now and with his big strong hands, he took the lead by turning Laura around and bending her over, placing pressure on the back of her neck. With his other hand he pushed his cock inside her, thrusting slowly, then more forcefully as his energy increased.

Laura took more than one sharp intake of breath... this was painful. He was far too big for her and it felt like someone was stabbing her in the stomach. "Stop, it's hurting... you're hurting me!" she cried. Jon wouldn't stop and for Laura, the pain became unbearable. "I'll... tell... mum," she tried.

Jon still had one hand on the back of her neck. He tightened his grip slightly. "You won't. Remember what happened to Lee? And don't forget who started all of this!" he said menacingly.

Laura began to cry. She needed to get herself out of the situation. She couldn't take the pain any longer and dropped to her knees. The bath water began to turn a shade of red as the skin stung between her legs.

Jon had to be careful. Too much noise would arouse suspicion downstairs. He got out of the bath unfulfilled, put a towel around his waist and went to his bedroom. Laura was left to clean herself up, eventually retreating to her own room. She had plenty of time to think about what she'd done, and felt guilty, dirty and compromised. She had no control.

Meal times were a little awkward for a few days as the dynamic changed between them. Jon would pop into Laura's room whenever he liked and pester her. He'd apologised to her for being so rough, but she didn't want to turn her back on him for fear of being grabbed again. Her body still needed to recover.

As the weeks passed, the pressure he exerted for her to give him more of what he wanted became unbearable. He'd put a finger inside her once and fucked her again over her own bed. She had choices, but none of them were good. Telling the police would have huge repercussions on her and the whole family. It would be the same if she said something to a school teacher. That option would also kill the popularity status she'd worked so hard to change. But Laura knew she had to do something, otherwise it would never stop. And so, she took the brave decision to tell her mother one afternoon after school.

She nervously approached Louvaine who had just finished up feeding the baby. "Mum... I've got something to tell you, but I don't think you'll like it."

Lou looked up at Laura, concerned. "What is it? You know you can tell me anything."

Laura took a deep breath. "A couple of weeks back on Tuesday, Dad... touched me," she said tentatively.

Louvaine frowned. "What do you mean, touched you? You two are always playing around with each other, and don't think I haven't noticed you showing all your bits and pieces to anyone who wants a look!" Louvaine was annoyed. Why was her daughter trying to cause trouble with her marriage?

Laura's eyes became tearful. "He put his... thing inside me mum."

"Don't be ridiculous, Dad's got a real woman, not some skinny little slut with dirty dreamt-up fantasies. I think you should go upstairs and do your homework. And when you come down later, put some decent clothes on for a change!"

Laura burst into tears as she stormed out of the living room. *How can she not believe me? My own mother of all people.* Laura cried on her bed for quite some time before returning to her homework.

When Jon got home that evening he felt the tension between the two women at the dinner table and knew better than to get involved. Later, he popped in to see Laura in her room to perk her up a little, but she clearly wasn't in any mood to have any fun. *Little prick-tease!*

In bed that night he put his arm around Lou and spooned up behind her. He began stroking her thigh and inner thigh. She didn't reject him, but she was also not especially receptive either.

"Lou, you know I love you, right?"

"I know you do," she said, brushing him on the leg.

"It just seems that you're so distant from me now since we had Jr."

Throughout the evening, Louvaine had been thinking about what Laura had told her. She knew it was all lies, but it also gave her an opportunity for self-reflection. Now that Jon had brought the subject up she realised that she didn't really have an answer for him.

"I don't mean to be distant... I just... well, I just don't know why I'm feeling like this."

Jon patted her bottom and turned over. "Not to worry," he said.

Lou lay there thinking and wondering. She decided that the next day, she'd pay a visit to the doctors.

When Louvaine explained about her feelings, or lack of, to the doctor, he identified the symptoms of post-natal depression pretty quickly and prescribed a course of anti-depressants. One week later and Louvaine had transformed into a different character. Although somewhat lethargic, her moods were less erratic and she found herself more appreciative of Jon, to the point of initiating physical contact with him again. Conversely, Laura ate and slept less, due to the anguish she felt about her position in the family. And in Jon's mind, he'd literally become king... now he had a choice of two women in the house.

* * *

CHAPTER 28

NEWS AND TRUTH ARE NOT THE SAME

Kim left a day's interval before contacting Marchand again. He said he had no new information, but would contact the funeral directors for an update. He promised to leave a message with her hotel reception if he had anything new. With at least a day to kill, she decided to devote some of the time to herself. What was the point in being in France if you couldn't wander round the wonderful shops the country had to offer? The hotel reception directed her to the Feydeau areas of the city centre as being the best places to shop – so that's where she headed.

The last few years had been somewhat lean for her business and Kim had been forced to neglect a small passion in life. Some women have an eye for clothes shops and Kim was definitely a member of that fraternity. She eventually hit the jackpot when she found herself in a place called the Passage Pommeraye. Built in the renaissance style, it was a fantastically cavernous treasure-trove of little boutique shops set out on three levels that sold anything from silver, jewellery, antiques, art, clothing and shoes to food, incense and perfumes. The ornate décor, wide staircases and wonderfully sculpted statues on each level gave an air of spaciousness and beauty that was definitely conducive to spending money. *England has much to learn*. Kim sauntered around purchasing some lovely scarves along with a white top and a flattering slim line skirt. On the top floor there was a large *parfumerie* that specialised in creating one-off perfumes for anyone who had the patience and was prepared to spend a little time with the perfumer. Time was something she had in abundance, so she opened the door.

As Kim ventured inside she was greeted by shelf upon shelf small brown bottles, which reminded her of the chemistry lab at school. A female assistant greeted her as she completed the task of transporting stock from a box to a cupboard.

"*Je serai avec vous dans une courte seconde.*" (*I will be with you in just a short second*).

Not wishing to disturb the woman as she finished her task, Kim made her way slowly towards the counter, removing the lids off one or two bottles to inhale the contents. The assistant finished unpacking the box and turned around to engage her new customer.

"*Comment puis-je... vous aider?*" Her voice trailed off in surprise at seeing the woman now in her shop. Kim turned to face the *parfumeuse* and was just as surprised to see Servane Fortier facing her, less than five feet away.

"I cannot believe it's you. How come you are here? Did you find Lee?" the woman asked. It had been about ten days since Kim had tracked Servane down to her home in Saint-Julien-de-Concelles when she'd briefly taken the runaway boy in and tried to help him.

Kim knew this was going to be awkward, but she tried her best to remain composed. "Hello Servane, I really wasn't expecting to see you again. Shall we sit down?" she suggested.

Servane walked past to the shop door, turned the sign from 'Ouvert' to 'Fermé' and locked it as she ushered Kim over to some chairs by a counter. Servane waited for the woman to answer her question. It didn't seem that she was going to like the answer.

"To answer your question Servane, yes I did find Lee. You'd been very kind to him so you deserve to know what happened." Servane's body tensed just a little and she began to rub a thumb along the back of her hand. "He'd been caught by the police in La Chapelle-Basse-Mer for trying to steal food from a shop, but he escaped their custody. They tracked his location to Ancenis and cornered him on the bridge that leads into the city. Lee must have felt like he no longer had anything to lose, because he jumped from the side of the bridge."

Servane's hand immediately went to her mouth as she gasped. "Is he alright? What happened?"

Kim paused. There was only one way to put this. "I'm sorry Servane, but Lee died because of the fall. I'm still here because there are things that need to be completed for the family." Kim didn't want to be too specific; besides, Servane would probably see the story in the newspaper soon.

Servane's eyes began to tear up. She took a tissue from a box in the draw besides her seat. Her mind had gone back to the words Lee had written to her on the 10 Franc note she knew she'd never spend.

Kim didn't really know what to do for the woman, but she offered a shoulder to cry on, which Servane duly accepted.

After thirty seconds or so, Servane pulled away, sensing Kim's discomfort. "I'm sorry," she said, "I know I should keep my composure."

Kim felt sorry for her, but her mind was now on extricating herself from the shop as soon as possible... the fun had just been taken out of her shopping excursion.

"I should go now, would you mind opening the shop door for me?" Kim said delicately.

Servane knew that she had imposed on Kim and apologised profusely. "Thank you for telling me what happened." She wasn't sure whether to shake hands or kiss both cheeks. In the end she did neither.

"I'm sorry to be the bearer of bad news." Kim said as she touched Servane on the arm and walked out of the shop. She took a leisurely walk back to the hotel, where a message was waiting for her at reception.

'*Your casket can be collected tomorrow after 1400h. Marchand.*' This served as a reminder that she needed to change up some more money.

* * *

The next day she called Marchand to thank him and tell him that she expected to be on a ferry home sometime late that evening. But she hadn't heard anything about the newspaper story yet and asked him to check up on Claude Lebesque to make sure that the story was indeed going live. By 1:45pm she was packed and checked out of the hotel. She drove the twenty miles to Ancenis, following the same ominous route across the bridge that she had taken once before. After asking for directions a couple of times, Kim found the funeral home. Even though it was in the centre of town, she was surprised at how rural the place felt.

"*Bonjour.* Can I speak with the owner please? My name is Kim, they should be expecting me," she asked as she was greeted at reception.

"I am Mr. Gonard, are you Miss Montrall?" Kim showed the man one of her business cards. He nodded his approval. "Can I see your copy of the medical certificate?" he asked. Kim retrieved the certificate from an envelope in her bag. Again Gonard nodded his approval and returned the certificate back to her. "Please wait a moment, thank you." He indicated for Kim to be seated in his office behind the counter whilst he went to a side storage room. She was relieved to see him return with a metal urn in his hand. Monsieur Gonard sat behind his desk and placed the urn at his side. On the desk in front of them both was an envelope. He opened it and showed Kim the certified copy of the death registration. She made sure to read it thoroughly, ensuring that all the pertinent details looked correct.

"Are you satisfied, Miss Montrall?"

"Is this everything?" she replied. "Is anything else required to take Lee's ashes back to his family in England?"

"No, just this urn," he said, gesturing to the container on his left. Kim understood the hint and retrieved 800 Francs from her bag. She put the notes on the table and pushed them towards Monsieur Gonard. He returned the gesture and slid the urn over towards her. "The urn must remain sealed as you cross any borders," he warned, as he showed her where the adhesive had been applied.

"Thank you for your help in this matter, Mr. Gonard." She stood up and shook the man by the hand. He escorted her out to the main reception and Kim walked back to her car. She placed the ashes of the unknown man and all of the certificates in her suitcase and drove to *La Poste*, which she'd seen on the way.

Outside was a telephone box that she used to contact Nancy. "I have the ashes and all the required certification," she said directly.

"Fantastic. And what of the news story?"

"It's not been published yet, but I do have assurances from the reporter that it will be published soon. Rather than stay here, I thought it best to return home. I have instructed the reporter to send me a copy of the newspaper article to my business address." Nancy paused briefly.

"And what's your appraisal of this reporter... can he be trusted? Is he committed to printing?"

"I couldn't stake my life on the story coming out." Kim instinctively knew what the next response would be.

"Stay put and make sure that you have the story in hand before coming back. Call me once you're on your way with an ETA or if there's a problem," Nancy said resolutely. "Anything else?"

"Nothing else to report," Kim said.

"Thank you, Kim." Nancy ended the call.

Kim drove back to Nantes to check back into what now seemed like her favourite hotel. They knew her name there now and gave her the same room she'd just vacated. Before checking in, she asked for a copy of the latest *Ouest-France* and checked every page first – nothing. Kim then checked in and immediately called Marchand.

"Commandant Marchand?"

"Oui?"

"It's Miss Montrall. I have been asked to remain in the city until the story is published. I would rather not stay any longer than I need to – would you mind speaking to Lebesque again to get a definitive day on when the story will run, please?" she asked politely.

"I will kick him for you, Miss Montrall, and I will get him to contact you directly – will this be satisfactory?" he asked.

"Merci, commandant. I appreciate your help very much," she said as she ended the call. Now, all she had to do was wait... with any luck she wouldn't run into anyone else she recognised.

Kim didn't have to wait long. She received a short call from Lebesque to say that the article would be in tomorrow's paper as promised. The next morning she skipped through the paper and there it was on page nine, with a 5×5 cm picture of Lee. She mentally translated as she read:

Runaway 7-year-old dies in Ancenis

A 7-year-old boy from England who ran away from home has died whilst jumping from a bridge in Ancenis, according to eyewitnesses. The boy, who died on 25th January, has been identified as Lee King. It is understood that he may have runaway from an orphanage after being mistreated by his mother and stepfather. It is believed that this remarkable young boy may have hidden himself inside a lorry destined to Nantes in December. Nobody knows how he survived for so long with nowhere to live, but what is known is that he ventured east through Saint-Julien-de-Concelles. A police source confirmed that the boy had been on the run after being caught taking food, and unfortunately, climbed and jumped from the suspension bridge in Ancenis when they tried to help him down. The official cause of death was drowning. The boy's family were unavailable for comment, but a representative of the family said, "We are all very saddened by the way Lee ended his short but eventful life. He was a brave and vibrant young soul, surviving with one small suitcase in a cold winter. He will be missed.

Kim purchased two additional copies from reception as she checked out again and headed back to Calais.

* * *

As she waited for Kim to complete her mission, Nancy gave plenty of thought to the promise she'd made to Lee. After all he'd been through and told her about, he deserved the retribution he sought. She'd always loved David, but when she looked at his achievements in the cold light of day, he was ultimately a disappointment. He was kind to a fault but hated confrontation. Whilst there's a time and place for restraint, confrontation can sometimes be a quick and simpler option. The whole business with Louvaine was a case in point. If he'd thrown her out of the home, Lee wouldn't have suffered so much and Laura would probably have been better off too. She didn't know how or where Lee had got his instincts from, but he was much more the son she always envisaged having. He had such strength of character. A bit rough around the edges and with a wildness sometimes, but with time these characteristics could be honed and shaped. He'd proved so many things already at such a young age: bravery, independence, intelligence and an ability to not just see people, but to see through people. Now that he would be under The Service's guidance, she was sure that between herself and The Chief, they'd be able to create something that England had never had before – a truly born-and-bred asset. Louvaine, Laura and Jon King would all need to be dealt with separately. Laura was flesh and blood, and even though she knew that Lee would want to reserve a special kind of physical punishment for her, Nancy decided to formulate a different plan. The first goal would be to create divisions, but for that she needed the story from *Ouest-France* in her hands.

* * *

If it wasn't for the money the agent had given her in Paris two weeks ago, Kim would've been broke by now. Tracking and locating people, especially in other countries, was not cheap and she hadn't been paid yet for any of the work she'd done for Nancy. It seemed that Nancy had just expected her to have endless reserves to go wherever she wanted her to go. At least The Service had known that field agents need cash to do the job. For the journey back to England, she was down to her last 200 Francs, which needed to cover her fuel and ticket costs – it was going to be a close call! In Calais whilst waiting for the ferry to board, Kim called Nancy again – this time reversing the charges. Nancy agreed the charge.

"Please be brief."

"I have the article. Will board the 1 o'clock ferry and should be with you before 5 o'clock GMT." That was the briefest she could think of.

Nancy gave a one-word answer. "Excellent," and ended the call.

Kim didn't take the abruptness personally; no agent did, it was just the way the business operated... and reverse charges were extortionate. The journey back was pretty uneventful and she was happy that everything had pretty much gone to plan – other than the encounter with Servane. But she didn't expect any blow-back from the woman. As she made her way to Nancy's home, Kim still quizzed herself about why Lee's life was being erased. The Service was clearly part of the story, so they must be arranging a new identity for him. But the one question she still couldn't answer was why.

She made good time and got to Sevenoaks by 4:30pm. Before this case, no interactions with her old handler had been conducted at her private home. But as Nancy had 'officially' retired, Kim guessed that she had been able to relax her protocol a little. As she lifted the barrier to Woodland Rise private road she couldn't help wonder again at how the other half lived. By the time Kim had pulled into the driveway and retrieved her bag containing the urn, certificates and two newspapers, Nancy was waiting at the front door.

"Welcome back, Kimberly – I'm sorry this little side-mission was put on you at such short notice. Come on in, the water's on the boil and I've made a fresh pot of chicken soup if you're interested.

Kim smiled; she hadn't had home-cooked food since she left her parents' home ten years ago. Feeling quite cantankerous, Kim handed the urn to Nancy. "I'm *so* sorry for your loss."

The smile left Nancy's face as she raised an eyebrow. She understood Kim's feelings but was unimpressed none-the-less. Kim saw Nancy's reaction, but she'd had enough of being used as a mule and maintained her poise. They both went through the house to the kitchen.

"Would you like a tea or coffee?" Nancy asked. She already knew the answer, she pretty much new everything about Kim's life, but she offered the choice regardless.

"I think I'll have tea for a change," which surprised Nancy. Kim sat down at the kitchen table and waited as she made a pot for them both.

"Would you like soup as well? I'm having some myself."

"Yes please," said Kim. Nancy played 'mother' and poured the tea for them both. She then brought over two bowls of soup for them both to enjoy. When she sat down, Kim handed her an A4 envelope with the medical certification of death and the death registration. Nancy put on her glasses read through them both carefully.

"And the news article?" she said, gesturing to the two newspapers.

"Page nine."

Nancy opened the paper and thumbed to the article. She immediately saw the picture and eagerly read through the short piece. "This is excellent. Just what we need."

"So, just what is it that you need, Nancy?" Kim probed.

Nancy knew that Kim was asking for an explanation. She removed her glasses and sat back in her chair, assessing how much information she should impart. "Whilst you were in France tracking Lee down, I had been briefing The Chief with updates. It was during this time that he formed an idea that had the potential to be mutually beneficial."

"Mutually beneficial?" Kim repeated.

"Yes. Lee has potential, but he could've fallen through the cracks, and still could. As much as David loves him, he really wasn't focussed on taking care of Lee when he really needed it. With everything that the boy's been through over the last couple of years, I'm sure you'll agree that he's become quite the interesting customer, don't you think?"

Kim nodded, trying to take in the consequences of what Nancy was saying.

"When Lee returned I agreed to facilitate a meeting. The Chief made a proposal that would provide opportunities that Lee would never have otherwise. I can see what you're thinking, Kim, but I can assure you that he was not press-ganged into making an uninformed decision – far from it. I made sure that he was given a balanced view. Lee made the decision himself. Ultimately, I think he needed and wanted a new life. I hope you'll now understand why this press story is vital. It marks the beginning of his new life."

"And what about David, does he not have any say in this?" Kim said, astounded.

Nancy sighed. "I agree with you Kim. That was the hardest part, and the ramifications were explained to Lee at the time. I gave him at least three chances to back out, but he made his decision and stuck by it. I know he was sad to effectively abandon his father, but I don't think he felt David was going to be enough for him. David's my son and I love him, but when the going gets tough, he's not the best in a crisis."

Kim nodded understandingly. "I think deep down Lee knew this, so in answer to your question, it is Lee that has ultimately decided for David."

"So where is Lee now?"

"I'm afraid that's going to be very limited information, I'm sorry."

"What does David know?"

"I've told David that lee shot himself with the police officer's gun when he jumped off the bridge, but I'll find a way of explaining the differences in the article when I see him next. I'm glad you thought to provide a couple of copies, as I'm sure he'll want to keep one in memory."

"So what's your plan?" Kim asked, teasing Nancy to provide more information. But Nancy just smiled and ignored the question.

"Outside of Lee, The Chief and me, you are the only other person with any knowledge of this; so I hope you'll see why we need a different final report. You'll also need to draft a more detailed report for The Chief's office when you submit your out-of-pocket expenses."

Kim nodded; it was just the opening she needed. "Talking of expenses, I'm all out of money. I literally have just a few Francs to my name at the moment. Do you have some money I could have as an advance before the final invoice?"

"How much do you need?" Nancy asked. She liked to play games with herself sometimes. When Kim had reversed the charges of the call earlier, she knew the woman needed money.

"Well, I expect the final bill will be around the two thousand mark, so will five hundred be manageable?"

Nancy walked over to the counter by the sink. She smiled to herself as she took out the exact amount contained within a blue tin. "Is this OK?" she asked. "You'd best count it."

Kim trusted Nancy, but was also wary of her former boss. Not wishing to offend she said, "I'm sure it's fine, and thank you. Speaking of reports and invoicing, do you want me to bring it over in person?"

"I think that would be the best. Shall we say one week's time at 7pm? I'll make sure that David's here. If you can give me a couple of days' notice regarding the amount, I'll try to make sure we have the balance for you when you come round."

Kim understood what Nancy had implied between the lines. She was teeing her up for reinforcing the story back to David next week. *Sometimes the job is just like shovelling shit.* "Before I go, I wanted to ask you about my future with The Service?"

Nancy knew exactly what Kim was asking. "As promised, I spoke directly with The Chief. I'm no longer in control of assignments as you know, but I expect that there may be a few more coming your way. I will just say that the problem in Paris didn't help, so you're going to have to be patient. Your pathway back may take smaller steps than you're hoping for."

The moment Kim had left the scene at Ángel's, she knew she'd hammered another nail in her coffin... these things were nearly impossible to come back from. "Message received," she said. And with that, both women rose from their seats.

On the drive back home Kim gave some thought to her future. Did she want to be set aside to the second-rate missions because they couldn't trust her not to screw up? This was a real dilemma for her and shouldn't be decided whilst driving. When she got home, she would be going out for a good drink; she deserved it and her subconscious could make the decision for her.

After Kim left and with the ammunition in her possession, Nancy looked at the kitchen clock. She might just be in time to catch the person she wanted.

"Theo Greaves – foreign desk?" was just the response Nancy wanted to hear on the other end of the phone.

"Hello Theo, it's been quite a while – would it be OK if we caught up this week?"

Although this was phrased as a question, Theo knew there was only one answer. "Good to hear your voice again. Of course. Tomorrow, eleven thirty, St. Paul's, south, in blue?"

"Perfect, let's have lunch," Nancy said as she clicked off the phone.

* * *

CHAPTER 29

PIZZA PLAN

Nancy arrived by St. Paul's cathedral at 11 o'clock. She always arrived early for meetings and the extra half an hour gave her a chance to have a good walk around. She couldn't believe how much the city had changed since she was last here, 6 years ago. The West End hadn't really changed that much, but this part of London seemed to be in a new state of metamorphosis, with cranes and new building works now part of the skyline. Nancy wandered around for twenty minutes to look for a suitable restaurant. There wasn't a huge range on offer other than sandwich shops, but she found what looked like a relatively new pizza place called Leoni's. Reconnoitre done, she headed back to the meeting point and waited – watching in the direction that Theo would likely be coming from. She jumped when a large hand grabbed her by the shoulder.

"You can't wait here, Madam!" She recognised the voice instantly as she turned to face Theo Greaves.

Theo was a big man and had the big personality to go with his fifty-two years. He had brownish-blond curly hair, with green eyes, rosy cheeks and a big chubby smile. Dressed in a dark suit, checked shirt, Macintosh raincoat, and brogue shoes, the six-foot-three colossus enveloped Nancy's slender frame with a big bear hug that nearly lifted her out of her shoes. He'd decided to surprise the woman just as she had surprised him with her call the evening before. He'd seen her from a significant distance away and decided to go the whole way around the cathedral to ensure he approached from her blind side. To his eyes nothing had changed. Nancy still looked as stylish as ever with a blue and white head scarf, dark navy-blue overcoat, black gloves and tights finished with heeled black crocodile skin loafers. *Always the classy woman*, he thought.

When Theo finally let go his embrace, Nancy smiled the genuine smile she'd rarely had the chance to use these days. "So good to see you again, young man." Although Nancy was a good thirteen years older, Theo had been the one and only subordinate who always got away with speaking to her as an equal. It was the same during his early years in The Service, and whilst she had always tried to cultivate a straight, distant relationship with all her agents, Theo wouldn't have any of it. That's just who he was and Nancy came to realise what a wonderful asset that made him. She pointed in the direction of the river and linked arms with Theo.

"I never thought I'd hear your voice again, what with you being retired now?" he probed.

"Well, you're right about the retirement, but I still keep in contact and up to speed. You know we never really retire; it's just the lifestyle that changes. I saw your piece on the Non-Proliferation of Nuclear Weapons treaty. Very thorough – such a shame about the non-signatories?"

"Great ideals but it's only a matter of time before someone starts testing again. Did you know that I got to go on Concorde in December?" he said, changing the subject.

"No, what was it like? I've thought about it but it's prohibitively expensive."

"Over FOUR THOUSAND POUNDS! And that's just one way. Luckily it was all-expenses. They took a bunch of us journos to New York for free so that we'd hype it up in the press *etcetera*. Three-and-a-half hours to get there, and after finding a return flight, eight hours to get back."

"What was it like inside?" Nancy asked.

"Great if you're..." he searched for his next words carefully.

"Not six-foot-three?" Nancy finished.

Theo's cheeks reddened a little more as he smiled and patted his stomach. "It's not a very spacious plane. Only a hundred passengers, but the service is second-to-none, of that you can be assured."

As they headed down the slight gradient towards the Thames embankment, Nancy gave a subtle gesture to her right.

"Leoni's?" suggested Theo.

Nancy nodded.

"That's one of my favourites. Have you been there before?" he asked.

"I've actually never even had pizza before – anything you'd recommend?"

"They do a wonderful pepperoni and mozzarella."

"Mozzarella?" Nancy enquired. She knew what mozzarella was but she liked how Theo acted like a son would.

"Mozzarella is this amazing..." He stopped, looked at Nancy and smiled. "You nearly had me there." They both chuckled.

"It would be lovely and chivalrous of you to order for me, though."

"It's always my pleasure, Nancy, you know that."

Other than in a professional setting, Nancy hadn't been anywhere near a man since she was widowed. There was something about Theo's bold and excitable personality that always made her feel warm inside, whenever she was in his presence. She repressed everything behind a veneer, but even though he was married, she still held a secret candle for him at times... when her thoughts were her own.

Leoni's was lovely and cosy, and they were seated at a corner table by the front window that was beginning to condensate. As a true gallant, Theo took Nancy's coat and scarf and seated her in the gentlemanly fashion. He ordered a large pepperoni and mozzarella pizza for them to share with two classes of house white. The waitress brought a plate of freshly made grissini with a fresh tomato sauce along with the wine and left the couple to their privacy. As Nancy reached into her bag and took out a copy of the *Ouest-France* newspaper, she enquired, "How's your French these days, Theo?"

"Ça va toujours – pourquoi?" (*Still fine – why?*)

"I wondered if you wouldn't mind taking a look at page nine and the story about the runaway boy."

Theo thumbed his way to page nine and read the story within twenty seconds. He looked up, both surprised and perplexed.

Reading his reaction Nancy quietly said, "He was my grandson, Theo." She let a tear escape the inner corner of her eye as a concerned Theo passed over his serviette.

"I'm very sorry, Nancy." He held her had across the table in support, something no other person would've dared try. "It says his name was Lee King?" he probed.

"It's a long story, so I'll spare you some of the sordid details. My now ex-daughter-in-law had an affair that broke up the marriage with my son. She shacked up with her new guy 'Jon King' and moved away two times so that we couldn't find or see the children. I eventually found her on both occasions, but during that time, she'd remarried and changed everyone's surname. As you can see in the paper, they eventually got rid of Lee to a children's home." Theo raised an eyebrow. He also widened his field of vision which would be imperceptible to the untrained eye. Nancy continued. "You see, my despicable ex-daughter-in-law, Louvaine, had had a baby with this man and I think she was pushing Lee out to make room for the new child. I also found out that they had been severely abusing Lee physically and I can't be sure that this isn't happening to my granddaughter, Laura, too. After being in the home for a couple of months, Lee had had enough and ran away. I think he'd lost his faith in everyone – myself included. I eventually traced him to France with the help of an associate and she tracked him down. We'd worked out a way to bring him back home and everything was going to plan, when he was cornered on a bridge. I suspect the French have massaged the truth a little and they were more heavy-handed that they would ever admit. I don't think that poor boy felt he had any choice." Nancy padded her eyes again, deliberately smudging a little eye-liner.

Theo pointed. "You've smudged a little bit."

"Oh how silly of me. I'm sorry; this is so embarrassing." she said, reaching for her bag.

"It's OK, Nancy; I can see this is difficult."

Nancy took out her vanity set mirror. She held it about twelve inches from her face and took a few attempts to wipe the smudge from her eye. It also gave her the chance to check the ninety-degree view over her left shoulder out of the restaurant window.

Whilst Theo felt for his former handler, he still wasn't sure what she wanted from him. Although he was beginning to get an idea, he really wanted her to spell it out. The waitress came over to their table with an absolutely humongous fifteen-inch, sizzling hot pizza. Nancy looked at Theo as if to say, *There's no way I can eat anywhere near half of this.* But Theo smiled.

"Don't worry, I've got this covered!" he said, which perked her up a little. The waitress sliced the pizza into eighths for them and topped off their wine glasses, before leaving for another customer. Nancy had genuinely never had pizza before and followed Theo's lead on how to get the slice to her plate and eat it. She refused to use her fingers though and instead picked up the somewhat blunt knife and fork wrapped within her own serviette.

"So, where do I come into this?" he continued.

"I was hoping, with a few amendments, you could get the story published in *The Mail* somewhere. I'd like to start applying some pressure?" Theo's instinct had been correct.

"I think I can get that done for you, but I'd have to give this to another reporter – it's... not exactly Foreign Desk material."

"I'd also like you to ensure that the story filters down to the *Hertfordshire Advertiser*," she said.

"I don't know anyone there, but maybe an anonymous tip could work?"

"There's one more thing." Theo smiled again. Nancy never changed – there was always 'one more thing'. "I'd like you to apply a little investigative pressure in person if you wouldn't mind. A couple of days after the story goes live, I'd like you to door-step the mother and intercept Laura separately to see if she's willing to share anything. I want you to be old-school with Louvaine but sensitive with the daughter. It's important to know if there's anything going on with her. I have written down everything you'll need here." Nancy handed him a well-penned

Basildon Bond envelope which was typical of the woman he'd known for so many years.

"Do you know whether they read *The Mail*?"

"Don't worry Theo; I'll make sure they get a copy."

"I have one more question, Nancy, and please don't take this as a discourtesy, but you have been retired for a while now – is this sanctioned?"

"You're absolutely right to ask. All I can say is that The Chief's office have full knowledge and have left this within my control. You are well within your rights to make contact with his assistant, but as is the usual practice, nothing will be confirmed to you. But it won't be denied either!" she said with a raised eyebrow.

"How much notice do you need on publishing date?"

"Can you give me at least twenty-four hours – I need to make sure the delivery is in place?"

"I will do my best, but I don't have control of final edit. How would you like me to contact you?"

Nancy smiled and began writing on a serviette. "Here's my number." Inside she caught and reprimanded herself. *Are you flirting with this man? For Christ's sake, woman, pull yourself together – he's thirteen years your junior and married!*

Now that the business was over, Nancy wanted to listen to what Theo had been up to for the past few years and what stories he was currently working on. He talked about his time interviewing Harold Wilson and how the man's mind had seemingly 'left the building' long before he announced his resignation... all while demolishing the remaining pizza.

"For a leftie, he actually made some sensible decisions – given the state of the world as it is. I'm glad he didn't send our troops into that god-awful war in Vietnam. I'm not so sure about Callaghan, he seems to be butting up against the unions, which is making the markets very nervous. What's your view?" he enquired.

"Well, you know I try to stay out of politics but I'm definitely in agreement with your appraisal. So you think I should sell my stocks and shares then?" she said with a wry smile.

"I've put all mine in a few US technology firms; they seem to be the future. In the office we're moving from old typewriters to new all electronic ones now. From what I'm seeing on my travels, I think the US is way ahead of us on the innovation front."

"So what's on your plate at the moment?" Nancy enquired.

"Seeing as anything significant that's happening in the world is in the Middle-East or South-East Asia, I'm constantly in and out of the area – I suspect I'll be assigned there again very soon. Other than that, I've been asked to help a colleague on a domestic story, but we're a long way off on that at the moment."

"What's the domestic one about, if you don't mind me asking?"

"At the moment, all I know is that there's some kind of activist pro-paedophilia group with alleged political ties. It looks like a long-lead one though."

Nancy's instincts prickled at this news. "I know I'm just a retired old colleague, but would it be possible to get an update on how you're doing with that one if you get any significant breaks?"

Theo was a little surprised to hear this, but Nancy had surprised him many times before. "Of course, and you're not old – the beauty of a woman with passing years only grows!" he said with a smile that created two small dimples in his cheeks. Nancy flushed, her body tingled and she found her smile hard to control. They both knew that he still had 'the gift' and chuckled to each other.

Theo looked out of the window and then at his watch. He caught the attention of the waitress for the bill. "I'd love to play all day, Nancy, but I do have to be back in the office before 1 o'clock."

"That's not a problem, Theo. If you need to head off I can see to the bill – it's the least I can do for your help."

"Are you sure, I hate to just leave you here on your own?" he said tentatively. Nancy placed her hand on his and indicated for him to go. The big man unfurled himself and rose like a sequoia from his chair. He quickly and slightly awkwardly put on his Mac, touched Nancy lightly on the shoulder, kissed her cheek and made his way out of the restaurant.

Nancy mused to herself as the waitress brought the bill to her table. She opened the vanity set again to check her make-up... and her rear quarter view again. The scene had changed but one thing had remained constant – a man in a black coat standing by a doorway on the opposite side of the street.

Walking back up the hill towards Fleet Street, Theo thought about today's encounter with his old boss. He was surprised she would be using her contacts for personal business, but he guessed that her time served to Queen and country owed her a few favours. He sympathised with her plight anyway and would do whatever she needed to help. The frisson of attraction swirled around his mind... could he really cross the line with such a woman? He checked back over his shoulder; the man had remained in place. He knew that the man wouldn't get close to Nancy, he was just an observer, but Theo still felt a little guilty anyway.

Back at the news desk, he followed procedural rules and called into HQ to confirm whether Nancy's actions were sanctioned and just as Nancy said; the assistant didn't deny any knowledge.

* * *

CHAPTER 30

THE SHEPHERD

Nancy looked at her watch. She had a couple of errands to run before heading home, but if her instincts were true, things could get dicey. After paying the bill, she put her coat and gloves on, but made sure to leave her scarf on the window ledge – just out of sight. She left the restaurant and walked down the hill at a slightly slower pace that was not in keeping with the rest of the human traffic flowing along the street. After about one hundred yards and nearing the river, she immediately turned back on herself, retracing her steps back to the restaurant. The damage was done. In less than a second she'd spotted the man in black walking down the hill. He'd kept his distance which meant he'd also had to maintain the same slow walking pace. He stayed on the opposite side of the street from her and continued walking downwards. Nancy didn't look at him directly, but kept him in her peripheral vision – taking in all of his attributes and features as they eventually passed each other.

The man rounded a corner and looked back at her covertly.

In the restaurant, Nancy stopped a scurrying waitress. "Excuse me; I think I may have left my head-scarf here a few minutes ago?"

The waitress looked around at where Nancy had been seated and found the scarf on the floor between the table and window ledge. "Here you go, madam."

"Oh, thank you very much; I'd forget my head as well, if it weren't screwed on."

When Nancy stepped outside the restaurant again, she walked back down the hill whilst putting her scarf on, scanning the forward horizon as she did so. There he was again... fifty yards, left-hand corner. Tail confirmed. She didn't think the man had been with her on the train to London, so it must have been through Theo. As she reached Queen Victoria Street, Nancy headed right towards oncoming traffic. As soon as she had the chance, she hailed a taxi and hopped in quickly.

"Where to?" the driver said.

"London Bridge, please." The driver switched off his 'For Hire' light and drove east past the man in black. From what Nancy could observe, he hadn't attempted to follow her. Just to be sure, she told the driver to head south over London Bridge and then head back west to drop her off at St. George's Cathedral in Southwark – which was just a couple of minutes' walk from Century House.

"If you don't mind me saying, it's a bit of a long way round when we could've just gone over Blackfriars?" the driver said innocently.

"I know, I've just had a change of mind – but it's extra cash, right?"

The driver smiled. "I'm not complaining," he said, as Nancy began writing some initial notes in a notebook that she always carried in her handbag.

After being dropped off at the cathedral, Nancy walked towards The Office, checking herself along the way. She entered Century House through the rear of the building this time. She would have liked to see The Chief, but the visit was unannounced, and as it turned out, he wasn't in the office anyway. Nancy enlisted the help of his assistant. She asked for her to make copies of Lee's Medical Certification of Death and the Death Registration; one for her and one for The Chief. Whilst the assistant made the copies, Nancy called David at work.

"Hi Mum, what's up? I presume you have more information now?"

"Yes, Kim got back from France late yesterday and dropped off the certificates for you. Would you like to come round for some dinner, we can talk a little easier then?" Nancy could hear the heave of David's sigh.

"Sure, I'll be round. Would half-six be alright, we've got problems on the production line here?"

"That's fine son, I'll see you then." She waited for David to click off before putting the receiver down herself. The assistant came back with the extremely well-presented copies, all now in separate files.

"Original, copy and copy," she said as she handed each file to Nancy. Nancy gave one of the files back to the assistant.

"Please can you put this one in Lee Powell's file and inform The Chief for me."

"Will do, Mrs. Walker. I hear you met with Mr. Greaves today. I do hope it was fruitful?" she enquired.

Nancy didn't change her expression. "Yes, the plan is proceeding. Do you have any updates on Lee?"

"I think The Chief's going to call you about that when he's bedded himself in to his new surroundings. I think he wants to give the boy a little time to adjust, if you know what I mean."

"OK, but I'll need to see Lee soon – he ran away the last time he felt neglected. Does The Chief have some time available tomorrow? I have another urgent item to discuss with him in person."

The assistant looked at the diary. "Would two thirty be OK?"

"Yes, that will be fine, but I'll need you to arrange for our best portrait artist to be made available for a 'POI' at least two hours beforehand – unless there's one available now?" Nancy asked.

The assistant didn't need to probe further; she'd been in the organisation for thirty years and knew the drill for enquiring about a 'Person of Interest' or POIs as they called them. "We don't have one now, but if you're happy to wait a little while, I'll make a couple of calls."

Nancy nodded and paced outside of the assistant's office whilst she waited.

Ten minutes later, the assistant waved Nancy back through her window. "You remember Patrick Arden?"

Nancy smiled. She had worked with Patrick many years ago. "Of course, a gifted man and the best, as I recall."

"He can't come in but has asked for you to visit his studio in Soho if that's alright?"

"Any particular time?"

"He said he'd be free all morning."

"Thank you, that should give me plenty of time."

"I thought so," the assistant said. "Here's the address. He'll make sure you're undisturbed."

Nancy took the piece of paper from the assistant. *The Chief's a lucky man to have someone so efficient and discreet,* she thought. Nancy left for the commute home – she had dinner to make for David and a lot of thinking to do.

Now that she'd briefly picked up a tail, counter-surveillance was key and Nancy made sure to be especially vigilant on each leg of the journey home. On the train she sat in a half-filled carriage and occupied herself with her own thoughts. The first thing she did was to take the notebook and pen from her bag and write more detailed descriptions of the man who'd followed her that afternoon. She also added more notes as she walked through the timeline of the day in her mind. Theo had approached her from behind. If he was genuinely playing a joke, that was fine, but it was also the best way to ensure she didn't see him or anyone else coming. Theo had looked over at the man in black at least twice whilst they were in the restaurant. The first time had been very subtle, but he hadn't masked it well enough. The second time was not subtle at all. Had the man in black given him a signal? Whether he had or not, Theo knew the man was there – of that she was certain. He continued the conversation with her and didn't signal to her in any way that they'd been followed. All roads led to one conclusion. Theo was compromised in some way, which meant she was now compromised too. She was angry at the position he'd put her in. But the biggest nagging question she had was why? If he knew he was going to be followed, why would he purposefully compromise her... she was retired, after all?

Maintaining her awareness, Nancy got off the train at Dunton Green, one stop earlier than she would normally. She made sure to be the last person to get off in her carriage and the last person to exit the station. She caught a mini-cab and asked the driver to take her towards Sevenoaks. Once happy that nothing untoward was happening, she told the driver to drop her at the train station, collected her car and drove home. As she reached the barrier to the private road of Woodland Rise, she was comforted by the fact that anyone who wanted to follow would be severely hampered by the location. The residents here could be quite nosy sometimes and always seemed aware of anything out of the ordinary. She also drew comfort in the fact that Theo had her telephone number. A secure line had been installed in the house some years back. It meant that all inbound and outbound telephone numbers were centrally collected before being routed to their intended recipient. If Theo gave her number to someone else, it could be flagged. As Nancy had been retired for a few years, she was no longer on the internal watched list. But the infrastructure was still there and she could get The Chief to reinstate this at any time.

When David arrived later that evening they were both in sombre moods but for different reasons. Nancy had set out Lee's urn in the front room. She certainly didn't want it in the kitchen. Unsure how David would react to the cremation, she braced herself as she ushered him through, where she had placed the urn on a small table decorated with a floral tablecloth. David stared quietly for a few moments.

"So this is it?" he said. Nancy nodded and put her arm around his shoulder. "I guess cremation was the best thing – I hadn't even thought about a burial or plots," he added.

"I think this way he'll always be with us, you know; not out of sight, so to speak."

"It's so small!" he said of the eight-inch-high container.

Nancy had also expected something a little larger herself. She felt the movement of David's shoulders as he began to cry.

"I'm so sorry, Lee, it's all my fault – I should've listened!" He picked up the urn and began talking to the brown and bronze striped container. Nancy remained silent and kept her arm around her son until he wiped his eyes and sat down on the sofa. Over on the side she picked up an A4 envelope and handed it to him.

"These are the original certified documents you will need to keep. They're in French but Kim says one is the medical certificate of death and the other is the registration. She wouldn't have been able to bring him back without them. It's important to keep them safe."

"I will."

"Do you know where you'll want to keep him?" Nancy asked.

"I don't know yet, Mum. When I get home, I'll probably put it... him... on the mantelpiece for now."

"That sounds right to me, son. Why don't you leave the urn here for a bit and come on into the kitchen; I have some shepherd's pie in the oven."

David and his mother sat in the warm kitchen talking for a couple of hours. It had helped relieve the tension in both of them, even when Nancy had to raise the subject of money and payment to Kim.

"I think her bill is going to be in the region of two thousand pounds. I've given her five hundred already, but she'll need the balance when she comes back with her report next Thursday." Surprisingly David didn't get angry like she expected. "Shall we say half each?"

David seemed empty and certainly didn't challenge the large sum. "Thank you, Mum, for helping. If I sign a cheque now, can you fill in the amount for me when you get the bill from Kim? I should be able to make sure I've got enough in the account if I pop to the bank tomorrow. I'm not sure I want to be round here and listen to her talking through the report." He looked down at the table.

"I understand your reticence, and it's entirely your choice, but aren't you forgetting somebody?" David looked up again. His mind had been so preoccupied that he'd neglected his daughter. His eyes began to water again.

"I don't know what to do, Mum. Even though Lou stopped her seeing me under duress, Laura still had the chance to see us both every other week when we found them again. She chose not to and I don't know if finding and forcing her to see us is going to make her an unwilling participant." Nancy listened. Everything David said made sense. She still hadn't confessed to knowing where the new address was. "Two grand is a lot of money and look where it got us with Lee. We could end up spending a load more money with Kim trying to find her again and for what – for her to reject me... again?"

Nancy sighed and rubbed her son's hand. "I understand what you're saying. Why don't we leave this for now? We can always revisit this again if you want to."

"To be honest, Mum, I'm not sure I want to. Dealing with Lou and all of that hassle is not something I want to go through again."

Nancy knew not to push the subject any further. "Are you sure you're not coming over when Kim arrives with her report? I'd arranged it for an evening so that you could be here, but if you don't want to be here, I should let her know so that she can do it during her professional hours."

"I'd rather not," he said.

"OK, I guess that's settled then."

After retiring from the kitchen to the front room, David signed the blank cheque and talked about work for a while. Nancy didn't really understand the reality of running a factory line, but letting David talk seemed to make him more relaxed. As he spoke, Nancy's mind wandered to the events that happened earlier in the day. It occurred to her that David could potentially be a serious weakness should somebody or some organisation wish to attempt to compromise her. She would need to formulate back-up plans if things started to turn out badly. She was annoyed that having retired from The Service relatively unscathed, now, of all times, she was facing potential danger.

"You OK, Mum?" David said. "You seem to be in a different world."

"I'm sorry, David, my mind's just wandered a little, that's all."

David looked at his watch and smiled. "You're not the first person I've bored to death about production issues. I should be going anyway."

"I'm sorry, David, I didn't mean to be rude."

"That's OK, Mum, it's getting late anyway." David turned to the urn. He gingerly picked up the ceramic container and the envelope. "I'll see you soon, yeah." He kissed his mother on the cheek.

After David left and Nancy had finished cleaning up in the kitchen, she poured herself a small sherry and sat in the front room armchair... thinking.

When David arrived home, he put Lee's ashes on the centre of the mantelpiece. He then went to the fridge, pulled open a can of beer and sat down on the sofa opposite the fireplace in silence. He raised the can once to the urn and drank the rest swiftly.

* * *

The next morning Nancy was up early and prepared as always. At 8 o'clock she rang Kim. "I'm sorry to call you so early, Kim, but I have a very full day ahead of me and I need to be out in thirty minutes."

Kim was already dressed and alert. "No problems, Nancy – what's up?"

"You're off the hook for presenting the report back to David next week. You can still deliver it on the Thursday but could we do the daytime instead? I can also go through your submission for The Chief's office."

"That's fine with me – any particular time in mind?" Kim asked.

"Would first thing be alright? We don't lose a whole day then."

"I'll see you at 9am, Thursday."

"Excellent. One other thing: is your invoice estimate still the same or do you have a more exact figure?" Nancy enquired.

"Hold on, I have a precise total." Kim went over to a file on her table. "£2,167 plus 12.5% VAT, which is £2,438." The dreaded VAT would often catch people out and Kim waited for a push-back or a sharp intake of breath at the other end of the phone, but Nancy took the news within her stride.

"Thank you, Kim, I'll see you next week." Nancy said as she put the receiver down.

It's always business with Nancy, Kim thought. There was never any room for emotional attachment.

Nancy filled out the cheque from David for one thousand pounds only. She didn't see the point in penny-pinching for the remainder of his share, considering what she'd put him through. She readied herself and then made her way into London again. Before heading into the notorious Soho district, she popped into the main branch of her bank to pay David's cheque in and withdraw enough cash for herself and Kim's invoice. From there, Nancy took a cab to the intersection of Berwick and Broadwick Street. She'd gone past Patrick Arden's Portrait Gallery deliberately; she got out and waited for a short while. Once assured she was alone, she headed back down the street and walked inside, where Patrick was wiping around each picture frame with a duster.

"Hello, Nancy, so good to see you – it's been a while." Nancy and Patrick shook hands. They had a professional relationship, not just through The Service, but Nancy also had one of Patrick's paintings hanging on her living room wall at home. He had the most amazing eye when translating a photograph to paint. She'd been so impressed that, ten years ago, she commissioned him to paint a picture of her late husband from a happier time. He was also an exceptional sketch artist, given the right information.

"It's good to see you too, Patrick, and a good chance for me to see your latest works. When did you move into your own gallery?"

"Oh, I decided to take the plunge about two years ago."

"Does it pay the bills?" she asked.

"Business is slow but profitable."

Nancy had a brief wander around the small gallery. She stopped at one picture. It was a different style to the others and by far the largest in the shop. A mosaic of small circles of many different varieties of shape and colour, each set in squares that were then set out in a diagonal parquet style. Nancy squinted and cocked her head to the left and then the right. Patrick laughed and gently put his arms on her shoulders, guiding her further back to the opposing wall.

"How about now?" he said. Nancy laughed at herself. There right in front of her very eyes was a portrait of Liza Minnelli in a red riding hood.

"That's wonderful, Patrick."

"I'm experimenting with a new style," he said. "The original picture was taken by Andy Warhol and I saw it in a magazine."

"It won't be long before it sells, I bet?"

"Here's hoping," he said, crossing his fingers. "Would you like a drink before we get to work?" Patrick understood the value in making sure an eyewitness felt comfortable before providing details. The end results were always better.

"Would a glass of water be alright?"

Patrick locked the shop door and switched the sign to *Closed*. He ushered Nancy through to the back of the gallery where he had a desk and two chairs set up. He popped over to a sink and filled a glass with water for his guest. Nancy took her notebook from her bag as he sat down with paper and a number of pencils ready to get to work.

"Is that a description of the POI?"

"Yes, I wrote it down approximately three hours after seeing him," she said.

"Good, why don't you read out everything initially and we'll go from there."

"This won't all be relevant but here goes, 5ft 10in – 5ft 11in. Dark woollen three-quarter length coat. Dark roll-neck jumper. All clothing clean and well turned out. Face shape, Slavic, square with a slight taper to the jaw line. He had a typical high forehead and hairline with dark brown hair." Nancy showed Patrick her own rough sketch of a shallow 'M' to represent the hairline. "Hair well-trimmed and over the ear. Two to three creases along the forehead. Ears were medium to large, of the pointed type, not rounded. Eyebrows, angled not round; medium density. Brow line slightly protruding, with slight crease to the top of the nose. Eyes green, piercing, but dark patches under and around them, like he'd not slept for a while. Nose, medium to large, angular top and ridge, to slightly more rounded at the tip. One crease each side from above the top of the nostril towards the outer mouth, but not reaching the lips. His mouth was straight and top and bottom lips were even in width, approximately one quarter inch each. He had a defined philtrum slightly angled left to right. It ran in line to the cleft. The jaw line to the chin was a rounded off 'V' shape. He had a small chin with a cleft, the dimple probably half an inch. There was a scar or crease just above the cleft, much like a rounded tick. " Nancy drew this out for him. "Protruding thyroid cartilage. Clean shaven. Skin texture good, no pocking, but definitely smokes."

This was all very helpful to Patrick. He began sketching out rough shapes on A3 and asking Nancy to refer back to her notes for more detail whenever he needed them, rubbing out and making changes as he went along. After an hour or so, they had both honed the image to enough of a likeness for Nancy's purposes. He packaged the sketch into a cardboard folio folder, tied the two ribbons to keep the contents secure and handed it to Nancy with his business card.

"That's perfect, Patrick – thank you."

"You're welcome. It was good to work with you again. Is there anything in the shop I can interest you in before you go?"

Nancy smiled. She couldn't blame the man for taking every opportunity that came his way. "If I had a wall large enough and the money…" She pointed to his latest work. "But next time I'm around I'll definitely pop in, now that I know you have your own place."

Patrick smiled. "I had to try." They shook hands and he let her out of the shop door.

Nancy walked westwards towards Regent Street. She looked at her watch. It was just after 1 o'clock. She popped into a small sandwich shop and bought a cheese and salad roll for later. On Regent Street, she caught a cab to St. George's Cathedral, again making sure she wasn't followed. Once at Century House she headed to the sixth floor Identity & Records section to speak to the Head Clerk, and showed him the sketch.

"Do you have any history on this POI?" The clerk was in his forties and Nancy knew he had a mind like a computer where faces were concerned.

"Looks familiar – Eastern Bloc?" he asked.

"I think that would be a good place to start. I have a two thirty on the 11th – it would be extremely helpful if I had something more concrete ready for the meeting." She smiled.

"I'll do my best, Ma'am."

"Thank you, I'll just be over in the corner by the window if you find something." Nancy took her roll and a newspaper from her bag and sat at a spare table leafing through the various stories of the *Daily Mail*. It wasn't her normal paper of choice, but she had suddenly become very interested in its contents, especially anything reported by Theo Greaves.

Just over thirty minutes later, the clerk walked over to where Nancy was seated. "Would you like to come with me, Ma'am? I think I've narrowed it down to three likely suspects."

Nancy was pleased. The Americans had recently come up with the idea of Identikits, but you couldn't beat the human brain for intuition. The clerk placed three pictures on his desk. Although similar, Nancy was really only drawn to one of them. But to make sure, she took out her vanity case, turned her back to the clerk, placed the mirror twelve inches from her face and asked the man to hold each picture behind her left shoulder. There was no doubt in her mind; the first picture was of the man in question.

"Florian Schäfer. 'The Shepherd', we call him – it's a literal translation of the surname." A small explosion fired off inside Nancy's brain. Schäfer was a name she'd heard before. "We believe he was born in Austria, but his allegiances are definitely further east. As you're not in active service, I don't have clearance to give you his file, I'm afraid – that would need to come down from upstairs – but I can give you a copy of the picture and the file reference number?"

"Thank you very much, you've been very helpful. We may send for the file in a bit, so you may want to have it to hand," she said. "Just one more thing, does this 'Shepherd' have a *modus operandi*?"

"All in the file, I'm afraid. From memory, I don't think we've been able to prove he's a hands-on type... but that's only based on what we can prove. He's a babysitter, I believe."

"That's very useful to know. Any illegal entries?"

"I can't be sure. My mind's good, but this is a huge archive now!"

"No problem, I'll wait here for the photocopy and will read the file in due course." The clerk went to the back of his office and made a double-sized copy of the image for her. Nancy's mind wandered back in time whilst she waited. Did Schäfer know who she was or was it a coincidence? Nancy didn't believe in coincidences; there was definitely a connection there somewhere.

"Here you go. I hope this helps." Nancy thanked the man and took the lift to the eleventh floor, where she waited patiently in the outer office of The Chief with his assistant for company.

At 2:35 The Chief finished a phone call and opened his door. "Come on in Nancy. No calls," he directed to the assistant. They both sat down. "I believe you have a POI to talk about?"

Nancy handed the sketch and photo copy to him. "Theo and I were followed to a restaurant yesterday and he then tailed me for little while after I left. All roads lead to Theo, I'm afraid."

The Chief buzzed his intercom.

"Can you get file reference i-5362 up to me as soon as possible, please?" He didn't wait for an answer. "Tell me more about this," he said.

Nancy walked him through the encounter in detail. When she'd finished, she asked, "Is this situation something The Service is aware of?"

"Not to my knowledge," The Chief replied. There was a knock on the door. The assistant entered with the file requested. The Chief turned over the front sheet and adjusted his seat round to sit side by side with Nancy, so that they could both digest the contents together.

SUMMARY: *Florian Schäfer. Born 17/10/49 in Klostermarienberg, Austria. Parents Lukas and Lillian Schäfer. Entry to the UK 1970 via*

Istanbul. Went to Birkbeck University and studied Psychology under the name Max Tost. Dismissed for spreading false rumours about his Psychology professor. Now runs a translation service and English teaching school in West London under the guise of Lukas Mayer. Ardent pacifist. Highly suspected Stasi or KGB.

Even though the details were sparse, they were enough to confirm to Nancy who Florian Schäfer really was. She turned back the front sheet and scanned through the list of people who'd requested to see the file. Theo's name was near the top just before that of his case officer.

In the late 1960s after a number of embarrassing public revelations, MI6 had established a whole swathe of information-control systems internally. One process was to literally log every interaction with internal documents. Theo's interaction was dated 1976, but he had been denied access to the file.

"So, any idea what he might want with Theo?" The Chief asked. He had a reasonable idea, but he also wanted to see how Nancy saw the situation.

Nancy remained calm. "If I had to guess, and this would be a guess," she said, "Theo's been recruited for his ties in the Middle East. Theo said that this was where most of the action is these days and he's been quite active in the area for a while. If the Stasi are still training pilots and terrorists, it would be a great 'hands-off' way to make introductions *etcetera*."

"That's an interesting hypothesis. Do you think Theo is a double?"

"Hard to say without knowing about the intel he handles. He may not be double in the truest sense of the meaning."

"How so?" The Chief asked.

"He may be an agent for us, but also working a second job for The Stasi or KGB on the side. If this guy has compromised Theo in some way, it may not necessarily be fully against Her Majesty's interests. That said, Theo's now been exposed, which means that he'll need to be monitored more closely." She pointed to the access log. "This may give us an idea of how long he's been compromised for." Nancy noted to herself that Theo's case officer *had* been allowed to view the file.

"And what about you? Why do you think this Schäfer followed you?" The Chief asked.

Nancy's mind churned back to 1960. She needed to be careful. The file hadn't disclosed anything, but she wondered if The Chief had made the connection. She kept her cards to her chest. "Purely judging by Theo's behaviour, he may have given the guy intel before our meeting. Schäfer was either purposely waiting to follow me, or he may have just been fishing. Either way, I'll be on a high threat alert from now on."

"Do you want me to have a Special Branch officer assigned to you?"

"I don't think so. Besides, I'm retired," Nancy said, as if it were nothing. But inside, she was now concerned for her own safety and wanted to change the subject. "Just as an aside, Theo said he was working on an unrelated longer lead story about an activist pro-paedophilia group with alleged political ties." Nancy deliberately added this to the conversation to see if her instincts where correct.

"Oh, right, what did he have to offer there?" The Chief enquired.

"That was it, I'm afraid – he didn't say anything else." Her instincts were correct; The Chief had the same reaction that she had had, and she knew it had piqued his interest – even if he didn't show it. "So anyway, I'm sure you've got ideas on how you want to deal with Theo, but I'm here to ask for a couple of favours."

"Of course, this is sterling work as always Nancy. What do you need?"

"Well, I wish to remain retired, and Theo has my number, so I need you to put my number back on the Watch List effective immediately, please."

"Done," The Chief said.

"I need Theo to be given the time to carry out the actions I've asked of him which will help cement Lee's story, and meet the boy's conditions. I've just asked Theo to print Lee's cover story and doorstep the mother. So I think about two weeks should cover it. After that, he's all yours."

"That shouldn't be a problem."

"And the other reason I came was to get an update on Lee and set up a time to pay a visit."

* * *

CHAPTER 31

HAM IN THE SANDWICH

Lee had never been in a Bentley before. On the day of his inauguration into The Service and after a final farewell to his Nan, The Chief had taken him down in the lift at Century House to the basement floor; where a chauffeur was ready and waiting for their arrival. Lee loved cars, and wanted to absorb as much as he could before getting in. He walked around the two-tone blue car, sliding his hands across all the curves and angles.

"I don't understand," he said. "This is a Rolls Royce Silver Shadow II, but it's got a different front grill and it says Bentley?" The Chief smiled. He was a bit of a car aficionado himself, which was why he'd chosen the Bentley instead of the standard Jaguar – and definitely not a Roller.

"Well observed. It's based on the Silver Shadow platform but with a number of variations. Let me show you." The Chief showed Lee the differences in ride-height, the special tyres, bonnet angle, height and positioning, and the change in suspension. "Here, feel the thickness of the body." He showed Lee where to feel under the top of the front wheel arch. "Bentley is owned by the same company as Rolls Royce, which is why they use the same body. But Bentleys are the more powerful, sportier versions."

"It's an inch thick!" Lee said.

"Yup, you would not want to get hit by one of these, she's built like a tank. Come, let's put your bags in the boot – it gets more interesting on the inside." The chauffeur got out of the driver's side and opened the boot for them. He took The Chief's briefcase but Lee wanted to put his own things in. The rear bumper protruded out so far that he had to almost throw the bags in. The chauffeur then opened the passenger side door, where The Chief ushered Lee in first. The main things he noticed were the exceptionally deep carpets, the plush leather seats and how roomy everything was.

"My Dad's got a Ford..." Lee stopped himself and looked down slightly. "I knew someone who had a Ford Granada," he said in a more subdued voice. "It's a really fast car too." The Chief pointed to the carpeted box that sat on the transmission tunnel between them, and signalled for Lee to open it. Lee did and smiled. "Just like Batman!" he exclaimed.

"Ha, yes, just like Batman." Lee looked at the phone. If this was his car, he would've loved to pick up the receiver, dial Louvaine or Jon and say the words that were now etched in his mind – *I'm going to come and kill you one day*. That thought had burned away within him whilst he was abandoned at the children's home and during his unhappy times in France. Their day would come when he was bigger and stronger, and the odds could be turned in his favour. But for now, Lee buried the thought deep inside.

The Chief gave an instruction to the chauffeur. "Can you head along the M4 – we need to go to Taplow, just past Slough."

"Right you are, Sir." The chauffeur glided the Bentley out of the underground car park and headed west towards their destination.

After their long and fruitful afternoon, The Chief still had one burning question. "There's something I'm dying to know, Lee. What made you jump from a bridge that could've killed you, if not by the impact, but by subsequent drowning?"

Lee thought for a second. "I didn't want to go back... I didn't want to be caught... I had no reason to shoot anybody – my life... didn't mean anything to me anymore."

The Chief put his hand on Lee's right forearm. "Back in the war, I was put in a similar situation myself once. You and I have a lot in common."

Lee was about to ask why when the chauffeur caught their attention. "We've got company, Sir. Rover SD1, dark brown I think. I haven't got the plate yet. Not seen this one before."

"How far back?" The Chief asked.

"Four cars, Sir."

The Chief pulled the centre armrest down between them and motioned for Lee to get on it to look through the rear window. "Be a good lad and get me the number plate, would you?"

Lee excitedly jumped onto the armrest, sitting on both knees and holding on to the seat-back. It was getting dark and took a little while before he could get the full license plate. "MLM... 929...P. I think that makes it a 1975 plate. There are two men inside."

The Chief opened the box by his left leg on the transmission tunnel, picked up the receiver and pushed a single button on the phone. "This is Ghost 1. Request intercept with contact, Rover SD1, index Mike-

Lima-Mike-nine-two-nine-Papa. Entering Motorway 4 westbound from the 205." The Chief listened briefly, replaced the receiver and amplified a command to the chauffeur. "Time for some dry cleaning."

"Yes, Sir," the chauffeur said with a grin.

"Dry cleaning?" Lee asked, confused, but still in position to look out of the window.

The Chief smiled. "Unfortunately, it's a game we have to play all too often, given the position I hold. Dry cleaning gets rid of dirty spots. So if you think you've been spotted, that's what you do; carry out measures to see if you're being surveilled. You are now in a perfect position to see if we are genuinely being followed. Keep an eye out to see if the target or any other targets accelerate to stay with us, but slow down when we do. With any luck we might have some fun with them in a bit."

As the car pulled off the A205 at Chiswick and entered the M4, the chauffer floored the throttle and kept his foot buried to the sumptuous sheepskin floor mat. The acceleration kept Lee's chest pinned to the rear seat as he kept his eyes just above the seat back.

"He's having a hard time keeping up," Lee said.

"Would you concur, Sergeant?" The Chief asked the chauffeur.

"I would, Sir."

"Time for phase two," The Chief said.

After one-to-two miles the chauffeur slowed the car down from one hundred to fifty miles an hour and moved the car into the inside lane.

"Keep your eyes peeled for the outside lane," The Chief instructed.

Lee watched as the Rover, which had maintained its acceleration, slowly washed off its speed to maintain a distance with the Bentley. "They've maintained their distance," he reported.

"I bet they're fuming now, Sir. They must know they've been made?"

The Chief didn't answer the rhetorical question, but tapped Lee on the leg. "Keep watching, we're just getting started."

After about five minutes, Lee could see the small flecks of blue light as a traffic police car began speeding into view in the outside lane. As the traffic began to pull left to let it pass, the police car drew level with the Rover which was already in the middle lane. Lee watched as the police signalled for it to pull over to the inside lane. The Rover complied as the police car pulled in front and slowly guided the driver to move to the hard shoulder, where they both eventually stopped.

Lee smiled. "The police have got them now," he said.

"Excellent!" The Chief replied. "All in a day's work in this job. Anything else we should be concerned with, Sergeant?"

"No secondaries from what I can see, Sir."

The Chief looked at Lee. "Sometimes they use a decoy that they know we'll easily spot, so that other surveillance gets missed."

Lee continued to look out of the rear window for a while as the chauffeur pushed the right pedal down again to maintain about eighty. When he was certain that there was nothing untoward happening, he climbed back down and sat in his seat. He kept quiet and watched the road signs.

The chauffeur pulled off at junction seven. "Directions from here, Sir?" he asked The Chief.

"Left at the next roundabout, then follow Bath Road to the fourth junction. Turn right at Berry Hill."

As they drove along Berry Hill and then right to Saxon Gardens, The Chief directed the driver to the house of Christopher and Deborah Powell. Lee's stomach tightened. This was going to be a big step.

As if sensing his trepidation, The Chief put his hand on Lee's shoulder. "Inch by inch, step by step, that's all it has to be for now."

It was nice of him to say, but it still didn't loosen the knots Lee felt. "Please stay in the car, I'll take it from here, Sergeant."

The Chief lifted the armrest back into position, opened his door and waited for Lee to follow. They both went to the boot and collected the shopping his Nan had kindly bought for him.

As they walked up the driveway towards the front door there was a piece of crucial information Lee needed. "How much do they know about me?" he asked.

"Good question, and one I'm glad you didn't ask in the car. They know you were sent to a home, that you ran away and that you wouldn't come home until you were promised not to be put back in the home again. They don't know who your parents were. They know that the only relative who will be allowed contact with you is your nan. We are getting the foster care paperwork drawn up and once that's in place, they'll enrol you into the boarding school we talked about. They both have ties with The Service and as well as becoming your official guardians, they'll be your handlers too." Lee frowned. "All agents have handlers. To put it in perspective, your nan was Kim's handler before she retired. When your nan first joined, she had a handler too. Any more questions before we knock on the door?"

Lee saw a slight twitch at the one of the front curtains. "No, I think they're waiting for us anyway."

The front door opened just before The Chief could ring the bell.

"Ah, Lee, I'd like you to meet Christopher Powell. Chris, this is Lee." The Chief put a guiding hand on Lee's back to coax him forward a little. Chris put out his hand to shake and Lee responded politely. He didn't really know what to say, so he remained silent.

"Pleased to meet you, Lee." He shook The Chief's hand too. "Sir. Come in both of you, Debbie's just upstairs preparing a room." The

Chief let Lee go first as they both walked past their host. "Just head left to the living room."

Lee looked around and took as much in as he could. *These people are doing alright for themselves.* The room was twice the size of any room his parents had. *They've also used a bit of air freshener too.* As they both sat on one of the comfortable sofas, Lee couldn't help but look at the sophisticated TV in the corner with so many buttons.

Chris called upstairs. "Can you come down Debs, our guests are here!" He had a commanding voice, but his facial expressions had been hard to read. *Was Chris really pleased to see him? Was he feeling just as awkward? Was The Chief ordering him to do this?* All these questions circulated around Lee's head. He was just wondering what 'Debs' would be like, when she skipped down the stairs. The contrast couldn't have been more stark. Chris was tall, fit, thin-faced with cropped hair; Debs was much shorter, rounder-faced, with red hair flowing to her shoulders.

The Chief stood as she came downstairs and Lee followed suit. Her face lit up like a Christmas tree when she saw the guests. She almost danced over to them with her arms outstretched. "Hello, Sir." Debs embraced The Chief, but her attention was quickly re-focussed on the boy next to him. She scooped Lee up in a bear hug so he couldn't move his arms, and swung him round in circles. Lee's face resembled a surprised seal whilst he was reminded that his ribs still hurt a little. The men watched from the sidelines.

"Aren't you a little cracker?" Debs said as she finally put Lee down and ruffled his hair.

Chris and The Chief laughed. "And this is my wife Debbie. Sorry mate, emotions aren't my strong point... but Debs on the other hand! If you're a good boy she'll give you a bone and take you for nice walk in a bit."

"Christopher!" Debs said playfully. "You can call me Debs if you like, Lee."

Chris walked over to his wife and put a hand on her shoulder and Lee's. Although The Chief looked a little apprehensive at Chris's last remark, Lee smiled. He didn't mind the guy's sense of humour – at least he had one. Although caught by the initial shock and unexpected exuberance of this new woman, Lee's heart warmed with the knowledge that someone had actually been pleased to see him. His mind briefly shifted backwards. How was it that a complete stranger could be so kind and embracing having never met him before, yet his own family would never go near him? Lee allowed himself to relax as Debs held his hand.

"Come on, I'll show you to your new room." She took him upstairs excitedly; it was as though she had a new playmate.

"Drink, Sir?" Chris asked as he ushered The Chief to sit over at the dining table.

"I don't suppose you have a single malt in there somewhere?"

"Neat or with ice?" Chris took a bottle of Glenlivet from the drinks cabinet.

"Neat is perfect, thank you."

Chris walked over with the bottle and two cut whisky glasses, poured half an inch in each and slid one over to his boss. "Debs has been bouncing of the walls ever since you called. When you first mentioned this as a possibility, she... we both set ourselves up for another disappointment."

"I think the three of you will make a good... family partnership," The Chief said, choosing his words carefully. "The boy's been through a lot, so the both of you are going to have to be patient. A short leash won't work with this one. He may be seven, but he's independent and resourceful."

"Example?" Chris asked.

"He ran away to France, lived on the streets, escaped from a police cell, jumped from a bridge and faked his own death. Does that give you a measure?"

Chris was no expert on kids, but he'd only played with a train set when he was the same age.

The Chief lowered his voice. "You may hear noise filter down the grapevine about two dead KGB agents. That boy also protected one of ours." Chris looked stunned. "I know," The Chief said. "One other thing for the both of you to bear in mind – the boy is highly intuitive, especially when he's being misled. You'll either have to be story perfect or be as honest as you can. I would suggest leaning towards the latter if I were you. He'll be a great asset for us all if nurtured properly."

Chris took this all in as Debs and Lee appeared at the top of the landing and made their way downstairs. Both men looked up. Lee seemed much happier and relaxed as he came downstairs.

"Would you like a drink?" Chris asked, addressing them both.

"I'll have a tonic water, what would you like Lee?"

Lee wasn't sure what he'd be allowed to have or what they had in the house. "I don't suppose you've got any cream soda or lemonade?" he asked tentatively.

Debbie noticed the way Lee had slightly retreated. Not physically, but she could see that something was going on there. "I'm not sure, why don't you come with me and we can see what we've got," she said, holding Lee's hand again and leading him outside to an adjacent garage. Debs stood Lee in front of an array of fizzy drink cans stacked on the floor. "I don't think we have cream soda, but you can see what else we have." Lee spied what he wanted and changed his mind… a can of ginger beer. It reminded him of his Nan. Lee was hungry. He hadn't eaten anything since lunch in the fancy restaurant, but he kept quiet anyway – ginger beer was treat enough.

When they got back to the table, Chris had Debbie's drink prepared on ice and Lee sat down with the adults. Both Chris and Debs left a short silence to prompt The Chief to speak, but Lee asked a question.

"What's that?" he said pointing to the men's glasses.

"It's scotch," The Chief said, "Want to try it?"

Lee looked around the table, as they all just looked at him. He cautiously lifted The Chief's glass and smelled the contents. It was like smelling petrol and a shock to Lee's nasal passages. He backed his head away immediately.

"Try a sip?" The Chief said, goading Lee. So Lee took a small sip and instantly reacted like a sneezing dog, shaking his head from side to side. The men laughed.

"How can you drink that? It's horrible!" he said, as he pushed the glass back to The Chief and *pssst* open his can of ginger beer.

"I haven't got a clue Lee, it's just that tastes change as you get older sometimes."

"Well, mine won't," he said. "I won't be touching that again!"

The Chief looked at his watch. "So I will need to be going soon – shall we all just walk through the rough plan?" It wasn't a question and The Chief addressed all three of them. "I know each of you know some of the plan already, but I just want everyone to be on the same page. We'll get the new birth certificate, and foster papers set up at our end. I'm expecting this to be completed within two weeks, and then Chris and Debbie will be legal guardians for you, Lee. A place has been reserved at Caldicot School and the fees will be paid through Chris and Debbie. As soon as the paperwork is ready, your new foster parents will enrol you in the school. I believe the school allows parental visits on Wednesdays and Saturdays, but we have set up a special dispensation for weekends. That way you can alternate between being with your foster parents and in receipt of the training I've spoken to you about."

"And my nan," Lee cut in.

"Apologies, and your nan. If things work out between the three of you and you all agree it's what you want, Chris and Debbie can apply to fully adopt you. That would mean they would be your actual parents in the eyes of the law."

"How far away is the school?" Lee enquired.

Chris stepped in. "It's about three or four miles away. Why do you ask?"

"I was just wondering why I have to go to a boarding school, if I could walk there or catch a bus or something?"

"Another good question, Lee and one I hope I'll have a good answer for," The Chief said. "Remember I said that Chris and Debbie both had ties with The Service?" Lee nodded. "Well that means there will be times when they are away from home, either at different times or at the same time. This means that they, myself and your nan need to be assured that you'll be looked after. This is why the boarding school was the best choice. Also, Caldicot is a very good feeder school for Harrow, which is an important place for you to attend when you're old enough. Does that help answer your question?"

Lee thought it through. Whilst it made sense logically, it was going to be a big change. But considering everything that had happened over the past few hours, another life change now seemed to be the norm, so he nodded.

The Chief continued. "My suggestion would be for the three of you to bed in for a little while, whilst the paperwork and enrolment is sorted out. Once you're in school, I'll arrange for your nan to come and visit." He looked around the table. "Is everyone in agreement?"

"Good with me," Chris said.

"I'm happy," Debs said.

They all looked at Lee. "It's good with me too," he replied.

The Chief raised his glass and everyone clinked theirs – Lee with his can.

When The Chief had finished his whisky and shaken Lee's hand, Chris then escorted him to the front door. The Bentley was waiting for him at the end of the driveway. Lee tried to listen to what they were saying, but not much else was said and the front lights of the Bentley soon wafted out of sight.

It was getting late. Back in the living room, Debs and Lee had started talking about the big adventure they were all about to embark upon. In truth, it was mainly Debs talking. She was so excited, Lee just listened. Chris sat down and listened too. He was a patient man and had heard Debs talk excitedly about the future before.

When he could get a word in edgeways, Chris changed the subject. "I don't want to bring the conversation down, but there's something I think we all need to discuss from the very beginning." Lee tensed inside and Debs wasn't quite sure what this was going to be about. "Lee, we... all of us need to understand why we are here and the parts we have to play from this point onwards. I think this is going to be the toughest for you, but I'm hoping that as time goes on, it becomes more than playing a part."

Lee frowned a little, but Debbie had understood where her husband was heading. "He's talking about having to call us Mum and Dad, sweetheart," she interjected.

Lee began to understand and Chris appreciated the relief his wife brought to the conversation, which allowed him to continue with greater fervour. "As you know, we are all part of The Service now. This means that we each have a huge responsibility to our country and each other. Any slip of the tongue or inconsistency of story could blow our cover or yours. In the worst of cases, it can get somebody killed." Lee had cottoned on now; he'd seen this first hand. Chris could see the boy's body begin to relax more. "So from The Service's perspective, we are now mother, father and son – which means that we all have to adjust how we act and what we say. From our perspective, we've never had a child. Nobody's ever seen us with a child and all of our friends and family currently all think we're a couple only. But we've been in this business for a little while know and can adjust. I can't speak for you, Lee, but I would imagine that it's going to be more difficult." He looked at Debbie for some support.

"I think what Chris is saying is that in public, we all have to act. Chris plays the character of Dad, I play the character of Mum and you play the role of Lee. When you're in a play, you have to call each actor by the character role. What's your favourite programme?"

Lee actually had to think. It had been a while since he'd watched a television set. "The Six-Million-Dollar Man," he said finally.

Debbie was vexed but Chris knew exactly what Lee was talking about. "Excellent choice! So, the character in that programme is called Steve Austin, but his real name is Lee Majors, right? But, you never hear anyone on the programme call him Lee or Mr. Majors – they all play their character roles. So what I'm asking you to do, whenever in public, is to call us both Mum and Dad only... even if you don't mean it right now."

Debbie felt that she should give Lee more reassurance. "But as time goes by and we get to know each other and we adopt you as our own, we hope you'll actually come to see us as more than your guardians." She put her hand on Lee's arm.

"Do you think you can manage it?" Chris asked.

Lee thought about what they'd both said. Inside he was confused and conflicted. It was torture to think about anyone other than his dad being his dad. It was just as hard to think about anyone else but Louvaine as his mother, even though she'd hated him and he'd just found out that neither of them were his parents at all.

Debbie and Chris watched as Lee wrung his fingers and bowed his head in thought. The last thing Debbie wanted to do was put the boy under too much pressure at such a crucial stage. "Would you like to think about it for a while?" she asked.

"Yes please," Lee said quietly.

Debbie and Chris nodded to each other. "It's getting late my love, and I expect it's been a big day. Do you think it's time to go to bed?"

Lee looked up pensively. "Could I have a biscuit before I go?"

"Of course, when did you last eat?"

"Lunchtime."

"What?" It startled Lee when Debbie raised her voice, but it was purely through concern. "No, no, no, come with me... let's get you a sandwich." She walked out towards the kitchen and beckoned Lee to follow. Like the living room, the kitchen was also more spacious than his parents had ever been able to afford.

Debbie crouched down face-to-face with Lee. "Put your arms around my neck." She said with a smile. Lee gave her a strange look but complied anyway. "Hup!" In a single movement, she'd put her arms around Lee's legs, lifted him up and sat him on the sideboard.

Lee smiled. The woman was pretty strong for her size. She whizzed around the kitchen with bread, butter and a knife ready in no time. "Right, what'll it be? I've got ham, cheese and corned-beef."

"Can I have some ham, please?"

"Coming right up. Any pickle? I have Piccalilli, Branston or mustard?"

"Just ham, please."

The sandwich was made, cut in quarters and on a plate within a minute. *She's definitely nifty around the kitchen*, Lee thought. He jumped off the sideboard himself. It was nice that Debs was trying, but he wanted to show he was independent too.

They both went back to the dining table where Chris had a newspaper open. "Do you read the newspapers, Lee?" he asked.

"I read the jokes and the sport sometimes, but the rest is just boring. Always seems to be bad news." Lee felt it was best to keep quiet about sometimes looking at Page 3 of *The Sun* when he and his friends got the chance.

Chris looked at Debbie. "He's right you know. But there is another way to look at the news as well, though."

Lee finished a mouthful of sandwich. "What do you mean?"

"Well, pretty much every paper has its own agenda, whether that be political or financial." Chris was about to continue when Debbie cut in, knowing full well that he was about to embark on one of his in-depth analyses.

"Shall we let Lee finish his sandwich and continue with this tomorrow? It is getting late after all."

Chris caught himself and smiled. In his own way, this was how he showed his enthusiasm for having Lee around, but he knew that Debbie was right. Best not overwhelm the lad so soon. "She's right mate, best not bore you with this tonight."

When Lee had finished the last quarter of sandwich and what was left of his ginger beer, Debbie took him upstairs and showed him which flannel and toothbrush was his to use. "I'll pop back up in a minute to tuck you in."

The independent part of Lee was about to say, "No, I'm too old for tucking in," but he held back. It might be nice for a change. He couldn't remember ever being tucked in at home. He washed, cleaned his teeth and then headed to what was now his room. Debbie had done her best to make the space as comfortable and welcoming as possible. It was lighter in colour than his room at home and the bed sheets were all freshly cleaned. She'd put his new clothes in drawers, cupboards or hung them in the wardrobe, but he didn't have any pyjamas. His mind flicked back to the times in France where he had to wash in freezing cold water fountains. He could survive not having pyjamas. He got undressed, leaving just his underpants on and got into bed under the nice crisp sheets. A couple of minutes later, Debs came back upstairs and sat on the side of Lee's bed. She stroked his hair and the side of his face for a while. *I could get used to this.*

She spoke to him softly. "Today's been a big day for you, I bet?"

Lee summed up his day in the simplest and only way he could see it. "This morning I had a dad and a mum – this afternoon I no longer had a dad and mum and found out I wasn't even theirs anyway." Lee searched his mind for the right way to say the next sentence, but Debbie ended it for him.

"And now you're here with us... two complete strangers?" she remarked.

Lee felt embarrassed. It made him sound ungrateful which he definitely wasn't. "I'm not complaining," he said. "It's just a lot to..."

"Cope with," Debbie finished. Lee nodded. Debbie thought for a little. "You know, there's only so much that The Chief was able to tell us about you. He first asked us to entertain the idea of having you a few weeks back. It's a big change for all of us. Sometimes, ingredients on their own can be just that... lonely on their own. Take your ham sandwich for instance. Bread, ham and butter on their own are a bit boring, right?" Lee nodded and smiled. He could see where Debs was going with this. "Well, I think we'll all make a very happy and mouth-watering, succulent ham sandwich if we all help each other and stick together."

"Which bit are you?" Lee asked.

"Well, I'm the butter of course. Dry bread and ham on their own... can you imagine that!" She laughed. Lee laughed too. This evening would definitely have been seriously awkward if Debs had not been around. "How about we talk a little more tomorrow? We can tell you more about us and our past, and if it's OK, you could tell us about you. Would that be a good deal?"

It seemed fair enough to Lee. He needed to hear about the two people he was going to be living with anyway. "Yes, sure."

"Oh, one more thing," Debbie said. Lee tensed slightly, fearing a telling off for something. Debbie seemed to sense this, because she softened her voice a little. "Please don't suffer in silence. If there's something on your mind or something we've forgotten, please tell us – this is Day One for us as parents as well, and we're bound to mess up somewhere."

Lee relaxed again. "OK," he said with a half-smile.

Debbie got up from the edge of the bed. "Do you sleep with the door ajar or closed?" she asked.

"Pulled to if that's alright."

Debbie turned out the light, pulled the door to and quietly went downstairs to cuddle up to her husband.

"How is he?" Chris asked.

"Well, considering we've all gone from zero to one hundred in about three hours, I'd say he was doing OK."

"What do you think of him?" Chris had a habit of not skirting around a subject; it was why she liked him.

"He's lovely little boy. Closed-up, but with a little reassurance he could be as emotionally enlightened as you one day," she joked.

Chris chuckled. He really had been lucky to be partnered with Debbie five years ago.

"The Chief spoke to me whilst you were upstairs earlier. What he said was only brief but his exact words were: 'Lee ran away to France, lived on the streets, escaped from a police cell, jumped from a bridge and faked his own death.'" Debbie turned to face her husband with a frown. "He also said that something else happened in France that ended up with the boy '*protecting one of ours*.'"

"Seriously?" Debbie said slightly incredulously.

"From the mouth of the man himself."

"Well, I've agreed with Lee that we'll have a show 'n' tell session tomorrow so that we can all get to know about each other's past. I suggest we talk a little about how we met, with inconsequential specifics of course, and then let him tell us about himself. We can then come back to the subject of 'mum and dad' if that all goes well." Debbie snuggled back into Chris's arms and relaxed her mind, content at having a new life in the house. Chris, on the other hand, gave more thought to what The Chief had said.

Upstairs, Lee hadn't gone to sleep. He tried to hear what was being said downstairs from the bed, but he could only hear the tones of their voices, like television background noise through a wall. He chose not to get up and open the door. They'd probably hear him no matter how quiet he tried to be. He had no reason to mistrust them and in the end it didn't really matter what they thought of him; this was a business arrangement with his nan and The Chief. Lee then focussed on the bigger issue for him – having to call them Mum and Dad. The way Lee's brain worked was that once a person had introduced themselves, the name that they had given was the one imprinted in his mind. It would be hard for him to see it them as anyone other than Debs and Chris. The anxiety of the problem kept Lee tossing in bed.

When the adults came upstairs, Lee kept still and closed his eyes to let the merest sliver of light filter through. The bedroom door opened. He could make out Debs' outline, but she didn't come in, she just pulled the door to again. Lee relaxed his face; it felt strange that someone cared. He thought about what the two had said about character acting. When he thought about his own situation, he was now another character of himself. Lee Powell had just come into being; Lee King was not of his choosing; Lee Walker was who he thought he was, but he'd actually been Joseph Merry from birth. It occurred to him that if his name could be changed that easily, then he would have to adapt to other people's name changes more easily too. Lee agreed with himself that although Debbie was Debs, she was also now a Mum. If she and Chris could accept a stranger in their home using their surname, then he could look at Debs as 'a mum' and Chris as 'a dad'. Removing the 'a' in time would be difficult, but not impossible. *It's amazing what one simple letter can do!* he thought to himself. Content that he had made enough progress in his own mind, Lee lay on his front, relaxed his body and snuggled up to the fragrant pillow next to his side.

* * *

CHAPTER 32

IN THE SADDLE

The next morning Lee awoke to movement in the bedroom opposite. He was still tired but decided to get up and synchronise with his new mum and dad. He was just changing his underpants when Debbie popped her head around the door.

"Ooh, morning, cheeky!" she laughed. She also noticed what looked like old bruises around his ribs. Caught by surprise, Lee scrambled to pull his pants up quickly. "Sorry, Lee, I probably should've knocked. Is there anything you'd like for breakfast?"

"Do you have cereals?" he asked.

"Sure, why don't you choose when you come down. We'll see you in the kitchen."

When he got downstairs, Debbie was making toast and offered to make some for Lee, but he had spied a box of Alpen which he'd only once been allowed to have at home. Debbie portioned out a good measure in a bowl for him and was about to pour the milk when Lee said, "Stop. Do you mind if I pour the milk myself?"

"Of course, sweetie, go ahead." Chris watched in the background. Once satisfied with the correct amount of milk on his cereal, Lee went and sat down at the kitchen table with Chris.

"So, how did you sleep in the strange house?"

"OK, I guess." Lee looked up at the wall clock which said 8:16. "Is this the time you normally get up?" he asked.

Chris chortled and looked over at Debbie. "We try to maintain a reasonable schedule, but when we have to be away, that can all go out of the window. We have to do whatever's necessary and sleeping patterns are secondary."

Lee wanted him to divulge more and faked a confused look on his face. "When has that happened, then?" he asked.

Chris saw what a good question he'd been posed. He loved playing mind-chess and could see this conversation was going to get interesting. Debbie brought over the toast, butter and jam, and sat beside Chris. Whilst answering, Chris buttered a slice, spread some strawberry jam and cut the toast diagonally into two pieces. "So, the way this job seems to work is that we can be sent off anywhere at a moment's notice. To give an example, in the past, I have received a call at 2 o'clock in the afternoon to be in Berlin overnight."

"What did you have to do when you were there?"

Chris analysed the question as he formulated his answer. Had Lee already made assumptions by asking the question? "My job was to shadow and report activity, so that's what I did."

Lee frowned again, his mind searching back to the previous week. Had Chris been like the agent he'd seen in France? The man had turned up very quickly after the shootings and it looked as though Kim had seen him before.

"What type of person did you shadow and how did you make sure you weren't discovered?" This was interesting.

Chris was now on the back foot. The landscape in Berlin was still delicate. There was only so much information he'd given his wife, something they'd agreed when they first began seeing each other... and The Chief had warned him about lying to the boy. He was going to have to do some blocking, but with a trade-off.

"Unfortunately, I can't tell you the type of person I had to follow. All of our reports are classified, I'm afraid. But what I can and would be happy to do, is teach you some of the techniques we use. Would that be of interest?"

Lee didn't think the man was going to spill the beans, but it had been worth the try anyway. "Definitely," he said. "Do you both do the same thing or do you have different jobs?"

Chris smiled. Lee would make a good fisherman. "Debs and I..." Chris started.

"You mean Mum?" Lee interjected.

The two adults looked at each other in shock. "Mum and I were both trained in similar ways and methods, but sometimes have to go about how we do our jobs differently."

"Why's that?" Lee asked.

Debbie decided to include herself in the conversation. "There are some jobs that only a woman can do. Picture this if you will. Our country needs information from a man. That man is known to like a drink or two and also likes the company of women. If you were The Chief, who would you send to extract the information?"

Lee smiled. He understood what his mum was saying between the lines, but he thought he'd make things a little more interesting. "How would you know if the man was going to be interested in you?" he asked.

Chris burst out laughing, swiftly followed by a dig in the ribs from his wife. She slowly got up from her seat and sat next to Lee, talking seductively as she did so. "Well, young man, there are very few men who can resist my charms when there's something that I want." She began to twirl her fingers through Lee's hair, which made him bury his head in his neck when it began to tickle. She moved her mouth closer and closer to the side of Lee's face and lowered her voice. "And you have something that I want, handsome man."

As she whispered into Lee's ear, the feeling was an excruciating mix between pleasure and pain. Lee and Chris were laughing. Just when he couldn't bear it any longer, his mum blew a big raspberry on the side of Lee's neck to finish the job. She'd got so carried away that Lee was on the floor by the time she'd finished with him. His stomach hurt from laughing so much. It was a feeling he'd never felt before in a family setting. Mum pulled him up by his arms, sat him back on his chair and went back to her place next to Chris.

"I hope that answers the question for you?" she said rhetorically. After Lee had managed to draw breath he asked them both how they'd met.

"I met..." She paused. "...Dad at a conference. We'd been paired together as a sort of training partnership and just hit it off really well." She looked at 'Dad' as she said this. "The conference led to us being on a counterintelligence Op together about five years ago. We were so good together we decided to get married. That was about four years ago now." She paused.

Lee didn't understand what a counterintelligence Op was, nor was he sure whether he should ask what was on his mind or not, but decided to test the waters. "And you've not been able to have a baby?" It wasn't meant to hurt, but he could tell by his mum's change of expression that that his question had hit her hard.

Chris put his arm around her, but she did her best to maintain composure. "I'm afraid I can't have children," she said.

"Sorry I asked," Lee said with genuine concern. "I didn't want to make you unhappy."

"That's alright, Lee," she said in a slightly harder tone than usual. "It's a genuine question and reasonable given where we all are now."

Dad continued where Mum left off. "About two years ago we'd mentioned to our handlers that we were going to try for a baby. It didn't go down too well at the time, but we both had plenty of work on. We'd tried for sometime but things hadn't worked out." Lee wasn't quite sure what 'trying' was. He had an idea, but would really need this confirmed by someone, some time. "About six months ago, we both got tested and we found out that Deb... Mum had a problem that couldn't be fixed. We'd told our handlers so that they'd know we'd continue to be on active duty. This must have been reported up, because three weeks ago we got a call from The Chief himself about you. And now here you are. Things move quickly in this world!" he said.

"So what do you do when you're not on duty?"

"Well, Mum works as a freelance journalist and I am a photographer. I also do a little bit of electrician work on the side sometimes."

"Are they well paid jobs?"

"If you're asking how we afford this place? Mum inherited the house in her mother's Will." Lee wasn't sure if it was the truth of not, but he at least had something to tell people if they really wanted to know.

"So tell us about you, Lee, how did you end up.... well, here, I guess?"

Lee thought about where to begin and how much information to divulge. The only way he could explain everything was chronologically.

"I used to have a mum, a dad and a sister. One day when I was supposed to go to watch a football match, my mum..." He paused.

Should he say 'my mum' anymore? He rephrased. "The mum came home with another man and I caught them together. I wrote a note to... the dad telling him about it. One night the dad left home, leaving me with the mum and the sister. They both hated me and made my life hell." Lee paused. Thinking about what to skip or include. "I asked him to take me with him but he didn't." Inside, an anger began to flare up towards David. "Eventually, the other man moved in. The mum stopped us seeing the dad and we ended up moving away, twice. They got married and changed our names. She made us call him dad, but I never did," Lee said proudly. "The sister did, though... she was a traitor. She also used to lie to get me into trouble all the time. The last time it happened, she said that I'd threatened her with a knife. The next day I was sent to a children's home." He paused again trying to compose himself. Debs went to put her hand on his arm, but Lee withdrew. He steeled himself. "After a while at the home I ran away, ended up in France in Nantes, mostly on the streets. My nan must've found out somehow because she sent a woman to come and find me. The woman eventually brought me home to my nan and the next day was when I met The Chief. He talked to me about his plans and I agreed. So here I am. Like you say, things move quickly." Lee had managed to walk through the story without losing his composure and without bursting into tears. It helped that he'd glossed over so much of the detail.

Mum and dad both looked at each other and Chris decided to probe further.

"The Chief said something about a bridge?" He said, looking to tease more information out from the boy.

Lee wasn't going to make it easy for him though. "I had to jump from a bridge to escape the police."

"How come?"

"Because they were after me."

Chris could see Lee was blocking. Although this annoyed him, he didn't show it on the outside. "So what steps did you go through to escape from the police cell?" he asked.

Now that was a better question, Lee thought. The Chief had clearly given his new dad more information. "What did The Chief say to you?" Lee responded.

Chris looked at Debbie as if to seek reassurance and then returned to Lee.

"He said you'd escaped a police cell, jumped from a bridge, faked your death and protected an agent."

Lee mused. "I escaped the cell by stealing some cell keys. As I said, I jumped from the bridge to escape from the police. They thought I'd killed myself when I jumped." He stopped briefly when thinking about the incident in Paris. "And I shot two people who were about to kill the person who'd come to find me."

Chris and Debbie's faces changed. Seven years old and he'd shot two people already. "How did you come to have a gun?" Chris asked.

Lee remained deadpan. His eyes sharpened. "It was the one I took from the police station when I escaped." Lee could see that both Mum and Dad were slightly taken aback by what he'd said.

"Why did you take a gun from the police station?" Mum asked, concerned.

Lee thought briefly. "I wanted everyone to leave me alone. If the worst came to the worst, I would've killed myself," he said matter-of-factly.

Mum got up from her seat and went back round to Lee. She gave him a big cuddle, which he didn't reciprocate. "That's all behind you now. This is a new beginning for you and for us. Let's try to make it a happy one, shall we?" Lee didn't really have the chance to answer clearly because his head was too deeply buried in his new mother's chest. "Let's leave it for now; I think we should clean up the breakfast things."

Debbie cleared the table and Lee helped with the wiping up. As she was washing the dishes, she asked, "How come you didn't want me to pour your milk for you?"

"'Cause you don't know how much milk I like." He didn't tell her it was because his sister used to deliberately torment him by drowning his cereal and then get him told off for using too much milk.

Chris remained at the breakfast table reading the paper. His eyes moved side to side, but his mind analysed what Lee had said. He'd clearly glossed over a lot of detail and summarised his situation to a bare minimum. Lee had almost goaded him into asking better questions. But the only small details the boy had provided were the note, his father not taking him, the incident with his sister and finally the incident about the bridge. Chris found it interesting how Lee's face changed when he talked about the shootings and potential suicide. There was no emotion in his voice or expression. The only conclusion Chris could come to was that there was a reason for everything that Lee did. Nothing was random and everything was calculated. He could see why The Chief saw potential.

When Lee had finished the wiping up he asked if it was OK to go out for a while.

Debbie and Chris looked at each other. Debbie quite apprehensively. "You've only just got here," she found herself saying.

Chris had remembered The Chief's warning – *long leash*. "I'm pretty sure if he could find his way around France he could find his way back – right Lee?"

Lee looked over at Mum.

"Please don't go too far," she said.

Lee tried to reassure her. "Don't worry, I just like going out." He went upstairs and put his sneakers and coat on. When he came downstairs he quickly popped back into the kitchen. "Do you have a spare key for later, or do you want me to knock?"

"Here," Dad said, as he unwound his own key from his key ring, "Back by 12 o'clock, please."

"Sure." Lee was at the front door before anyone could say anything else. Debbie quickly shot to the front room window to see which way Lee would go. Chris followed on more sedately.

"Aren't you going to follow him?" Debbie said.

"I wasn't planning to. He's clearly used to being out and about and The Chief said not to keep him on a short leash."

"I'm worried about him. Why is he going out already, is it something we've done?" she asked.

"What do we do when we find ourselves in a new territory?"

"Know your territory," she said with a sigh.

"I'm pretty sure he's probably trying to get to know his bearings."

"I know what you're saying is right, but can't you keep an eye on him anyway... for me?" Debbie looked at Chris with eyes he couldn't refuse. Complying was definitely non-negotiable.

He rolled his eyes and sighed. "OK, OK." Chris put his running shoes and jacket on and went out in the direction Lee had headed.

* * *

Saxon Gardens was a quiet road where none of the houses overlooked each other. Lee turned right out of the driveway and soon came to a dead-end, so retraced his footsteps past the house and to the entry of the road. He'd sort of already seen what was on the left when he arrived the night before, so decided to turn right and venture further up the hill. The place reminded him of his nan's where you could ride a bike safely without too much problem with motorists. The hill wasn't steep but it was long, which Lee knew would make it cool for going down at full speed on a bike... or as much speed as he dared. He just needed a bike. He thought about broaching the subject with Chr... his dad – he'd be able to cover so much more ground with a bike. Lee spent some time thinking about the bike or bikes he'd really love to own. His friend Richard had a mauve Raleigh Tomahawk which was OK, but Lee would've loved a 5 - or 10-speed racer instead. His mind wandered back to the last time he'd seen Richard, which now seemed like such a long time ago.

As Lee walked further up the hill and round a bend, the pavement finished on both sides, and the road, dominated by trees, narrowed. Lee had always been taught to walk towards oncoming traffic, but wasn't sure what to do when he first heard and then saw two horses, mounted by women, trotting synchronously towards him. He decided it was best to maintain consistency and walk at the same pace on the same side. The women could move the horses around him anyway. As they got closer and closer, Lee began to get a little apprehensive. Whilst they didn't look particularly large from a distance, the sheer size of the beasts had a way of sneaking up on you. As they were about to pass one another, the two ladies stopped talking and drew their rides to a halt.

"Hello, young man, how are you?" one of them asked.

Lee needed to be as natural as possible, but his leg began to shake at the sheer size of the chestnut horse standing nearest to him. "I'm alright, thank you."

"Where are you heading?" the woman asked as her horse began paying Lee some attention by sniffing his hair.

"I'm just out for a walk to explore the area, is there anything interesting up that way?"

"Shouldn't you be in school?"

Lee began to get annoyed. He was just being polite and here was this nosey parker giving him the third degree about being in school. *Still, she had a point,* he thought. He remained calm.

"I'm being enrolled soon – I just got here yesterday, so I want to make the most of my free time by exploring."

The woman weighed up what Lee had said and whispered to her friend. "We can both show you around if you like?" Lee ducked when the woman's horse tried to lick his hair. "Chester!" she barked, and pulled at the reins.

"I'm not supposed to go with strangers," Lee said as he glanced back down the road where he'd just come from. Just as he did so, he saw a very slight movement by a tree on the left-hand side.

"Words of wisdom from your parents, no doubt, but everyone's a stranger until you say hello. It's up to you though, we're not going to force you – but we do know the area pretty well and can show you around."

Lee thought about it. He'd become used to being on his own and working things out for himself, but it also made sense to get a helping hand whenever you could. Besides, he wanted to know what the movement had been down the hill. He had an idea, but it might be fun to confirm it. "OK, but I have to be back by 12 o'clock," he said.

"No problem. We're not going to be that long anyway. Where do you live?"

"Just down the road at Saxon Gardens." Lee was wondering how he was going to get on top of such a huge animal. The woman took her left foot out of the stirrup and leaned down towards his arms.

"Here. Grab my arm, and when I pull you up, put your left foot in the stirrup there." The woman was surprisingly strong for her size and managed to get Lee up half way so that he could eventually get a foothold. "Right, hold on to my neck and climb your way onto the saddle in front of me. I'll move back a little." This was scary. Lee had never told anyone he didn't like heights, and this horse was high.

Chris watched from behind a tree, intrigued by what he was seeing. He couldn't afford to blow his cover, but the boy was about to get on a complete stranger's horse. He decided to see how this played out. Debbie wouldn't appreciate his decision, that's for sure.

Once finally on and astride the saddle, Lee was able to stabilise his heart rate. The woman could feel the boy shaking and decided that introductions were in order before setting off. She put her right arm around Lee, whilst he grabbed the reins as tightly as he could. "My name's Mary, this is Charlotte." Charlotte smiled and said hello. "You've met Chester and Charlotte's horse is called Mimi."

Lee didn't quite know if he was supposed to talk to the horses or not, but he stroked Chester's mane anyway. "My name's Lee," he said politely.

"Happy to meet you, Lee; now we're not strangers." Mary put her arms around him and held onto the reins with both hands, whilst keeping Lee between her elbows. She gave a 'click-click' with the side of her mouth and the two horses started moving. The body movement felt very strange to Lee. He could barely split his legs enough across the saddle and the ride was harsh. To say it was uncomfortable was an understatement; his inner thighs hurt and his testicles had already started to ache. He kept an eye out for where he'd seen the movement before. He leaned forward again as they neared the spot, scanning as much as possible – but he couldn't see anything. *Maybe it was my imagination?* he thought.

Just in case someone had been there, Lee spoke to Mary in a loud voice: "So we're definitely going to be back before 12 o'clock, right?"

"Yep, probably about eleven-ish. That way you'll get to see most of the surrounding area," she said, just as loudly. If Dad was following, he'd at least now know what he was up to. Mary had a natural rhythm in keeping with her steed which caterpillared from her hips and torso up Lee's back. He could feel the woman's soft bumps on his shoulder-blades and decided to lean back slightly and try to relax. He kept his hands firmly attached to the saddle though, just to be sure.

Chris watched on in amazement as Lee bounced past on horseback chatting away with the two women he'd never met before. When he watched him get on the stranger's horse, Chris thought the boy naive. But when Lee had sent him an obvious message he knew that was definitely not the case. Getting a tour of the surroundings on horseback might have been a good idea for Lee, but for him, keeping up and under cover had just got harder – especially if the riders decided to go across country or for a gallop. He followed the horses back down the hill towards home. About half a mile past Saxon Gardens, the riders veered left along an unmade path. He reached the path just in time to see both horses cantering across a field. *That's it, I'm done,* he thought, and walked back towards home. He'd just have to trust that Lee would come home OK as he'd indicated. Chris had never really lied to Debbie before. He'd withheld information but he was now seriously considering what to say to his wife.

As he opened the front door Debbie popped her head round from the living room. "How is he, darling?" she asked, looking behind her husband.

"You won't believe me, but the boy's gone off horse riding with two women!" he replied with a wry smile.

Debbie was about to shout at her husband, but reined in her frustration. She knew that Chris would've had to make split decisions and was usually exceptional at the calculations. "How the hell did that happen?"

Chris explained what he had seen. "There was no way I was going to keep up once they got a good head of speed."

Debbie began to start searching for her shoes.

"Where are you going?" he asked.

"To go and find him, of course!" There was panic in her voice.

Chris stopped her in her tracks and held her arms firmly. "That's not everything." Debbie's head jerked back slightly. "He sent me a message after getting on the horse. He'll be back before 12 o'clock." Debbie's mouth opened in surprise. "If he's not back by then, then I will go looking for him."

"So you're saying he knew you were there?"

"Yep," said Chris. "Somehow he knew. I was careful too. But it looks like I need to brush up on my skills!"

* * *

Chris looked at his watch when he heard the key in the front door turn. *11:18. Lee definitely sent me a message.* Debbie had been fidgety most of the morning, keeping herself busy by tidying until Chris told her to calm down. They were both in the living room, Debbie researching council planning applications and Chris reading a New Scientist magazine.

Lee took off his shoes and coat at the front door. "Hello!" he called out. "Where should I put my coat and shoes?" Chris came out from the living room and showed Lee where to put his coat in the cupboard by the door. Lee's shoes were muddy so he was instructed to put them by the back door for now, until the mud dried.

"Our wanderer returns," Dad said to Mum, as he sat back down with his magazine.

"Did you enjoy your time out?" she asked in a familiar tone.

Lee knew where this was heading. It was not like he hadn't been asked about his whereabouts before. It seemed like all adults did the same. Start with an easy question and then ask the big one, like 'Where did you go?' He began by being deliberately vague. "Yes, it was really good, thanks."

"That's good, what did you get up to?" she asked. It was a variation on the same theme. Whilst he would've probably lied to his previous parents, there didn't seem to be much point in this case – especially if he'd been followed.

"Well, I went up that hill and met a couple of nice ladies on horses. We got talking and they agreed to show me around. So one of them popped me on her horse and we did a huge circuit around the area."

Mum acted surprised. "Didn't anyone tell you to not go off with strangers?" she asked.

Given what he'd observed of Debbie in the short time he'd known her, her reaction was quite restrained. This reinforced Lee's assumption that he had definitely been followed up the hill. Mary's simple but wise words had stuck with him. "Everyone's a stranger until you say hello," he countered.

Mum and Dad looked at each other. What Lee had said was hard to refute, but they also knew how dangerous going off with strangers could be. "Oh, but Lee, you really need to be careful, my love. Going off with strangers can be dangerous – you've seen the adverts, haven't you?"

Now that's more in keeping with Mum's natural state, Lee thought. He also thought it would be a good opportunity to drop a hint about a bike. "Yes, I've seen the adverts, but they were just being friendly and it's not easy exploring without my bike."

Chris was secretly impressed. *That was subtle.* He had to smile at the kid's boldness. "So, where did you end up going?" he asked.

"We went across lots of fields, through a place called Hitcham, where they keep their horses and back down along the river Thames. I didn't realise the Thames was here too, I thought it was in London."

"Sounds like you had a productive time out, then. Should we ask what your new friends' names are?"

"The horses or the ladies?" Lee teased. Dad pulled a face and raised an eyebrow. "The ladies were Mary and Charlotte and their horses were Chester and Mimi. Chester and Mimi are brother and sister."

"Well, I guess you better get cleaned up. I'll make you a sandwich before I go out," Mum said. Lee winced as he tried to get out of the chair; the insides of his legs were seriously aching.

Mum made both of the boys a sandwich before went out which just left Lee and Dad at home for the afternoon. Lee had been eyeing up their television ever since he'd arrived. He'd never seen one that big before and with so many buttons. "Can we watch the TV?" Lee asked. He really wanted to see if it was as good as it looked.

"Sure," Dad said.

He went over, switched the wall plug on and then the television. The picture expanded into view from a small dot to full-size within a second. Lee was impressed; his parents'... former parents' TV took ages to warm up. "Which channel do you want?" Chris pushed button one, then two and then three. There wasn't too much on in the afternoon on a week day, so they both agreed to ITV.

"How comes there are so many buttons, there are only three channels?"

Lee had unwittingly picked the right question to ask, because the floodgates just opened. Dad eulogized about the 'Blaupunkt Werke Java TV 16 Colour'20-inch screen, the electronic station search with automatic tuning and 16-fold memory, and two buttons for manual channel tuning in particularly difficult reception areas.

This was all very well, but it still didn't really answer his question. "So why all the buttons then if there are only three channels? What do you do with channels four to sixteen? And I've never heard of Blaupunkt before."

Dad knew that it was technology for technology's sake; Debbie had asked the same questions when he'd bought it.

"Blaupunkt is a German company. I got the TV in West Germany a year or so ago. They have more channels over there, so it made more sense I guess – but look at the picture, isn't it wonderful?"

Lee couldn't really argue, the picture was good. "It is a nice TV," he said. "Sounds good, too."

Dad smiled. At least someone appreciated a decent piece of kit. As they both sat and ate their lunch, Chris couldn't help but confront the elephant in the room – he needed to say something. "How did you know I was there?" he asked. He knew Lee wasn't stupid and he really wanted to know where he'd gone wrong with his surveillance.

Lee thought about how to answer the question. He considered playing Chris along for a bit, but he could see that the man was desperately in need of the information. He also realised that if he annoyed his dad now, it might backfire on him at a later date. They'd both been good to him and so maybe he should be more forthcoming. He also wanted a bike. "It was only a slight movement in the tree that I just happened to see, that's all." Lee kept quiet about his suspicions before the sighting. He'd realised that Deb's inquisitiveness would never allow him to just go off unchecked, having only known him for a day. He'd felt subconsciously that one of them was keeping an eye on him. It just made sense for them to do it anyway.

"So why did you really get on the horse with that woman?"

"The same reasons as I said before. I also wanted to check the tree, but I didn't see you."

Dad nodded thoughtfully. "That was a nice little 'not-so-subtle' hint about the bike. What did you have before?"

Lee smiled and tried withhold a laugh. He'd got the conversation on the table, now he needed to find a way to close the deal. "I had a Tomahawk before, but it was getting too small for me and they're not very fast." Lee knew this was a little white lie, but he figured there was no way his new dad would find out what bike he really had.

Chris decided that it was his turn to tease a little. "Tomahawks are expensive aren't they? There must be cheaper bikes out there. What about a Budgie?"

The smile instantly disappeared from Lee's face. This was not going to plan at all. He frowned. "The Budgie's a baby's bike – it's even smaller than a Tomahawk."

"Oh, I didn't realise that," Dad said innocently. "I'm so out of touch – what do seven-year-olds ride these days then?"

Lee wanted to play it cool. Casually, he said, "I think they go for racers now." He wondered if Dad had his own bike and if he did, whether he'd get as excited as he did about the television. "What bike have you got?" Lee asked.

"I have a Peugeot 10-speed – want to see it?"

"Definitely!" Lee said excitedly. They went out into the garage where Chris's bike was neatly hooked onto a bracket on the back wall. It was pristine, pearlescent white and just the sort of bike Lee had dreamed of. Dad got it down from the wall and showed Lee around the gears, brakes, slimline wheels and razorblade saddle.

"Can I have a go?" Lee asked.

Chris was defensive about his pride and joy. "It's a bit big for you, mate – I'm not sure you'll be able to handle it."

"Can I at least see if I can reach the pedals?"

Chris lifted Lee on and held the handlebars with both hands. But even when Lee sat on the top frame, he could only just reach the pedal at its top-most position. "See what I mean?"

Lee didn't hide his disappointment. Being a kid was a pain sometimes. He wished he was bigger for a number of reasons. Dad saw the disappointment on his face and sympathised with the boy's plight. He'd been a kid once and remembered what it felt like. He lifted Lee carefully from the bike and replaced it on the wall.

Back in the living room, Lee just sat down and watched television. Chris could see that the boy was unhappy, but didn't really know what else to say.

But although Lee seemed despondent, he was really quite happy that he'd sown the seeds in his dad's mind. Maybe his plan would work.

* * *

CHAPTER 33

COUNTDOWN

Wednesday, and Nancy picked up the phone after four rings; it was Theo.

"I've managed to get your story in Friday's edition. You know how it is, Friday's often the slow news day."

"That's excellent news – thank you, Theo."

"How do you want me to handle the interaction?" he asked.

"Seeing as they'll get it on Friday, let's give them the weekend to stew over the story... assuming it gets read, of course. I would suggest first thing on the Monday. You'll have to play it by ear, but if the husband goes to work first, catching the wife and daughter on their own will have the best impact. Put the frighteners on them, but watch out... the wife can be feisty. If you can make things loud enough so that the neighbours can hear, that would also make life more interesting. Once you've been well and truly told where to go, I would suggest approaching the daughter. If you can catch her on the way to school, that may work but she may need time to process what's happening. It might be best to follow her and find out where she goes to school

– she'll probably be more relaxed at the end of the school day. As I've said, softly, softly. But let her know that the situation's going to get worse and that you may be able to help her if she can tell you anything about what's been going on with the family," Nancy explained.

"Sounds fairly straightforward to me. I'll post an anonymous note to the Herts Advertiser whilst I'm in the area."

"That's perfect. Can you update me the same day? I don't mind what time."

"No problem." Theo clicked off.

Nancy made another call. "Can you confirm the location of the last call to this number please?"

"I can't give specifics at the moment, but the general area is Putney, South-West London."

"Thank you," Nancy said as she put the receiver down. She looked up at the clock in the living room. There was enough time for her to drive to St. Albans. It was a meagre task that had to be done, but she no longer had the advantage of a vast network of people at her disposal. Some things would just have to be done the old-fashioned way.

Two hours later, Nancy sat in her car down the road from Louvaine King's home. Given the woman's propensity for moving, she felt it best to ensure the address was still the correct one. When Laura walked up the driveway at 4:15pm, Nancy couldn't help but be amazed at how she'd grown up. Even in her pristine school uniform, she was clearly well on her way to womanhood. Nancy wanted to shout out to her and take Laura back home, but she knew she had to go against her heart this time. With the address confirmed, she drove to the nearest newsagents.

"Oh hello there, I'm wondering if you can help me. My husband was supposed to sort out our daily paper delivery, but I haven't received anything yet."

"What's the address?"

Nancy gave Louvaine's address to the woman.

"No, I'm sorry but we don't have anything set up yet. Would you like to set something up now?"

Nancy tutted. "That would be helpful, thank you." Nancy gave her name as Mrs. King and two pounds to put on account until the next payment was due. "What sort of time are the papers delivered in the morning?" she asked.

"Our lad usually heads up that way at about seven to seven-thirty."

"OK. Is there anything else you need from me?" Nancy asked.

"I just need to know when you want to start your first delivery?"

Nancy thought briefly. "Friday will be fine, thank you."

"Friday it is, Mrs. King. Anything else you'd like while you're in?"

"Do you have any useful husbands behind there somewhere?"

The assistant smiled. "The useful ones sold out long ago, only useless ones left I'm afraid."

"No point in having two," Nancy said as she made her way out of the shop.

* * *

The next day, Kim arrived at Nancy's at 9 o'clock sharp as planned. Nancy greeted her in her normal fashion and made a coffee for them both, but said that they would need to be done by 10:30 – she had somewhere else to be that day. She put on some reading glasses and read through the family report first. It was thorough, and documented her time from Bracknell through to the collection of Lee's ashes in Ancenis. It omitted specific names where possible, such as Lee's interaction with Servane, the names of any police officers and time spent near Paris.

Each section was broken down from a billing perspective to give the agreed grand total. Nancy double checked to make sure there was nothing that could cause a problem if it ever got into the hands of anyone else. She was satisfied. She went over to the sink, retrieved the balance of £1,938 owed in cash and handed it to Kim.

It was the second report that Nancy was most interested in, though. This one had to be detailed down to the minutiae. She pored over each sentence. "So, you think you were drugged?" Nancy asked, maintaining her focus on the report.

"It's the only plausible explanation. I'd had two glasses of wine and when I woke up, I'd never felt that fuzzy before."

"You mean, when you were woken up," Nancy corrected.

Kim remained quiet.

Nancy went through the report again, this time taking a pencil from a wall shelf and highlighting a couple of areas that she thought would need to be revised. "You have to remember, Kim, that there was a verbal report from another agent and Lee. The agent's final detailed report will be in soon. Whilst it might be unflattering, you cast doubt on all past and future work with us if you leave vagueness or ambiguities in yours. I'll leave it up to you, which is why I've only used a light pencil, but my advice would be to make a couple of amendments." Nancy removed the glasses and looked up at the clock.

Kim knew the woman was right. She had no choice but to open herself up to ridicule. "I'll make the amendments and send the report in tomorrow," she said.

"I think that's a worthwhile choice," Nancy said as she stood up from her chair. "Thank you for everything you've done and I'm sorry to have to push you out of the door, so-to-speak, Kim, but I really do have to get ready to shoot off soon. Will you let me know how things go with future assignments?"

"Sure," Kim replied. Whether she would or not would be another matter, but there was no other way to answer the question.

After Kim had left, Nancy put everything work-related away in the hidden safe behind a false back in her bedroom wardrobe. She made sure everything was secure and fixed small traps around the house – some microscope slides under the carpet by the front and back doors and small pieces of Sellotape with one end stuck to each door, the other trailing on the carpet. As she eased the car out of the driveway, she waved to her neighbour across the street who'd just put out the rubbish. Nancy had estimated her journey at anywhere between 1-2 hours depending on traffic. She was eager to see how Lee was getting on in his new surroundings. Nancy had been given background files on Chris and Deborah Powell when the whole arrangement had been made with The Chief and she'd trusted his judgement on their suitability for the job, but there was nothing quite like being face-to-face, to get a true flavour of who they were. When she'd called a week ago, Lee had been out with Chris and only Deborah had been around. They'd had a quick chat about how Lee was settling in and Nancy was intrigued to see if Deborah was as kind as she'd sounded on the phone. Traffic wasn't too heavy and Nancy had used counter-surveillance measures along the way. She arrived at Saxon Gardens before 12 o'clock.

Lee heard the car pull into the driveway, immediately ran to the front door and was at the driver's side before Nancy could pull the handle. He opened the door for her, and gave her a big hug as she side-saddled out of the car. It had only been two weeks since they'd last seen each other, but so much had changed for Lee that it felt like months.

"How's my not-so-little detective? You seem to get bigger every time I see you."

"I'm really happy, Nan – Mum and Dad are really good with me." Lee said excitedly.

This felt peculiar to Nancy. Even though this was the cover, it felt strange that Lee would already be addressing the couple in such a way. She clearly had to adjust herself to get used to the change. As she looked at Lee, she could physically see the changes in him. Gone were the constant frown-lines and back was the carefree smile he'd had years ago.

"I'm so happy to hear you say that, young man, I've been keeping my fingers crossed every day that things would be better for you." Nancy closed her car door and put her arm around Lee's shoulder. "I've got a few bits and pieces for you in the boot, if you wouldn't mind giving me a hand?"

Lee didn't need a second invitation. He darted round the back and pushed the boot button, whilst Nancy locked the driver's door. She smiled at the look on Lee's face when the latch wouldn't open and held up the jangling keys. Rather than come back to collect the keys, Lee opened his hands for his Nan to toss them to him – which she duly did. It was these little behaviours that were important for her to maintain in him. He was not, and never had been, subservient. If her long-term goal was to be achieved, Lee would lead and only follow when the situation suited.

By now, Debbie and Chris had both appeared at the front door. They looked at each other wondering if they should walk out to meet their visitor or wait on the doorstep. Debbie couldn't wait and walked out towards Lee and Nancy, who were both now pulling bags and boxes out of the car. Lee looked up.

"Nan, this is Mum, but you can call her Debs," he said. The two women shook hands.

"So glad to finally meet you," Debbie said with her customary warm smile. Chris had followed behind and also shook Nancy by the hand.

"This is Dad, but call him Chris," Lee said whilst not wavering... or looking her in the eye. He still found the sentence hard to say – especially to his Nan. Lee ducked under the handshaking to fetch one last box from deep in the car. His new parents showed a certain reverence towards Nancy. They'd heard of her by reputation only, but that was enough for anyone in the know to be alert at all times.

"Is that everything?" Nancy asked.

"Yep," Lee said as he jumped up to reach the boot lid. He locked it and then double checked the button before handing the keys back to his Nan. Dad took the bulk of the bags with Lee, whilst Mum walked in behind with Nancy, already chit-chatting about how good the last two weeks had been for them. Once inside, Dad and Lee put the bags in the living room whilst Mum took Nancy's coat. Lee bounced back from the living room. It was nice of his Nan to bring presents, of a sort, but he could feel that they were all probably clothes.

"Come on, Nan, I'll show you around," he said. Lee led her upstairs to his room, downstairs to some of the other rooms and finally into the garage where his new pride and joy now resided... a five-speed, small-framed Raleigh Racer in metallic blue. Chris knew he'd been played when he took Lee out to buy it. But there were going to be lessons in responsibility attached that Lee would need to learn; such as keeping it working in perfect order at all times.

"What do you think Nan, isn't it cool?"

"It looks lovely, darling. It's a huge step up from the little one round at mine. Can you fit on it?"

Lee smiled. "Not quite on the saddle yet but Dad said it wouldn't be too long."

There it was again... a sharp little pin-prick to her heart. *If Lee can get used to it, so can you,* she thought to herself.

"Do you mind if I ask how you've managed to start saying Mum and Dad so soon? It's not a criticism, I'm actually very impressed."

Lee's smile receded a little as his face became more serious. "When I arrived they were both every kind to me. I figured that after what you'd told me, a mum and a dad could be anyone if I was going to be an agent. So I sort of saw them as name badges at first. But I like them, which makes it easier now."

Nancy smiled warmly and bent down to Lee's height. "This is an important lesson. This ability to adjust your mind this quickly will stand you in good stead in years to come." She brushed his hair. "Well done," she whispered.

Lee felt a warm glow of approval inside, something he'd not felt in a long, long time. As they made their way back to the living room where Chris and Debbie were waiting, Nancy remarked at what a lovely house they both had. Debbie encountered the same warm glow that Lee had just felt, whilst Chris's internals remained on high alert.

Nancy indicated for Lee to open the gifts she had brought for him whilst they all chatted about what the family had been up to since Lee's arrival. During their previous phone conversation, Debbie and Nancy had divided up the clothing purchases between them, with Debbie getting Lee fitted for his uniform and PE clothing, and Nancy providing other necessities. Lee tried his best to seem thankful for the pants, socks, T-shirts, jumpers, pyjamas and dressing gown, but none of these things were quite to his taste. He wondered if he'd be this bland when he got old. But however boring the clothes were, he still had the manners to thank his Nan... she was only trying her best after all.

"Why don't you put your new uniform on for your Nan, Lee?" Mum suggested.

Clearly it wasn't a suggestion as Nan said, "Oh yes, I'd love to see that. When does he start?"

Lee went upstairs as Dad spoke. "This Monday. We're actually going to miss him a bit; it's been good having someone around, hasn't it, love?" Debbie nodded. As they spoke, Nancy looked around the room, noticing the newspaper on a side table.

"Well, it looks as though he's settled in very well with you. You've done a good job. I can see a positive change even in these two weeks."

"We just want to do our best for him, but..." Debbie trailed off not knowing whether to raise her concern.

"But what?" Nancy enquired.

Debbie looked at Chris for support, but he wasn't quite sure what she was about to say. "I'm just wondering how he'll take to being at a boarding school?"

Nancy nodded, acknowledging the reservation. "The only thing I can say is that over the last six months or so, Lee has continuously had to make new adjustments, so I think he will adapt. I'm hoping that the move here and the school will give him the new foundations he needs. The Chief did say that you can visit regularly at the school, though?"

"I know, but it's not quite the same. We've all really bonded and I'm worried that those bonds will perish with a lack of contact."

"I understand what you're saying, Debbie, but I think you both need to have faith in yourselves. Loyalty is a huge part of Lee's make-up. Stay loyal to each other and you'll be fine. Besides, I believe The Chief's managed to get you a dispensation for the weekends too, so I don't think it'll be that bad."

Debbie put on a brave face, but was not convinced.

"I'll also be popping down every month and you can always contact me by phone, so there'll be good support system in place," Nancy finished, as Lee came downstairs in his blue shirt, dark trousers and navy jumper with school emblem. "Somebody looks dapper in his uniform!"

Lee's shoulders slumped as his eyes rolled. He never understood why adults got so worked up about a school uniform.

"We just need to conquer the double-Windsor, and we'll be there," Chris added.

Nancy motioned for Lee to do a little catwalk presentation in front of her. "Are you looking forward to school on Monday?" she asked.

Lee shrugged. He really didn't know whether it would be a good experience or not.

Nancy smiled. "Don't worry; you'll have your Mum and Dad here for support if you need anything."

"How often will I get to see you, Nan?"

"How does every month sound – would that be OK with you?" Nancy read Lee's despondency. "I know, young man, it's not ideal for me either," she said softly. "But this is not an ordinary life or path we follow. We sacrifice a lot for the greater good, I'm afraid. Think of it this way. You'll get to see your Mum or Dad most Wednesdays and two weekends a month; with the exception of when they have to both be on assignment. They will also begin some of your training... which reminds me, Chris, how are you getting on with the training plan?"

"It's in draft form right now. Debbie and I just need to make sure we're happy with the ways, means and timelines before we submit it to HQ."

Lee was intrigued to see what this plan about his life looked like, but he got the feeling that this was something only the adults wanted to control. Still there was no harm in asking. "Can I see this training plan?" he asked.

Chris looked at Nancy for direction.

"In broad terms, I expect that Dad and Mum will teach you tricks of the trade. Individually at first which will require lots of practice on your part. Think of this as homework. As you get better, they'll probably combine some of these tasks together so you'll have a sort of puzzle to solve based on a number of tasks. If you've proven yourself capable, then you'll be required to carry out a mission. Does that about cover it, Dad?" Nancy asked.

"Yes, that's pretty much it. We can't give you details, Lee, because the second and third stages need to be in 'field conditions.'"

"What's field conditions?" Lee questioned.

Nancy subtly held one finger up at Chris. "When an agent is active, they are considered 'in the field.' These are the times when your training really matters, along with your ability to plan ahead and think on the spot. It sounds a bit daunting, I know, but do you remember all of the things you did to escape the home, travel to France, live day-to-day in the middle of winter, acquire assistance when needed, elude authorities, find food and clothing and protect yourself and others?" Lee nodded. "Well this will just be a more advanced way of doing some of the things you've already done, that's all."

Lee felt relieved. His Nan always had a way of making things clear, unlike other people. She never talked down to him. To others she seemed cold, but to Lee she was like a Fox's Glacier Mint – 'clear and refreshing'.

"Speaking of things done, you all might want to pay special attention to tomorrow's edition." Nancy pointed over to the *Daily Mail* on the side and then looked at Lee. "Our plan is in motion."

Chris looked at Debbie, then Nancy. The Chief hadn't told him about another plan. "What plan is that?" he asked.

"I can't say specifics, but I am carrying out my orders," she said, saluting towards Lee. Lee spluttered. He'd never seen himself as being in charge of his Nan before. "Shall we go for a little walk?" she continued, indicating Lee only. He understood.

"I'll go and get changed – won't be long."

Nancy and Lee's new parents chatted whilst he was upstairs. Chris was intrigued to know more about the shootings in France. Nothing had been in the national news.

"Can I ask what happened with Lee in France?"

Nancy steepled her fingers. "What have you been told so far?"

Chris needed to be careful. He didn't want to antagonise such an influential woman. He decided truth was the best option. "My understanding is that Lee shot two KGB agents whilst protecting one of ours."

Nancy was annoyed. This sort of information had a habit of biting The Service back in political ways that agents often didn't understand. "Where did you come by this information?"

Chris sensed her displeasure and realised he'd probably said too much. "It was something The Chief touched on the night he brought Lee here," he said, choosing to leave out what Lee has also disclosed.

Nancy thought briefly. The man must have had a reason for saying something to Chris. If she said nothing, they might always be wary of Lee. It was time to put this issue to bed. "One of our agents had compromised themselves just outside of Paris. I wouldn't have expected an agent to put themselves and a seven-year-old in that situation. I had jokingly given Lee an order to look after the agent, but he took it seriously and followed through with the only means he had at the time. This is all that should be said on the matter."

Both Chris and Debbie understood what Nancy meant. Chris regretted asking, because she would now most definitely brief Lee about what to say – thus cutting off an information supply.

Nancy knew that she'd been a bit terse. "Don't worry, I would've asked the same question if I were in your position," she said. Lee came downstairs dressed sensibly for a walk. "Let's continue our parley when we get back." Nancy rose from her seat to meet Lee and headed towards the front door.

As the door closed, Debbie looked at her husband. She didn't need to say what she was going to say, because Chris already knew he'd screwed up – but she said it anyway. "Nice one!"

"I know, I know, I'm sorry, OK." There was nothing else he could say. Debbie just looked at him, shook her head and forgave the screw-up.

Both Lee and Nancy enjoyed being out in the crisp fresh air. As they took a left at the end of the road, Lee spoke first.

"I heard what you were talking about when I was upstairs. Is something wrong?"

Nancy looked at him as they kept on walking. "I'm going to ask you a couple of questions and I promise to explain why afterwards. Did Chris by any chance ask you about the shootings and if so, what did you say back to him?"

Lee needed to focus his mind back a couple of weeks. "It was after they had told me a bit about themselves. Dad asked me about the bridge. He said The Chief hadn't given him much information, so I said I escaped a police cell by stealing some keys. I jumped from the bridge to escape from them, and they thought I'd killed myself when I jumped. He also knew about Paris, so I just said that I'd shot two people who were about to kill the person who'd come to help me."

"Can I ask you what your motivation was for telling them that you'd shot two people? I presume they were quite shocked?" Nancy asked.

"I wanted them to know that if it came to it, I'd have no hesitation in doing what had to be done," Lee said proudly.

"OK, now I'm going to tell you why I asked you the questions. This business is all about information and leverage. The art of a top agent is to be ghostly. Power isn't just physical; it's mostly psychological." She pointed to her temple. "In the mind. I know you like James Bond, but that really isn't the real world. Tell me, now that you've told them that you shot two people, do you think they will think of you differently?"

Lee's head bowed a little whilst he thought for a minute. "So you think they'll be more wary of me now?" he asked.

"Correct. I know that's what you wanted, and that would work with, say, boys at school or bullies etcetera, but this is a different game. In this game you want people to be open and trusting of you. The more open they believe you are, the more they want to tell you – especially those with big egos."

"Egos?" Lee questioned.

"People with high self-esteem or self-importance, yes? Do you know anyone like that?" she asked.

One person instantly burned their way to the forefront of his mind. "Louvaine King," he said resolutely.

"Louvaine King, indeed," Nancy resoundingly agreed, as she ruffled Lee's hair. "So, now, time for you to put your thinking cap on. What's the play with Mum and Dad?" she asked.

Lee didn't understand the question, but this was all going to be part of his new education. Nancy rephrased it. "What do you think your approach should be with Mum and Dad now?"

Lee took his time to think about this one. It was a difficult question and hard for him to answer, but he tried his best. "Well, we've all been getting on really well for the last two weeks. They're kind and I like them both, especially Mum. I don't really want that to change. If the question about the gun hadn't come up today, everything would've been fine. I did as you asked and looked after Kim... that's part of the job isn't it... following orders?"

"Hmmm, that's an interesting perspective, young man. Maybe I'm looking at this the wrong way," Nancy mused. "Let me think this over whilst we walk. Just rewinding back to the subject of Louvaine, the article in the paper tomorrow will be about you and the incidents that led to your death. It was already reported in France, so I wanted there to be a credible trail to follow."

"I'm not sure I understand, Nan?" Lee said.

"So, the death of Lee King has been reported in a French newspaper as 'under dubious circumstances.' Let's say that somebody in the English press picks up on it and reports the story. Let's say that they, or someone else, decide to try and follow up on that story, to see if they can locate the King family. Let's say they start investigating what happened, how do you think the family will react?"

"They'll probably just move again," Lee said despondently.

Nancy tried to reassure him. "I agree it's a possibility, but I don't think they can just move away so easily now. And besides, the reputational damage will have been done if, for example, their names are revealed in the local press. This is called 'shaking the tree.'"

"You mean like an apple tree?" Lee said.

"Absolutely! We shake the tree to see what falls out. We can then react, swiftly if necessary, to what's landed. You never know what can land right in your lap." She smiled.

"But you already know where they live," Lee said.

Nancy could tell that he wasn't really impressed. "I know this isn't the kind of revenge you were hoping for. You want them all to be put through as much pain as they've put you through, right?" Lee nodded. He didn't tell her that he just wanted them all dead. "Well, I made a promise to you that I am going to keep." She stopped and turned to face him. "Some punishments are physical, but some of the most brutal punishments are psychological, because they stay in the mind forever." She pointed at her temple again. "Do you trust me?" she asked. Of course he trusted her; he wasn't sure why she'd asked and it made him feel sad. He nodded. "Then trust me as I update you on progress. You know what they say, 'Hell hath no fury like a woman scorned,' and I am a woman, am I not?" This brought a smile back to Lee's face again. Nancy was happy that Lee was back on-side, but she wasn't just doing this for him... it would be for her and David too.

* * *

When Lee and Nancy had got home from their walk and sat down, Chris apologised for pursuing things he should probably have let go.

Nancy surprised everyone, including Lee, when she apologised herself. "It's me that should be sorry; it was entirely my fault. I've been set in my ways for too long, but Lee convinced me that I... we should change. I sometimes forget that we're all just human and it's only natural to be inquisitive. Why don't you tell Dad and Mum everything that happened when you got to Paris, Lee – excluding names please?"

Debbie and Chris looked at each other in surprise. Nancy knew that she needed to repair the relationship and Lee was happy to oblige, recounting the story in a more detailed but factual form. When Lee had finished, it was evident to them that he had actually been a bit of a hero. The concerns they'd had about a cold killer living in their household fell away. Neither of them had ever had to shoot somebody, and Chris wondered if he'd have done the same if he'd have been in Lee's position.

Nancy put her arm around Lee's shoulder in support. She thought about asking him to leave the room so that she could talk to Chris and Debbie alone, but decided that there was nothing she was going to say that would be too controversial. "There are a couple of things that I wanted to cover off with Mum and Dad before I head back – would you like to stay and listen too?" she asked.

"Sure," he replied.

Nancy began by talking about the additional training Lee would be receiving. Both she and The Chief had felt that Lee needed to settle in here and at the school first. So the plan was to start one weekend per month from Easter term. This would extend to two weekends per month from a date to be agreed.

Even though this was something that The Chief had outlined, and what they'd agreed to, it still didn't stop Debbie feeling a little low-spirited.

"What sort of training is this going to be, Nan?" Lee enquired. Throughout this whole situation, no one had actually told him this, other than what had been discussed earlier that afternoon. Chris and Debbie wondered the same thing.

Nancy needed to be careful here. "It will be with The Special Forces, but I don't have the full details yet," she said.

Chris was immediately jealous. Before joining The Service, he'd originally applied to get into the SAS, but had ultimately failed during 'Officers Week'.

Lee had seen a logo of something similar on an Action Man box before. "Is that to do with The Army?" he asked.

Nancy looked at Chris and motioned for him to pick up from where she'd left off. She knew exactly what was on his file and wondered whether he'd been able to get over his perceived failure.

"They're a very select part of The Army, where only the best of the best are recruited. There's a very high failure rate for soldiers and an even higher failure rate for officers," Chris explained.

Nancy decided to cushion some the impact on Chris. "You won't actually be in the SAS – the Special Air Service – you will just be receiving training from some of their specialists."

"Special Air Service?" Lee sounded bewildered.

Nancy and Chris smiled. "It's confusing I know, something to do with them originally being a parachute regiment," Chris said.

"What sort of specialist training will there be?" Lee asked excitedly.

Nancy looked at the time; she didn't want to outstay her welcome.

"How about I let Dad answer that one for you in a bit, as I'm going to have to make a move, my darling, or be stuck in traffic for ages."

Lee didn't want his Nan to leave; she'd barely been there a few hours. But he'd at least got to see her again, he supposed. He walked her to the coat cupboard by the front door and jumped her coat off the peg.

"Don't forget the paper tomorrow," she said to all of them as she put her coat on. She shook the hands of Chris and Debbie and gave Lee a little peck on the cheek.

"Ergh, you taste like dead bodies," she said playfully.

Debbie momentarily stopped breathing, her eyes wide open in surprise. The woman clearly had a dark sense of humour, but Lee just laughed.

"How many dead bodies have you kissed, Nan?" Lee replied, just as playfully.

Nancy laughed. "Nice come-back young man," she said as she ruffled his hair. "I'm glad I got to see you before you start school and I'll be in touch as we progress." Lee hugged Nancy for five seconds before letting her go.

As Nancy drove off, with a wave in the rear-view mirror, an upsurge of emotion hit her like a ten-foot ocean wave. The picture in her mind was of the last time she'd seen her beloved husband – the one and only dead body she'd ever kissed.

* * *

CHAPTER 34

COMMENCE FIRE

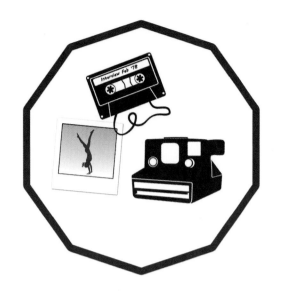

Early Friday morning and the newspaper landed on the floor with a crisp thwack as the over-sprung letterbox snapped closed. By the time Jon had made his way downstairs and opened the door, the paperboy had long gone. He shrugged, put the paper in the kitchen, gathered his keys and coat, and left for work. Not long after, Laura got up and went to the kitchen for breakfast. Whilst her mother attended to Jon Jr., she made herself some porridge, noticing the Daily Mail sat on the kitchen table. It was strange seeing it there because her parents didn't usually read dailies unless Jon sometimes brought a *Sun* or *Mirror* home from work – both of which were too crude for her academic tastes. She had ten minutes and began thumbing through the pages, scanning the various headlines as she ate her oats.

Laura dropped her spoon. There on page ten was a black and white picture of Lee under the headline:

WHY WAS A 7-YEAR-OLD BOY KILLED IN FRANCE?

Lee King, a seven-year-old boy who was forced to run away from a children's home in Suffolk, has drowned in France, having jumped from a bridge in an apparent suicide. In a statement, French police said they believe he had stowed away in a container lorry, travelling nearly six hundred miles to a small town near Nantes, just before Christmas. However, the reason for the suicide is unknown. A police investigation is ongoing but it is alleged that the boy may have been the victim of family abuse in St. Albans, where he resided before being transferred to the children's home. Did you know this boy? Please get in touch with our news desk if you have any information.

Laura couldn't eat any more. She folded the paper around the story and ran upstairs to her mother who'd just finished getting the baby ready for the morning.

"Mum, you need to read the paper," Laura said, holding the story under her mother's nose as she held the baby on one hip.

Louvaine took the paper with her right hand – she immediately recognised the picture of Lee and began reading. She sat down on the nursing chair in Jon Jr's room. It was as though someone had punched her in the abdomen, sucking the air right out of her. She tried to regain her composure, asking Laura where the paper had come from.

"I don't know, I just found it on the kitchen table and saw this as I was flicking through."

Louvaine looked at the picture and words again as the baby began to grip the paper with his tiny red hands. Her concern wasn't that Lee had killed himself, but that the article mentioned the town where they lived.

"I think you should go to school and don't say anything to Dad when you get home –this will all blow over."

By the way her mother responded Laura sensed that she really wasn't that concerned – certainly not about Lee, anyway. As she packed her things and left the house to walk to school, her mind swirled in thoughts of the clashes she'd instigated, the fibs she'd told and the beatings Lee had endured, all because of her. Her mother had used her like a pawn by passively encouraging her to keep tabs on her brother and help keep him in line. For the first time, Laura cried on Lee's behalf. She'd made his life a living hell and now he was dead. *You're going to hell for this*, she thought. She was so wrapped up in her own thoughts that she didn't notice the big man get out of his car.

Theo Greaves walked on the other side of the street, eventually overtaking Laura's position. The girl was clearly upset, constantly rubbing her eyes with her jumper. If this was about the article, he could move up the timeline of the intervention. The best way to test his assumption would be to doorstep the mother today and see what reaction he got. He took a left as Laura carried on walking and when safe, doubled back and maintained a safe distance until she reached her destination. He thought about speaking to her before school, but Nancy was right. It was sometimes better for people to stew for a while. Theo walked back towards his car and took out his 'typical journalist' equipment of a recorder and camera. He made sure the equipment was primed and ready, walked up the driveway and knocked on the front door. He put on his best smile.

"Oh, hello…Mrs. King?"

Louvaine looked up as she held her baby on one hip.

"Yes, can I help?" Louvaine didn't see the man's camera until he'd swung it round and taken a photograph. "What are you doing?" she protested.

"I'm following up on today's story about your son, Lee. Can you tell me what happened?" Theo held the recorder towards the woman's face.

"Who are you?" she asked, flummoxed and searching for time to think straight.

"My name's Theo Greaves of the *Daily Mail.* Can you tell me what happened?"

"I don't know what you're talking about; this is the only son I have," she protested, indicating the baby she was holding.

She was about to close the door when Theo jammed his size thirteen on the door base and read from a piece of paper. "Louvaine King, Jonathan King, Laura King and Lee King. That's your family isn't it? This is the newest addition, right?" he said a little more forcefully.

"I don't know what you're talking about; now get off my fucking door!" she shouted.

Theo raised his voice a lot louder. "I don't think you want to cause a scene, Mrs. King, as this could get a lot worse for you. Can you tell me why you sent Lee to the children's home?"

There was the sound of a door opening and Louvaine's worst nightmare began to unfold. The neighbour next door popped her head out and asked if she was OK.

This was just what Theo needed. "Sorry to bother you, madam, but do you remember young Lee King who used to live here? He recently killed himself."

The woman's eyes widened like saucers. "What, young Lee?"

"Don't say anything, he's a scumbag journalist!" Louvaine shouted at the woman. But the damage had been done. She tried to push the big man away from her door, but nothing she could do had any effect. At seventeen stones (238lbs), Theo was not going to be pushed anywhere. He took another picture of her as she stuck two fingers up to the camera.

Perfect, he thought and directed himself back towards the neighbour. "Did you know that she sent her son away to a children's home and he then committed suicide last month?" The neighbour shook her head and looked at Louvaine, stunned. "It's in today's *Daily Mail*," he added. Theo turned back towards Louvaine. "This is your chance to give me your side of the story, Mrs. King," he said, making sure his foot was nowhere near the door opening.

"Get lost, you fat fuck!" Louvaine slammed the door shut, as the baby started to cry. She leant against the door. She wanted the floor to engulf her there and then.

Outside, the woman asked Theo if what he said was true.

"I'm afraid so, madam," he said without any enjoyment. "Did you know the boy?"

"Not that well, really. They've only been here about six or eight months."

"What was he like?"

"He was a nice kid, but as I said, I hadn't really got to know him that well."

Theo pulled a fresh rolled-up copy of the day's paper from out of his pocket and showed the picture on page ten to the woman. "Was that him?" The woman nodded. "Thank you, madam, I really appreciate your help."

"Please don't include me on anything, will you?" she asked.

"Don't worry, I never asked your name, so I won't quote you. I just needed confirmation that the boy lived here, that's all," he said, and made his way back to the car. Although the timeline had changed, everything had pretty much gone the way Nancy said it might. Theo drove off in search of a telephone box and updated Nancy on the morning's events. Now all he had to do was wait.

Nancy called Directory Enquiries and acquired the telephone number for the Newsagents she'd been to the day before and cancelled the paper subscription. She then went out and purchased a couple of copies for herself.

Louvaine spent the whole day in turmoil. Should she tell Jon when he got home? What would she say to anyone else that knocked on the door? What would the neighbours think of her? The rumour was bound to spread now that next door had heard what that oaf had said. She'd planned to take the baby out in the pram, but she couldn't be sure the man wasn't still around, so decided against it.

* * *

Laura also had a difficult day. Her form teacher and friends noticed she looked off and asked if she was alright. But she didn't want to talk about anything and kept pretty quiet the whole time. When the last bell went, she packed up the books she didn't need and put them in her locker. Two girls from her class walked out of the school with her. Both were quite excited and tried to raise her spirits by talking about meeting the boys tomorrow. But when Laura thought of boys, the picture of Lee in the paper came flooding back.

"Are you going to meet us in town tomorrow as planned?" one of them asked.

"I'm not sure. I haven't been feeling too well today, so I'll give you a call tomorrow morning, yeah?" Laura said. The girls split off in two directions, with Laura now walking alone. She was so absorbed in her own thoughts that she didn't hear or observe the approach of the big man from across the street.

"Laura, Laura King?" he said, as caught up to her side.

Surprised, she stopped and looked up at the man. "Yes?"

Theo kept his hands in his pockets to try and not scare the girl. "I'm sorry to bother you, my name is Theo Greaves. My colleague has written an article in article in today's *Daily Mail* about the sad suicide of your brother, perhaps you've seen it?" he asked in a soft voice.

Laura gasped – her face one of instant concern. "What do you want with me?" she asked as she started walking again.

Theo matched her pace. "I really hate this part of my job but I wanted to talk to you to find out a little bit more about Lee and the family."

Laura froze. What could she possibly say that wouldn't ultimately come back to her? "I shouldn't talk to you; you'll get me in trouble."

"What if I said that I'm trying to protect you?" he said, raising his voice slightly. Theo touched her on the shoulder lightly, which was enough to stop Laura in her tracks.

"What do you mean, protect me? Protect me from what?" she asked.

Theo bent down to her level and raised an eyebrow. "Why don't I tell you what I know, you can tell me if it's true or not, and if it's not you can put me right – does that sound fair? There's probably going to be a few more articles about this once the local press get hold of the story and everyone here will know. Wouldn't you rather they get the right story? They'll just make it up with lies otherwise." Laura considered what the man was saying – Theo knew he was close to convincing her. "Don't worry, we can go somewhere and sit down. It can be as public or as private as you like and I'm definitely not going to abduct you or anything," he said with a smile.

Laura made the moves in her mind; she could come out of this blameless if she was careful. She pointed to the monument opposite, which had a couple of bench seats. It looked the safest place as any to her.

They both sat down and Theo took out his cassette recorder.

"Why are you doing that? Laura asked.

"I just find it easier than having to write notes. Look at my big fat fingers!" He held up his right hand. Laura smiled nervously. "Also, there's no chance of me misquoting or changing anything, because it's all here. It's actually for your benefit too."

Laura agreed somewhat reticently, which gave Theo his cue to begin as he switched on the recorder.

"So, Laura, could you confirm that you are happy for me to record this conversation and that your name is Laura King, daughter of Louvaine King and sister of Lee King?" Even though she was out in the open, Laura felt like she was in an interrogation cell. Theo could see the apprehension in her face. Laura nodded. "Could you speak, it's just that the tape can't see your face – that's all," he said jovially.

"My name is Laura King and yes, my mum is Louvaine and Lee is... was my brother," she said pensively.

"Thank you Laura. Did you read the article in this morning's *Daily Mail* about Lee?"

"Yes." Her voice was very soft.

Theo looked at her face. "Looking at your expression, I guess you're feeling quite sad about his death?"

"Yes. He didn't deserve that," she said solemnly.

Theo knew he needed to be careful. "Do you know why Lee was sent to the children's home?" Laura hesitated, and Theo tried again. "I know what happened in France is not your fault, but it would really be helpful to understand what happened to him leading up to his death."

Laura needed to stall for time. "You said you'd tell me what you knew so far," she said quickly.

Theo could see that the girl needed to compose herself a little. There was no harm in a little give and take, he thought. "So what I've been able to piece together is that Lee was taken to a children's home a fair way from here. I'm not sure why, but he was clearly unhappy there and ran away just before Christmas. The French police think he managed to stow away in a lorry in England and travel all the way to Nantes, and from there he lived on the streets for a while. I'm guessing that he was on the run, because there was an article in a French newspaper stating that the police had tried to capture him after he stole some food." Laura tutted and shook her head. Theo continued. "So as you can see, I have a picture of what happened after Lee ran away from the home, but it's open to interpretation as to what happened before." Theo decided to pursue the theft avenue with Laura. "I take it that Lee had stolen before?" he asked.

"Yes... I'd caught him stealing once before but that wasn't the only time. Mum also thought he was stealing too. She found toys and sweets in his room that no one in the family had bought for him."

"Did Lee do anything else? Really bad things that made your parents want to give him away?"

A needle pierced Laura's heart. It was her fault he was sent away, but how was she going to get out of this? Laura began slowly. "There were... problems... with my dad; well our stepdad. They didn't get on and he used to hit Lee... a lot." Laura was doing fine now. She had an idea; a nice way to get back at Jon for doing those horrible things to her – and her mother too, for not believing her. "Before Lee was sent away, Dad had really gone to town on him and nearly beaten Lee unconscious. I saw the bruises all the way up his ribs and on his face. He was the main reason Lee had to go." *Yes, this was good*, she thought and none of it was technically untrue.

"Do you think they... your parents, were making way for the new baby?" Theo asked.

This caught Laura slightly off-guard. How did he know about the baby? She shrugged. "Possibly."

"This is a difficult question for me to ask you, but it is important – so I hope you'll understand," he prepped. "Have your parents ever hurt you or done anything that would potentially hurt you, like Lee?" he asked delicately.

Laura was about to instantly respond with an emphatic 'No', but stopped. She thought again. What would happen if she told the man about her dad? "What did you mean when you said you were trying to protect me?" she asked.

Theo now knew there must be something. He couldn't really protect her as such; it was more like damage limitation.

"I can make sure that your name's not mentioned in the story. But if there's something else going on I can try to help as best I can."

Laura looked down at the pavement and thought for a little while longer. "He's been... doing... things to me," she finally said.

Theo was actually surprised. "You don't have to go into detail if you don't want to, but are you saying what I think you're saying about your dad?"

Laura nodded. "He took a picture of me too."

Theo put a big hand on her shoulder. "How old are you, if you don't mind me asking?"

"Eleven," she snivelled.

Theo was angry. He tried to find a tissue, but didn't have one on him. Laura just used her jumper again as she'd done earlier that morning.

"When did this begin?" Theo asked, containing himself as best he could.

"After Lee went, I guess."

"Can I ask what he's done to you?" he said in a soft tone.

Laura wept a little more. "He keeps coming into my room and forcing himself on me, putting his thing in me, hurting me." Laura cried and Theo put her head on his chest.

"Have you been able to speak to anyone else about this... your mum, school teacher or friend?" he ventured.

"No," she said quietly.

Theo wasn't surprised but decided to push one step further. "What about telling your real dad, or a grandparent, or someone else?"

Laura sat up and shook her head. "I don't think so."

Theo turned off the recorder. "Would you like me to come home with you and have a little *chat* with your parents – I can be quite persuasive?"

Laura was adamant. "No, that's just going to make my life worse – they might get rid of me, just like they did Lee."

Theo backed off and brought his mind back to the mission. "OK, if that's what you want. I'm just a reporter, but here is my telephone number just in case." Theo handed her a card. "I suggest you keep it safe. Will you be OK getting home, or do you want me to walk with you?"

The last thing Laura wanted was for a reporter to be near her house. She'd definitely be in trouble with her mother then. "No, it's OK. I need to get home before it gets dark anyway," she said.

"Well, thank you for talking to me Laura; it's helped with the background information about Lee. Can I give you some advice?" Laura nodded. "There might be others who pursue this story locally. You should try to stay as clear of everything as possible, and let your parents take the brunt of any potential issues, yeah?"

"I will," she said as she walked off towards home leaving Theo sat on the bench contemplating.

A couple of minutes later, Theo walked away in the opposite direction towards his car; stopping at a telephone box to update Nancy. He gave her a précis of the conversation with Laura and even played a little bit of the tape for her. "What's the play now?" he asked.

Nancy thought quickly and decisively. Dealing with the revelations would need some time. But her priority would be to recover Theo's tape – she didn't want it in the open or duplicated. "It's pretty bad and best not discussed over the phone, can we meet today?"

"Of course. Where do you have in mind?"

"There's a small village called Datchet just south of Slough and east of Windsor. Let's meet at the train station car park in two hours. What car do you have?"

"I have a green Jag, registration HHP 23M."

"Thank you, Theo, I'll see you soon."

After putting the phone down, Theo wrote a note, located the *Herts Advertiser* offices and handed it in along with a copy of the *Daily Mail* at the reception.

Nancy was already parked at Datchet train station when Theo arrived. She watched him drive in and, rather than blink her lights at him, she waited for a minute to see if he had any company. Assessing the car park as clear, Nancy got out and walked over to the Jaguar. Theo opened the passenger side door and she sank down into the plush leather armchair of a seat. They talked for a long time, with Theo giving a full verbal report of the encounter with Louvaine, the neighbour, and finally, with Laura. He played the tape in full on the car stereo, filling in aspects that weren't completely audible.

By the end, Nancy was clearly angry – her knuckles white in comparison to her reddish hands. "This isn't what I expected Theo. You did an amazing job getting Laura to talk... but this is bad."

Theo could see the woman was distressed. He put his hand around hers, feeling the tension beneath. "What do you want to do? Personally I'd cut the guy's bollocks off, but I suspect that's just a short-term measure."

It was crude and not far off what Nancy would dearly like for the man, but that's not how she operated and Theo knew that too. "I've tipped off the local newspaper as you asked," he said.

Nancy prioritised what she needed in her mind. "Would it be OK if I have the tape?" Theo knew that these things could be used as leverage and this was a sanctioned personal job. He ejected the cassette and gave it to Nancy. "Any copies?" she asked as a matter of course.

"No copies."

"How quickly do you think a local reporter will act on your tip-off, if at all? And when do you think they'd need their story ready for print?"

"I'd be surprised if their reporting staff worked weekends, so I would expect if anything was going to happen, it would have to be done by Monday, possibly Tuesday at the latest. They distribute on Thursdays," Theo replied.

Nancy thought for a while longer.

"Is there anything else you need me to do?" he asked.

Nancy felt a little bad about using Theo for personal donkey work and if it had been under different circumstances, she'd have thought about inviting him for a drink. But he was now a marked man and it was time to cut ties. She put her other hand on his and rubbed it gently. "I don't think there's anything left Theo. I may need to speak with the authorities on this one, so the landscape will need to be clean. I'd like to thank you again for your work on this, though."

"You're always welcome, Nancy."

Nancy got out of the car, shut the door and bent down to take a farewell look at Theo Greaves.

* * *

Louvaine had felt on edge for much of the day. She'd spent the whole time thinking about the reporter, the story and what to say to Jon and Laura. She went through a number of stories she could use to justify her actions if she was asked. She'd thought about blaming the whole thing on her ex-husband. But whilst she could get him into trouble for the car accident seven years ago, she was still a willing accomplice when it came to keeping quiet and accepting Lee into the household.

In the end she'd called the solicitor she'd used for her divorce for advice. He'd passed her on to another partner in the firm with more expertise in criminal law. When she read the article, described what had happened that morning and talked through her thinking about how to handle the situation, the solicitor simply advised her to not say anything and keep quiet to any enquiries. When she asked why, he explained that everything she'd done up to the point of having Lee removed from the house was open to interpretation from a legal standpoint and would cast her in an unfavourable light. However, the removal of the boy from the family home was fully legal and done through the appropriate channels. Anything that happened to him afterwards was the responsibility of the children's home and not hers. Therefore, if she maintained that standpoint, there would be nothing anybody could do... legally. As for reputational damage, the article had just speculated abuse. She would just have to ride it out using the same reasons she'd given to Social Services. It may not win her any friends, but it would be much more favourable than an investigation into her affairs.

The call had put her mind at some ease, and rather than make a big deal of it, she decided to mention the article to Jon at the dinner table. She gave Jon the page to read. His reaction was somewhat different to hers.

"It's a shame it turned out like that for him," he said genuinely.

Louvaine snapped. "What about the last part?" she said, stabbing her finger at the paper.

Jon re-read the last few sentences. "I don't see the problem. It alleges there was abuse, but there wasn't. You were pregnant when you fell over, he busted my car and he threatened Laura here with a knife. The way I see it, you did the right thing for the family."

Laura remained silent but Louvaine smiled. "You've got a point there." She rubbed Jon's hand. "Just so you know, a reporter knocked on the door this morning about this article." Jon and Laura were both surprised, but for slightly different reasons. "Don't worry, I didn't tell him anything, but Kathy next door came out and overheard some of the commotion."

Jon got angry. "What, some guy from the paper coming to our home – do you want me to find him?"

"I don't think that would be a good idea, he was pretty big," Louvaine said. Laura's stomach wrenched. "Anyway, I spoke with a solicitor today and his advice was that we must stick with what happened. Lee had become out of control and a danger to the family. Everything that happened after he went to the home is their responsibility, not ours." She looked at Jon and Laura. Laura was surprised at how callous it all sounded. "We mustn't say anything to anyone and it will blow over."

Laura excused herself from the table – she no longer felt like eating.

* * *

CHAPTER 35

A NEW CASE

On the whole journey home from Datchet, Nancy let her subconscious turn scenario after scenario over in her mind. Laura was eleven years old. If she was older, things might be easier logistically. She'd be more self-sufficient. But she wasn't like Lee. Nancy doubted that she'd run away, knowing that Lee had killed himself. She needed to find the balance between rescuing her granddaughter from this vile situation and her promise to Lee – otherwise her plans could go up in smoke. Only one scenario gave her hope, but it would need to be played expertly.

The next day at 10am, Nancy made a phone call to Hertfordshire Social Services. Lynn Franks was not on duty that weekend, so Nancy left a message for her to call as a matter of urgency. With nothing better to do for the rest of the weekend, Nancy retrieved some old recording equipment from the loft and hooked everything up in such a way as to be able to make a couple of crude sound copies on tape. As long as the voices could be heard against the background noise, she was happy.

* * *

On Monday morning, Nancy received the call she was waiting for.

"Morning, Nancy, I was wondering when you'd be in contact. I take it you've found Lee? Fred's been going out of her mind and the Bury St. Edmunds police are none the wiser."

From this question alone Nancy knew that Lynn was not a *Mail* reader.

"Thank you very much for calling me back, Lynn. We did find Lee but I'm afraid he was eventually found dead, in France of all places." Nancy paused. "He'd killed himself before we could get to him."

Lynn was staggered. The death of a runaway was always a high possibility, but it was the first time she'd been so closely involved. "I'm so sorry, Nancy, I really am. He was such a lovely boy during the brief time I got to know him. How did it happen?"

"That's very kind of you to say Lynn. The coroner's report stated the cause of death as drowning. As you can imagine, it's not been easy. The problem is that things have got a little complicated and I was hoping I could come and meet with you, today if possible? I can give you more detail then."

Lynn looked at her schedule. "I don't have a lot of free time I'm afraid, could we do later in the week?"

"Do you remember I said there was also a daughter at risk?" added Nancy. "Well that risk has now become grave." She hoped that would be enough for the woman to rethink her priorities.

Lynn felt guilty. She'd been partially responsible for a young boy's death. "OK, I'll make some calls and shift some things around. Can you get here for 1 o'clock?"

"Thank you, that sounds perfect. I'll ask for you at reception," Nancy said, and put the receiver down.

Lynn hung up, still stunned by what Nancy had told her – and first thing on a Monday morning. *I hope this isn't an omen for the rest of the week.* She immediately made a call to Fred to give her the bad news.

At 1 o'clock, Lynn met Nancy in reception and shook her by the hand. "I have the same empty office ready for us if you'd like to follow me."

After they'd both sat down, Nancy opened a large bag she'd brought and put a copy of the *Daily Mail* on the table.

"I appreciate you seeing me at such short notice, Lynn. You may want to turn to page ten." Nancy slid the paper over.

Lynn immediately saw the picture of Lee and began reading the related article. "What happened? How comes this made the national newspaper?" she asked.

"Lee's father and I had hired a private investigator to try and locate him after he went missing from the home; that's who I called when I was last here. The investigator eventually managed to locate Lee in France, but unfortunately was too late to save him. The investigator remained in France on David's and my behalf to deal with all of the paperwork, police and arrangements for bringing his ashes back to England. Unfortunately, during that time, a French newspaper picked up on the story. The investigator thought it might be useful to give the story to someone in this country. I agreed. The aim was just to 'shake the tree' as such. I needed to see if my granddaughter had been having any of the same problems Lee had encountered."

Lynn interrupted. "I did interview Lee the second time I saw him, but he was very evasive about what was happening at home."

"I want you to listen to this and tell me what you think." Nancy pulled out a large portable cassette recorder with integrated speaker from her bag. "It's an informal interview between a reporter and Laura."

She pressed play and pushed the volume to its highest. Lynn listened intently as the moral drama unfolded. She had a number of questions, but when the tape stopped, it was Nancy who spoke first.

"I can see you have questions and I'm happy to answer any you have, but essentially, I need to know what Social Services would normally do in this situation."

"Well, I was not expecting this to be honest, Nancy, it's very serious. I need to know if any of this recording was taken under duress of any kind? It doesn't sound like it, but any court will throw it out if any doubts could be cast."

Nancy nodded in appreciation. "From what I know and what we can both hear, the recording was done out in the open and, for a journalist, quite sensitively – wouldn't you agree?"

"Agreed," Lynn said. "Can the journalist potentially be called as a witness if something like this went to court?"

"The journalist was a man by the name of Theo Greaves from the *Mail* and yes, he would be able to testify if required."

"Do you have a copy of this tape that I can have?"

Nancy pulled out a cassette copy from her bag along with a file. "I recorded the cassette and have also typed up the transcript of the recording for you, which I'm sure you'll find helpful."

"I have one last question before I give an opinion. When I interviewed Lee, he told me that Laura had continually lied to get him into trouble, which ultimately, in my view, led to a lot of his physical abuse. What's to say that your granddaughter isn't manipulating the journalist for some perverted reason?"

Nancy mused. The woman had posed a very good question. "I agree with you and I think it's something to be wary of. The only thing that would verify the story would be to find the picture or negative if it indeed exists. Are those the lines you were thinking along too?"

Lynn nodded in answer, drew a deep breath and then shook her head slowly. "Well, you may not like what I'm about to say, but my professional opinion would be as follows: there would need to be a police search of the house to look for the evidence. Along with the search warrant, our department would have to take the girl into temporary care for her own safety."

"Would this happen in all cases?" Nancy asked, concerned.

"I'm afraid so, Nancy. There's no avoiding it. We are obliged to do what's best for the victim in the first instance. Our number one priority will be to remove her from the danger as quickly as possible."

Lynn could see that Nancy was anxious about the whole thing, which was exactly what she wanted Lynn to see.

"How long does it normally take for you to get everything in place with the warrants and police etc?" Nancy enquired.

"A day, possibly two, depending on the judge. I'm sorry, Nancy, but having heard this now, I have no choice but to do my job."

Nancy's shoulders slumped. "Would it be possible to do me a favour?"

"I can try," Lynn said.

"Would you be able to arrange for Laura to be taken Alexandra House?"

Lynn was taken back a little by the question. "Wouldn't you want her to go back into your or her father's custody?" Lynn asked in surprise.

"I would and I'm sure David would too. But he's now out of the country on business and spends at least two days a week away. He would need to make some significant adjustments first before he could properly care for Laura. And, if Louvaine gets wind of any involvement from me, it could seriously jeopardise any case you bring against the husband. At least if Laura was at that home, I'd know where she was and could get to know her again once the dust settles. She didn't even mention us on the tape, so I don't want to force her to stay with me or David if she doesn't want to. My hope is that with a bit of time, she'll see that being with true family is where she belongs."

Lynn nodded. She'd also been surprised that the girl hadn't mentioned her father or Nancy on the tape. From what she'd seen and heard, everything made sense. "Are you sure you're happy to trust me and Fred again?" Lynn asked in a self-deprecating way.

"I don't think you can fully stop someone running away, but I'm hopeful Fred will have learned a few lessons from Lee and keep a better eye on Laura... would you agree?" Nancy asked.

"I'll make sure of it. She's not as useless as it seemed and I still feel guilty about Lee. I tried calling the number he gave me for you, but I couldn't get any response. I should've acted quicker and driven to you directly."

Nancy was a little surprised that she'd missed the calls, but put a reassuring hand on Lynn's. "I can assure you that the guilt is shared. This is our chance to try and make something right for Laura now."

Lynn's mind also roamed back to Lee. "Would it be alright if I keep this article? I will also need to close off Lee's file here and although devastating, Fred will need to be updated about what we've discussed. She's genuinely messed up over the whole situation."

"Of course, keep the paper."

Lynn folded the paper, and stood to indicate that the meeting was now over. "Well, Nancy, it looks like I have a mountain of work to do this week. I'd rather handle this myself if that's OK with you, so I'll need to reassign some of my other cases."

Nancy took the hint and stood too. "I appreciate everything you're doing, Lynn. Can I just ask that you keep me in the loop as to when the search and visit will take place and then when Laura has been placed at the home safely?" Nancy tore a small strip from the newspaper and wrote her number down. "I doubt Lee gave you the wrong number, but here it is again. This is not to be passed to anyone or to go on file... I trust you'll understand?"

"Of course and yes, I'll definitely keep you informed." Lynn definitely didn't want to get on the wrong side of the Secret Service.

* * *

CHAPTER 36

TAKEAWAY

In just a little over twenty-four hours, Lynn had everything lined up. She called Nancy on the Tuesday afternoon, getting through first time, to say that she, a colleague and the police would be knocking on the family door at 6 o'clock the next morning.

"Thank you for letting me know Lynn, I really appreciate the quick turnaround."

"My feet haven't touched the ground since we spoke yesterday," Lynn said. She was just about to say goodbye when Nancy spoke again.

"Lynn, we may have a little fly in the ointment."

"What's that?" She asked exhausted.

"I've been informed that your local press have somehow managed to get hold of the story and may be looking to go much deeper than what the *Daily Mail* wrote." Nancy said.

"What do you mean? How much deeper?" Lynn asked, her brain now somewhat frazzled.

"I honestly don't know; it's only recently come to my knowledge."

"Shit, that's all this situation needs. Have they approached the family at all?"

"I'm afraid that's something I just don't know. I hope not. I'd hate for the family to be scared off. But I've been thinking. If they haven't, you could potentially use this to your advantage."

"How so?" Lynn asked.

"Well you know what the police are like; they love a little bit of publicity – especially for something like this."

Nancy was about to continue when Lynn cut in. "How's that an advantage to me? It's not going to be good for the girl."

Nancy took a silent deep breath and continued. "I agree. But think of it this way. If you control the press, what they are allowed to cover and the narrative, a story that Social Services have acted swiftly to uncover a potential paedophile will be a win for you and the police."

Lynn thought about this for a minute. Nancy remained quiet.

"What would you suggest?" Lynn asked.

"Well ultimately this is your case and it will be your decision how you conduct it. But I would say that firstly you should enquire at the *Herts Recorder* news desk whether anyone is looking for information on the story. Secondly, if they are, ask to speak to the covering reporter and say that you have some important information relating to the case. If you do get to speak to him or her, then that would be a good time to come to a co-operative arrangement. Tell them when the search is going to be and tell them that the police will take a dim view of any photography of any children but that the adults will be fair game. They'll know that they can't mention the children's names by law anyway. Lastly, I would tell them that if they want to work with you again, they must stay on public property at all times and not hinder any action by the police or yourself. The police can handle any comments if you want to keep a low profile."

"That all sounds fine, but why would I want to work with them again?" Lynn questioned. She really wasn't happy about the situation she could potentially be in.

"Whilst it doesn't sound as though Jon King is likely to be a serial offender, these stories give hope and courage to others in similar situations – as well as the decisive action by dedicated public servants, of course. There have been a number of excellent studies on this. This story may just uncover another abuse victim that you wouldn't have known about before. We can't let these sorts of people get away with abusing young children, and as much as we despise the press, they can play their part if managed properly."

"Can I think on it?" Lynn asked. She was already under tremendous pressure.

"Like I said, this is your case and it's your decision. They may not be pursuing it anyway, which would certainly make things less complicated. The one thing I would ask is that if you do work together, I'd like to have a copy of all photographs and the story when it gets published, if that's alright with you?"

"OK, let me think. I'll be in touch." Lynn hung up the phone, undecided on what she should do next. Everything Nancy had said made sense; it was just way out of her comfort zone.

* * *

It was 5:25 on Wednesday morning and Lynn was sat in a small briefing room in the St. Albans police station along with four officers, a reporter from the *Herts Advertiser* and another Social

Services colleague. After the call with Nancy and speaking with the reporter over the phone, she really didn't feel comfortable being in the situation on her own. The senior police officer had briefed them all on their roles and how he wanted the operation handled. There were to be no rogue officers taking things into their own hands. The police would go in first, then Social Services only. The press could take photographs and if given the signal, ask questions of the adults only. Lynn had spoken with Fred and given her all the details she had about Laura, which were sketchy at best. But her information could follow on afterwards. The most important thing was to get her out of a potentially abusive environment.

At 5:50am two officers knocked on the front door and rang the doorbell of the King family home, whilst the other two had got themselves into position by the back garden. Lynn and her colleague stood about ten feet behind and the photographer placed himself to the side to get the best reaction shot.

The door opened and an annoyed man with blond hair appeared in a dressing gown. He was visibly shocked to see two police officers standing tall on his doorstep. It was a good shot for the reporter.

"Mr. Jon King?"

"Yes?" The man looked confused. The officers moved past the front door within touching distance of him.

"Mr. King, I am hereby arresting you on suspicion of raping a minor. You are not obliged to say anything unless you wish to do so, but what you say may be put into writing and given in evidence." He held up two letters. "We have a warrant for your arrest and to search the premises. Handcuff him, please," he said to the second officer, who swiftly pulled Jon's arm behind his back to administer the cuffs.

Jon began to struggle and shout. "What are you fucking talking about? I haven't raped anyone. You must have the wrong person. What are you doing?"

The lead officer wasn't going to put up with anything from a child rapist and swiftly gave the man a disguised punch to the stomach, sending the wind from his lungs, enabling the other officer to do his job more efficiently. "Don't worry, sir, everything will be explained down at the station." He radioed for the two other officers to come back to the front of the house.

Louvaine heard the commotion going on downstairs and came belting down the steps to see her husband lying face flat on the floor with two police at the entrance. "What are you doing in my house? That's my husband, get out, you've no right to be in here!" she shouted, instantly coming to Jon's defence. She didn't really know why he was in handcuffs, but she was damned if she was going to let anyone come into her home and arrest him.

The lead officer spoke. "Madam, I do have the right and your husband is being arrested for the rape of your daughter." Louvaine was briefly stunned into silence. She looked down at Jon.

"It's not true, Lou, she must've made something up!" Jon said as he strained to move his head to the side to see his wife. The officers from the rear had now made their way to the front and positioned themselves in front of Lynn as back-up to their colleagues.

Louvaine wasn't quite sure what to do, but she was angrier now. She shouted upstairs for Laura to come down and tell the police it was a lie.

Laura had been looking out of her bedroom window and listening to the commotion going on downstairs. Her heart raced and palpitations commandeered her lungs. What had she done? She stayed where she was, hoping her mother wouldn't call again.

But that hope disappeared instantly as Louvaine shouted once more. "Laura, get down here now!"

The lead officer could see the situation getting messy and potentially leading to the intimidation of the key witness. He directed his attention to the other officers. "Get him out of here now."

Louvaine tried to push one of them away, but they just levered her off. Two officers pulled Jon up to his feet and began marching down the driveway – his dressing gown flapping openly in the wind.

It was another good shot for the reporter who chanced his luck at asking a few questions. "Is it true that you had sex with your daughter, Mr. King? Is she more attractive than your wife?"

Jon spat in the reporter's direction. "She's just a prick-tease and a liar, that's what she is," he responded angrily, and instantly regretted it. The police officers secured Jon in the back of one of the police cars. The reporter made sure to get a few more pictures without any interference from the police. By now, most of the street had heard the fracas and were either watching from windows, or braving the cold outside their front doors.

With two officers now inside and the main risk in the back of a car, Lynn and her colleague made their way into the house.

"What are *you* doing here?" Louvaine asked, surprised. Laura was beginning to make her way down the stairs.

"I'm sorry, Mrs. King, but we have to take Laura away from the home until this situation is resolved," Lynn said in a stern voice. The bottom instantly fell out from under Laura's feet as her legs began to buckle – holding on to the banister for immediate support.

As Lynn began to make her way towards Laura, Louvaine snapped. She struck Lynn in the face and pulled her hair back with such force, she fell to the ground. "You're not taking anyone from here you bitch!"

she spat, as the lead police officer restrained her and Lynn was helped by her colleague.

Louvaine kicked out at the officer, who by this time had seen enough.

"Mrs. King, I am arresting you for assaulting a social worker and a police officer in the line of duty. You are not obliged to say anything unless you wish to do so, but what you say may be put into writing and given in evidence." He kicked her legs apart, dropped her face first onto the stairs and put a pair of handcuffs on her.

Louvaine looked up the steps to Laura, with a snarl. "What have you done, you little tart? He's only ever been nice to you!"

Laura was in tears and conflicted inside. On one hand she wanted to save the family, but on the other, she didn't want her dad touching her anymore. "I'm sorry, mum!" she cried.

The lead officer pulled Louvaine up to her feet.

"You can't arrest me, I've got a baby upstairs... you can't arrest me!" she shouted and tried to twist away from the officer.

By now Lynn had got to her feet. She couldn't stand the woman when they first spoke on the phone and she definitely hated her now. "Don't worry, Mrs. King, we'll take good care of that for you," she said with a cold sneer to taunt the woman.

Before she had the chance to do any further harm, the lead officer turned Louvaine about and instructed one of the other officers to take the woman out to an awaiting vehicle. "Make sure you put her in the other car, I don't want them talking to each other. And keep an eye on both of them!" he shouted.

The waiting reporter had managed to get a glimpse of the fracas inside and approached the apprehended woman on the way to the car taking photographs as he did so. "Did you know your husband was abusing your daughter?" he asked loudly.

"Get lost, you scumbag," Louvaine replied with disdain.

"Were you in on it? Did you abuse Lee too?" he said, twisting the knife.

"I said fuck off, you cunt!" The officer forced her into the back of the second vehicle.

Inside the house, Lynn climbed the stairs towards Laura, who was still holding on to one of the balusters. "I don't think you'll know me, Laura, but I've been here before," she said softly.

Laura looked sceptical. She hadn't seen the woman before, so how could this be true?

"I was here to collect Lee when your mother gave him away. My name is Lynn. Please, can you come upstairs with me?"

The full force of what she'd done to Lee and now what she'd done to the family hit Laura harder than anything she'd ever known before. Lynn held out a hand and guided Laura upstairs to her room. Her colleague followed, but made her way into what was now the baby's room.

"I don't want to go!" Laura wept half-heartedly.

"I'm really sorry Laura, I hate doing this – but it's the law, I'm afraid."

Downstairs, the lead officer gave orders to the remaining two men. "Right, turn the place over. You know what we're looking for – leave no stone unturned." They each took different downstairs rooms to go through.

Lynn gently coaxed Laura to pack some of her belongings, but she also had questions she needed to ask the girl. "As you can probably gather, we listened to the recording of the interview you had with the reporter last week. Please don't blame anyone; he had a responsibility in law to inform the authorities with anything like this. But, do you know where your dad keeps the picture you mentioned?" Laura genuinely didn't know and shook her head. "What about the camera he took it with; do you know where he keeps that?" Lynn asked.

Laura snivelled and thought for a bit. "I think it might be in the garage."

Lynn called down to the lead officer. "You may want see if it's in the garage – we think the camera may be there."

Laura felt sick. If they found the picture of her, the two women and all those men downstairs would see it... they would see her.

When Laura finished her packing, Lynn asked her to get dressed and help her colleague next door with the baby's things. She then began transferring the bags to her car. The reporter took photos which he knew would add to the drama of evidence being removed from the home.

Both saddened and ecstatic, the lead officer found what they were looking for in an envelope inside a tool box. The picture had a small amount of creasing damage, but it was clear what the depiction was... a young girl in an open-legged handstand position with the picture taken from an angle above. He walked upstairs and showed it to Lynn first. She sighed. It was sad that the story now had more credence, but relieved that they hadn't just completely violated a family on the basis of hearsay.

The officer showed Laura the picture. "I'm sorry to have to ask, but is this the picture you spoke of in the interview?" he said as softly as he could. Laura nodded and cried. Both social workers cast a look at each other.

"Are there any other pictures we need to be aware off?" he asked. Laura shook her head. She had no words to say. "We're going to need her to come down to the station to make a statement," he directed towards Lynn. The officer then put the picture in a see-through plastic bag and went downstairs to continue with the search. While Lynn and her colleague collected and packed things for the baby, Laura sat on the bed comforting the five-month-old in her arms.

When they'd finished, the three of them stood in the bedroom. Lynn put an arm around Laura. "It's time to go," she said softly.

Downstairs, the police were finishing up with their search. They'd taken anything they'd needed, but made sure to leave as much mess and as many broken artefacts as possible. They all walked out together whilst the reporter made sure to keep a distance. He'd made a deal not to approach the girl, but still took photographs anyway, knowing they couldn't be published.

Laura looked around. She could see all the different neighbours either on their doorsteps or huddled together in mini-groups gossiping about her and her family. Maybe it was for the best that she was going away for a bit. But she wondered what it was going to be like when she came back. She helped Lynn's colleague put Jon Jr. in his cot and secure it in the car and was just about to squeeze in with him when Lynn directed her to her own vehicle.

"I should be with the baby to stop him moving around in the car," Laura said.

"Don't worry, my colleague has done this before, he'll be safe, I promise. Anyway, there's more room in this one." She ushered Laura into the passenger side.

Just over a mile into the journey, the police cars branched off, heading to the station. Lynn followed the police to the right whilst her colleague turned left.

"Where's she going?" Laura said, concerned.

"The police need a statement from you, which is where we're going now. Hopefully it won't take too long. It wouldn't be a good idea to take a small infant into a police station; they're really not geared up for that sort of thing."

At the station car park, Jon was taken in first through a secure rear entrance and formally charged and processed by the duty Sergeant. They brought Louvaine in ten minutes later to make sure neither could speak to each other. Lynn parked her vehicle at the front of the station and was escorted with Laura to an interview room well away from the holding cells. The young girl felt nervous in the stark grey 18×12-foot box. It was really designed with criminals in mind, not for victims.

As they waited for the police, Lynn remarked to Laura, "This is a horrible place. My advice would be to try and get this over with as quickly as possible. Just make sure you're honest and don't feel that you need to defend yourself or your stepdad – just having that picture of you is a serious enough offence as it is."

Laura nodded. She knew that Lynn only wanted the best for her, but it was hard not to try and think of a way out of this whole situation. *Couldn't I just say the entire thing was a misunderstanding?* she thought to herself.

The interview itself wasn't quite as painful as Laura expected. The same man that arrested her father was also the one leading the interview – along with another officer who wrote everything down. He was authoritative but not unkind and made sure to give her the time she needed to gather her thoughts. The main thing he used was a copy of the transcript from Theo's recording, to talk about Lee. Laura was happy to furnish or confirm information about the abuse Lee had endured. What she didn't realise was that the officer was deriving a picture of how her mum and dad operated within the family group. He asked for more detailed information about what happened in the lead up to Lee being removed from the home.

Lynn paid special attention to this to see if everything dovetailed from her conversations with Lee months ago. He then asked if Laura had received any abuse from either of her parents whilst Lee was still at home. Laura had initially said no, interpreting 'abuse' as physical only.

"Did your stepfather touch you in any way that may just have seemed a little strange at the time?" Laura stopped in her tracks, only now making the connection. She looked at Lynn.

"If there is anything, even something small or minor, it's important to let us know," Lynn said.

Laura paused. "Well, there were a few times that he touched me on the bottom, playfully," Laura said, partially defending her dad.

"Can you give any examples?" the officer asked. Laura spoke about getting her letter of acceptance into Grammar school and a couple of other general examples.

This was all leading up to one of the more difficult questions the police needed to ask. "Can you recall the first time when your stepfather touched or did something more serious to you?"

Laura's memory raced. Her mind went back to the time she'd lied to the police about Lee being kidnapped. She felt the same now as she did then. "There was a time, in the bathroom. I was in the bath as usual when he came in to go to the toilet." Laura was nervous now; this was getting serious. But she'd started and had to go through with the lie.

"Was this a usual occurrence?" the officer asked.

"No, it was the first time."

"And was this before or after Lee had been removed from the home?"

"It was in November, so after," she said.

"Do you remember the date, by any chance?"

"I think it was the 8th, Wednesday night is my bath night."

The second officer continued making notes.

"Please continue, Laura."

She'd now had some time to think a little more about her story. "I wasn't sure why he did that, as I said; it was the first time. But we're not allowed to question what Mum or Dad say or do. After he'd been to toilet he just took all of his clothes off and got into the bath with me."

"Didn't you find that strange?" the officer questioned.

Laura wasn't happy about being treated like five-year-old. "Of course I found it strange – wouldn't you?"

The officer maintained a calm demeanour. "I'm sorry, continue."

"I was at one end by the taps. He started talking for a bit, asking me how school was going. His thing was sticking up. I tried to be polite but I wanted to get out. As I got up and turned around, he grabbed me from behind and... forced himself... inside me."

"Did you scream or shout? Where was your mum at this time?" he asked.

"Mum was downstairs; she's always busy with the baby. If I'd screamed, he would've beaten me like he did Lee. I told him that I was going to tell Mum, but he just said that I wouldn't and to remember what happened to Lee."

"So he threatened to beat you?" the officer asked.

"No, he meant that they would get rid of me too." Laura sniffed, somewhat relieved that she'd managed to give 'her side' of the story convincingly.

The next question the officer had to ask was abhorrent, even for his years of experience – but it was the job. "I'm going to ask you a question now that I hate to have to ask, but it's something I have to do." Lynn had an idea what the man was leading up to. "When your stepfather forced himself inside you, did he injure you in any way?" The question was as delicate as he could put it, but he looked to Lynn to help him out a little more here.

"I think what the officer is asking Laura, is did your father cause you to bleed?" The officer nodded in appreciation.

"Yes, there was some blood and it hurt for weeks after," Laura said. The officer asked a few more questions about whether Jon had repeated the assaults. He asked her whether she'd ever had sex before, to which she'd said no. He then asked whether Laura had considered telling someone about it; her mother, a schoolteacher or friend. When Laura revealed that she'd told her mother, all of the adults in the room took a sharp intake of breath. The officers were even more surprised when Laura explained the response she'd got. Lynn was less surprised, having had a couple of dealings with Louvaine. *I hope this woman goes to jail as an accessory too.*

The lead officer then turned his attention to the recording made by the *Daily Mail* reporter. He read out a copy of the transcript that he'd been given as part of the evidence bundle to execute the warrants.

"*There were problems with my dad, well our stepdad. They didn't get on and he used to hit Lee a lot. Before Lee was sent away, dad had really gone to town on him and nearly beaten Lee unconscious. I saw the bruises all the way up his ribs and on his face. He was the main reason Lee had to go,*" the officer read out loud. "Could you walk me through how this particular incident came about?"

Laura started talking through how when she and Lee were doing the washing up, he had threatened her with a knife.

The officer cut in. "And how old was Lee at this time?"

"He was seven," Laura said sheepishly. Just saying it out loud sounded absurd. Lynn also listened intently, having been the only person in the room to question Lee about this.

"A seven-year-old?" the officer questioned.

Laura needed to cover her tracks. "Well, he was nearly the same height as me and that's what it looked like at the time!" she retorted.

Lynn saw the chink in the girl's story, but remained silent – *no need to complicate the interview at this point.*

The officer continued. "And what happened after that?"

Laura described how she'd gone upstairs to tell her parents and how Jon had gone racing downstairs, hitting and punching Lee all around the hallway and that even though her mother was heavily pregnant, she'd also kicked and punched him.

"And what happened after that?"

"He was sent upstairs and mum started making phone calls." She looked at Lynn.

"I can make Lee's file available to you if needed. But for the purposes of this statement, it was me that Louvaine King made contact with after the incident." Lynn looked straight into Laura's eyes. Laura looked away.

After the preparation and signing of Laura's statement, the officer told her there was one more thing that needed to be done. "I've asked a doctor to come to the station to give you a quick medical examination."

"I don't understand, why do I need an examination?" Laura was confused – they'd yet to cover much in the way of human biology at school.

The officer again looked over to Lynn for assistance.

"They need to check that you are OK inside after what happened with your stepdad. Don't worry; I can be there with you if you need support."

After the two officers left the room, Laura waited pensively with Lynn. The anxiety was in not knowing what to expect from the examination. Lynn tried to make her feel a little better by saying that what Laura was about to go though was pretty routine for most women. But it didn't really do much to ease her mind.

After the doctor had completed the examination, the police took a quick statement from Lynn regarding Louvaine's assault and took a picture of her facial bruising for evidence.

It was after 11 o'clock before they were both finished at the station. Lynn bought them both a nice breakfast in a local café before heading back to the car for the next leg of the journey. She was tired. The last few days had been full-on and she'd been up since 4:30 that morning.

"Where was Jon Jr. taken?" Laura asked.

"Looking after young infants takes specialist care. My colleague has taken the baby to safe and secure place that only looks after under three-year-olds. I'm really sorry, but for security purposes I can't tell you at the moment. Your mum or dad could coerce you into saying something and we just can't take that chance until everything gets sorted out," she said, genuinely concerned. "The place I'm taking you to doesn't cater for small infants I'm afraid – that's the only reason you're being separated."

Laura began to get nervous and started looking around – her head darting left and right. "So, where are we going now, then?"

"It's a little way away from here, but don't worry, they'll take good care of you whilst things get sorted out with your parents."

Laura's mind whirled. "What's going to happen with them?"

Lynn needed to be careful. These questions from children were always a minefield. "I'm going to be frank with you Laura. I'm really not sure. It doesn't look good for your... stepdad. As for your mum, I would imagine that she'd just get a rap on the knuckles or something for the assaults. I'm not sure what they'll do about not doing anything to help you – I guess it just depends on the judge." Lynn looked at her face in the rear-view mirror. A red mark had appeared under her left eye where Louvaine had hit her. "Can I ask you something?" she said as Laura put her hands between her thighs. "I know that this is sensitive, now that Lee is... dead, but did he really threaten you with a knife?"

For Laura, it was as though Lee had really stabbed her through the heart from the grave. Her lies and stories had come to haunt her. She didn't answer.

"I think it would help rest his soul if he knew if there'd been some truth after his suicide. Also, you can't be put on trial for that," she added.

Laura contemplated the question. It was something that had been bothering her conscience for many nights after Lee left the house. "No, I... exaggerated," she said guiltily.

Lynn didn't look at Laura. She focused on the road. It was better that way. She wouldn't have to show her feelings towards the girl in her car. "I found bruises all over Lee's body after I collected him. Was he beaten a lot?"

Laura felt exorcised from the answer she'd given to the last question. "Well, it wasn't every day. It was just when he got in trouble." She paused. "But when he did get in trouble... he really did get in trouble."

Lynn sighed inwardly. He was such a nice kid. *They generally are. It's the parents that screw them up.*

"Can I ask why you exaggerated... about the knife incident?" Lynn needed to know why she would do that to her brother, but Laura stayed silent. Even though she knew she was an accessory to Lee's eventual death, she didn't want to implicate herself or her mother any further.

They'd been on the road for a while now and Laura was getting anxious. "We're miles away from my school. Please, where are we going? It's a good Grammar school."

There was no good way to answer this question. Lynn had to bite the bullet. "It's a little way yet, but from memory I don't think they have a Grammar school there. We can check when we arrive."

Laura began to get annoyed. Why wasn't this woman answering her questions? What was she hiding? "I asked where we were going," she said, frustrated.

Lynn just wanted what was right for the girl and really didn't appreciate the tone. "We're going to a place called Bury St. Edmunds. You'll be there until everything gets sorted out with your parents," she said in a slightly clipped tone.

"I've never heard of the place. Why couldn't I have just stayed with a neighbour with the baby until mum gets back from the police station? From what I see on the news these days, she'll probably be home today anyway," Laura said, trying to exert some intellectual authority.

Lynn could see what Laura was trying to do, and the girl clearly had a brain. But Lynn had experience, vast experience and that would trump an academic any day of the week. "Let's play this out shall we? You and the baby stay with a neighbour and your mother comes home. What happens to you when you get indoors?"

Laura knew immediately, but needed to save face through belligerence. "She'd tell me off."

Lynn laughed. "Really, that's what you're sticking with? Think again Laura," she said harshly. "You've seen what the police did to your home, you saw how she reacted to me and the police and to the arrest for assault. You're telling me that she's just going to tell you off? I'm sorry but your mother doesn't strike me as the forgiving type!" Laura knew the woman was right, but she hated to lose an argument. Lynn sensed the cogs whirring and decided to drive home the advantage. "And before you kid yourself about your mother, think about this. After Jon King is charged by the police, he may not be remanded in custody. I've seen it happen before. What do you think will happen if he comes home and you're there? Do you really think he's going to apologise and just say, 'It's water under the bridge'?" She paused. "I don't want to be nasty to you Laura, but there are some very harsh realities you need to face here. They could even do to you what they did to Lee. That's why you need to be a distance away from them for a while until things can be worked out. I also doubt life will be much fun at your Grammar school once people start gossiping either."

Laura rested her head on the B-pillar and gazed out of the side window. Lynn was right; her life was now in ruins. She cursed herself for talking to the reporter. Maybe she could've dealt with her dad differently to persuade him to leave her alone. Now she'd single-handedly wrecked the entire family. "What's going to happen to Jon Jr.?" she asked without making eye contact.

Lynn didn't want to commit to anything here. She knew what she wanted to happen. She knew it would be best for the child to be as far away from its parents as possible. In her view, the parents should both be sterilised... as a minimum. "He'll be cared for by someone else for a while. My colleague and I will have to write reports based on the facts we know and provide recommendations. This will be combined with all the other information that's provided and finally reviewed by a judge, who will make a final decision."

Laura absorbed what the woman had just said. Her thoughts moved away from Jon Jr. back to her own needs. Her entire future was now in the hands of a social worker. The woman sitting right next to her had the power to dictate what happened to her future. She realised she had to be careful, and remained quiet for the rest of the journey... deep in her own thought.

Lynn left the girl alone. It had been a rough morning for everyone and it wasn't going to get any easier when they arrived at their destination.

* * *

As the car pulled into the driveway in front of the big house, Laura read the sign in the distance by the front door: *Alexandra House for Children*. She was angry. She looked sideways at Lynn. "You didn't say anything about a children's home!" she said incredulously.

"I'm not sure what you were expecting, Laura – it's not like we could leave you alone in a hotel now, is it?" Lynn said. There was something about the girl she couldn't warm to. Apart from being a spitting image of her mother, she seemed to have the same mannerisms too. She also thought about how the other kids would react to her here. Lynn already knew the answer, but that would be for Fred to deal with. They both got out and went to the rear of the car. Lynn carried one sack and gave the other two for Laura to carry. As with Lee before, Lynn took Laura round to the side entrance and knocked on the door.

An old lady answered with a cheerful smile.

"Hello, Lynn and hello, young lady," she said.

"Laura, this is Fred. She manages the home. Fred, this is Laura."

Laura had no reservations about questioning Fred's name. "Is that Fred short for Winifred, then?" she said as if she already deduced the answer.

Fred smiled afresh. "Not quite, my dear, just a nickname that stuck over the years. I wish I'd thought of that fifty-odd years ago though." Laura looked her up and down. Fred had seen the look before. It didn't bother her too much... residents had a habit of changing over time. "Come on in, both of you, it's warmer inside."

Fred put the kettle on and then said she'd show Laura to her bedroom. She walked Laura through the living area and up the stairs to the only unoccupied room she had. There was a radio playing in one of the other bedrooms down the hall, but other than that, there were no other signs of life. She opened what would now be Laura's door and put the bag she had on the bed. The bedroom itself was quite spacious compared to what Laura was used to at home, but it was cold and sparse. Her mother had really made an effort in their new home to make Laura's room a comfortable place. This room just had a bed, carpet, curtains, a wardrobe, a couple of shelves and some drawers.

"Why don't you put your bits away and when you're settled, meet us back downstairs in the kitchen. We can have a good chat with you over coffee," Fred said.

Lynn hadn't really had a great deal of time to brief Fred on the entire situation the day before, so whilst waiting for Laura to come down again, she went into more detail about Lee's death and how Laura's situation had come about.

Fred was upset about Lee. She'd really liked the boy's spirit and had already informed the local police that they could close the missing persons file – which was probably still empty anyway.

Lynn then recounted what had happened that morning, which had turned out far messier than she'd hoped for. She gave Fred a typed letter containing all of Laura's pertinent information and also gave her a warning. "Keep a *very* close eye on this one Fred. Neither of us can afford for her to go missing."

"There's only so much I can do, Lynn, you know that – but I understand your concern. How long is she going to be here by the way? I need to know about school registration etc."

"This is between you and me, but from what I've seen and the report recommendation I'm going to give, I'd start the registration process this week."

Upstairs, Laura had put some of her clothes on hangers in the wardrobe. When she went to put the rest of her clothes in the drawers, there were still a few items in them. It was mostly school uniform and a few T-shirts. She could see that whoever had lived in the room before was probably a young boy, but there were no name-tags in the clothes. As she looked around the room, her attention was taken up by the shelves behind the bedroom door. There were a few little toys, the likes of which she'd seen before. Thinking back she thought Lee may have had the same ones. But it was the solid silver moneybox shaped like a duck in the corner that really drew her attention. It was uncanny that whoever had been before had exactly the same moneybox her brother had once had. She picked it up and shook it, but it was empty. Memories of Lee returned in her mind. For once she saw him in a good light. She packed up the belongings and took them downstairs to the kitchen, where Fred and Lynn had been going over case files.

"I wasn't sure what to do with these?" Laura asked as she placed the pile on the table. Fred and Lynn looked at each other.

"Maybe Fred can sell the uniform?" Lynn directed to Fred, who nodded. "It's up to you if you want to keep the rest."

Laura looked confused; she really wasn't sure why she'd want kids' toys – especially a boy's.

Lynn read her reaction. "They were all that was left of your brother after he ran away," she said softly.

Laura's heart dropped like a heavy stone. Lynn got up and pulled a seat out for her to sit on; she didn't want the girl fainting and hitting her head on the cold tiled floor. Laura began to cry. Her tears were genuine and the release of everything that had happened that morning and the over the last six months. The part she'd played in her brother's death and the destruction of her family were too much to bear. And now, here she was in the very same children's home that Lee had been sent away to. Lynn put a comforting arm around her. "If you don't want to keep them, that's fine too."

Laura shook her head. She didn't want to see the toys or moneybox again. It was bad enough that she'd have to sleep in the same room and the same bed tonight.

"Why don't I take it from here?" Fred suggested.

This was Lynn's queue to leave. There was never any good time during a 'drop-off', but this seemed like the best way to break ties. Lynn knew what the woman was saying and stood up to give Laura a summary of what would probably happen over the coming weeks. "As we've talked about, there's going to be a lot going on with your family before any decisions can be made about how and when you can return. I'm going to keep Fred as updated as I can, and in turn she'll pass on anything to you. If you need to get in contact with me, Fred has my number. I'm sorry to have to say this, but there is a chance that you might need to testify against your stepfather.

Laura looked a little stunned. In her mind, this could only make things worse. Her mother would never forgive her for that. "What if I don't want to testify?"

Both women understood Laura's anxiousness.

"Well, it will be your choice, Laura," said Lynn. "But all choices have consequences and it might be worth thinking about what might happen if you didn't testify. Think about what we discussed in the car." Laura said nothing and sat quietly. Lynn gave her a rub on the shoulder and picked up her bag and keys.

Back in the car, she looked at her eye again in the rear-view mirror before starting the engine. As she drove home, she began to ponder about Laura and how she would settle into the home. She wasn't like Lee, but would she run away or make her way back home? She also wondered why Nancy had been so distant from this situation. Although Nancy had already given an answer, it seemed as if she was she trying to punish Laura. There was a whole heap of questions she wanted to ask the next time they spoke.

When Lynn got back to St. Albans, she knew she'd be working until the early hours. It wasn't until 1 o'clock in the morning that she finally finished typing up her full report on Laura which was fully cross-referenced with Lee's. She looked at her diary and shook her head. She needed to get home and get some sleep.

* * *

CHAPTER 37

SCHEISSE

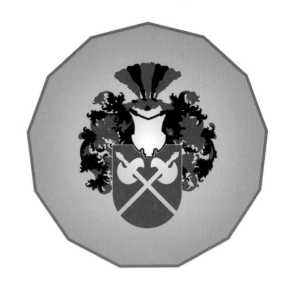

IS THERE A CHILD RAPIST IN ST. ALBANS?

A man was arrested in St. Albans yesterday and charged with the assault and rape of an underage girl. Jon King, pictured above, who described his victim as 'just a p***k-tease' was arrested by police in the early hours of Wednesday morning along with his wife Louvaine King, who was also charged with assaulting a police officer. Sources say that the man may also have been in possession of indecent images. We are unable to name the victim or victims for legal reasons. But a spokesman for the police said that they are also following up links on alleged physical abuse of Lee King, whose recent suicide in France was reported in the national press last week.

Lynn read the headline on the front page of the *Advertiser* and looked at the picture of a partially nude menacing man flanked by two policemen. It was pretty sensationalist for the local rag, but the young reporter had wanted to make name for himself. Lynn guessed he was trying to make it to the big leagues. They sat in a small room just behind the reception at the *Advertiser* offices. As agreed, he gave her photocopies of the unedited pictures he'd taken the day before. Although it didn't make any difference to him, out of curiosity he asked Lynn why she wanted them.

"They'll go into the file just like everything else. I'm very thorough when it comes to the children I'm responsible for," she said.

As she got up to leave, the reporter shook her hand. "It was great doing business with you. I'm going to be following this up to the conclusion of the case. It's the best story we've had here for a long time. Get in touch with me first if you come across anything else you need a hand with."

Lynn smiled politely. "I appreciate everything you did." She began to see the benefit of having a press contact as she made her way back to her own office. Now that she had everything she needed, she phoned Nancy. It was getting towards the end of the week and Lynn still had other cases to deal with.

Nancy could tell that the woman was a little frayed on the other end of the phone.

"Would you like an update over the phone or does this need to be in person?" Lynn asked.

"It would be better in person, but you sound like you're burning the candle at both ends – are you OK?" Nancy was genuinely concerned for Lynn; she understood how stress impacted people differently.

"You don't know the half of it. This one really kicked off and I'm behind on my other cases."

Nancy was intrigued, but guessed that Lynn would have been in contact earlier if things had gone badly.

"Look, I've clearly asked you to go above and beyond with this case, Lynn, so how about you decide the meeting time and place, and I'll pay for the food. I hope that will be incentive enough for you to pick somewhere you like?"

The pressure lifted from Lynn's shoulders. She could now do things at her own pace, rather than be swept up at what seemed like someone else's. "Do you want to meet me here again next Tuesday at about twelve thirty? I have a place in mind." Lynn wanted to be the 'secret squirrel' herself for a change and Nancy was game. "I should also be able to give you the latest updates by then too."

"That sounds perfect. See you next Tuesday," Nancy replied.

* * *

In the afternoon of Laura's first day at the home, Fred took her round and introduced her to all the other residents at Alexandra. She decided to use her first name only, knowing that the kids would find out who she was eventually – she just didn't want it to come from her. Quite a few of the boys smiled at her, especially Gordon – but not so much the girls. Laura wasn't impressed with anyone she met. They were all broken rejects whom nobody wanted anymore. She stayed downstairs for a little while to be sociable, but none of the children really held any interest for her intellectually. For Laura, this home was just a temporary situation until everything could be patched up with her mother. Then she'd go back home.

Her attitude must have been apparent, because when she met Angela, Fred's fifteen year-old second in command, the girl smiled and spoke with an air of sarcasm, "Welcome to Alex, you're one of us now."

This rankled with Laura. She certainly wasn't *one of them*! Her limbs were fully intact for starters.

After the debacle surrounding Lee's disappearance and having felt that Fred had made her out to be a tell-tale, Angela's relationship with the home's manager had been a little frosty. Even though Fred had explained to her that she already knew about the knife-threatening incident from Lee's social worker, Angela still hadn't forgiven Fred for not explaining this to Lee before he ran away. She'd really had a bond with the little guy, so it hit her quite hard when Fred had given her the news about Lee's death and Laura's arrival the day before. Angela gave Laura a little time to settle in but knocked on her door after dinner – there was something she needed to know for sure.

Laura really didn't want any company, she was too busy consoling herself over what had happened that day, but being older, Angela opened the door anyway. "Do you mind if I come in?"

"If you have to." Laura pouted.

Angela walked in and looked around. Laura was sat on her bed reading.

"The first few days are always tough. Lee was the same when he arrived," Angela said, testing Laura's reaction. The girl on the bed was just as Lee had described his sister and there was no way the name 'Laura' could be a coincidence. "Your surname is King isn't it?" Laura nodded. There didn't seem a lot of point in lying. Angela gave a short smile. "I'm no expert but this seems to be the very definition of irony, wouldn't you say?"

"I don't see why it's any of your business," Laura responded.

"Well normally, I guess that would be the case. But I'd grown quite fond of young Lee. He was a great kid and he told me all about you. He told me how you lied about things to get him in trouble, so that he'd get beaten up. It was because of you that he ended up here wasn't it?"

Laura began to get annoyed at the intrusion. "You haven't got a clue; he wasn't exactly a saint, you know."

"I know that, he was a typical seven-year-old. But he only hit back at people who'd bullied him and he definitely didn't threaten you with a knife, did he?"

Laura had had enough of the questions and snapped back. "You don't know anything, so why don't you just get out and leave me alone!"

"Oh I will, don't you worry, but there are some things you need to know. Firstly, I'm the oldest and have been here the longest. When Fred's not around, it's me that's in charge. So don't be thinking you can be a bitch to any of the other kids here, because we won't have it. Secondly, when Lee ran away, he stole twenty-five quid from me and my boyfriend. You'll be repaying us both back."

Laura sniggered. "You believe everything you hear from a thief do you?" She felt like hitting the girl.

"I wasn't sure before, but now I've met you, yes I do. If he was a thief, he was at least an honest one. And just so you know. I didn't know your surname, but Lee described you perfectly."

Laura got up. Even though there was a two-year age gap, they were both the same height. Laura looked down her nose. "Why don't you get lost and take your little spastic arm with you – I'll do whatever I like."

Angela wasn't intimidated and just smiled. "If that's the way you want it. But you're just as responsible for Lee's death as those scummy parents of yours. Enjoy your stay here!" She walked out of Laura's room and headed downstairs for a quick conversation with Fred.

Laura sat back down on her bed. Day one and she'd already made an enemy without even trying. She tried to focus her mind. Even after all that had happened, Jon had given her some good advice: 'See what makes girls popular and emulate it'. *It worked in school, so it must be easy enough to translate here*, she thought.

* * *

Tuesday couldn't come any sooner for Nancy. It wasn't usual for her to be the one anxiously waiting for information, but the weekend had passed very slowly. To pass the time, she'd been in contact with The Office for an update on The Shepherd and Theo. The Chief hadn't yet made a decision about Theo, and counter surveillance had yet to get a fix on Florian Schäfer; which was a little more disturbing. She'd made up her mind that it wasn't a coincidence she'd been followed, and busied herself with cleaning, shoring up the place and making sure that nothing of any importance was out in the open. During retirement, her home had been kept spotless, but now Nancy made sure to sprinkle Hoover dust in and around key areas. If she were to have an unwelcome snooper, she was hopeful she'd know about it. Nancy removed all of the family pictures from around the house, except one, and took them down to a concealed basement in the back garden that not even David knew anything about. It was there that she took her Smith & Wesson Model 36 out of retirement. Giving the .38 Special a good clean, she rigged up a small cushioned area and gave the gun a couple of test firings. From now on, and until she felt safe again, the 'Chief's Special', as the Americans called it, would be near to hand whether inside or outside the home. Before leaving the house Nancy placed a number of different traps by the main entrances, drew the curtains and made a quick phone call, leaving the receiver off the hook and making sure to inform the person on the other end that she was leaving. It was time to meet Lynn.

Lynn had chosen to eat at a pub just out of town. Even though Nancy had said nothing, Lynn explained that the place had just reopened and apparently now did a stonking pub-lunch. Nancy smiled... *at least it wouldn't be an expensive afternoon.* The women managed to get a small booth in the saloon area that amazingly had waitress service. After ordering their non-alcoholic drinks and food, Lynn proceeded to get down to business. She gave Nancy a copy of the local paper to read along with copies of the reporter's photographs. Nancy scanned through everything. This was good news indeed.

"Can you walk me though what happened? The more detailed the better," Nancy asked.

Lynn did just that, all the way up to dropping off Laura, when the waitress arrived to serve their food.

The additional arrest and removal of Louvaine and the newborn were not unintended consequences. In fact, knowing how Louvaine would react, Nancy had hoped the woman would create full-on collateral damage for herself.

As they both tucked into a roast beef dinner with all the trimmings, Nancy gave kudos to Lynn. "You're right, this place is spot on. So have there been any updates in the last week?"

"Well, after Laura gave her statement, Jon King was formally charged and remanded in custody. Louvaine got lesser charges and she's back at home now, but the baby is still in social care for the moment. She's petitioning to get him back."

"And what about Laura?"

"That's the strange one. I haven't had any enquiries to have her returned. It seems a little odd, don't you think?"

Nancy looked at Lynn and shook her head. "Louvaine's a nasty woman and this has been a nasty business all round. I feel sorry for my son who wasted so many years of his life with her, but I'm also glad that he's now out of it – even though it's cost him a great deal. The greatest suffering has been for the children, though. Lee's dead and I can only wonder what Laura's fate would be if she were to go back."

"Do you think she's rejecting Laura in the same way she rejected Lee?" Lynn enquired.

"It sounds like it, from what you're saying, which doesn't surprise me. It makes you wonder what would happen to the young baby in years to come. Is it a boy or a girl?"

"It's a boy. Nearly six months old."

Nancy exhaled deeply. "That's such a shame. I'm sure all of these things have a subconscious effect on young babies. And if his father gets convicted, you can imagine what it's going to be like growing up with that kind of stigma." It wasn't really a question to Lynn, more Nancy ruminating aloud. "How has Laura settled in to the home?"

"I think the whole day was a complete shock to her. I checked in with Fred earlier today. She hasn't exactly endeared herself to some of the other children and seems to spend most of her time on her own in her room. Fred got her registered at the local school. I don't think she's going to find it any better there either – it's certainly not a 'nice Grammar school', that's for sure."

Nancy thought for a while. She looked genuinely conflicted.

Lynn thought too. *Was this the time to ask Nancy what her plans were?* "If you don't mind me asking, I'm wondering why you don't take Laura in yourself? It's quite normal for a child to go to a grandparent during times like this."

"Believe me, Lynn; I've thought about it a great deal. I would take Laura in a heartbeat, but there are a couple of problems. I live on my own. If Louvaine and Jon decided to cause a problem or take Laura back, it would just be more unsettling to her. Being pulled in two directions at any age is never good, but it's especially bad during the adolescent years. But I could put up with that if not for my second problem."

Lynn frowned. "What's the problem?"

Nancy looked around. "You cannot tell anyone about what I'm going to say, do you promise?"

Lynn put up three fingers in a Girl Guide salute. "I promise," she said, concerned.

Nancy blew her cheeks out in preparation of what she was about to say. It was going completely against her principles. "At this moment my life may be in serious danger. There is an East European agent on the loose and I have to take precautions. I don't think that potentially putting Laura in the crosshairs would be a good idea, do you?"

Lynn laughed. *This is the stuff of films. Surely the woman is over-exaggerating?*

Nancy remained straight faced as Lynn's laugh subsided.

"Are you serious?" Lynn whispered.

Nancy picked her bag up from the seat and showed Lynn the contents. Lynn gasped.

"I have rarely had to carry this, but this afternoon or any other time, when I go home – I may have to use it."

Lynn's expression fell abruptly. Nancy could see the penny had dropped. "I just can't take Laura right now. But when my situation is resolved satisfactorily, I'll be in a position to do something positive where she is concerned. Can you understand now?"

Lynn nodded. "Can't you get someone to protect you?"

"There are people out looking for the agent as we speak and it's most likely that they'll find him first, but I must be careful. The Service won't assign someone to me indefinitely; it's just not the way we work," Nancy replied.

"I hope we weren't followed?" Lynn said, nervously looking around.

"I wasn't followed to your office and we weren't surveilled at your office or on the way here, I can assure you."

Lost for words, Lynn went back to her meal. When they'd both finished she had one last curious question for Nancy. "Does anyone in your family know about what you do?"

Nancy shook her head. "Outside of The Service, the only person that knows what I do is you." Lynn felt both honoured and uneasy at the same time. "Will you make sure to keep me updated with court dates and Laura's status?"

"Of course. I'm sorry I laughed earlier, Nancy – it all just sounded a bit 'Len Deighton' to me."

Nancy smiled. She'd read the books too.

The two women discussed the arrangements for regular updates about Laura, settling on every Tuesday for the moment.

"Just one other thing," Nancy said. "If you don't get through to me on the first occasion, don't try a second time. It means that I am out or there's a problem. I'll call you when I can. If you haven't had any contact with me for more than one week or whatever interval we've agreed, do not contact me. Is that clear?"

"Sure," Lynn said pensively. She was really concerned now.

* * *

Florian Schäfer drove past the east entrance to Woodland Rise twice. There was an unmanned barrier, which didn't seem a problem – but he wanted to know what his entry and exit strategy would be. Using his map, he drove around the one mile of countryside to reach the opposite entrance to Nancy's road. The barrier to this entrance was also closed. He got out of the car, raised the barrier and drove through – leaving his exit open.

Weeks ago when Theo had met with Nancy, Schäfer had followed the woman as far as he'd dared. He wasn't sure whether he'd been made or not. He didn't discount the possibility. Instead of following her taxi, he took the gamble of hailing a cab of his own, and headed in the opposite direction. He paid the driver and waited at a bus stop diagonally opposite Century House, the infamous MI6 headquarters. The bus stop was a perfect cover, out in the open and yet no one would question his being there – people came and went all day. He used the cover of looking up the road for the oncoming busses to mentally log the comings and goings from the building. Playing a hunch was a waiting game and Schäfer could wait for hours on end. He had a good nose for it. He hadn't seen the woman enter the building, but ninety minutes and nine cigarettes later, his hunch finally bore fruit. She walked out of the front entrance of Century House and ordered a cab. He flagged one down himself and followed her to Charing Cross station. Eager to do well for his KGB paymasters, Schäfer waited for the woman to get on the train before boarding himself. He sat in one of the compartments at the rear-most carriage on the left-hand side and patiently waited. At each stop, he opened the window briefly for some 'fresh air', surreptitiously looking down the train to see who was getting off. At Dunton Green he saw his target disembark – the only problem being that she was only one of two people. He couldn't risk standing out so blatantly. The next station was Sevenoaks, so Schäfer got off the train there and crossed the bridge to the opposite platform for the journey back to London.... he'd definitely be paying Theo a visit when he got back. There was a fifteen-minute wait for the next train and Schäfer was hungry. He went to the main station entrance where there was a small newsagent and bought some crisps and a can of coke. As he turned around to go back to the platform, he couldn't believe his eyes. The woman had got out of a taxi about eighty yards away and was now entering the driver's side of another vehicle. Sometimes things just fell into your lap. He took a pen from his pocket and wrote the vehicle registration on his hand as she pulled out of the car park. *Excellent*, he thought. He didn't need to follow her any further; he'd get someone to locate her address for him and await orders. He tore off part of his cigarette packet, transferred the licence number and headed back to the London platform. Although he couldn't confirm it, his gut feeling was that the woman must have made him at the restaurant. He admired how cool she'd been in the situation and realised how careful he would need to be.

* * *

Number seven was the house he was looking for, as he cruised slowly along the rise. When he found it, he pulled the white van straight into the driveway; something Schäfer had '*borrowed*' the night before – '*Phil's Carpet Cleaning*' adorning both flanks. The woman's car wasn't there. He'd been given the go ahead by his superiors and walked up to the front door like any normal visitor would. He rang the bell twice, but no one answered – just as he'd hoped. He looked around. There was an alarm box on the front of the house. The surrounding bushes and deciduous trees gave some cover, but not as much as they would in the summer months. He moved quietly around the perimeter looking for any openings or weaknesses. Nancy Walker hadn't left any windows open and all doors were locked. Curtains were also drawn which made life a little more difficult. The back door was the best option for entry to the kitchen. Schäfer looked around the door frame and between the shut lines – locating the alarm's magnetic read switch at the top of the door. He took a thin strip of magnetic material from his pocket, bent it into an 'L' shape, and with some Sellotape, stuck it in place between the door magnet and receiver switch. Schäfer then expertly picked the lock and gingerly opened the door 2-3 inches, looking top to bottom for traps. At the very bottom of the door he noticed he'd broken a small paper tab that had connected the door to the wall. "Verdammt!" he hissed under his breath. He'd just have to find a way to repair it later. As he opened the door further ajar he kept his gaze upwards for any string traps at the top of the door. His heart then skipped a beat as he heard the most almighty crash. He was briefly indecisive. Should he go inside or leave? His hand had instinctively moved across his chest to draw his weapon if needed. The houses seemed far enough apart, so he stepped inside. He felt the slight crackle underneath his boot. He instantly knew what it was. "Scheisse!" The woman had left multiple traps. The worst of them was a stack of china plates that he'd unwittingly pulled from a cabinet through a homemade pulley system she'd rigged up using fishing line. Not only had the plates smashed into pieces on the clay-tiled floor, but the woman had also made sure that the plates had been laden with talcum powder. Cursing under his breath, he had to admire the old lady. He left the mess on the floor; there was no way he could clean up, replace the paper and glass traps and replace the broken china. He closed the door and walked around the mess inside. He'd decide later whether to make the place look like it had been burgled or not.

Schäfer began working each room as quietly as he could. He searched cupboards, opened containers, and moved rugs, felt underneath the carpets for differences, looking for secret hatches in floors and walls. The place felt too clean. He initially couldn't put a finger on it, but then realised what it was. There was only one picture on display in the house: a portrait of a man he recognised on the hallway wall. He stood and looked at it momentarily before moving upstairs to carry out the same process... not noticing that the phone receiver was still off the hook in the living room, adjacent to the kitchen.

On the other end of the phone, a listening agent had been alerted by the doorbell and the sound made by the smashing of the chinaware. There was a protocol. If Nancy had accidentally made the sound or had an issue, she had thirty seconds to get to the phone and verify her status using a pre-defined code word. The listening agent hit the tape record button and remained silent – watching the wall clock as the second hand continued past the deadline. She picked up another phone and made a call to Emergency Response.

"Possible B&E. Nancy Walker. Thirteen fifty-two Zulu. Recording. Connection still active."

The Emergency Response Overseer was the custodian of all contingency plans for all agents, buildings and VIPs within The Services' remit. When the listening protocol for Nancy Walker was re-initiated by The Chief, the Overseer was advised and had made sure to apprise himself of the details in her file. Immediately after receiving the call he contacted the Emergency Response Squad Leader, Mike Finny.

"Possible B&E. Nancy Walker. thirteen fifty-two Zulu. 7 Woodland Rise, Sevenoaks, Kent. Suspected foreign operative. What assets do you have near the location?"

Finny looked at his map. "I have assets with me at Dover – one hour fifteen, or Central London – one hour thirty?" It was the overseer who was responsible for making that decision; Finny would be responsible for mission execution.

The overseer decided. "Move assets from Dover. Will have police there for a perimeter. Contact should be by the name of Chief Inspector Tom Barnes."

"Orders?" The squad leader asked.

"Priority apprehend, non-lethal force. Lethal force approved only if target poses lethal threat."

"Yes, sir." Finny clicked off.

The overseer then called the contact number for Tom Barnes.

"Chief Inspector Barnes, this is MI6 Emergency Response. We have reason to believe that there has been a forced entry to number 7 Woodland Rise; I believe you're aware of the address?"

"I am, yes."

"Good. We have an armed unit converging at approximately fifteen ten Zulu. We need containment and perimeter set up. One unit at each end of Woodland Rise, one unit in Wilderness Avenue directly behind the property and one unit in Parkfield directly south. Units must run silent and must not approach the house. My unit will be headed up by Mike Finny, access to be unhindered. He will take control of the situation on arrival. No other traffic either motorised or on foot is to enter or exit Woodland Rise. Can you confirm you are able to provide back-up?"

"I'll take command myself." Barnes didn't want anyone else calling the shots on this one. "Is Mrs. Walker on the premises?" he asked, concerned.

"Unlikely.".

"I'll get right on it now; we'll have units in place within ten minutes. Anything else I need to know?"

"We don't know if the potential target is armed," the overseer said.

"Understood." Barnes clicked off and shot up from his desk. He went to a cabinet and pulled out his own, very unused, holstered pistol. "Cancel my diary," he said to his assistant, as he strode out of his office towards the main incident room.

After selecting eight other officers to move out in four different cars, Barnes gave each car a leader and each leader a location. The importance was stealth and to get to the locations as soon as possible. Barnes then gave specific orders over the vehicle radios as they drove. There were lots of questions from a couple of the other officers, but the chief inspector just repeated what he'd been asked and reinforced to the men what their role would be in the operation. The north and south units were to be on the lookout for anyone acting suspiciously moving away from the scene, whilst the east and west units were to let nobody in or out without his order to do so. Barnes himself would be at the west end of Woodland Rise. All police units were in place by 14:15.

* * *

Upstairs, Schäfer finally found the alarm control box in the closet of the old woman's bedroom. He took an armful of hanging items out which gave him time to work. Without cutting the wires, he disconnected the audible alarm and phone signal cables. He'd seen most alarm systems before, but this one was a little more advanced. There was another cable labelled '*Remote*'. It could only be a remote connection to a police station.

Schäfer disconnected the cable and jumped when he heard a huge thud within the wall behind. *Das ist nicht gut.* He got up and checked outside. The bedroom window looked out from the front of the house. There were no visible movements. Schäfer took more clothes from the closet, laying them on Nancy's bed to give him better visibility and then began feeling and padding the back wall further. There it was. As he pushed, a latched door opened to reveal a Chubb torch and drill-resistant safe. He'd seen the type before, but this one was slightly different. It must've been custom-made, because it had a combination *and* key lock.

Schäfer thought about his next steps. Breaking into the safe would take way too much time and he didn't know when the woman would be back. If he left now, she'd definitely know someone had broken in and his journey would be wasted. He could turn the place upside down to find the key, or he could just wait for the woman to return and 'convince' her to talk and open the safe. He decided that a further search could bear more fruit. Besides, he could always wait for the woman anyway.

* * *

On the drive back to Sevenoaks, Nancy's thoughts alternated between the good news that Lynn had given her to what her movements would be when she arrived home. As she turned left into Woodland Rise a car was straddled right across the road barring her entrance to the gate. A man was stood by the car; he indicated for her to stop. Nancy kept calm and slowly edged her left hand inside her handbag. Another man got out of the rear of the vehicle, a man she recognised. Tom Barnes walked over to the passenger side of Nancy's car whilst instructing the officer to remain where he was. Nancy unlocked the passenger door to let Tom in.

"Glad to see you Nancy, but we've been alerted that you may've had an intruder. We're just holding the perimeter for now; a squad is on its way."

Nancy moved her handbag to her right side and patted Tom's arm as he sat down. "Good to see you again, Tom and thanks for the heads-up. What's the status?"

"We received the call a while back. We're expecting a team imminently, led by someone called Mike Finny."

The officer who'd initially barred Nancy's entrance left his position and approached the chief inspector. "Can I speak to you, sir?" he said, politely indicating for his boss to get out.

"Don't worry, lad. We need to make sure this lady is kept informed of everything."

The officer appeared surprised, looking over at the well dressed old lady. Nancy's expression remained unchanged. "Yes, sir. We've had a radio from the east team of a Mike Finny asking for you personally."

"Tell the east team to send him round to us ASAP. We'll coordinate action from here."

"Yes, sir." The officer jogged back to the car, somewhat confused, and relayed the message.

Within three minutes, a plain black van had pulled into the road entrance and parked next to Nancy's car. Finny, Barnes and Nancy all got out of the vehicles and introduced themselves. Finny hadn't expected Nancy to be present which he initially thought would be an obstacle to the mission. But Nancy expertly took control.

"Is the van well-lit? If so, let's put the intercept plan together inside."

Finny nodded and opened a sliding side door. Barnes signalled for his officers to remain at their posts. It was a tight squeeze, but there were six people now in the van. Barnes closed the door. There was no need for introductions; instead, Nancy immediately called for a light and a map.

"Tom, do you just have men at the road entrances?" she asked.

Tom pointed to the other locations on the map. "We have units north and south to keep a small perimeter."

Nancy then gave the squad a concise layout of the surrounding land along with a room-by-room description of the house. "What's your plan?" she asked.

Including Finny, there was a total squad of four. He needed to use his manpower wisely. "The plan was to make one pass to recce what we can. Stop on this bend here where there's a blind spot and double the team back on foot, two to the front, and two to the rear. If you have keys, it'll make our lives simpler."

Nancy paused. She herself had been thinking as Finny explained his plan. "If the intruder is who I think it is, he's Stasi or KGB. He'll be armed. If he's downstairs it's less of a problem, but if he's upstairs, he'll have the high ground on you. So, how about this? Why don't I go in first?" Tom was about to protest, but Nancy put her hand up to stop him. "I don't think he wants to kill me. I suspect he'll be looking for information. If I go in first, he'll be unlikely to expect you. I'll try to draw him into the kitchen at the back of the house. If you give me five minutes before you drive by, you can continue your plan from there. I may need to disable some traps; nothing harmful, just noisy. You'll need to be quick. I suspect he will want to take me back upstairs again." Everyone looked at each other. "It's where I keep the safe," she said, somewhat exasperated.

The men all exhaled with relief. Finny wasn't happy about the plan, a potential hostage in the mix was never a good idea.

Nancy knew what he was thinking. "I'll be going in with protection. It's in the car. I'll try to make sure I'm on the east wall if I'm downstairs when you enter. If he ends up keeping me upstairs, you'll need to enter the house dead silent from the rear and hold position until he comes down. DO NOT hesitate... no matter what you see, is that understood?" she ordered. Barnes looked at Finny who then looked at Nancy – her eyes as steely as any soldier he'd ever seen. "And Tom, nobody comes in or out until you hear from one of us... agreed?"

He begrudgingly agreed as Finny and his men all nodded to the plan. "Right, let's go then," Nancy said, indicating for someone to let her out of the van.

Barnes instructed his officers to let Nancy's car and the van through the barricade, but only Nancy continued whilst Finny kept the van's engine running. He radioed all units to be on high alert. Nancy put her coat on for the drive and placed her pistol in her left-hand side pocket. She was right-handed, but had learned to shoot effectively from both sides. She took a deep breath. It was crunch time. It seemed like the past had caught up with her.

* * *

PART 5

(1931 – 1961)

CHAPTER 38

THE WAR

In 1931, after achieving a distinction in the Higher School Certificate, Mary Roberts, the daughter of a butcher from Hastings, was accepted into Girton College, Cambridge. She was the first person from her family to ever go to university. Her father, David, always knew she was intelligent, even as an infant. And so when she was five years old, he began contributing ten shillings a week religiously into a scholarship fund for this exact purpose. From the first time Mary set foot in Cambridge, it became clear that women were still second class when it came to education. Girton was a segregated all-female college but instead of bonding with other women in solidarity or joining any political movements, she set about formulating symbiotic relationships with male students and professors at the other more established colleges.

Mary was particularly interested in the electromagnetic spectrum within her mathematical physics studies and showed a particular aptitude in signal processing and interpretation. Before leaving university with her diploma in 1935, she'd been approached by one of the male professors to meet with a contact from the British Security Services. Although she didn't think so at the time, the meeting must have gone well, because they'd asked her to change her name, take on a new persona, sign The Official Secrets Act and go to work for Telecommunications Research Establishment near Ipswich. So, Nancy White began her first job as a communications assistant for a new technology that could detect aircraft called radar. It was a challenge being a woman in an all-male establishment, but with a lot of hard work, her talents brought recognition. Her skills were used in creating and proofing schematics, as well as finding continuous ways to improve signal quality and accuracy. During her spare time, Nancy also undertook firearms and combat training.

With another war in Europe seemingly inevitable, Britain was already starting to secure its defences. This detection technology was quickly being expanded into something called the 'Chain Home' – a network of pioneering early warning radar stations set across the south and eastern seaboard of England. In 1938 Nancy was asked by her handler to attend the International Telegraph and Telephone Conference in Cairo with a male counterpart who would act as her boss. Although the conference itself was aimed towards world governance and regulation, it was also used by many secret service agencies around the world to trade in the shadows. By cultivating a demure style and paying careful attention to her looks, Nancy could garner any male attention as she needed. She was the honey-trap to her boss's straight, business-like character. She was prepped with a new cover story and passport, with orders to listen to and assess technical discussions and illicit information.

The trip to Cairo was more successful than Nancy expected. She'd saved her boss from going down a dead end, when a supposed scientist had offered to sell certain technological secrets from an unknown source. They'd both listened and her boss had been game, but as they'd dug deeper into the science, Nancy had warned that the claims the man made were somewhat preposterous.

Nancy also had her eyes on a handsome man she'd noticed at the hotel on the conference's fourth day. Stefan Winkler had looked in her direction a couple of times. Her attraction to him – a tall, hastily dressed man with dark hair and smooth skin she just wanted to touch – took her completely by surprise. He seemed shy and would look away every time she glanced back in his direction. Something told her that he wanted to talk to her, but she had the feeling he wouldn't come over if she was constantly by her boss's side.

Her instincts were correct. After she excused herself from a very dull speech about the regulation for counting of words, Stefan followed her from the conference room to the hotel bar.

"Excuse me, I… er… Do you mind if I talk to you?"

Nancy wasn't sure if his nerves were real or part of an elaborate act, but he didn't seem to have much time. During their conversation he said that he was from Vienna, Austria (which had just been annexed as part of the Germanic Reich), and that his earlier speech covered just part of the science and technology he had access to.

Nancy didn't quite know how to deal with this but tried to keep calm for both their sakes. Eventually, she made a decision. "Perhaps you'd like to come upstairs?" she said.

He hesitated, and once again she took charge. Making their acquaintance look like a discreet rendezvous to the barman, she linked arms with Stefan and walked with him towards the staircase.

Stefan was quite startled at this bold move by the young woman and was even more surprised when he got to her room. She gave him a notebook and pen and asked him to write down what he wanted, what information he could get his hands on and what he could give in return for his freedom... "Assuming I've read the situation correctly," she added.

She was right. She kept him talking and writing until her boss came to find her and knocked at her room, where she explained everything. Her boss took over from there, but Nancy listened intently, taking in every little detail of how deals were made in this arena. They hatched plans and agreed to send unidirectional messages via the BBC World Service. Stefan's responsibility would be to acquire all the information and get to Paris Gare du Nord railway station at the designated time. Her boss made it clear that because of the impending war, it was a one-time only offer. If he was any more than an hour late, they'd be gone.

During the conference, which lasted from February to April, Nancy and her boss did a roaring trade. She was even approached unsuccessfully by a Yugoslavian and a Hungarian, whom she worked out were both recruiting for the USSR. When they weren't actually in seminars, her boss spent a great deal of time explaining some of the intricacies of the job. Their partnership worked extremely well, but he knew that their conversion rate would probably only be five to ten percent.

Stefan managed to put himself in that percentile when they met again in Paris in June. Nancy was once again reminded of how handsome he was – always a good sign.

Before heading to England, Nancy was tasked with assessing the documents Stefan had provided; the proof Britain needed that he'd kept his side of the bargain. For one night she'd rented a small gîte in a quiet village just outside of the city where document reviews were peppered with gradually more passionate physical exploration. Stefan was no expert under the sheets, but what he lacked in technique, he made up for with repetition and stamina.

Back in England, they were separated when Nancy returned to the research establishment to continue her work. She was thanked for her exemplary service, but when she enquired about Stefan, all she was told was that he would go through a debriefing period. As time went on, she became less and less certain that she'd ever see him again, and tried to put him out of her mind.

After three months had passed, she was contacted again and told to visit the Ministry of Information in Bloomsbury, London. With the exception of her handler, Nancy knew nothing of the other people in the room that day... a day that would change her life forever. The plan put to her was so outrageous that she couldn't stop herself from laughing, but none of the men in the room found the suggestion funny.

Their plan was for Nancy to join the Women's Auxiliary Air Force and live with Stefan as a married couple with new identities. They would both go to work at a new RAF facility being built in Ventnor on the Isle of Wight for the Chain Home project. Housing would be provided, and as well as working on the cutting-edge technology of the time, Nancy would also be responsible for reporting in on Stefan.

Eventually she stopped laughing and looked at their serious faces. They meant it!

"How long will the assignment be for?" she asked.

The room fell silent. Then her handler plucked up the courage to answer. "Nobody really knows."

Nancy questioned the reality of living in a community where her husband would sound German in a country that hated all things German. Her handler shared her concern, but the best response he could give was that Stefan had been given linguistic lessons over the past month, and he might pass as a Belgian. "No-one has anything against the Belgians… and besides, hardly anyone will know what one sounds like."

If the room full of men wasn't intimidating enough, they applied even more pressure by stating that Nancy's decision was required before leaving that day… she'd be doing a great deed for her country.

Nancy's father may have been a butcher, but he was also a businessman. He'd always taught her that nothing comes free. This had been ingrained so deeply, that Nancy instinctively countered the group with her own terms.

"If I do this for 'King and Country,' then I'll need some things in return."

The men looked at each other, not expecting a negotiation. "What's your request?" asked her handler.

"I want my role within the security service to be expanded to more field and foreign recruitment opportunities," she replied. "And as I don't receive a salary for my espionage work, I want the marital home to be purchased, with the deeds placed solely in my name."

Nancy looked at the faces of each of the men as she spoke. One of them went so red, he looked almost about to burst. She was asked to leave the room whilst the committee deliberated. Nancy had never expected to get both of her requests through. Asking the British government to stump up the cash to buy her a property was so preposterous that expanding her duties would seem like nothing in comparison. It was a diversion.

When she was called back in, she expected to be berated. But to her amazement, the group had agreed her terms – her handler giving a respectful nod of approval.

On 19ᵗʰ August 1938, Nancy and Stefan had wedding photographs taken and officially became Mr. & Mrs. Stephen and Nancy Walker.

Surprisingly, given the lack of romantic courtship period, Stephen and Nancy worked well as a couple. They were both very dedicated to their roles, even though they worked in separate buildings – and often spent hours discussing technicalities when they were at home together. Home life was fun, even when the war officially started. Stephen would bring Nancy fresh flowers every Saturday. As the war continued and rationing became the norm, Stephen would pick flowers from wherever he could. It always made him unhappy every time Nancy needed to leave home, concerned she might never come back. But he still brought flowers home even when she wasn't there.

For Nancy, these were indeed dangerous times, but she enjoyed the thrill of being out there. Away from home, she went by the codename of 'Massette', the French translation meaning 'mallet', which helped secure her tough reputation throughout the network. She learned a lot about people and her own instincts, and became an expert at reading body language, facial expressions and eye movements. She found that most men were reckless when it came to the potential of sexual engagement. They would promise and deliver so much more at just the merest flirtation. Nancy became one of the most productive assets England had, leading to some key foreign defections that became high-profile within the Ministry of Information. This led to her level of authority increasing in addition to the human and financial resources she now oversaw. As months turned to years and Germany's occupation of Europe spread further and further westward, Nancy began to distance herself by building up her own network of foreign and British contacts. Being out there was fine, but being caught by the Germans or Russians was a guaranteed death sentence, whichever way you looked at it. She deliberately established herself as an enigma – rarely to be seen, but well informed and far reaching in her ability to inflict damage to her enemies.

This didn't stop Nancy interacting with people. She wasn't inhuman and had social needs just like anyone else. She just had to be careful that she herself wasn't being played, making sure that business meetings were carefully staged and that she played a completely different character socially. These activities helped her build up her own little business interests and financial independence on the side. The war was going badly and if she was going to survive when it eventually ended, she wanted to do so comfortably. Nancy was results-orientated and saw her role as head of a business rather than just a playmaker for the government. Promises were made and deliveries had to be met. She ran a tight ship, with no exceptions. If an asset was cast off, they were either made an example of to others, or never heard of again. This of course led to Nancy becoming a target herself.

Each time she returned to England, she never went directly to her home, but took a circuitous route to protect the location. As part of Nancy's original obligation to keep an eye on Stephen's comings and goings, she'd asked the next door neighbour to keep a log for her when she was away, having spun her a line that Stephen had once been unfaithful. But Nancy would still watch the home from a distance for at least a day or so, just to be sure.

She was always joyful to see her husband. They both enjoyed the physical side to their relationship and homecomings were definitely something they both looked forward to. In August 1943 whilst in Italy after facilitating diplomatic arrangements and just weeks before the Italians surrendered to the Allies, Nancy received some disturbing news from a doctor she'd seen privately... she was pregnant. She'd been savvy enough not to see her own physician because in Britain, her private life was not her own. She had serious reservations. *Did she want to keep the baby? How would it affect her career now that she'd established herself so well? Was she absolutely sure that Stephen was the father – the dates were close?* She was definitely attracted to him, he was protective in a gentle way, looked after her as best he could and of course brought her whatever flowers he could afford. When it came down to it and when she really thought about him, she realised that she'd actually come to love the man. But when she got home after receiving the news, Nancy found she had an even bigger problem to deal with.

Before officially arriving home Nancy watched her own house and her husband's movements in the usual way. But something was different this time. One late afternoon, a visitor she'd never seen before went to the house. The man only stayed for ten minutes, which seemed a little odd. Nancy continued to keep a watch until Stephen finally appeared after dark. She followed him at a distance to the RAF base, where he showed his pass and went through security. Nancy waited. There was only one entrance to the site. Thirty minutes later and after there had been a change of guard at the gate, her husband exited Ventnor station. He wasn't carrying a case or bag, but to her trained eye, she could see that he'd definitely put on a little weight around the legs and midriff. Nancy continued to follow her husband as he walked westwards away from the base, towards the St. Lawrence radar station. Rather than confront him, Nancy kept a good distance behind – she wanted to see how this was going to play out. Was Stephen heading to a 'Dead Drop'? She couldn't help questioning what she should do.

She didn't hear the man a hundred or so yards behind her, tracking both of them.

Instead of walking to the radar station, Stephen took a left turn that led to a large house at a dead end. As he rounded the bend, a cacophony of sounds split the air – gunfire and shouting in the distance, followed by the air-raid siren. In the distance, spotlights searched across the landscape… but not in the air.

Stephen was caught in two minds. He wasn't a soldier and deplored violence; he was scared. If he went further, he'd be heading towards the gunfire. The drop-off was supposed to be a straightforward one at the house, and then he'd just go home. He nearly jumped a foot when he heard a familiar voice call out loudly to him from behind.

"I think you should come home now, Stephen, before it's too late." He knew it was Nancy before he spun round. He searched his mind for an excuse for being where he was, but his mind failed him.

"What are you doing here?" he asked shakily.

"I'm following you. It sounds like our commandos have found something or someone. Who were you going to sell us out to?" Nancy's voice was stern and cold. She drew closer to him so they could see each other's outline.

The man who'd followed them moved to one side and slowly approached, keeping close to the bushes – hoping to overhear what was being discussed.

"I-i-it's not like that," Stephen stuttered, his heart beating nineteen to the dozen. "I'm sorry darling. They have my family back in Vienna!"

Nancy inferred from this that the man who'd visited their home was either German or worked on their behalf. She thought about Stephen. She still loved him, but she had the greater good to think about too. She gave him an ultimatum.

"I want you to listen because I will only say this once. You can come back with me now as Stephen Walker and we can find a way to sort things out, or you can continue down this path as Stefan Winkler to your fate. But you won't be taking whatever it is you have around your waist and legs that you took from Ventnor." Nancy hadn't taken the gun from her coat pocket, but her hand was keeping it warm. She desperately wanted Stephen to make the right decision.

Stephen thought about his options. He hated the Nazis and what they'd done to his family and country. Britain had been good to him, and Nancy was a truly wonderful woman. More gunfire could be heard in the distance along with what sounded like speeding trucks.

"If I come back, what will become of my family?" he asked.

"I'm afraid I can't guarantee anything for your family. Austria is well and truly isolated now. But if you give away *this* country's defence secrets, I guarantee that they won't just let your family go or send them off to Switzerland for a happy life. I know you're not that naive. They'll just make you give them more. Your family may already be dead Stephen, I mean; do you have any proof that they're still alive?" Stephen said nothing. "And what about the millions of lives that are at stake here... will you sell out all those women and children?"

"I don't want to kill anyone," Stephen's voice was dejected. "You know that. I've just been forced into a corner and I didn't think I had a choice. I'm so sorry."

The German was now close enough to hear what the couple were talking about. His asset had been compromised.

Nancy wanted her husband back, not just for herself, but because he still had a key role to play in the development of the radio countermeasure system. She could hear the noise of the trucks getting closer and needed to think quickly. She took a chance.

"It wouldn't just be the women and children from the mainland you'd be affecting – you now have a wife and child here that you'd be consigning to a death sentence if you give away information to the enemy." Nancy paused to let her words sink in.

Stephen began to shake. Are you saying what I think you are?" he said nervously.

The German slowly drew his pistol from its holster.

Nancy wasn't sure that she could've put it any clearer. "Yes, Stephen, you're going to be a father." She hated the idea of using her pregnancy as a weapon like this, especially as she wasn't completely sure it was his child. But so much was at stake here; she could deal with the ramifications later.

Stephen walked towards his wife to put his arms around her, but as the distant gunshots got closer, Nancy put one arm up to his chest. They might be husband and wife in name, but if he was going to try something, she might have to shoot him there and then. *At least the background gunfire would hide the shot.* "This is difficult for me, so I need to be sure whether you want to stay or go," she said firmly. Stephen began to answer when Nancy heard the sound over her left shoulder… the sound of a weapon being cocked. Her heart raced, though she tried her best to control it.

Stephen moved her arm away and put both arms around Nancy. He could feel her body shaking as he held her tightly. Nancy took a step over to her right and eased her gun out of her coat pocket, then put her arms around Stephen's waist and turned him slightly to the left to become an unwitting shield if she needed it

"Of course I want to stay with you, darli…"

A loud shot rang out behind, cutting Stephen's sentence dead. His brain took a while to figure out what was happening as he twisted round to look behind him. A second shot; this time a flash came from the bushes fifteen yards away by the side of the road.

Stephen's body twisted sharply as he fell backwards. Now Nancy knew where the gunman was, she crouched and fired off three shots in quick succession. She thought she saw the man fall back into the bushes, as separate machine gun fire could be heard getting closer to the house.

Nancy ran over to the bushes and found the gunman still breathing, his body searching for air as blood spluttered through the side of his windpipe.

"Who do you work for?" she asked urgently, but she didn't really expect him to answer. Not only because a bullet had gone right through his throat, but because he'd probably rather die than give anything to the enemy. The trucks were getting closer and Nancy was worried about Stephen. She grabbed the tails of the gunman's coat, yanked them up to cover his face, put the barrel of her pistol to his forehead and shot him one more time. Then she quickly searched the dead man's pockets. Grabbing what she could, she ran back to Stephen, who was lying in the road trying to get to his feet. Relieved that he was still alive, she helped him up. Even with the searchlights switching back and forth, it was hard to see where he'd been hit.

"Can you walk? We've got to get out of here, now!"

"I think so," Stephen said, holding his right side just below the ribs.

"You can lean on me, but we have to run. Those trucks and the gunfire are getting closer."

* * *

Back at their home, Nancy drew all the curtains and lit a single candle. In the living room, Stephen stripped off his clothes. He'd been lucky. The bullet had scorched through the files he'd taped to his side and grazed his torso. All the files that were taped to his arms, legs, body and back had helped save his life. Nancy pulled the tape from his skin with great pleasure, removing large tracts of hair as she did so.

Stephen looked sheepish. He realised that he'd nearly got them both killed. He'd nearly got his unborn child killed too.

Nancy did her best to remain calm as she dressed the wound with iodine and a bandage, but inside she seethed. When the civil defence sirens sounded again to signal the all-clear, she turned on the lights. Stephen got dressed again whilst Nancy looked through the pile of files sat on the table. Everything was there if you had the right resources – which the enemy had in spades. All the engineering and electronic specifications, including all of the long- and short-distance frequencies used to detect incoming aircraft. The difficulty now was how they were going to explain the disappearance of the files or even get the files back to on to the base again.

Stephen could see how disappointed she was in him and not much was said between the two that night. He went to bed like a scolded child, but Nancy stayed downstairs, thinking. She went through the papers she'd taken from the dead man that evening. 'George Smith' was a thirty-two-year-old writer, according to his identity card... although with a magnifying glass, Nancy could see it was forged. The address was probably forged too, but worth checking out nonetheless. She'd also taken the man's keys which she put in her coat pocket just in case.

At 4:30 the next morning, she shook her husband awake. "Get up, we have work to do. When you've washed, come downstairs in your underwear and bring your suit with you."

Stephen was about to question his wife, but could see by the look on her face that now wasn't the best time. When he came downstairs to the living room, she began taping all of the files back in place and then watched her husband put his clothes on. She wondered if he'd had any help on the base that night.

By 5:30 they were out of the door and walking to work together. Nancy had even made their lunches before they left home. The same night security guard was on duty which was what she was counting on. He checked both of their IDs and lunch bags, before letting them through. Nancy had a good idea where the files had come from but made Stephen show her the way whilst nobody was around. She was about to tell her husband to put the papers back in their rightful places, when another idea came to mind. The files had been crumpled and someone would soon notice the bullet hole and blood damage to one of them, which in turn would raise an alert and make everyone a tampering suspect.

She told Stephen to go to his work station, whilst she took the files. She placed them on the base commander's desk with a note. Back in her office, she called her handler to give him a version of the events that had happened the previous evening. What made her story more plausible was the fact that he already knew about the other incident in St. Lawrence: the Germans had tried to invade the island, trying to steal radar equipment from the St. Lawrence station. He commended her on her good work and hung up. A few hours later when the base commander inevitably summoned her to his office, she covered for Stephen. "I can't say where from, but I'd received a tip-off that there was going to be a theft or an invasion. I'd been watching Ventnor all day and saw a man I didn't know walking away with a large package last night. I followed him, as he headed towards the house on Wolverton Road near St. Lawrence. He must have realised he was being followed because when he turned a corner, I'd lost him. As it turned out, he'd stopped and concealed himself between two bushes. As I continued walking, I heard the cocking of a pistol to my left and turned just he appeared behind me. He fired his weapon but just missed – just giving me enough time to fire back three times." Nancy pointed to one of the files on the base commander's desk. "You can see the blood-stain and bullet hole are a testament to that." Nancy watched the base commander's face, not sure if he had bought everything she'd said. She added, "I don't think it's a coincidence that it happened as the German's had tried to invade the St. Lawrence base – there was gunfire there too. I tried to question him but he'd taken one to the throat and wouldn't talk, so the last bullet was through the head."

The base commander listened intently. He knew Nancy was commanded by higher authorities, but he was still astounded by the story. He'd been up for most of the night in conversations with high-ranking military types discussing what to do about handling the news of the attempted invasion.

"Is the body still there?" he asked.

Nancy shrugged. "I don't see why not, unless someone else has moved it since."

"Take me to it, then."

He drove her the mile or so to the scene. The body was still in the same position it had been left in the night before. This wasn't the first person she'd killed, but it was the first person she'd shot herself. She uncovered the corpse's head to get a good look at what was left of the man's face. The vomit-inducing sight and smell instantly imprinted on her senses, but she managed to keep her composure... being a butcher's daughter definitely helped.

The commander drove them both to St. Lawrence where his counterpart agreed to include the body amongst those of the other German forces killed in the invasion. The three of them also discussed further security measures at all the bases. Nancy suggested that all personnel must now be fully searched when going on or off base. There should be no special treatment for senior officers and women either. The commanders agreed, along with a host of additional oversight and administrative accountability measures. As far as the 'invasion' was concerned, there was no invasion. There was a 'military readiness operation' that night and all records to the contrary were to be erased – orders from the very top.

That evening when Stephen and Nancy left work for home, they were both physically searched before leaving the base. The security guard felt strange and didn't quite know how to handle the search of a woman... especially with her husband standing there. But Nancy just told him to search her as he would a man. On the walk home Stephen said how irritated he was by someone else having his paws all over his wife. Nancy understood his reaction, which in some ways was a little endearing but she was in no mood for an argument and was firm in her response.

"All I wanted to do was come home to give you the wonderful news, but we were both nearly killed last night, I've had to kill a man *and* I've had to lie to cover for what you've done. It's a small price, don't you think?" And with that, the conversation was over. Stephen apologised again, but it was going to be a long while before they could get back to any semblance of what they once were.

* * *

The prospect of a new baby arriving came at the worst time for Nancy and the country. In the early months, Nancy considered finding some way to get rid of the child growing within her, but her heart wouldn't let her kill something so innocent. She also feared that Stephen would no longer have a reason to stay and help the allied effort. Nancy took her last mission in Europe in December of 1943. Bombings became so regular on the island due to its proximity to German-occupied France, that she relocated to a quiet area near Ipswich – where she could continue her work with the Telecommunications Research Establishment. Stephen would visit whenever he could, always with flowers.

Their beautiful baby was came in the May of 1944 and named David in honour of Nancy's father. Stephen was overjoyed to see that he had a son, whilst Nancy was relieved that the child was endowed with a thick, dark mane of hair.

By this time, the tide had begun to turn in the Allies' favour. U-Boats and German destroyers were routinely being sunk or scuppered and the shear bulk of numbers the Americans contributed played a significant part in keeping the Germans at bay in France. But the V1 and V2 rocket attacks that came shortly after were game-changers for the research facility – and kept everyone up day and night.

When the war eventually ended, Nancy sold the house on the island and the family moved to a small hamlet near Malvern in Worcestershire. The Telecommunications Research Establishment had also moved and changed names to the Radar Research Establishment, where Stephen continued his work on radar, infra-red detection and semi-conductors, amongst other things.

Compared to what the couple had seen elsewhere, Malvern had received very little in the way of bomb damage and was an ideal picturesque place to start a new life. It would take years for the rest of the country to properly rebuild itself. Nancy continued her work for The Service and was fortunate that a significant part of her contact and asset base across Europe had managed to remain alive during the latter stages of the war. Every allegiance had to be completely re-evaluated, as territorial and influential lines were redrawn by the Allies.

The most significant gains were made by the Russians. Nancy was fully aware of the power struggle now taking place between the USSR and the Americans, and made sure to cultivate new relationships across the Atlantic and in the Eastern Block. Although not strictly her turf, she also quietly stepped up her domestic recruitment as well. She made sure that there was never just one agent embedded within any given organisation under surveillance. This even stretched to having her agents established within Britain's own domestic services, such as MI5.... it was always good to know what the left hand was doing.

During this time, Nancy also had someone investigate the history and whereabouts of Stephen's family. He'd told her a lot about them, which gave her contact a significant amount to go on. In the first instance, she needed to know if they actually existed and what had happened before, during and after the war. Similarly to Germany, Austria and Vienna had become divided up into a number of territories overseen by the British, French Americans and Russians. Stefan Winkler's family had hailed from the eastern region now occupied by the Russians, which made the acquisition of information extremely difficult because Nancy's remit had been to tread very carefully in the region.

Her real assignment was to pave the way for the arming of a secret Austrian army, not ponder about personal issues. Stephen badgered her regularly for news, but for much of the time she had nothing, which sometimes bubbled over into arguments.

Her contact eventually came through, but the news wasn't good. Stephen was devastated to learn that his parents had been killed along with his younger brother. But also explained that there was no death record of his sister, Lillian, which meant she could still be alive somewhere. It was a small sliver of hope that helped Nancy counteract the gloomy depression Stephen had fallen into.

The Service also reorganised itself post-war, and in 1956, Nancy was put in charge of all European operations. It was a huge role because it actually incorporated all of Eastern and Western Europe and well as parts of North Africa. All operations in these areas of the world, or that impacted them, went through Nancy first.

As tensions between the USA and the USSR heightened into what the press termed a 'Cold War', the world began to change at a rapid pace. The industry had become obsessed with technology and miniaturisation. Radio transmitters and electronic circuits were being developed without the need for wires and the transfer of documents and pictures across borders was now almost completely carried out through the use of microdots. In the old days, each country knew that most espionage traffic was fed through local embassies, but new technology meant that cells could now operate independently, without any need to communicate through embassies whatsoever. This was all well and good for your own people, but it made the hunting of foreign spies exponentially more difficult. More than fifty percent of all leads came from some form of human error or a simple element of luck. Being caught between two huge powerbases determined to annihilate each other and the rest of the world along with them was a tricky position to be in for Britain, but Nancy did her best to navigate the torrid waters. This could not be said about politicians who seemed happy to give away any advantages Britain gained to the Americans.

Home life had become somewhat routine for the Walkers. After minor complications during David's birth, Nancy was told that she wouldn't be able to have any more children. So David was the apple of her eye. Whenever she could, she'd spend time with him reading, talking and nurturing his creative side. Stephen also played a part helping with homework and academic studies, but with both parents often working long and difficult hours, David's interests migrated towards sports and practical subjects at school. His grades in academic subjects were average at best. Stephen couldn't understand why David was unable or unwilling to comprehend what he characterised as simple mathematical theories, and David couldn't understand why his father could barely run, kick a football to save his life or fix things around the house.

These fundamental differences began to cause an emotional rift between father and son, culminating in Stephen devoting more time to work-related pursuits rather than being at home. With Nancy also often away, David would spend most of his time hanging out with his friends. When she was there, she could see the divide widening between Stephen and David, but even though her son's academic abilities were also a disappointment to her, she wouldn't abandon him. He deserved someone to love him for who he was, not just for what apparent use he did or didn't have in this world.

* * *

In 1955 Austria finally achieved independence, but it wasn't until 1956 that being able to visit his homeland could be considered safe for Stephen. He took a month's well-earned break from work and after agreement with Nancy, who arranged the visas, went back home to see if he could locate his sister.

During the German occupation, life had been dire and sometimes gruesome for the Winkler family. During the invasion, their home had been thoroughly ransacked. Soldiers had not only stolen anything of value, but when her parents had tried to resist, her mother had been raped and shot in the back of the head; whilst her father was nowhere to be found. Fortunately for her, Lillian had been working behind the bar at the Ratskeller beneath the city hall. But it was she who'd come home to the devastating discovery. It was she that had clean up the human remains and bury her mother. It was she that had to find out where her father was and if he was indeed alive. Not Stefan, not her big brother who'd just left them before the war began to suffer the atrocities of the Nazi regime. She often wondered if he'd known what was going to happen – the inadequate note he'd left the family not really explaining anything:

Dearest Mother, Father and Lilli,

Our country needs help but to do this, I must leave you. I cannot say where I'm going but I truly hope you will understand one day.

Your loving son and brother, always.

Stefan

She wondered what he'd meant by having to leave to help. He was a very clever scientist and she could never understand the concepts he'd tried to explain to her. *Was he a spy? Had he gone to work for the Germans with the aim of giving away their secrets?* Even if he had, it still didn't matter to her. He'd just left them to their fate without so much as a goodbye.

Despite her hatred for all things German and their people, Lillian still had to smile and make polite conversations with the soldiers that frequented Ratskeller. Rather than be shot or carted off to some labour camp, authorities had seen fit to allow her to keep her job... after all, a pretty girl behind the bar was good for morale. During this time, many officers and soldiers had tried and mostly failed to arouse any romantic interest in her, except one. Lillian had been secretly courted by a Lieutenant, Lukas Schäfer. As it turned out, Lukas was different from all the other German's who'd just assumed she was there to bestow pleasure when they wanted. He was part of a small secret group of soldiers with allegiances to the Russians, giving away German infantry positions and numbers whenever he could. He had helped to locate where Lillian's father had been taken, who had been carted off to join the Jews at Mauthausen labour camp. Unfortunately, her father had subsequently been shot during his internment, but as horrific as that was; she appreciated Lukas's determination to help her anyway. With Lillian's help, they became a very successful team. After the war, Lukas remained in Austria and they married in 1948 – which gave extra credence to their cover. In 1950, Lillian gave birth to a son they named Florian.

Stephen eventually found Lillian living in Klostermarienberg, a territory which had only just been relinquished by the Russians. He'd waited for so long to see his sister again, anxiously thinking about what he would say to the sister he'd abandoned so selfishly before the war. But for Lillian, even reuniting could not dispel the resentment she felt at what he had done. The pain was too great.

She despised the reappearance of her brother, with whom she'd had no contact for eighteen years. He tried explaining what had happened and why he'd left the way he did. How devastated he was about the deaths of their family and the guilt he felt. He told her how happy he was that the war was finally over and about his family back in England. He asked for her forgiveness which she wouldn't commit to.

It was Lukas's idea to let Stephen stay for a couple of days, and although she wasn't happy, Lillian knew why he had suggested it. Over the days they all discussed what they had each done during and after the war. On the second day Lillian and Lukas put their cards on the table. "Forgiving you is going to be hard for me, Stefan. You just left us to deal with the German regime by ourselves. The rest of our family are now dead," said Lillian.

"But they didn't die because I left and I probably wouldn't be here now if I'd stayed, would I?" Stephen countered. He glanced at Lukas. "I mean no disrespect of course." Irked by Stephen's comment, Lillian tried to keep calm... *he was probably right after all.*

It was Lukas who spoke next, acting as the peacekeeper between estranged brother and sister. "Things are very different between our two countries. Although we are now independent, we still struggle for a truly united Austria – we don't like being carved up like Berlin. Perhaps you can write to each other and maybe help your homeland from England, *ja?*"

"I'm not sure how I can help rebuild our country?" Stephen said, confused.

In a smart act of tenderness, Lillian took Stephen's hand in hers. "Don't worry, we will show you how to do this."

On the journey back to England, Stephen contemplated what he would say to Nancy. His feelings torn between two families, if there was a sliver of hope of redemption with his sister, he had to help her if he could.

Once home, he explained how he'd eventually found Lillian, but said that she really wasn't happy about seeing him. Nancy could understand why. If she had any siblings and they had done what Stephen had... there was no way she'd be in a forgiving mood either. "The war has done terrible things to so many people, perhaps she'll come around. Will you be seeing her again or writing?" she enquired.

"Maybe I'll write to her," he just said despondently – which saved him from lying.

* * *

Over the next three years Nancy received intelligence reports on Lukas and Lillian. She'd been told that they were conduits for the KGB and made sure that any letters sent by and to Stephen were secretly screened before reaching the intended recipient. But unknown to her, these weren't the only communications Stephen engaged in.

In 1959 he was asked to join the Admiralty Underwater Weapons Establishment at Portland in Weymouth. The Admiralty felt that his outstanding work on radar detection would be transferable into the research of underwater weapons and detection systems. David was in his last year at school and Nancy didn't want to uproot the family until he'd at least left school and decided what direction he wanted to take in life. She also didn't want Stephen to resent her for limiting his career opportunities. In the end they agreed that rather than commute the three-hundred-mile round trip each day, Stephen would stay in Havant during the week and come back home at the weekends. It wasn't ideal, but perhaps the absence would make each heart grow fonder.

Things worked out quite well from a relationship standpoint until 1960, when Nancy received news from one of her moles in MI5 that there were a number of people under surveillance at Portland. Of the names given to her, Stephen's wasn't on the list, but she was now extremely concerned. The story was that the CIA had received intelligence that documents from the Underwater Weapons

Establishment had been reaching the Russians. MI5 had a number of people under investigation, including a low-level clerk, his mistress and a businessman in London. But there were also documents getting through that the clerk and his mistress didn't have access to.

Nancy quietly had Stephen put under surveillance whilst he was away from home. Letters retrieved from a post box he'd posted to and that she'd analysed showed that Stephen was passing information to the low-level clerk and that he was also providing the document names in separate letters to Lillian. The documents themselves were passed from the clerk to the London businessman, who in turn took frequent journeys abroad to liaise with his KGB contact.

Nancy felt disgusted, not just with Stephen, but with herself for allowing the opposition to use him like this. If word got out about what he was doing, her career would be over. She had to take care of her own business... and quickly. He was no longer her husband; he'd betrayed her. He was an agent gone bad and had to be eliminated. She still had an interrogation kit secretly stored away at home, but now she was going to need something a little more subtle... and lethal. From a contact via a supply chain in Amsterdam, she acquired two vials of Ricin.

Two weeks later on a Saturday evening when Stephen was home, Nancy slipped a slow acting sleeping drug into his evening tea. At 1 o'clock on the Sunday morning, a muted alarm went off under her pillow. Mildly comatose, Stephen was none the wiser. Nancy switched on the bedside light and pulled down Stephen's pyjama bottoms. He didn't feel the small prick of the needle into his groin, as Nancy injected the lethal dose of Ricin into his bloodstream. She wanted the toxin to act slowly and made sure that the injection was in the vein, and in an area that wouldn't be seen by a coroner – if it ever came to it.

Stephen didn't stir. She hid the injection equipment and turned out the light; rested her head on her pillow, watching Stefan Winkler take each breath closer to his last. As a young girl she'd been brought up with Christian values, but she realised that God had nothing to do with what Stephen had done to the country and his family – and God certainly had nothing to do with what she'd just sentenced the man to. Becoming godless was the only way she could reconcile murdering the father of her only son.

Stephen woke up a little fuzzy, but drove the way to Havant as usual on Sunday afternoon. It was now a waiting game for Nancy.

On Monday evening, Stephen showed signs of having the beginnings of bad cold. Even though he felt bad on Tuesday, he still went into work. But by the afternoon, he was advised to go home after vomiting twice in the research office. He went back to his lodgings and called Nancy, asking for her advice on whether to find a local doctor. She volunteered to go down to help him, but when he said he didn't want her to worry, she insisted. She also advised him to see if he could get some aspirin to help lower his temperature.

Nancy didn't rush the 140-odd miles from home and eventually arrived at the lodging house in the early evening. After knocking on Stephen's door a couple of times without any answer, she asked the manageress to come and open the door and stay; just in case she needed any more help.

As the manageress opened the door, she screamed. Nancy saw it too. Stephen lay on his back, a brown pool of bile beside him with crusty stains cascading from each corner of his mouth. The manageress fainted and Nancy was just able to catch her before the woman fell and hit her head on a chest of drawers. She stepped over her and checked to see if she could find a pulse on the traitor, but Stefan Winkler was dead.

Nancy looked at her watch and walked over to a side table. Taking a lithium salt pill from her purse, she crushed it with a key and divided the powder into two small piles. She scraped the first pile onto a small scrap of paper she had in her bag and funnelled the drug into her mouth – washing it down with some water from a jug on the side. She then quickly searched around the room to make sure he had nothing work-related stashed anywhere.

She found nothing. There was a snort from the manageress, so Nancy quickly dabbed what was left of the grainy powder directly into her eyes. The lithium stung with a searing pain immediately drawing tears and inflaming her top and bottom eyelids. After cleaning the side table, she walked round the bed and kissed Stephen lightly on the forehead before reviving the manageress. *Goodbye... Stefan.*

The women comforted each other, but it was the manageress who called the local police on Nancy's behalf. They were very understanding, as both women were visibly upset and shook uncontrollably – the lithium salt providing Nancy's stimulus. What followed was fairly procedural: Nancy and the manageress gave statements and a coroner eventually gave a cause of death as asphyxiation. No underlying cause was on the report other than symptoms of flu and a possible allergic reaction to aspirin.

The hardest thing for Nancy was breaking the news to David. Even though father and son weren't the closest, David was still devastated by the loss. Nancy took some time away from work and made the funeral arrangements. The intimate cremation took place in Worcester, where Nancy had made sure that none of her husband's work colleagues were invited. The last thing she wanted was to have the MI5 investigation extended to her affairs. Rather than keep her husband's ashes in an urn, they were placed in a memorial on site at the crematorium. In the early hours one week after the cremation, Nancy had one of her most trusted 'Cleaners' discreetly remove the file, blood and tissue samples for Stephen Walker from the Portsmouth coroner's office. Once in her possession, she destroyed the evidence.

From the pay-out of the life assurance policy she'd taken out on Stephen and some proceeds from her European business interests, Nancy had no reason to live in the family house any longer. Kent was where she was born and where she wanted to return to. She wanted to live somewhere equidistant from London and the coast, and in 1961, found her dream home at number 7 Woodland Rise, Sevenoaks.

* * *

PART 6

(March 1978 – April 1978)

CHAPTER 39

KILL OR BE KILLED

As Nancy pulled onto her driveway behind the *Phil's Carpet Cleaning* van, Schäfer watched from the bedroom window. A neighbour walked across the road from the opposite home to intercept her.

"I saw you leave earlier – that van's been there for an hour or so?" the woman said questioningly.

As much as Nancy appreciated the vigilance, it was the last thing she wanted right now, when time was of the essence.

"Thank you for looking out for me, but I've been expecting him. Look, I've got to check he's done the job properly – I'll pop over a bit later if that's alright?" Nancy knew the woman wanted to stand and gossip for a while, so she patted her left arm and turned towards the front door. Relieved that her neighbour seemed to have got the message, Nancy knew she'd have to make amends later.

Schäfer knew that the sight of the van would cause Nancy to be more vigilant on entry, and used the neighbour's interruption to slip back downstairs into one of the reception rooms without casting a shadow through the front door window.

Outside, Nancy cocked the pistol in her pocket, removed the safety and carefully opened the front door, making sure to unravel the main trap that had been set to break the front door window if sprung. She left the door on the latch.

"Is anybody there?" she called out as put her handbag down and picked up a broom handle with her right hand from inside the coat cupboard. She listened intently as she slowly walked past the porch door into the hallway; if he was still there, she didn't want to be caught off guard.

"I'll take zat."

Nancy turned as quickly as she could, but Schäfer sprang out of the front room on the right like a snake, and twisted the broom handle out of her hand. As her momentum spun her round further, he kicked her right ankle, sending her stumbling backwards. Nancy fell down on her back with a thud, just managing to keep her head from bouncing off the floor. Schäfer seemed to glamorise the hunt, standing over her menacingly with the broom handle. As he looked down at her, he hesitated for the briefest of seconds... but Nancy didn't. Three loud shots rang out from her left hip; all three hit Schäfer in the abdomen and chest and he fell backwards, wide-eyed and stunned – blood now oozing from his wounds.

The old woman got up to her feet in front of him – her gun now trained at his head. "Didn't your mother ever tell you *not* to play with your food?" He'd severely underestimated her.

Mike Finny and the squad heard the shots as they passed by Nancy's home. The plan instantly changed as he reversed the van back to block the driveway exit. All four got out and split equally, two to the front door, two to the rear.

Schäfer kept quiet, his breathing short and shallow as he slowly moved his right hand towards the gun holstered on his left hip.

Nancy moved quickly round to the man's head and made sure he could feel the hot steel of her gun barrel to his temple. "I suggest you take that out v-e-r-y slowly, Mr. Schäfer, and throw it over there as far as you can."

Knowing he was out-manoeuvred, he did as he was told, just as two men eased through the unlatched front door wearing black overalls and balaclavas, with guns pointed.

Finny assessed the situation. "You OK?" he asked.

"Bruised but fine. I need you to help me search him. His gun's over there."

Finny bound the man's wrists and began patting his body to check for weapons. It was a detailed search but not detailed enough for Nancy. When the other two men entered the house from the rear, Nancy asked them to tie the man up and blindfold him.

"What about his wounds?" Finny asked. The man was still bleeding profusely.

"I have medical supplies if you wouldn't mind lifting him and following me," she responded.

Finny told one of the squad to stand guard by the front door. Then he grabbed the man's feet whilst the other two hooked him under the armpits. They followed Nancy through the house and out of the back door.

Ten yards in front on the paved terrace was a dry hexagonal water fountain with a four-foot vertical centre piece. Nancy pushed this forward so that what looked like a solid concrete square slab hinged backwards ninety degrees, revealing a secret underground stairwell.

The woman said nothing – just proceeded to walk down the steps, switching on the lights at the bottom. The two men looked at Finny, who in turn just shrugged as if nothing would surprise him anymore. They followed Nancy down the steps into a fully stocked and well-thought-out bunker. But it was just what Nancy affectionately called her basement. Schäfer groaned in agony as the squad dumped him on the ground like a sack of potatoes. Nancy riffled through a couple of drawers and retrieved some scissors, a torch, a scalpel, pliers, bandages, hypodermics, vials and a weird metal device shaped like a duck's bill.

"Strip him down, please. Everything will be cleaner this way." The men did as they were asked, cutting his clothes away with the scissors she gave them, taking care *not* to spare the captive any pain.

Nancy found a chair and asked the men to sit the now completely naked captive on it. She whispered to Finny. "I need you to choke him out – but leave him alive, please."

Finny looked at the old lady with a whole new level of respect... she certainly wasn't someone to be messed with. He casually walked behind Schäfer, nodded briefly to his squad and snapped his right forearm around the man's neck – placing his left hand over his nose. Schäfer struggled as much as he could but the pain in his abdomen was unbearable and the other two men were keeping his legs in position. Finny could feel him trying to manoeuvre his trachea into the soft space between his biceps and forearm, but it was only matter of time before he succumbed to the overwhelming force of the larger men. Finny relaxed his grip as he felt Schäfer's resistance tail off.

Nancy checked the man's pulse and nodded in approval at Finny. "Keep his head still, please."

Finny put his palms on both sides of Schäfer's head as Nancy pushed the duck-billed piece of metal into his mouth.

"What *is* that thing?" one of the squad members asked. Nancy and Finny looked each other. "It's a speculum," she responded drily. But the man was still none the wiser.

Finny smiled at Nancy. "I'll tell you later," he said to his colleague, as Nancy pushed the thumb blade and wound the screw to keep the duck-bill open.

With his mouth fully open, Nancy picked up the scalpel and shone the torch inside Schäfer's mouth. After a minute of carefully poking around, she found what she was looking for. She exchanged the scalpel for the pliers and pushed Schäfer's head back slightly. With a couple of short tugs, she removed a cap that covered one of his hollowed-out molars and placed the contents on the side. She would look at them later. Nancy gave one last look around his mouth again just to be sure she hadn't missed anything, before removing the clamp. The man was still bleeding, but not quite as profusely. She had to act quickly. It wouldn't be long before Schäfer came to. Nancy asked Finny to untie Schäfer's wrists – she needed to inspect his forearms. Gripping with her right hand, she pressed her thumbs all the way up his left arm searching for a small lump. There it was, just above the inner elbow crease between two tendons. Nancy took the scalpel and cut a small incision into her captive's skin – pushing the small metallic pellet out like a splinter. The three-man squad looked on in awe – they'd never seen this done before, their jobs being to hand over the people they captured, or eliminate them. Nancy instructed Finny to re-tie Schäfer's hands as she placed the pellet next to the molar contents on the side.

Schäfer began to stir.

"How long do you think he'll survive in his current state?" Nancy asked Finny. She needed a second opinion to compare with her own.

Finny looked at the captive's wounds but he really didn't know how much damage had been caused internally. "There's two exit wounds and he's still bleeding. It's only a rough guess, but maybe a couple of hours. He may just go into a coma first."

Nancy nodded her appreciation and pierced a hypodermic syringe needle into a small sealed vial.

Schäfer came to, slightly groggy at first, but then began shouting in a slightly Germanic accent. "You stupid old hag – you shot me! I came to clean your carpet!"

Nancy took the man's blindfold off, his eyes now adjusting to the new light. "What are you doing?" He looked at the men for support. "She's a monster, can't you see? Let me go!" He could feel the searing pain in his stomach and dared to look down at the maroon sticky blood flow slowly pouring onto his lap.

Nancy smiled. "What is your name, Mr. Carpet Cleaner?" she asked simply.

Schäfer tried to remember the name on the side of the van he'd stolen, but in his current situation, the name eluded him. "Lukas Mayer – I work for the company," he said, spluttering in anger. He started to shake erratically. The temperature in the basement was pretty cold and his breath could be seen each time he spoke.

Nancy looked at Finny. "Would you mind tilting Mr. Mayer's head to the right, please?" she said calmly. "Don't worry, Mr. Mayer, this will help you relax and then we can get to know each other properly. You never know, we may even be able to patch up those wounds for you."

Schäfer began to resist, but Finny just lent into the job with more pleasure. Nancy injected a small dose of Ketamine into Schäfer's carotid artery which was now clear to see as he struggled against Finny. She stood back and waited for the man to calm down. He tried his best to resist for about 30 – 40 seconds, but the drug went straight through to the brain. Schäfer's head slowly rocked back and forth. Nancy acknowledged the behaviour and then picked up a second vial from the side table. Extracting what she needed, she didn't worry about sanitising the needle... cleanliness was going to be the least of Florian Schäfer's problems today.

"How are you feeling, Mr. Schäfer – is it helping with the pain?" Nancy asked.

"It's... Mayer... Stu… pid... wo-man."

Nancy injected the man with the second serum. Finny went to help, but Schäfer was compliant enough for Nancy to manage by herself. She then addressed Finny and the squad members.

"Gentlemen. I'm going to have to ask you to leave this room for a while, whilst I speak with our friend here alone."

They all looked at each other. This was not the usual protocol, but then, nothing they'd done that afternoon was usual protocol. Finny spoke up. "I don't think it's wise to leave you here with him alone, Ma'am."

"I understand your concerns. I'd like one of you to stay by the entrance just in case." She gave further instructions about informing Tom Barnes and The Chief that everything was under control. "I will report directly."

With an upturn of his head, Finny instructed the other two men to leave the room.

"I'm just going to check the bindings before I go," he said.

"Thank you," Nancy responded. "And don't worry, I'll be alright," as she tapped her coat pocket.

Finny gave a short salute and began walking up the steps to the entrance.

"Please close the hatch after you," she said.

Finny looked back, but Nancy just continued busying herself by getting another chair from across the room. She placed it six feet in front of the naked, blood-stained man and calmly watched as the Sodium Thiopental began to go to work.

"How are you feeling, Mr. Schäfer?" Nancy asked in a calming manner.

"I… am… not… Schäfer. Am… Luk… as." The man's head wandered from left to right in a daze. Although he was quite calm his skin shivered continuously.

"It's cold down here; would you like me to get you a blanket?"

Schäfer said nothing. Nancy stood up and walked over to a cupboard. She pulled out a large folded picnic blanket, placed it still folded on Schäfer's lap and sat back down on her seat.

The texture of the wool on his leg felt wonderful, reminding him of his childhood.

"I just want you to know that I'm not an unreasonable person. I'll gladly put the blanket over you to keep you warm; I just need you to confirm your real name for me. What's your first name, Mr. Schäfer?"

His body was in shock. The drugs had taken the edge off, but every time he looked down at his wounds, the glistening crimson mess seemed to get larger and inflate the pain he felt. He was sure he was going to die and paranoia began to settle in. "You... you... prom... ise?"

Nancy nodded her head.

"Flo... rian," he stuttered.

As she picked up the blanket from Schäfer's lap she asked, "What is your mother's name, Florian?" Nancy hesitated putting the blanket around Schäfer's body.

Schäfer felt tormented. She was just inches away, so close; he could smell the cleanser she'd used. His mind swirled – he just wanted the blanket around him. "Lill… ian, Lillian. That's her name."

This was good for Nancy. They'd now set a baseline for future discussions. She carefully put the blanket around the man's body to try and make him feel as comfortable as possible. She'd also now established an element of trust.

"Is that better for you now?" she asked. Schäfer nodded a very elongated yes. "Your wounds look quite bad, Florian. I'd like to get them seen to for you, but I need you to tell me why you came here, to my house?"

Schäfer hesitated. In the malaise that filled his mind, he wanted to hold out. He knew he should, but his body was also telling him that he needed fixing, fast.

"Florian, are you still with me? I need to know why you came here."

The man's willpower relented. "You… killed… my… uncle. Mother… said you… killed… Stefan."

This was interesting news to Nancy. "Did your mother say *why* she thought I killed your uncle?"

The shudders in Schäfer's body began to reduce slightly. He wanted to go to sleep. Nancy couldn't allow him to relax too much or pass out; she needed more information. She repeated the question a little more forcefully. "Florian, why does your mother think I killed your uncle?"

"She told me… you never trusted him… and he said that if anything suspicious were to happen, if he died… you'd be responsible for it."

So the man, her husband, a traitor to both countries, had taken out an extra insurance policy against her, just in case.

Nancy thought about what course of action to take next. She had to keep cool – she still needed more information. "You may find this hard to believe, Florian, but your uncle died whilst he was living away from me, where he worked. He called to tell me he wasn't well and had died by the time I arrived at his lodging room. I was with the manager when we both found him."

"Mother didn't know that. She knew about you, he used to write to her. Then one day she just stopped hearing from him."

Schäfer sounded genuinely upset for his mother. All this for an uncle he'd barely ever seen? Something seemed off. "Do you remember how old you were when you last saw Stefan?"

His injuries were beginning to take their toll. "Six," he answered drowsily. Nancy sensed the deterioration in him and was about to change the line of questioning when Schäfer continued. "But he sent us pictures and wrote quite often. You have a son, *ja?*" This sent a jolt through Nancy's spine. None of the letters she'd had intercepted included any pictures. Stefan must have been finding another way to get information out of the country.

Schäfer's head began to nod from side-to-side, the colour draining from his face. She had to find out his connection to Theo. "It was very upsetting for us as a family when we lost Stefan." Nancy paused. "I was just wondering how you came to meet with a good friend of mine, Theo Greaves?"

Schäfer giggled. "Ah Theo, he is... funny man... you know." He coughed.

"Yes, Theo's one of my favourites." Nancy admitted.

Schäfer laughed, which then hurt his stomach. His face contorted in pain. "You'll have... to get to the... back of the queue old lady... he likes them much younger." Schäfer laughed in pain again. His wounds began seeping blood as he coughed.

Nancy could hear by the gurgle in his cough that he didn't have long. She was also a little put out by Schäfer's comments. Theo had been so captivating at the restaurant, and it seemed she was just one of many who'd fallen for his charm. She decided to use this embarrassment, this hurt, to her advantage. Knowing that Schäfer would want to inflict some sort of pain on her before he left this world, she swallowed her pride and asked the question as if hurt by the man's last comment.

"What do you mean? I know he's married, I've met his wife."

Schäfer coughed and laughed again. He could see that the old lady had designs on Theo Greaves. Breathing had become much more difficult and laboured.

"You mean *wives*... old lady... wives." Nancy tried to act indifferently, but Schäfer could see she was wounded. "Egypt, Turkey..." the words hung in the air, as his lungs filled with blood and he began to suffocate.

Nancy asked one last question. "When did you first meet?"

Schäfer could barely maintain consciousness. He breathed out, breathed in... and breathed out for one last time. Nancy sat silently for a minute to take in everything he'd said. She checked, but Schäfer's pulse had finally stopped.

The contents of Schäfer's tooth still lay on the side so she decided to take a closer look. The method of hiding and transferring information inside fake molars was fast becoming outdated, but it was still standard issue in the Eastern Bloc. Nancy opened the drawer and took out a pair of tweezers and a large magnifying glass. With the tweezers, she carefully opened both of the small scrolls of what felt like wax paper to reveal the contents. Each scroll consisted of one small negative and a number of microdots. Nancy couldn't read the dots with the magnifying glass, but with some time, was able to make out places along the Israeli/Syrian border from the negatives. She rolled the contents up, put them back on the side and went outside to where Finny and the other two men were still waiting. It was getting dark.

"I need to make a phone call," she said.

The Chief had been made aware of the situation and was on high alert when Nancy's call was put straight through.

Nancy got to the point. "Our visitor has expired. It's unlikely he would've survived transportation anyway. I didn't get that much out of him before he died, but he did have a molar and cyanide capsule. I took a quick look at the two negatives in the molar and the information ties back to the Middle East – which puts Theo slap-bang in the middle of it all. Schäfer said Theo is compromised – wives in Egypt and Turkey apparently."

The Chief sighed at the other end of the line. "Can you come in and give a verbal report?"

"Of course. What do you want done with the body?"

"Can you tell the squad to take it to Camberwell? We'll get an autopsy done for the file and then decide from there. You can bring the other evidence here. I'll have the arrangements made and wait for you."

"Could you also arrange for 'the cleaners' to come down tomorrow?" Nancy asked. "The place is a bit of a mess."

"Will do, see you in a while," The Chief said.

Nancy glanced at herself in the mirror. She was looking a little worse for wear and her coat had three scorched bullet holes in the left side pocket.

She went back outside to where the men were waiting, each peering inside the basement.

"Orders, gentlemen. We are to remove the body and take it to London. Please untie him and gather all of his clothes. As the hallway is a mess with blood, feel free to tear as much carpet up as you want to transport the body to the van. I'll be coming with you, as I'll also need to go to HQ."

Finny looked at the men as if to say 'Don't ask any questions,' and headed down into the basement with Nancy. She picked up the evidence from the side and placed it in a small plastic kitchen bag from the drawer.

"Don't take the body through the house. I'll get the driver to bring the van to the back gate for you."

After Nancy had made various practical arrangements with the patiently waiting police officers, she thanked them and stood them down. Back in the house, she went to the kitchen first to retrieve a black dustbin bag before making her way upstairs to her bedroom. Schäfer had been kind enough to leave her clothes in a reasonably neat pile on the bed. Nancy got down on her knees and shuffled inside the closet to take a closer look at the alarm box and safe. There was no damage, but the booby trap would need to be reset. When Schäfer had disconnected the cable labelled 'Remote', two high-strength one-inch bolts automatically dropped from the inside the door into the safe chassis. They were independent of the locking mechanisms, which meant that even if you knew the combination and had the key, the door still wouldn't open. Nancy reconnected all of the cables again, and reset the bolts the way she'd been shown by the manufacturer. After replacing the clothes from the bed onto the closet rail, Nancy undressed and put the clothes and shoes she'd been wearing into the dustbin bag. She would have them incinerated. She put on a pair of trousers, shirt and jumper before making her face and hair more presentable.

Downstairs, the men had done everything she'd asked and were waiting in the black van. She put on a new overcoat from the closet and closed the front door on her way out. The two police officers had gone and managed to take the cleaning van with them. Woodland Rise had finally returned to some form of normality. Nancy got in the back passenger seat and sat behind Finny. A couple of minutes went by without a word being spoken, but the silence was eventually broken by the driver.

"Can you tell me where we are headed, Ma'am?"

"Camberwell Police Station, they'll be expecting us. Once we're finished there, I expect you'll be required to make statements at HQ." The driver looked at Finny who could also feel the looks from the other squad members in the back of his head. Nancy knew what they were all thinking, and as always, silenced the awkwardness with a statement.

"In case any of you were thinking of omitting or covering anything up in your statements, don't. You are to be clear, truthful and consistent in everything you say. For the avoidance of doubt, I shot Florian Schäfer, who was armed, three times when he tried to capture me in my own home. When he was apprehended and tied to the chair, I gave him a sedative. I then asked you all to leave whilst I interrogated him; before he finally succumbed to his injuries – it's that simple."

The men all shrugged... it was no skin off Finny's nose. They had no real jurisdictional powers and they'd all followed orders.

As they continued towards London, Nancy began to feel dull pains on her right elbow and on her back, where she'd been thrown to the floor by her assailant. To take her mind off her injuries, she thought about her future. If Schäfer had found her address, so could someone else, which meant that she was no longer safe. But any moves she made now would have to be considered in the context of how she, her family or network could be leveraged. Nancy also needed to consider a cover story for the information she'd extracted from the man during the brief interrogation. Her cards, as always, would need to be carefully played.

At Camberwell station, the van had been directed through the rear entrance and the body transferred to a small morgue in the basement. The mortuary assistant said that he'd been instructed to keep it on ice until further notice. This was a little concerning. Without control, Nancy's fate was in someone else's hands. It was never a feeling she'd liked, and one that she'd mostly avoided throughout her career. So she kept the bag of clothes with her, rather than hand them over too.

It was getting late by the time they arrived at HQ. After thanking the team for their help, Nancy headed straight to the 11th floor where The Chief was waiting. There was no assistant this time and as soon as she entered his office, The Chief got up from his desk and gave her a reassuring hug. Nancy winced in pain.

"I'm sorry, how silly of me. Are you alright?"

"I'm fine. Just a few bruises where I hit the floor." Nancy reached into her coat pocket and handed the small plastic bag over to The Chief. "Other than what we discussed, I'm not sure what this pertains to, but the transport mechanism seems a little old fashioned to me."

"I agree, but maybe that's the double-bluff. Did you get any other intelligence out of him?"

Whilst in the van on the journey to London, Nancy had been thinking about everything she'd extracted from Schäfer and how it potentially tied into the conversation she'd had with Theo in the pizza restaurant. She decided to take a risk and further implicate Theo – after all, he'd just nearly got her killed.

"He said that Theo was heading back to the Middle-East soon, but he was pretty vague about why. I initially thought it may have been to do with his wives, but I suspect the information hidden in the tooth may throw up something different. There wasn't much else. He was bleeding quite badly and it was hard to keep him conscious. I'm wondering if this also has something to do with the Americans, though."

"How so?" The Chief asked.

"Just something Theo talked about when we met last month. He seems to have a few ties across the Atlantic, including financial ones." The Chief didn't react to this, which Nancy found interesting. *Was it something he already knew about?*

"We had Special Branch pick him and his wife up today so we can ask him. They have them both at Scotland Yard. The Specials also found fake British, Egyptian and Turkish passports, cash, photo-reduction equipment and a bunch of files. We've got people working on that as we speak. But first we need to understand what we have here."

The Chief made a phone call. Five minutes later, there was a knock at the door. "I need a full analysis on the contents of these." He handed the plastic bag to the analyst who'd been retained to work overnight. "Please report as soon as you have something."

"Yes, sir," the analyst said as he left the office.

Nancy decided to address what from her perspective was of greater concern. She'd devoted her entire life so far to The Service and wanted to make sure that she could feel safe for the rest of her retirement. "Can I ask what your intentions are with the body?"

"I'll be honest, Nancy, it's put us in a difficult position. We can't just cremate it and send the ashes back. And when word gets out that Theo's been exposed, Russia will put two and two together. Whichever way we look at it, we're going to get repercussions. Do you have any suggestions?"

The Service was good at 'accident management', so Nancy wondered why he asked the question. She thought for a minute.

"He stole a carpet cleaning van. If the police are still in possession, perhaps we can arrange an accident? It's not perfect, I know, but hopefully there'll be a report of the theft on file to help the timeline."

"That may solve the immediate problem, but we also have to assume that you and your address are now compromised," he said.

Nancy knew exactly what he meant; she'd also given this a great deal of thought on the journey up. Her life in suburban Kent had been a happy one after Stephen died, but she could no longer stay at Woodland Rise and expect to live for very long. She was a blown agent and now understood how Kimberly Montrall would have felt after the incidents in Spain and France.

The Chief let his last statement hang there, as they both looked at one another as if communicating telepathically. Letting a blown agent go was never an easy process, especially one as devoted and experienced as Nancy.

"If I go dark, I'll still need access to the whole family," Nancy said with an air of resignation.

"I'm not sure that's a good idea."

Nancy knew that her delicate position was tenuous. "I think you'll get more out of Lee if I'm still around." The Chief gave a subtle nod. *She's right.* "And what if I told you that I think Lee's sister would be another useful asset for your new programme if directed carefully?" It was Nancy's one last act of desperation.

* * *

CHAPTER 40

THE AFTERMATH

The Chief was weighing up Nancy's usefulness in his mind. He was intrigued by what she proposed but The Service had much more pressing things to attend to that evening. However, even in retirement, she'd been a very loyal and a good asset. In the end he agreed that she could still maintain limited contact with Lee via Debbie and Chris. How she managed the rest of her family was down to her, but David would be off limits and they would discuss Laura at a later time.

Nancy's life as she knew it had come close to disintegrating. Going 'dark' would severely impact her personal life and any professional relationships she still maintained. She asked if she could be present at Theo's interrogation, but The Chief shook his head.

"Other than the ER team and myself, the files will show that Florian Schäfer killed you today."

Nancy's heart skipped momentarily. The reality of the situation had just kicked in. "Will this go to press?" she asked worriedly.

"I think it's entirely likely. I'll give you a day to sort yourself out before going to print. Call me tomorrow from a phone box once you've decided on a plan – use the code word 'Empress'. Only you and I will speak in the future."

Inside, Nancy was devastated, but outside she managed to maintain her demeanour and just agreed with what The Chief had said. What choice was there, really? She would've done exactly the same in his position; it was just crushing to be on the other end of something like this. There would be time to grieve later, but for tonight and tomorrow, she had plans to execute.

The last train from Charing Cross had long since gone, so The Chief paid for Nancy to take a taxi. At just after 11 o'clock the taxi arrived at Century House to take her back home. The driver was happy for the long fare as he lived in Croydon, halfway towards Sevenoaks, which meant that he wouldn't have to come back into London that night. Like most cabbies, he tried to engage Nancy in some harmless chit-chat, but tonight was not the night, and she politely asked him to drive quietly whilst she made furious notes under a vanity light in the back seat. Thirty minutes later she sat back and drew a big sigh. David was all the official family she had left and she wondered what her death would do to his fragile emotional state.

As she immersed herself in ways to shape the wording of a letter to him, the driver cut through her thoughts. "I'll need directions once we get within a few miles of Sevenoaks, love – I know how to get there, but I've never actually been there, if you know what mean?"

Now that she'd ordered her thoughts a little, Nancy was happy to engage in a little conversation as she directed him to the west entrance of Woodland Rise.

"Bit fancy, having your own barrier isn't it?"

Nancy smiled at the man and said, "Don't worry, I'll walk from here." She thanked him, gave him a five-pound tip, and took the black sack of her belongings.

After the driver pulled away, Nancy began the quiet walk home. It was only a third of a mile, but the fresh air would do her good; she expected to be up for most of the night. As she walked along the footpath, she was tempted to add her sack to one of the piles at the end of each neighbour's driveway ready for the morning rubbish collection, but it would be sloppy, and she didn't take the chance.

She entered her home via the back entrance. Once inside, she headed straight to the dining room, lit some kindling on the log fire and stoked it up until the flames radiated enough heat for her to back away. Nancy took each item from the black bag and fed them into the fire one by one. Then she braved the outside cold and went down to the basement, where remnants of her interrogation still lay. She collected the ropes along with anything else that could be burned, and brought them back to the fire in the dining room.

On her second visit, she concentrated on removing all items that would look out of place in any normal garage: drugs, syringe kits, speculum, bullets, gun-cleaning equipment and targets. Everything went in the plastic bag. Then she picked out two large travel cases and took them into the house. She stoked the fire again in the dining room, pressing her hands to the heat and adding another log for good measure. Before heading upstairs she checked that nothing was out of place in the other downstairs rooms. The burgundy address book by the telephone could stay; it didn't contain anything she couldn't leave behind. The hallway by the front porch was a mess, but the cleaners could deal with that as well as the basement.

Upstairs, Nancy removed the entire contents of the safe and placed them on her bed: ninety-five thousand pounds in cash, two cast gold bars, a small envelope containing six uncut diamonds, her black address book, a number of A4 manila files and two envelopes, held together with an elastic band, containing new identifications and a number of document files. Nancy unravelled the elastic band and took out one of the IDs, which she placed on the pillow. As she went through the contents of the files, she placed all of the documents David would need – house deeds, her normal passport, birth, marriage and death certificates, life assurances, some bank books, safe code and her Will – into one file and put everything else into one of the suitcases. The safe she left open, with the key in the lock. Into the cases, she packed enough clothing essentials to get by on, without making it look like anything had been removed from the wardrobes, shoe cupboards and drawers. Nancy looked at her hands. She took off her rings and bracelet and placed them in her jewellery box, but kept her petite gold earrings in. After finishing her packing, she zipped up the cases and carried them out to the top of the stairs. Before descending, Nancy took one last look in every room, each one evoking memories of David or the grandchildren. There was something missing and made a mental note to replace all of the family pictures before she left.

Downstairs, the wood in the fireplace had turned to ashes but still gave off enough heat to be stoked up again with a couple of new logs. From the basement, she retrieved all of the family pictures she'd hidden in a blanket the day before. It took just a few minutes to replace them all around the house. The thought of keeping one circled her mind. *But the dead don't keep mementos.*

Nancy made herself a cup of coffee, took out some writing paper and a pen from the dining room cupboard and sat down at the table. She sighed. This was the letter she thought she'd never have to write. Her eyes welled up as she wrote the final words to her son. Tears fell, smudging the last few words just a little. Nancy pre-dated the letter to May 1977, folded it into a matching envelope and wrote her son's name on the front.

She looked at the wall clock – 2:35am. Thursday was going to be a long day. Nancy needed some sleep before the cleaners arrived. She sealed the letter, doused the fire, switched off the light and went upstairs to bed.

The alarm went off at 6 o'clock as always. The three hours had helped, but Nancy still felt drained. She went downstairs to put the kettle on and make a single phone call to the local taxi service. The car was booked for 6:45, which gave her enough time to get washed, dressed and carry the heavy cases down to the front door. Everything else she needed was placed inside her handbag. There was just enough time to drink a coffee she'd made when the taxi arrived. She'd given the controller instructions on the phone, and the driver flashed his headlights instead of beeping his horn to signal his arrival. He was also good enough to take the bags for her. Nancy hid her keys under the front door mat as the man hoisted the cases into the boot. As they quietly rolled off the driveway, Nancy kept her view forwards; there was no point in looking back.

About ten minutes later, the driver pulled up outside Sevenoaks train station. "That'll be a quid, please, love," the driver said, getting out of the car and opening the boot. He put the cases on the pavement as Nancy gave him the pound note and thanked him.

As he drove away, she didn't head inside. She had a call to make and there was a telephone box twenty yards from the entrance. She dialled the number and rested the two pence piece on the coin slot as she listened for someone to pick up at the other end.

"Hello?" the gruff voice answered.

Nancy pushed the coin into the slot. "Tom, it's Nancy."

C.I. Barnes had been in bed when his phone rang. He immediately sat up when he heard the woman's voice. "It's so good to hear you're OK, but why the pay phone?"

"I need to meet you – I'll explain everything then. Can you get to Sevenoaks train station?"

Tom was a little disturbed but didn't want to ask any unnecessary questions. "Twenty minutes be alright?"

"Thanks, Tom, I'll be waiting in the Station Café just opposite."

Eighteen minutes later, Tom Barnes entered the café dressed in a tracksuit and trainers. He ordered a tea and sat down opposite Nancy, who was nursing her own cup of coffee.

"Thanks for coming at such short notice, Tom; you know I wouldn't ask if it wasn't so important."

C.I. Barnes looked Nancy up and down. There were no discernible marks on her and she looked as demure as always. "What went on yesterday?" he asked. "My lads were a little stumped, to say the least."

"It's the usual answer I'm afraid – I really can't tell you much."

Tom's face was a picture of disappointment, as he shook his head and sighed.

Nancy realised that even though their mutual favours had pretty much evened out over the years, their friendship was also important. "Look, if I do tell you, your career and those of your subordinates will be finished... are you sure you want to know?"

Tom nodded. "I would hope we trust each other by now," he said.

Nancy did trust Tom; so much, that she was about to entrust him with her son's affairs. "Yesterday, a man gained access to my home under the pretence of cleaning my carpets. I suspect it may be leaked that he was a professional burglar. After I got home, he tried to make me show him where I kept the valuables. However, there was a struggle, which resulted in my death." Tom jolted at Nancy's last statement, but she put her hand up to avoid him interrupting. The café owner brought a tea to the table and went back to the counter. "I'm not sure what The Service is going to say about this 'burglar' or if the story is likely to change before it gets to the press. What I want you to know is that whatever the official story is – or is required to be – I need you to go along with it for my sake and my family's. Can you agree to that?" Tom nodded without saying anything. "The real story is that a KGB agent had managed to compromise me through another British agent. I was lucky to be forewarned and he died yesterday at my hands. The Service will be conducting their own investigation as to how and why this happened. In order to save other lives, there is a price to be paid. Nancy Walker must officially die. That's the 'unofficial' version of events and all I can say." Nancy slid an addressed A4 envelope under the base of the table towards Tom, which he accepted. "Inside that envelope is everything my son, David, will need to wrap up my affairs once The Service has announced my death. All I ask of you is to make sure that he gets everything and is guided sensibly to not ask too many questions. You never know, I may need to contact you at some point in the future. Will you do this for me?"

"Of course. Am I likely to be contacted about what happened to you, or should I just keep my eyes peeled in the national press?" he asked.

Nancy shrugged. "Right now, I don't know how things are going to be dealt with. The one thing I do know is that Nancy Walker's death will need to be officially publicised and David will need to be informed by someone." She passed another smaller envelope under table to Tom. Without needing to look at it, Tom knew what this was. There wasn't a cop worth his salt who didn't know what a stack of notes felt like. "That's for any inconvenience you may have to go through," Nancy said.

Tom went to push the money back towards her as if he didn't want to accept it, but she just put her hand up again with finality. Tom nodded in compliance and put the envelope in his trouser pocket. Nancy's left hand was resting on the plastic tablecloth when Tom put his free hand on top and gave it a squeeze.

"Am I allowed to know your new name and where you're headed?"

Nancy shook her head, glanced at her watch and stood up. "Stay for a little while, Tom. You may've seen a ghost, but at least it was a friendly one." She put on her coat and picked up the two suitcases that she'd wedged by the entrance.

Tom gave a subtle wave and watched as Nancy Walker exited his life for the last time.

At the station she bought a newspaper and ticket to London, boarding the first train to go her way. She was lucky to find a seat during the busy commuting time and a kind gentleman helped put her suitcases on the overhead rack. Nancy had a feeling that the man wanted to engage in further conversation, but she just smiled politely and opened her paper. There was still much to think about. Memories came flooding back of her first ever train journey alone, lugging what felt like a whole wardrobe to her digs after being accepted at Cambridge. At the age of sixty-five, she had never imagined she'd feel that way again. A sense of unease and trepidation lingered in the back of her mind.

In London, she hailed a cab and made her way to the Midland Bank main branch in the city, where she closed two savings accounts totalling four thousand pounds. With that done, she walked outside to the nearest telephone box and made the call.

"It's Empress calling," she said to The Chief's assistant.

"I'll put you straight through," the voice replied. Nancy listened to see if the assistant conveyed anything else in her voice, but if she did have any feelings, the woman was well trained at hiding them.

"How are you holding up?" The Chief said.

"I'm alright. I didn't expect this level of change at my age."

"I'm genuinely sorry about that, but there are so many moving parts to protect."

"I understand. I would've done the same. The place is ready for cleaning. Keys are under the front door mat. The whole of the downstairs will need to be done and there's a basement under the water fountain in the back garden that will need to be sanitised. What's the story going to be?"

"We've located the stolen vehicle, so it's going to be manslaughter at the house during what was thought to be a burglary gone wrong, followed by a police chase resulting in the man's death through dangerous driving. We've managed to enlist some help from our domestic friends."

"And what about our friend from the *Daily Mail*?" Nancy said with a harder edge. The Chief sighed briefly. She knew she wasn't going to like this answer.

"Because of the information you provided, we still need to keep him in play... for now at least. I know it's not what you want to hear, but all I can say is that we *will* resolve everything – I promise." Nancy knew that The Chief couldn't go into any more detail and it would be wrong for her to push the subject any further, even though from a personal level, she wanted to know everything.

"What protocol do you want me to use to make contact with my grandson?"

"Use the same as you used today in the first instance. We'll make contact with the family first to advise them on the situation. Can you give it a couple of weeks before calling? We need to let things settle down... I imagine you've got a fair bit to sort out yourself?" he said with raised intonation. He knew Nancy wouldn't reveal where she was heading, but hung the bait out anyway.

"I do indeed," she said. "And thank you... for everything."

"We'll speak again, Empress," The Chief said remorsefully, before ending the call.

Nancy took her notebook from her bag and crossed out another couple of tasks from her list. Apart from finding somewhere to live, everything else had now been done. She had an idea of where she wanted to go, but just needed to jot down a few new items before making the next leg of her journey. Nancy desperately wanted to add Theo to the new list, but she had to trust that The Chief's plans were valid and that he'd find a way to make things right in the end.

She looked at her watch; it was still before 10 o'clock. Nancy flagged down another taxi. The driver was a little terse and didn't even bother to help with her bags – and therefore didn't receive a tip.

The journey took her to the National Safe Deposit Company in Queen Victoria Street, where a man was pleased to open an account for her and where she then deposited all of the valuables and documentation she'd been carrying around London that morning. She kept three thousand pounds for herself and hailed another taxi from outside the main entrance. "Old Gloucester Street, please," she said to the more helpful driver.

On arrival, Nancy buzzed the door of No.27 and was let in without the need to identify herself on the intercom. British Monomarks was a postal service that could offer her the absolute privacy and discretion that she now needed. Whilst it was Nancy Walker who entered the building, it was Vivienne Cooper who completed the application and paid the receptionist a year in advance with cash. It took less than twenty minutes to set up a mail collection and storage service, at what would now be her new official London address in Old Gloucester Street, W1.

Vivienne wrote the address in her notebook and took three address cards before asking the lady at reception to call her another taxi. From W1, the driver took her to Paddington station. Even though it was a relatively short journey, she was more than happy to engage the man in conversation; it was a great way for her to acclimatise to her new persona.

Like most British Rail stations in London, Paddington was a filthy place to be – even if you were just passing through. The moment Vivienne walked inside and onto the concourse, she could feel the oppressiveness of the diesel smog in her lungs. The once-elegant arched metal and brickwork was covered in thick soot and looked as though it hadn't been cleaned since the station was built. The unions and successive governments were all to blame for the decline in investment. She made two quick calls to confirm a place to stay before purchasing a one-way ticket to Windsor. This was a city location with plenty to offer; she could hide in plain sight or find somewhere to live remotely. There were nice rural walks, but it also had the advantage of being close to Lee and the M25 for Laura. She bought a magazine and boarded the next available train.

The Castle Hotel was just a ten-minute walk from the train station. Even though it was only lunchtime, the few hours of sleep she'd had, coupled with lugging two heavy suitcases around London, had taken their toll. After checking in for an indefinite period to a lovely room at the back of the building, Vivienne put the '*Do not disturb*' sign on the door, lay on the bed, and slept.

* * *

Back at Woodlands Rise, the cleaners visited the former home of Nancy Walker. Outside, two police cars sat parked by the driveway, whilst the entire front entrance had been cordoned off with tarpaulin sheets. Two Special Branch officers stood guard, whilst two others canvassed and took statements from the local neighbours, including the lady opposite.

Inside, the cleaners had been through the house, tipping chairs, smashing things, pulling everything out of cupboards as well as removing valuables like Nancy's jewellery box. Two bullets were removed from the walls in the main hallway with the holes then hit with a hammer to disguise their original size. Crime scene photos were taken whilst another scene was being staged in the dining room using an actress. A woman with uncannily similar looks and size to Nancy changed into clothing from her wardrobe before being made up to look severely bloodied, bruised and disfigured. The final set of pictures was taken before the basement was sterilised and checked with a fine-tooth comb. Blood stains and signs of a struggle were left in the dining room, as well as other places around the house. The telephone had rung three times, but the specialists simply ignored the sound and continued the work they'd been tasked with. By 2 o'clock they'd finished and were off the scene, although two police officers remained conspicuous outside.

At Sevenoaks police station, Tom Barnes was visited by Inspector Brand from Special Branch. After his early morning meeting in the café, Tom knew it would only be a matter of time. One day after the incident they came with a prepared file in hand. *These guys were efficient, that's for sure.*

Knowing he had a previous relationship with the 'deceased' made things a lot easier and they went over each document in detail to familiarise him with what was now the 'official report' on what happened to Nancy Walker on 29th March 1978.

Tom Barnes had two big questions. "Who's dealing with all of the funeral arrangements and how are you going to explain the lack of a body to her son?"

The senior officer responded calmly. "We'll oversee the arrangements, but we'd like you to deal with the son to make sure he doesn't... overreact."

"So you want me to deliver the bad news, is that what you're saying?"

The Special nodded.

Barnes gave him a derisory look. "And what if he needs proof of his mother's death?"

"An actress was used for the crime scene pictures, and when they're added to the file they'll be gruesome enough to make anyone's stomach churn. We should have them by tomorrow. We *hope* that you'll be able to convince the son not to want to view or identify the body."

"And if he still insists?" Barnes asked.

"If the worst comes to the worst we can delay with a post mortem and get the actress to play her part again. But that's an extremely tricky operation that should be avoided. Do you know the son?"

"No, I've not met him before – so I have no way of knowing how he'll react."

"Then I think it will be better to be armed with the pictures before you speak to him," Brand said. "I'll have them on your desk first thing tomorrow morning. We need to get this thing wrapped up ASAP, so you'll have to break the news to him tomorrow too. Here's my card. Call me after you've spoken to him – there are people high up who want to know which way the wind's going to blow on this one."

"I'll do my best," Barnes answered. It was disconcerting to know how similarly the east and west governments could act at times. If he hadn't been so deeply involved, Tom wouldn't have believed that the British government could participate in such an immoral deception. After the Specials left, he read through the file again and wrote a couple of lines in his notebook as an aide-memoire for breaking the news to David.

On Friday 31st, C.I. Barnes arrived at the station early, as usual – he always liked to be at work by 7:30, just to show the troops what was expected. His assistant gave him a sealed envelope as soon as he arrived. He opened it in his office and took out the pictures. He was amazed at how similar the actress resembled Nancy. The men he saw yesterday hadn't been kidding about how horrific the pictures were made to look. What he saw in front of him was barbaric. A female victim, aged between 60 and 70, with severe trauma to the head and neck. The woman's jaw and left eye socket looked broken, covered in blood. A ligature had been pulled extremely tightly around the neck, showing what looked like haemorrhaging and bruising underneath. The images all looked plausible but Barnes wanted to put them to the test. He put them back in the envelope, went downstairs and located the man he was looking for.

"Inspector."

"Sir?"

"Do you remember that private little job you did last year helping that old lady to get a forwarding address from a landlord in town?" Barnes sat down at the man's desk.

"Sure, me and Constable Jones – is there a problem?" Inspector Gray said defensively.

"Can you get Jones now? There's something I need to ask you both." A few minutes later the three of them were all seated around Gray's desk, the two subordinates nervously wondering what this was about.

For the sake of Jones, C.I. Barnes repeated the question he'd asked Gray a few minutes ago.

"I'd like you to look at these," he said, pulling the large-form pictures from the A4 envelope. "Is this her?"

Jones, who'd been with the police for two years, recoiled – whereas Gray was seasoned and focused on analysis of the pictures.

"Yep, I'd say so wouldn't you, Jones?" he said.

Jones inhaled deeply. "Yes, Guv."

"What's all this about, sir?" the inspector asked. "I assume she's dead? Was she local?"

"I can't really say at this moment. I just wanted to get a second opinion that's all."

"Well, we're sorry for your loss there, sir... she was a friend, right?"

Barnes could feel the inspector digging deeper than he felt comfortable with. "Thank you, Inspector, that'll be all." He nodded to Jones and left Gray's desk to head back upstairs. Back in his office, Barnes sat behind his desk – contemplating his next move. Special Branch had insisted that this be wrapped up as soon as possible, but all he had for David was the home address Nancy had written on the envelope she'd given him. No telephone number or work address. He asked his assistant to find every David Walker in the telephone book. There were only three and none corresponded to the address in his possession. He had no choice and prepared to visit David's address himself. The clock showed 7:55. The man could still be in for all he knew, so he told his assistant to rearrange all of his morning meetings and left the station with the now complete file.

* * *

Vivienne stirred, still dressed in the previous day's clothes. She looked at the digital clock/radio by the side of the bed. It was 6:01am... *had she imagined the noise by the door?* She got up and looked through the peephole, but no one was in the hallway. She opened the door to find four neatly stacked newspapers which she duly placed on the bed. Hunger gnawed at her stomach, but before leaving the room for breakfast, she desperately needed a relaxing bath. Forty-five minutes later she was checking through each paper thoroughly. Nothing! No news of her or anyone like her, or Schäfer for that matter. She desperately wanted to pick up the phone to call David – to somehow apologise for everything she was about to put him through, but she looked in the mirror and reprimanded herself. *Get a grip on yourself!*

Vivienne left the '*Do Not Disturb*' sign on the door whilst she went downstairs to eat. The Castle hotel certainly had plenty of choice, but knowing she might be there for a few months, Vivienne didn't overdo her intake. French toast, marmalade and Earl Grey tea were enough to rejuvenate her for the day ahead.

* * *

David had tried telephoning his mother a few times in the week without success. It wasn't unusual for her to be out now and again, but he'd tried at different times during the day on Wednesday and Thursday without success. But today was different. When he tried calling whilst getting ready for work, the line was dead, which was a little disconcerting – but not unheard of. The GPO were never that good at installing or fixing telephone lines, so he made up his mind to pop in to see his mum after work.

He looked at his watch; it was 8:15 and time to leave. After locking the front door, he got in his car and was about reverse out of the shared driveway when another car pulled up behind him. David bibbed the horn, but the car didn't move. Instead the driver switched the engine off. This was annoying; he was going to be late. David stepped out of the car and walked back towards the other driver who had just opened his own door. David subdued his initial reaction when he saw the driver.

"Do you mind moving? I've got to get to work," he said.

As Tom Barnes got out of the car, he put on his cap purely out of instinct. He was sure this was David; he could see a resemblance to Nancy in the man's eyes. He couldn't believe his luck. "David Walker?" he asked.

"Yes, what's the problem officer?" David replied, confused.

Barnes needed to be careful. He didn't want to cause a scene out in the open. "Don't worry, you've not done anything wrong – but I would like to speak with you about a private matter if you wouldn't mind. My name is Chief Inspector Tom Barnes." He closed and locked his car door, which indicated to David that he had little choice in the matter.

David showed the man in and walked upstairs to his apartment, which was the entire top floor of a converted house. "I need to call work to tell them I'm going to be late," he said, ushering Barnes over to the sofa.

However, Tom needed to maximise the effect on David. "Do you mind if we sit at the table?" he said, indicating the small dining table at the rear of the living room. "It's much easier on the back at my age. I think it's best that we talk first before you call your employer; I'm sure they'll be understanding."

David felt uneasy now. *Had something happened at work? Was he unwittingly part of an investigation?* He sat nervously at one end of the table as Barnes sat in the middle position and placed the closed file in front of him. David tried to work out what was inside, but there was nothing written or typed on the front. It was just a blank file.

Barnes hesitated briefly, before exhaling a long breath. Everyone hated this part of the job. "David. There's no easy way for me to say this, so I'm just going to tell you what I have to tell you. I just need you to remain calm if you can."

David was now on high alert. This didn't make him calm at all – in fact, he was now more agitated than ever.

"David, two days ago a man broke into your mother's home."

David immediately froze, eyes widened. "Is she alright? Where is she?" He wanted answers immediately.

Barnes continued. He knew he mustn't be derailed. "We believe he was a burglar, or that was his intention anyway..."

David cut in again. "Where is she? Where's my mother? I need to make sure she's OK!"

Barnes tried to remain calm again. "David. Your mother walked in on the man... who was armed..."

Calm hadn't worked and David's anger and impetuousness got the better of him. In the blink of an eye, he reached over for file in front of the chief inspector and tried to grasp it... pulling it towards him. Barnes was just a little too slow to react and only just caught the front of the file. In the instant that David pulled, the front cover between Barnes's fingers curled back revealing the black and white scene-of-crime photographs. David couldn't help but look... it was human nature. But within an instant, he'd wished he hadn't. There, sprawled all over the table were pictures of his bloodied, bruised and beaten mother... he instantly recognised her face and clothes. David's eyes welled up and he immediately retched and vomited, just missing the table.

Barnes wasn't sure what to do to comfort the man and instead, pulled all the documents back into the file. He wanted to spare David the pain of seeing them again, but crucially, didn't want them examined too closely. Barnes got up and took a cup from the side, filling it with tap water. He offered it to David, but the man wasn't interested. He just lent forward with his hands over his eyes, crying like he'd never cried before. Barnes felt for what David was going through in that moment. He wondered how heartless Nancy could truly be to allow her own flesh and blood to suffer like this. There was no way he could do the same thing to his own wife, or children if he'd had any. He put a consoling arm on David's shoulder. David didn't shrug it off; he just continued to shudder in shock.

"I think it might be best if I call your employer, David," Barnes said. "Is that alright with you?"

David didn't give a damn about work. He'd lost dad years ago which he didn't think had affected him. He'd only just started to get over the loss of Lee and now he'd lost his mother – the bedrock of his entire existence. *What was the point in living now?*

"Who should I call?" Barnes continued.

David stood up quickly enough to surprise the chief inspector, but there was no malice intended; he just wanted the man in uniform to go away. He didn't need to pick up his address book; David just dialled the number and said "Ask for the office," before walking over to the front of the apartment where he stared blankly out of the window.

Tom passed on the news of David's bereavement.

David had had time to think and after Barnes put the phone down, he asked: "Have you caught the burglar?"

"I know it's no consolation, but he's also dead. Got what he deserved if you ask me."

David turned to face the chief inspector, his eyes red and sore. "How?"

"Police responded to the burglar alarm. There was a car chase where he ended up crashing the car he'd stolen and killing himself. Normally we don't let the public read police case files, but I was a friend of your mother's... do you want to read this if I remove the pictures?"

David hesitated. He wasn't sure whether he wanted to know more or less about what had happened. Images flowed across his mind like the flicker of a film projector. In the end he agreed.

Initially, David paced up and down as he read, but Barnes suggested he sit down; psychologically, people's reactions were calmer when they were seated. David sat on the sofa and Barnes got a chair from the dining table and brought it over to be near him... he wasn't kidding about his back troubles.

As David pored over the report, key phrases imprinted on his mind. '*Three shots to the chest*', '*hit with a blunt weapon multiple times to the face*', '*broken fingers*', '*strangulation*' and '*cause of death yet to be determined*'. He felt sick and his hand shook when he handed the papers back to the chief inspector.

"I'm sorry, David." Barnes said. David looked at him, but said nothing. The chief inspector was nervous. He really didn't know how David would react to what he was going to say next. "This is hard for me to say, David, but there is the matter of formally identifying your mother's body?" Barnes watched the words sink in, as David's eyes welled up again and his head bowed.

"I'm not sure I can face it, seeing my mother... like that... I couldn't even do it for Lee."

Barnes knew what had happened to Lee, but chose to keep David focused. He sighed in sorrow and sympathy. "It's not a pleasant thing to have to do; the memories stay with you for life." Barnes wanted to see if the man would look for an easier way out before making any suggestion to him.

David's chest hurt as he sat in thought. "You said you were a friend of my mum's?"

"I always will be, David," Barnes said softly.

"Have you seen her body?" David asked.

It was an odd question and one that caught Barnes off guard. He didn't like lying but he could stretch the truth a little. He had seen her body... it was just that it was alive when he last saw it. "Yes, David. Why do you ask?"

"Would you be able to identify the body on my behalf? I just don't think I want to see her that way. It was bad enough seeing the photos and the report."

"Well, it's not usual for this to happen, but you are entitled to appoint someone else to identify a next-of-kin or relative in these circumstances. Is that what you would like to do?"

"It feels like you've already done it, so I suppose there's no need to go through it again?" David said.

Barnes nodded slowly. "Could you do me a favour, David, and write your request on a sheet of paper and sign it to that effect? It just covers me personally and means that all of the other funeral formalities can proceed normally."

David got up and walked over towards the table, pulled out a writing pad from a nearby drawer and wrote as the chief inspector had asked. He signed the note, tore off the page and handed it to Tom.

Barnes read it and put the note in the file, his pulse rate reducing with every breath. "Once your mother's body is formally identified and the coroner has completed the autopsy, I'll have an officer contact you with regard to releasing everything for a funeral. I'm not too sure what your mother's last wishes were, but I have some important documents in the car that I managed to retrieve from the house for you. Would you like to come downstairs to get them?"

David felt exhausted. He agreed soullessly and followed Barnes outside to his car.

After handing over the A4 envelope of Nancy's documents, Barnes took David's phone number and gave him his own. "Call my office if you need anything. Are you going to be OK?" David didn't have an answer to that question; he just shrugged and walked back into his apartment.

Tom Barnes reversed and pulled away from David's address. It was a sick business Nancy had been in, still was in for all he knew.

Inside, David walked around the apartment like a purposeless zombie. Eventually, he cleaned up the mess he'd made on the carpet by the table, pulled the curtains and went back to bed. His mind churned with possible ways of killing himself.

Back in his office, C.I. Barnes made the call back to Special Branch. "It's done. I've been round and broken the news. He's asked me to identify the body which, as far as I am concerned, I've officially done as of this call. It's now over to your bods to sort everything out regarding follow-ups and funeral arrangements."

"Thank you, Chief Inspector Barnes, my boss will be glad to hear the situation is now clear. We'll be in touch." After clicking off the phone with C.I. Barnes, Inspector Brand began putting his fast-track plans in motion.

* * *

CHAPTER 41

MASSETTE

Vivienne finished writing the letter in her hotel room using a set of blank stationery she'd purchased that morning. Even though 'Nancy Walker' had officially retired years ago as far as MI6 were concerned, 'Massette', her alter-ego, still remained active in Europe and further afield – acting as a conduit for people or organisations that needed special contractor services. Her black address book was one of the most valuable in the industry... if you knew how to use it. It was definitely something governments would kill for, which made her wonder whether this was what Schäfer had been looking for all along and whether Massette was also compromised.

The letter had been carefully written in a straddling chequerboard code, where only she and the recipient had the decryption key. Providing they both used the same key to encrypt and decrypt, the message could be understood. Vivienne had a different key for each and every operative in her black book, and thumbed 'A' for '*Angel*'. The note was simple:

PO BOX 777
27 OLD GLOUCESTER STREET
LONDON W1
ANGEL
HAVE NEED FOR YOUR SERVICES.
TWO TARGETS. KLOSTERMARIENBERG AUSTRIA.
LILLIAN AND LUKAS SCHAFER.
CONFIRM ACCEPTANCE, PRICE, TERMS.
MASSETTE

She placed the letter in an envelope, addressed it to a mailbox destination in Switzerland and put the letter in her handbag.

Downstairs, she approached the hotel receptionist. "Do you have a Yellow Pages I can look at, please?" The lady duly handed her the two-inch thick book, and Vivienne thumbed through various sections. Not quite finding what she was looking for, she asked the receptionist to call for a taxi.

"There should be one just outside, madam – there's usually one waiting."

Vivienne thanked the woman and walked out to the waiting cab. "Do you know where I can find a group of reputable car dealerships?" she asked.

The taxi driver raised an eyebrow and smiled. "I can take you to some dealerships, but I wouldn't trust them as far as I could throw 'em."

Vivienne smiled back. At least the guy had some integrity. "Where would you go if you were me?" she asked.

"It all depends on what you're looking for and what your budget is, I guess."

"Well, something safe, reliable and not too old, if that's any help?"

The driver thought for a minute. "There are few places on the way to Slough if you want to take a look there?"

"That sounds fine with me. Can I borrow you for the morning – off the meter?"

The driver smiled again. This was definitely a much better proposition than sitting around. "Twenty-quid?" he suggested eagerly.

Vivienne raised her own eyebrow. "Alright, but for that I'll be requiring your mechanical and negotiating skills as well."

"I'll do my best, madam. Hop in – your carriage awaits."

That morning the driver took Vivienne to three different dealers. The choice was finally reduced to two cars: a VW Golf and a Volvo 240 DL saloon, each used and priced similarly. The taxi driver said it came down to what her priorities were in terms of safety, fuel consumption and resale value. Colour also came into it for Vivienne; she needed something that would blend in with all the browns, reds and golds that she saw on the roads these days . But there was one thing that the dealer had said that stuck with her. "No one will go near you on the road in the Volvo – it's built like a battering ram and the other guy'd always come out worse off in an accident." After some fierce haggling by the taxi driver, Vivienne eventually decided on the burgundy Volvo.

It wouldn't have been the driver's first choice, but at least the woman would be safe, if not as stylish as she looked. His eyes stuck out like saucers when she pulled out the large envelope of notes from her bag.

Vivienne and the taxi driver parted ways at the dealership, driving off the forecourt in different directions. Back in Windsor, Vivienne parked her car at the hotel and used the rest of the day to familiarise herself more with her surroundings. For now, she had to pass the time until her story broke.

* * *

CHAPTER 42

DIVIDE AND CONQUER

What happens to a spy who appears to be playing two super-powers off against each other under the auspices of Her Majesty's government? Theo Greaves and his wife, Janet, had been arrested and had already been held separately at Scotland Yard for thirty-two hours. Theo knew when he signed up for the job that the powers-that-be could hold him indefinitely, but he hated the idea that Janet should suffer the consequences of his decision making. When questioned the first time, he'd said nothing, dismissing the evidence that the police found at his address as 'tools of the trade'.

The interview had only been thirty minutes, but it was just a taste of what was to come. The police hadn't shown their hand because operatives were still carrying out another deeper search of his home. When they found additional listening equipment built into the walls, he was questioned again, this time for two hours.

Having had time to think between interrogations, Theo suspected that their incarceration was something to do with Schäfer; *had the man been picked up and talked?* Clearly something had happened – *perhaps to do with Nancy?* He'd given Schäfer her name and telephone number. *If the man had gone after her, maybe he'd been made? Had Nancy figured out who he was? She was clever.* Theo decided to hold firm with his story – after all, it was in the training manual; what did they expect? Thoughts swirled around his mind for hours after the police questioning, the most critical being how he would protect his position. But Janet was a lever they could use against him. If only he could speak or get a message to her somehow. But at times of national security, the normal custody rules would be thrown out of the window. They could do whatever they wanted with her. He'd asked to see her, to make sure she was being treated fairly; but all requests were denied. He requested a lawyer at least five times, but neither he nor Janet were given permission to seek counsel. One of the secretaries at the branch had posed as Janet Greaves and called the news desk at the *Daily Mail* to tell them that Theo needed time off for a bereavement, so, for all intents and purposes, no one knew they were there.

Janet Greaves didn't really understand what was going on when the police first questioned her. She kept asking why she'd been detained without a good reason, seeing as she'd not been charged with anything. The Chief had been kept fully updated and during her second interview, the police revealed what had been found at the house. Signs of distress began to show when the nightmare hit that her sweet, enigmatic husband could be considered a spy. The police still weren't sure at this stage that they weren't a partnership in more ways than marriage, and so focused their attention on why many of the bank and share certificates were in her name, as well as probing her further about her husband's movements and trips abroad.

Things didn't look good for Theo. In fact, things were looking bad for MI6 and Great Britain as a nation, given the information they had from Schäfer's tooth. The documents contained in the microdots showed Israeli plans to infiltrate Syria and plant booby-trapped mines that would be activated by nuclear transmitters. The transmitters were connected or to be connected to the telephone cable between Damascus and Amman. This in itself wasn't the real issue. After all, the countries in the Middle East continued their tit-for-tat disputes almost on a daily basis. The real issue was that the nuclear material and transmitters were provided by the Americans. If this came to light, especially to the KGB, the USSR would see this as the US meddling in the region again. Not that Moscow was innocent on that front either. But for an area of the world that had been in continuous conflict for nearly four-thousand years, the United Nations didn't need another reason for the Russians to supply more arms to the Palestinians. From the dates and film evidence, the plan should have already been executed by now, but confirmation would ultimately be needed to test the validity of the information.

With this evidence in hand, MI6 and Special Branch knew they really had to turn the screws on the two suspects. In the same routine as before, Janet was taken from her detention cell and escorted to an interview room via a route that wouldn't bring her into any contact with Theo. Inspector Brand and Sergeant Rhodes, the two officers she'd spoken with previously, arrived shortly afterwards and greeted her with the usual pleasantries. There was only one difference this time – they had the extra pressure of The Chief of MI6 watching everything from behind the medium-sized two-way mirror in the interview room.

Like Theo, Janet had been stripped of her watch when she'd been processed into custody. There was no natural daylight in her cell or in the interview room; fluorescent lighting was constant at all times, so her best guess was that it was in the afternoon.

"Hello Janet, I trust you have been treated alright?" Brand said, as he and Rhodes sat down at the table opposite.

It wasn't really a question but Janet still complained. "No, not really. I've been given food, but I need a bath and a change of clothes. I haven't done anything wrong and you haven't charged me. Even I know that that you're not allowed to hold anyone this long, especially as you haven't even let me see my husband or a solicitor. I'm not going to say any more to you unless you either let me go, let me see my husband or provide me with a solicitor." She folded her arms and pursed her lips; she meant business.

Brand had seen it all before and showed no signs of being discouraged. He'd always been pleasant and straightforward with Mrs. Greaves and felt that they'd at least built up a level of mutual respect.

"You know what, Janet, I totally agree with you. Honestly, I'd hate to have been put in the position you're in at the moment; so I'm going to be clear and straight with you. Right now we have a whole heap of evidence that points to either your husband or both of you being regarded as traitors to Her Majesty and that will result in charges under the Treason Act. Surprisingly enough, it's the one conviction that can still be punished by the death penalty in this country, although most sentences are usually between ten and twenty-five years' imprisonment. We're going to talk to you about what we now know and I would strongly implore you to help us put the jigsaw pieces together, because this will help you, I promise. It might even help your husband, but that will be your choice as we talk. Does that sound fair enough to you?"

"Well if you're trying to scare me, you're not," she said adamantly. "Because unless you have something to charge me with, I know you'll have to let me go eventually."

"You're correct Janet, but any decision on what to charge you with lies with the man sitting behind that glass to your left and a judge who will go by his recommendation. I'd rather not let that situation happen; I'm just informing you of the seriousness. As I said, if we can present what we have and open a dialogue, I think it could have a positive impact on you both. Is that OK?"

Janet looked over to her left. Brand could see the woman trying to see past her own reflection, like all interviewees. They never could, but it always gave him a measure of the person in front of him.

Janet turned back to face him. "OK, but I'm not promising anything."

Brand nodded as Sergeant Rhodes opened the file and passed a sheet of paper to Brand.

"So I'm just going to go over what we've discussed to date."

Janet tutted. "You've already done that and I told you I didn't know anything about anything twice before."

"I know, Janet, but this I need to keep everything in context for the person making the decision, and we'll come to the new evidence very soon, I promise." Brand talked about the bugs found hidden in the walls of their home, the confidential files the police had found in their study, stacks of cash and share certificates for US technology companies, all in her name, and the fake passports – one of which had her picture and a similar date of birth. He didn't waver as he read through the list; he wanted The Chief to assess the woman's subconscious behaviour. "Is there anything you want to say about what we found before I continue?" Brand asked.

"Like I said before, I didn't know anything about that stuff – I only go into Theo's study to clean sometimes."

"And you're saying that Theo never discussed why you might need a fake passport or why you have share certificates in your name, and you never saw anything to raise your awareness whilst you were cleaning?"

Janet knew about the share certificates because her husband had shown them to her. But he'd said that he'd put them in her name for tax reasons, so as far as she was concerned, he was just following sound financial advice. It certainly had nothing to do with spying, so she remained unforthcoming on the matter. "I'm saying that the equipment could've been in the walls before we moved into the house for all I know, and there's nothing against the law about having cash or share certificates as far as I'm aware," she reiterated.

Brand nodded. "And the passports and confidential files?" he said, noting what she'd conveniently omitted.

"I don't know anything about them, as I said before. My husband's a journalist, so maybe they were something to do with a story he was writing?"

Brand could see that the woman was beginning to change her tune slightly from the previous interviews. *Was she trying to protect her husband, or herself?* Whatever her motives, he sensed a chink in her armour. Brand decided not to linger and pushed on. "So, I said we'd come on to the new evidence quite quickly – tell me, do you recognise this man?" Rhodes passed over a picture Florian Schäfer and put it in front of the woman, whilst Brand watched her eyes.

Janet looked at the picture. Her eyes darted downwards before she looked back at Brand. "No, should I?" she said matter-of-factly.

"We believe Theo does. Did you know that he is a KGB agent, Janet?" Brand waited. He wanted to see whether her reaction would be normal or forced. Janet remained stoic, her face not registering a reaction.

"We have reason to believe that Theo has been passing information between the USA and the USSR, which is why we found the cash and why you have shares in your name. He's using his position to play a very lethal game, Mrs. Greaves. I can't tell you everything, but the information we think your husband passed on could lead to a war in the Middle East and have further much more far-reaching consequences."

Janet began rubbing her fingers together in nervousness. She caught herself and put her hands on her lap, where the two officers couldn't see them.

Brand continued; he really wanted to press his advantage. "And Theo's actions have led to two deaths in the last five days, one of which was a murder." Brand gave a subtle look left to Rhodes, who opened the file again and passed over the crime scene pictures of Nancy Walker. "This poor, innocent sixty-five-year-old lady was killed on Wednesday because of your husband." Janet recoiled slightly at the horrifying images put in front of her. "I'm sorry to have to show you these, Janet, but as you can see – this isn't just about passing on a little bit of harmless information anymore; people are being murdered. British citizens are being killed and we can't allow that. If a war breaks out in the Middle East, more innocent people will die. There will also be severe diplomatic repercussions for this country, which could actually lead to more British deaths... they always do." He let his words sink in and watched Janet react. She began to lose a little colour in her face, but Brand was not prepared to give her a break to compose herself.

Janet pushed the pictures of Nancy away, not wishing to be exposed to them anymore, and thought seriously about her position and her relationship with Theo.

Brand slid the picture of Schäfer back in front of Janet. "Do you know this man, Janet?" he asked again. "This man killed the pensioner you've just seen."

Even though Janet was in two minds about whether to say anything, she still shook her head and denied knowing him.

Brand had conducted enough interviews in his life to know when he was close to a revelation. He knew the woman was on the precipice; he just needed to tip her over the edge. He signalled again to Rhodes who took two separate piles of papers out of the file, each with a black and white photo clipped to the top right-hand edge. Brand unclipped one of the file images. "Do you know or have you ever seen this woman before, Janet?"

The woman shook her head again. "No…?" She was genuinely puzzled.

By the way she reacted this time, Brand knew she'd definitely been lying before. He took the second picture from Rhodes. "How about this woman, do you know or have you ever seen this woman before?"

"No, I haven't. Should I have?" she enquired.

"The first woman is from Egypt and her name was Chione Tarek-Amin. The second woman is from Turkey and her original name, before she got married, was Kadri Özmen. But they now both have something in common. They're both now married to your husband."

It was like watching a perfectly decent building being hit with a wrecking ball. Janet's face contorted in such a way that neither Brand nor Rhodes knew quite what the woman would do next. All colour left on her face ebbed away. As she started to shake, her eyes began to well up. Brand asked Rhodes to go and fetch some tissues and a beaker of water for Mrs. Greaves. Two minutes later, Janet finally had something to wipe her tear-stained eyes with; her three-day-old mascara leaving black river deltas on her now stressed face. Brand put Schäfer's picture in front of the woman again. He wanted her to know that he hadn't bought her previous denials. "Now tell me, Janet, have you seen this man before?"

Janet Greaves had had enough. She was tired, she'd been cooped up for days trying to defend her husband who all this time had been leading a triple life. *I'm not going down for that bastard!* She couldn't do this anymore. She didn't want to be embroiled in wars or murders. She thought for a few seconds before finally answering. "Yes, I have seen him before."

It was just the breakthrough Brand wanted. He gave himself a mental celebratory pat on the back, but remained poker-faced. "Please, tell me more?" he encouraged.

Mrs. Greaves wiped her eyes once more and fought to regain her composure. "If I tell you what I know, I need to know what you can do for me?"

"*Shit!*" Brand thought. He was close to getting a confession and this woman now wanted to barter! "Mrs. Greaves, do you realise how serious this matter is?" he said, losing his cool.

"Yes, I do realise how serious this is, Officer. Serious enough to know that it's my husband you really want, not me. Especially given the information I have. I'm just a casualty in all this."

Brand was annoyed and it showed. He looked over to the mirror on his right and then looked back at Janet Greaves. He'd underestimated her. Brand readjusted his tie knot to reset himself. "I'll need to speak with the boss, Janet, but I tell you now, if he thinks you're stringing us along, he's likely to prosecute you as an accomplice to your husband."

Brand got up and walked out of the interview room to the adjacent viewing room.

Janet Greaves finally caught sight of herself in the mirror as her head motioned left to the imaginary steps she thought it would take Brand to arrive next door. She'd taken a big risk by trying to bargain, but if her marriage was over – and it was sure as hell going to be over – she needed to have some way to start her life again.

"What do you think, sir?" Brand asked as he entered the viewing room.

With a wave of one hand The Chief instructed the stenographer who was also sat in the room to stop transcribing. "You've done a good job so far..."

"Brand, sir – Inspector."

"Well, Brand, what's your instinct on her; is she playing us?"

"I've been thinking about that, sir. I think she knew about the passports and possibly the files. But if the wives thing was an act, she should definitely be on television. Is she an agent in her own right? That remains to be seen. We've certainly never had a whiff of her before."

"We didn't get a whiff of Theo until recently, Inspector – so we shouldn't just trust our noses."

Brand felt like an idiot for having made his last statement.

"Nevertheless," The Chief continued," there are other time pressures and we'll have to release her soon. Our focus must be on what she knows and how long this has been going on. If she is an agent of some kind, we can keep tabs on her afterwards."

"Yes, sir. Does that mean you're going to offer her something?" Brand asked.

"Tell her that if she tells us everything that she knows, and if what she tells us is damning enough that Theo can't get out of it, we'll let her go."

"OK, sir. I also have an idea. Do you mind if I try something to gauge the validity of what she's telling us?"

"Of course, but just remember the long game. Keep it along the same lines as you started and don't let her agitate you again."

"Yes, sir." As he turned and left the room. Brand wanted Janet to think that he'd spoken up for her in the meeting room next door "Did you hear any of that?" he asked Rhodes as he re-entered the interview room.

"No, sir, how bad was it?" Rhodes asked.

Brand just gave a short sigh and sat back opposite Janet Greaves. "So, Janet, after a very heated discussion, the boss has agreed to let you go, but under one condition. If what you tell us has no bearing on any case against Mr. Greaves, the deal is worthless, is that understood?"

Janet nodded. "I'll also need the money and share certificates back as part of the deal so that I can restart my life," she stated.

Brand kept cool even though Sergeant Rhodes nearly told the woman where she could go.

"I'm afraid all evidence will need to remain with the police as part of the prosecution's case, Janet. Once Mr. Greaves has been sentenced, the police will be duty-bound to return them to you. Are we in agreement?" Brand asked.

Janet really wasn't in a position to bargain any more. She'd done the best she could in the circumstances. "OK," she said.

Brand drew her attention back to the picture of Schäfer. "So, Janet, what can you tell us about this man?"

"Well, his name is Lukas. The first time I saw him was when I came home from shopping one afternoon. They were talking in the drawing room – him and Theo. I didn't want to interrupt them, but when the man came round again, Theo introduced him as a contact for a story he was writing. Theo would sometimes tell me about some of the big stories he'd written, but he never really involved me in the detail of how he researched them. Anyway, the man looked shifty and I had a bad feeling about him. I wasn't happy about Theo bringing a foreigner to our home – Theo always seemed to be on edge when he was there."

"You said 'foreigner' – did Theo tell you where he was from?" Brand probed.

"No, but I know a German accent when I hear one; I've seen the war documentaries on the television," she said resolutely.

"And how many times did he come to your home?" Brand asked.

Janet wondered if this was a test. "Three times. After that I told Theo that I didn't want him in the house again."

"So, did you ever overhear what they discussed?"

"Well, as I said, Theo never really involved me. But the last time he was there, I heard them talking about money and oil prices, if that's any help."

"Everything's helpful at this stage, Janet," he replied. "You said Theo was on edge whenever Lukas was at your home – do you think the man was somehow exerting pressure on him?"

Janet paused for a few seconds whilst she thought. "I think so. As I said, I don't know what it was all about, but he was very confident that Theo would 'come through', the last time he left the house."

"You said that the man had been at your house three times. Do you remember how long ago it was when you first saw him and when the last time was?"

Janet looked at Brand. *He really doesn't know.* "I don't really remember exact dates, but the first time was probably just over a year ago, I think. The last time was maybe nine months ago," she said tentatively.

"Is there anything else you can tell us about this man, Janet?"

"No, not really. Like I said, he came to the house. They would talk privately and I asked Theo not to bring him home anymore. That's it."

Brand looked at the mirror and then back at Janet. He shook his head. "I'm not sure this is going to be enough, Janet. All it shows is that Theo knew this man. And if Lukas had been to your house, Theo could just rope you in to the story in court by saying that you also knew him. We need something of more substance, more proof of what Theo has been doing?"

Janet Greaves realised that that they were either playing 'dumb' very well or they just didn't have it. It was time to play her one ace card and hope that it got her off the hook.

"Did you know about the American?" she asked. Brand and Rhodes briefly looked at each other. Now she knew – they didn't have *that* piece of the jigsaw.

"Please go on, Janet."

"I wasn't sure it was related initially, but the German's visits were always a day or two after Theo had been visited by an American financier. He was the man who arranged the purchase of the shares in my name. All I had to do was sign the purchase documents."

"Did you see Theo give this man any money or write him a cheque for the purchases?" Brand asked.

"No, I was only there to sign the documents. Theo just told me what they were and that it was better for tax reasons. I assumed he paid the man after I signed."

"Did you get the name of this man?"

"Oh yes, James Kramer, a very charming man for a Yank."

"And what did he look like?" Brand probed.

"Well, he was about the same height as Theo, but slimmer. Dark hair with glasses. Always wore a nice suit."

"And what sort of age is he?"

"Maybe thirty-five-ish," she mused.

"And did your husband's behaviour change when Kramer visited? Any changes before, during or after?"

"No, not really. He just wanted me to make sure that the house was clean and tidy... you know, to make a good impression. Come to think of it, he was always happy after the man had left."

"How often has Kramer been to your home?"

"Oh I don't know, maybe five or six times... it's all in the diary, you know."

Brand was momentarily stunned. His men had missed something, which was bad enough, but to have this now revealed in front of The Chief of MI6 was embarrassing. He did his best to keep calm. "And where do you keep this diary, Mrs. Greaves?" he asked.

"I'm telling you about this because I don't want to see anyone else killed because of anything Theo's involved with. There's a lot of... personal stuff in there... things that I want to keep private – you understand?"

"We'll do our best to be as discreet as possible, Janet," Brand said. This didn't fill her with a great deal of confidence, but if could get her out of this situation, it was worth it.

"I keep it on the bookshelf with all the other books. It's brown and looks like a normal hardback – it just doesn't have any title on the spine."

"This is very helpful, Janet. We'll need to see if this has been catalogued in evidence. Do you think you'd be able to give an accurate description of James Kramer to one of our sketch artists in the meantime?" he asked, hoping to regain some credibility for the diary oversight.

"I guess so."

"Do you remember the first and last times the American visited your home?"

"I'm not sure about the first time; maybe February last year. But the last time is easy – it was last Monday," she said.

"Is there anything else we should know about, Mrs. Greaves? Any other visitors, odd changes to Theo's behaviours, irregular comings and goings, etcetera?"

"I don't think so, other than work colleagues. I've long since stopped worrying about Theo's comings and goings because he never comes home at the same time each day. But I think the diary should help you. And please don't call me Mrs. Greaves anymore; I'm going to start getting used to my maiden name from now on," she said resolutely.

"Well, I'd like to thank you for the help you've given us today, Janet. If the information in the diary pans out, I'd like to get you released as soon as possible. In the meantime, Sergeant Rhodes here will escort you back to the holding cell whilst we arrange for the sketch artist for you. He'll also arrange for some food and drink to be brought to you."

Brand waited until Janet had left for the holding cell, escorted by Rhodes, before going next door. "What do you think, sir?" he asked of The Chief.

The man waited as the stenographer picked up her things and left the room. "First of all, let's get hold of that diary. Start with the first and last entries of both men, and then see what's contained in between. Make sure you're there when she gives the description to the sketch artist. Afterwards, I'll need a copy sent to me and to this man at Gower Street." The Chief wrote a name down on the nearest piece of paper to hand. "That way we can all cross-reference what we have on this man. How much longer do you think you can keep her for, before it really starts to become a problem?"

"At best, overnight, sir. We've already breached protocol and a judge could deem the evidence inadmissible if a good defence lawyer brought it to light."

"Understood, Inspector. Best not hang around – I think we both know what needs to be done before the morning. Update me this evening. I also want to be present at Theo's next interrogation... even if it's in the middle of the night."

"Yes, sir."

* * *

To Brand's relief, Janet's diary had been collected as part of the inventory of evidence... it just hadn't been analysed yet due to the manpower being split across three other cases. With the weight of MI6 bearing down on them, the Inspector's boss had prioritised this case above the others. Rhodes was put on the diary, whilst Brand accompanied Mrs. Greaves to an intimate room where the artist went to work on the composite sketch. Brand subtly watched the woman throughout the exercise to ensure she wasn't giving the artist a confused picture of what the American looked like. When they'd finished, he told her that once they'd got a full work-up on James Kramer, they'd have enough evidence to question Theo on. If things worked out, she'd be able to leave within the next twelve hours, once her statement had been typed up and signed. When Janet voiced her complaints, Brand reminded her that spies and people associated with them are treated a great deal worse in Russia. She backed down a little after this.

Rhodes had gone through Janet's diary meticulously throughout the late afternoon. Although some of the woman's entries were quite titillating or somewhat emotional, he only made notes and attached coloured tabs on the relevant pages to the case. A copy of the James Kramer facial sketch had been couriered to MI5 in Gower Street, as well as MI6's Identity & Records head clerk and the Head of US Operations. The Chief had smoothed the way with his opposite number at MI5 for the operational help needed, and a call had been set up between the two services and Special Branch to go over any information they'd been able to pull together. 5pm on a Friday wasn't exactly the most popular time for the meeting, but given the potential consequences, everyone went above and beyond to provide what they could, based on the picture, name and possible job role.

During the meeting, Brand was able to verify dates when the man had been in the country. MI6's US Operations had drawn a blank, even with the assistance of Identity & Records. It was MI5 who came through with goods. James Kramer was an American representative in the UK for Peerson Wealth Management: a US company domiciled in the Cayman Islands that acted as a tax haven for 'select' clients. The company was also believed to act as an intermediary between national representatives who need to quietly move wealth across borders through legal entities and shell companies. From the limited information MI5 had, the organisation and Kramer himself were well connected. The suspicions were that it was a CIA front for quietly transacting business around the world through a legitimate company. The MI5 file also contained two pictures of Kramer along with more detailed information that hadn't been disclosed on the call. In the spirit of sharing, they agreed to provide a copy of the file for the case that could be picked up in an hour – a job given to Rhodes after the call ended. It was also agreed that no moves were to be made on Kramer without agreement between the two departments.

It was past 8 o'clock by the time the four members of the team had gone through the copy of the MI5 file. The Chief, Head of US Operations, Brand and Rhodes all agreed that the sketch artist had managed to draw a remarkable resemblance of the American from Janet Greaves' description. What they needed now was an approach plan for Theo's next interview to achieve maximum compliance.

Brand spoke first. "Sir, I think we know the main areas to focus on and ultimately what we want to extract from the man. My question to you is: what do you want to do with him afterwards?"

The Chief tilted his head. "What do you mean, Inspector?"

"Well, if you don't mind me asking, sir, are you planning to burn him or turn him? Whichever you choose subtly changes the way we approach the interview. If he starts pleading for a deal, I'll need to know what the scope is."

"I see what you're getting at," The Chief said, nodding whilst contemplating scenarios. "I think that we'll get more out of him if he thinks there's a chance he won't get burned. Does that make sense?"

"I believe it does, sir. Shall we get cracking?"

"No time like the present, Inspector."

The Chief, Ellis – Head of US Operations – and a stenographer stationed themselves in the viewing room whilst two uniformed policemen were sent to collect Theo from his cell. Brand and Rhodes discussed their strategy and paid a quick visit to Mrs. Greaves' cell before entering the now occupied interview room to sit opposite Theo – Rhodes now holding a much larger file than before. Anything of comfort had been removed from Theo's cell after his non-cooperative stance during the previous interviews. His cell hadn't been designed for a man of his size and any position he manoeuvred himself into would only remain comfortable for minutes. With barely any contact and two lukewarm meals provided, any time he had dozed off had left him with severely numb limbs when he awoke. The chair he now sat on was cushioned on the seat and back.

Theo knew this was all by design, but made the most of the comfort anyway. As he looked at the two officers in front, he wondered whether they actually had anything on him, or whether they were looking to bluff their way through another interrogation. *Was the thicker file for show?*

"Hello, Theo," Brand started. "Sorry you haven't had any contact for a while, but as you can appreciate, a lot of evidence is required for a sensitive matter like this. How are you holding up?"

"It was nice of you to remove the cushions from my cell... a bit childish, don't you think?" Theo said sarcastically.

Brand wanted to smile. It was just the type of reaction he liked. "Well, unfortunately we've got a shortage of cushions at the moment, so we had to give them to your wife – I hope that was OK?"

Theo tutted. "I wasn't born yesterday, Inspector," he said, somewhat vexed.

Brand ignored the snipe and gave a quick glance over to the mirror on his right. "So just for the record, I am Inspector Brand and this is Sergeant Rhodes of Special Branch and the record of this interview will be kept as per the previous two."

"Who else is behind the mirror, Inspector?" Theo asked. He had a pretty good idea but couldn't be sure.

"I won't lie to you, Theo – this investigation has widened significantly, so there are a number of interested parties. That said, let's get down to business, shall we – I'd rather not have to keep your wife here any longer than necessary." Theo didn't react to the last comment, which Brand read as him having confidence in Janet not to say anything. "Before we get into the specifics of what we know now, I want to absolutely crystal clear with you. This is going to be your last interview with us. You may see that as a good sign, but I can assure you it's not. There WILL be finality to this interview, the outcome of which is totally dependent on you. So, please keep this in the back of your mind during our discussion."

Brand looked Theo in the eye as he made the statement. He wasn't expecting the man to react, so long as he analysed and absorbed the position he was in. Theo said nothing and Brand nodded to Rhodes, who passed over the picture of Florian Schäfer. Brand turned it around and placed it in front of Theo in the same way he'd done with Mrs. Greaves. "Can you tell me how you know this man?"

The moment Rhodes took the picture from the file, Theo knew who it was. He decided that his strategy was to not let the police rile him up in any way, so he kept his face, eyes and emotions as impassive as possible. "I don't know him – who is he?" he asked, remaining motionless.

Brand had been well schooled in the art of the interview. In fact, he had the best closing rate of all the Specials in the country. He knew that the more 'impassive' the subject, the more likely they would be suppressing some form of guilt. Almost telepathically, Rhodes passed over the crime scene pictures of Nancy Walker, and Brand put them in front of Theo.

Theo frowned. He instantly realised what he'd done, but hoped he could pass this off as a gut reaction to what was an awful scene. But inside, his stomach was tied up in knots. During the many hours in his cell, he'd had plenty of time to go over things in his head. Nancy had come to him for help in a personal situation and he'd betrayed her by offering her up to a foreign agent. He tried to remain calm.

"Now, I know you know who this is, Theo, as you met with Nancy Walker on the 8th February this year, didn't you?"

Theo felt cornered. If The Chief was behind the glass, or his handler for that matter, there was no way he could deny the meeting.

Brand turned the screw just a little tighter. "Would you like me to tell you how she died, Theo?"

"Yes, I had a meeting with Nancy, there's a record of that; but as I said, I don't know who the man is." They'd obviously done some homework since they last interviewed him. He was walking a tightrope as thin as a filament right now.

Brand had had enough of the man's denials. It was getting late and so time to start boxing him in. "He broke into her home, hit her repeatedly with a blunt object, strangled her to near death and shot her three times. Do you think she deserved that, Theo? Do you think her only son deserved to have his mother killed in that way? Had she done something against you, Theo?"

"No, of course not – I liked Nancy; we had a good working relationship," he conceded. "I just don't know who this man is, that's all!"

Brand looked the man dead in the eye. "Do you remember when I said this was going to be your last interview with us? And that the outcome of this interview will be totally dependent on you?" Theo nodded. "Well, in that file in front of Sergeant Rhodes, we have enough evidence and sworn testimony to guarantee you a stint in prison. So, door number one, you're absolutely, one hundred percent guaranteed a thirty-year stretch. That'll take you to about seventy-six, won't it?" The question was rhetorical, as Brand was in no mood for an answer. "Or, you could trade that prize for what's behind door number two, Theo. But I promise, the only way you're getting door number two is if you start telling me the fucking truth."

Theo tried to remain calm. Something the Inspector had said concerned him. *Sworn testimony. Had they somehow got Janet to incriminate him in some way? She wouldn't would she? He knew his wife. She was steadfast, reliable – they loved each other... didn't they? Who else could they have got statement from in such a short timeframe?*

Theo was taking too long to think, and Brand lost his patience. He gathered up the photographs and signalled to Rhodes. "OK, have it your way then." They both got up from their chairs and turned towards the door.

Brand's decision took everyone by surprise. In the viewing room, The Chief seethed. The Inspector had played hardball and blown the interview. Even Theo was startled by the inspector's reaction. But just as Rhodes knocked on the door to be let out of the room, Brand turned back to Theo. "Just so you know, we'll be prosecuting your wife as an accomplice. There's no way either of you could've afforded to purchase those shares on just your salary, especially with the other wives you're supporting. The powers-that-be may wish to save face and just give you and your wife up to the Russians. I'm pretty sure they'll have a couple of spare places in a gulag somewhere for spies who supply disinformation."

Theo was so dumbfounded that his mouth actually opened; *this guy really had done his homework.*

The door opened and Brand went to leave.

"OK... OK," Theo said, resigned to the fact that this was his best and only real option.

Rhodes nodded to the officer outside to close them in again, and they both walked back to the table. Inside the viewing room, The Chief gave a wry smile and sat down again to watch part two of the interview.

Rhodes passed over the photo of Schäfer once more.

"Tell us how you know this man and if he has a name, Theo?" Brand said.

Theo sighed. "His name is Lukas Mayer. We met a couple of years ago at the Arab League summit in Riyadh." Brand motioned for Theo to continue. "We were both covering the same story but from differing points of view. Mine for the paper, and he was completing a thesis in Middle-Eastern politics. It made sense to get the perspectives of other nations involved or who had skin in the game. So we had a few energetic debates in a compound where we could be served alcohol, and that's how we first got to know each other."

"Well, that all sounds innocent enough, Theo, but tell us – when did the situation change from one of casual acquaintance to something more... serious?" Brand asked.

"A few months later I happened to be in the pub with a few work friends when I saw him across the bar. So I invited him over for a few drinks. A few hours later after the guys had left and it was just the two of us, he made a play. I'd had a suspicion in Riyadh, but the discussions seemed harmless enough and I hadn't seen him again – until then, of course. He told me about a financier who had excellent connections across the stock markets. I must've said something about my finances in our previous conversations, because he knew... a lot... about my... indiscretions."

"What are we talking about here, Theo? I need you to be specific."

"Do I have to? You apparently have all the information," Theo countered.

"Humour me, Theo. We weren't in the pub with you."

Theo let out a deep breath. "I have two other wives, one in Egypt, the other in Turkey. None of them know about each other, and it was bleeding me dry financially."

Sergeant Rhodes took a pen from his pocket and a blank sheet of paper from the file. "We're going to need you to write down their names, dates of birth and addresses please," he said.

Whilst Theo wrote down the details, Brand continued his questioning. "Are these women just housewives, Theo?"

"No. Chione works in the Ministry of Petroleum in Egypt and Kadri has a job at the national airline."

"So, how are they bleeding you dry then, if they have jobs?" Brand asked.

"There are certain laws and traditions in these countries. Women can't rent or buy houses or cars by themselves; it's the husband's responsibility."

"So, you're saying that Mayer knew all this and offered you... something?"

"He said that he could arrange for cash payments to be made to me and that the financier could make sure any money was well invested and off the books, so-to-speak. All he asked for in return was that I pass on anything that the man gave me."

"And what was the financier's name?"

Theo knew there was no point trying to cover this up anymore. He'd introduced the man to his wife and the inspector must've got the information out of her in some way. "James Kramer," he said.

"So just to be clear, payments would be made to you from Mayer and then given to Kramer to invest on your own behalf?" Brand asked.

"Yes. I wouldn't have to invest with the man, he just recommended it."

"And how much did he say these payments would be?"

"He said they'd start at a thousand pounds, but double once trust had been established."

"And so what happened after Mayer made the proposal to you?" Brand asked.

"I said I'd have to think about it."

"How long did you thing about it? How did Mayer react?"

"He was fine at the outset. He suggested that I have an initial meeting with Kramer so that the man could really show me what was possible with the money and my situation."

"Did you take up Mayer's offer to meet with Kramer?" Brand asked. He knew it sounded like a stupid question, but it was mostly for the written record.

"Eventually, yes."

"So, I just want to clarify a few things. When did this meeting in the pub take place? When did you first meet Kramer? And how were communication protocols established between each of you?"

"The pub meeting was before Christmas of '76. I initially met with Kramer in early January."

"You're an experienced man, Theo; you must've known what was happening here?" Brand asked cynically. "Why didn't you report it?"

Theo was annoyed at the situation he'd put himself in. Thinking about it now, if he'd have been smarter, he probably could've reported the contact and been able to keep some of the money. Now the government would probably want all the money back.

"I thought about it, I really did. I made some discreet enquiries internally about them once things were established. But when nothing came back, I just thought it would be some easy money for literally just being a postman. I was behind on the mortgage payments and Janet had no idea that we could be out on our ear within a month or two," Theo conceded.

"And what were the communication protocols?" Brand asked, not wishing to be side-tracked.

"I'd be called at work by the American. Meet at my home for the financial advice and contact Mayer to arrange a meet the next day."

"So what I don't understand," Brand asked, "is how you could invest money you didn't have with the American, if you were paid afterwards by Mayer for trafficking?"

Theo sighed. He'd well-and-truly screwed up. He was going to have to come clean. "The American was paying me too. He was paying me to keep quiet about what I was passing to the German."

"So, how many times did you meet with Kramer?"

Theo's eyes darted to the top left of his sockets as he did the arithmetic. "I'd say five times."

"And how much were you paid by Kramer and Mayer respectively?"

"Twelve thousand from Kramer and seven thousand from Mayer," Theo said painfully.

Brand decided that Theo should be the one to explain what he'd been surmising all along. "So, in broad strokes, I'd like you to tell us what you think was actually going on here?"

Theo turned his head left and gazed toward the mirror for a moment, before returning his attention to the inspector. "I'd say that the CIA were behind the whole thing. They made Kramer look like a mole, sympathetic to the Russian cause, and passed the intel via me to Mayer."

"How long do you think it would take the Russians to cotton on to the fact that they were being duped?" Brand enquired.

"Well, that's the thing, Inspector. All of the information has been genuine so far. It looks like the US have taken a leaf out of the Russians' manual and are finally playing the long game."

"What makes you say that, Theo?"

"I looked at what Kramer gave me."

Brand sat back in his chair. Caution was required from here on. "OK, Theo, we'll come back to that in a bit," he said, giving himself time to think. He motioned for Rhodes to pass over the pictures of Nancy. "What I'm not understanding is why this man broke into this woman's home, beat her half to death and then finished the job with a gun. I think you can shed some light on that, can't you?"

Theo felt disgusted with himself when he looked at the pictures. She'd definitely not deserved to go like that. "Are you certain that Mayer did this?" he asked, more in hope than anything.

"We are one hundred percent sure, Theo. Mayer is just a false identity anyway. His real name is Florian Schäfer."

Theo bowed his head slightly. "During the meeting with Nancy in February, I noticed him standing across the street. He must've been keeping me under tabs. When I left Nancy, I looked to see if he'd followed me back, but he didn't – he stayed where he was. I guess he followed her after she left the restaurant. That night he invited himself into my home and asked me who I'd met and for more details on her. I initially resisted, but he threatened to expose me to my wife. So, I told him her name and said she was just an old colleague – all I had was the telephone number she'd given me. I never thought it would end up like... that," he said, gesturing towards the photos.

"Did he say why he wanted information on Mrs. Walker?" Brand asked.

"He just said that he needed to know for himself who she was and to be sure that I wasn't playing the wrong game. I gave him my word and just said that she'd asked for a personal favour... which was the truth. I never said anything about the arrangement. I don't know why he'd want to kill her – she's... she'd been retired for years," Theo said, correcting himself.

Brand paused briefly before his next question. "Are there any other people involved in this particular scheme?"

"No. And my wife certainly isn't involved."

Brand resisted the urge to ask which one, but was definitely curious about where the two foreign wives worked and their strategic value. "Are you absolutely sure about this, Theo?"

"Cross my heart," Theo said, mimicking the action that went with the saying.

Brand collected up all the evidence in front of Theo and gave it to Rhodes.

"Thank you for your time, Mr. Greaves. I'm going to suspend this interview for now, as I think we could all do with a break. Just so you know that I'm being fair, I'm going to need to take what you've said today under advisement with the powers-that-be. I'll have you escorted back to your cell for now."

Theo felt a little uncertain. "What happens now? Are you going to let Janet go?"

"You know as well as I do, Theo, that some decisions are above my pay grade. As for your wife, I don't see any reason to hang on to her, but again, that's for seniors to decide. If it helps in any way, I doubt there'll be much in the way of any procrastination." Brand turned and knocked on the door, and Rhodes followed.

Five minutes later, The Chief, the Head of US Operations and Brand sat alone in the viewing room. "I didn't think you'd want me delving deeper into potential US secrets, sir, but I think we managed to get a decent amount from him – assuming it's all true, of course."

"I appreciate that, Inspector – thank you. Any reason to think the story's a fabrication?" The Chief asked.

Brand looked at both of them. "My gut feeling says that the story is what it is. I'm sure if we put a forensic accountant on the job, the money side of things would probably be there or thereabouts. Timeline-wise, things seem to fit, based on what the missus was saying. The national security elements will need to be handled by you. I'm happy to be involved, but you'll have a better view of the chessboard than I do. The things that stick out for me are why he marries twice, one in the Egyptian Ministry and one in an airline. They seem well placed for other activity, not just coincidence. The other issues are what happens with Schäfer's body and how are the Russians going to react?"

"All good questions, Inspector. Your views, Ellis?" The Chief asked.

Ellis was a thirty-year veteran of The Service, and had risen quietly through the ranks over the years. At 5ft 5ins with short dark hair and thick-rimmed glasses, she looked the mumsy type, which was all part of her indistinguishable persona. Even in a room of three, she'd been barely noticeable until this point. But her intuition was razor sharp, and she always had the ability to call a situation correctly as far as the US was concerned.

"I think the question is, what was the relationship between Kramer and Schäfer and whether the Russians will replace the German? Will the Russians buy it that Schäfer went off-piste with a 'perceived' burglary and died in the ensuing car chase? Whatever his motives were, we need Greaves to remain innocent of them. If we burn Greaves, then both the Americans and Russians might get scared off or move to someone else. I don't see a great upside in sending Theo to prison, if he can be kept on a short leash for the foreseeable future. We can limit his exposure to British national interests. It all depends on the quality of the intel coming through from the American, of course. If the Russians suspect something, we can leave him exposed; the same with the Americans. Going forward, there may be ways to exploit the Egyptian and Turkish wives. There would need to be punitive action against Theo. Enough to make him think twice about branching out on his own again, but not too heavily that he makes plans to swap sides, sir."

"There's a lot of 'ifs' there, Ellis," The Chief said.

"I agree, sir, but if our supposed allies are doing things behind our backs, wouldn't it be best to have some knowledge about it?"

The Chief could see that Ellis made sense. "If we can verify the intel from Theo, would you be prepared to take responsibility for him and his actions?" he asked.

"So long as I have full control, sir?" Ellis replied.

"If the intel holds up, he's all yours," The Chief agreed.

Brand was a little piqued so say the least that all the work he and the rest of his officers had done was about to be wasted. "And what do you want to do with Mrs. Greaves, sir?" he asked in a slightly more tense tone.

"I don't see a reason to charge her for now. Ellis, can you make sure she keeps quiet? I doubt Theo will have much say in the matter."

"I'm sure she can be persuaded, sir," Ellis said. "Do you want me to do the in-depth interview with Theo this evening for the US intel?"

"I don't see why not, seeing as you're both here." The Chief then directed his attention to Brand, knowing full well that the man was disgruntled at not being able to take the spy down. "Inspector Brand, you have been exceptionally helpful and efficient in this investigation. I'm afraid I can't ask you to be involved in the next interview. But I believe we still have the dirty work to complete to tie up the loose ends of Schäfer's demise. I'll have the Filthy Squad pick up the body from Camberwell. The car accident will need to end in a burned-out wreck. Once they've done their job, the body will need to be sent over to Kent where you'll need to tie up the investigation – someone's soon to be enquiring about a missing person, I expect. The local force can then keep and process it in the normal way."

"Yes, sir – I'll make sure everything's properly wrapped up," Brand said, the disappointment clearly showing in his voice.

The Chief put a reassuring hand on the man's shoulder as he walked out of the room. "Don't worry, Brand... you won't remain an inspector for long."

* * *

CHAPTER 43

COVER UP

The 'Filthy Squad' were so named because they literally got all the crappy clean-up jobs that could land them anywhere in the world. As always, they'd been ruthlessly efficient at dealing with Schäfer's body, making sure that jagged steel rods had been placed in the entry and exit points before the van impact to completely destroy the evidence of bullet wounds. They put the American intel back inside the tooth and the poison capsule back in his left arm before the staged accident. When Brand got the charred body back, it was barely recognisable as human parts. At least the skull was mostly intact for any dental record identification that might be done at a later time. He too had been ruthlessly efficient in wrapping up the case with the aid of CI Barnes. They'd agreed that Kent police would keep the remains in the morgue for one month whist a next of kin could be established. The cause of death had eventually been classified as combination of internal injuries sustained in the accident, burn shock and asphyxiation due to lack of breathable oxygen in the vehicle during the fire. A special marker had been put on Florian Schäfer's and Nancy Walker's file that any release of information must be requested from the Station Chief and Special Branch. But Brand and Barnes were not out of the woods yet. There was still the issue of what to do about the lack of a body where Nancy Walker was concerned. Until a body was either ashes or in the ground, there was still the risk that David may still want to see or touch his mother before she was finally laid to rest. Over the weekend, with permission from CI Barnes, Brand assigned a 'liaison officer' to visit David Walker and provide any assistance with the difficult steps needed after a death in the family – so long as that assistance culminated in the decision in favour of a cremation.

* * *

Stephanie Munroe had flown through training school at the top of her class in 1975 and made detective sergeant within two years. Not having to wear police uniform definitely worked to her advantage, and she wasn't afraid to use her looks to achieve what she wanted. Although she had the ability to capture a man's attention from fifty paces, she'd also proven the ability to capture and apprehend an assailant at any distance if needed.

When Brand had briefed her on what would need to be a short mission, expediently executed, she was happy to oblige. After all, her ultimate goal was to make it into MI5 one day. Chief Inspector Barnes had only broken the bad news to Nancy's son the day before, so when Detective Sergeant Munroe went round to visit David early on the Saturday morning, she wasn't sure what to expect. The door finally opened on the fifth ring of the doorbell.

"Hello, David?" she asked. David was dressed in a hastily put-on pair of jeans and nearest T-shirt he could find. He looked tired. He'd slept, but only for the last few hours. The night before had been a combination of alcohol, takeaway food, cigarettes and more alcohol – which Munroe could smell the moment he'd opened the door.

"Yes, who are you?" If he'd had the energy to be taken back by the woman's svelte figure, he would've – but for now he was still hung over from drowning his sorrows the night before.

"I'm Detective Sergeant Munroe. Chief Inspector Barnes has asked me to come over and see how you are, can I come in?"

David's senses had started to return and he now began to take in the beauty of the woman who stood before him. She stood 5ft 11in with heels, her sharp blue eyes gazing directly at him. Individual strands of her long blonde hair gracefully brushed the contours of her neck in the morning breeze. "Sure. Sorry about the mess," he said apologetically.

The spring mornings could still be chilly and Munroe gave a short 'fff' intake of breath as she stepped over the threshold. David's flat wasn't the worst she'd seen, but it was clear that the man didn't have a woman in his life. "Take a seat," he said, gesturing towards the sofa, "I just need to wash and get decent."

"Don't feel you have to do anything special for me," Stephanie replied, but David had already turned and left for his bedroom. Instead of sitting down, Munroe walked around the place, taking in as much as she could about David's life. Pictures of family, a framed diploma in management on the wall, trade newspapers and an urn on the mantelpiece. She put down her handbag, removed her suit jacket and started tidying up the living room. Plates, cups and glasses by the sink, papers straightened and table and sideboards wiped of ring stains and crumbs. She was starting to fill the sink with soapy water when David came back to the living room, somewhat embarrassed.

"Please, you don't need to do that," he said, walking over to the kitchen space.

But Munroe ignored his request. "Do you have any rubber gloves... don't want to ruin these," she said with a smile, holding up her red-tipped fingernails.

"No, I don't."

"Well, you wash and I'll wipe then." She handed the dishcloth to David. He'd washed his face, cleaned his teeth, changed and brushed his hair. All small but notable improvements, she thought. There was a brief silence between them as David began washing the glasses. He really wasn't sure what the woman wanted. That and the fact that in her heels they were the same height... which was a little intimidating.

He decided to come right out and say it. "I know what you said at the door, but I still don't understand why you've come round here, sergeant. I doubt it's usual for police to do someone's cleaning up and this is a really bad time for me."

Munroe put a comforting hand on David's shoulder. "You're right David, this isn't usual and I certainly wouldn't do this for anyone, but it's precisely because this is a bad time that I couldn't bear to see a man potentially degenerate like this. I don't mean to pry, but my guess is that you probably hit the drink pretty hard yesterday?"

David looked away. "My mother's just been horrifically murdered and my seven-year-old son killed himself three months ago – what would you do to get rid of the pain, sergeant?"

"You're right David, I shouldn't have said anything – but please, call me Stephanie." He'd forgotten 'Detective' when addressing her rank, but she doubted this was malicious in any way.

David relaxed a little. "That's a nice name," he said a little shyly.

Stephanie smiled and thanked him. "Although I introduced myself as Detective Sergeant, strictly speaking, I'm here as a friend rather than in an official capacity. As a friend of your mother's, Chief Inspector Barnes was genuinely concerned for you and he asked me to come and see you as a favour."

"How did he know my mother? I'd never seen him before yesterday. I certainly never saw him visit the house."

"Honestly, I don't know. Perhaps you could ask him the next time you see him?"

David shrugged. "Yeah, maybe," he said, returning to the last plates in the bowl. He really didn't want to see anyone at the moment, although he could make an exception for the woman standing in front of him.

"I know it's a touchy subject," Stephanie ventured, "and please feel free to tell me to shut up, but have you been to the house yet or thought about what you want to do about funeral arrangements?"

David fell silent. As his shoulders began to shake, he bowed his head shamefully, tears falling in the dirty sink water. Stephanie took a deep breath and put her arm around David's shoulder. She had a stronger grip than he expected. He wiped his face with the back of his hand and shook his head. "No, my thoughts were... elsewhere."

"I understand. I'll help you... if you want, but only if you want it and feel that I'm not overstepping myself?"

David knew that he didn't have had a clue what to do in situations like this; his mother had dealt with all the arrangements for his father and Lee. "I'm going to need all the help I can get."

"OK, well how about we give this place a quick spruce up... tidy home, tidy mind, as my mother used to say."

David perked up enough to go along with what the woman said. In all fairness to himself, he probably would've gone along with anything she suggested. The woman had such an energy about her and she didn't hang around. She had David doing all sorts of odd jobs whilst she tackled some of the bigger ones. It briefly took his mind off the situation and reminded him of how his mother would tackle the cleaning around the house when he was a young boy.

Stephanie was true to her word. Ten minutes later, and the flat looked far more habitable.

"Thanks, Stephanie, I think you were right about the tidy mind. I just need to take a paracetamol. Would you like a drink? I can't believe how rude I've been not to offer you one before."

"To be honest David, the state the place was in before... I'm not sure I would've accepted," she said with a smile. "But I'd love a coffee now if you have one... milk, no sugar, please."

David gestured for her to sit down whilst he made them both a drink.

"CI Barnes said he gave you an envelope of your mother's documents. Have you gone through them yet?"

"No, I felt like I'd been hit by a bulldozer yesterday; I couldn't bear it."

"Would you like to go through them together? There may be some important things in there."

David brought the two coffees over and handed one to Stephanie. "It's around here somewhere."

"Is that it on the table? I may have moved it," she said.

David picked up the envelope and emptied out the contents between them on the sofa. She had nice legs through the sheer stockings, for sure.

Stephanie picked up an envelope simply titled *'Last Will & Testament'*. "Do you want to open it?"

David wasn't sure whether he did or not and indicated it was OK for Stephanie to open it instead. She took out the document carefully and scanned through the contents. "So, it looks like this was drawn up just a few months ago in December. Did something happen to make her want to change her will? Once you get through all the legal mumbo jumbo, it basically says that you are the main beneficiary. It also says that under no circumstance must any of the proceeds of the inheritance wind up in the hands of... Louvaine King or Jon King?" Stephanie looked at David for some affirmation.

His face changed from gentleness to anger. "It's a long story. Suffice to say that the bitch used to be my wife and then ran off with both my kids with this guy Jon. Between them, they were responsible for the death of my son." David glanced up to the urn on the mantelpiece as he spoke. "I'm not sure what was in the Will before, or even if she had one, but I'm glad mum had the intelligence to make sure that that bloodsucker can't get her hands on anything."

Stephanie decided not to press any further; post-marriage counselling was not part of what she'd signed up for. "There's a bit in here about setting up trusts for the children and that the solicitor who drew up the Will can set them up for you. I guess this is to stop any monies reaching the... adults," she said carefully.

"I guess that will all go to Laura now," David said, in a quietly concerned tone.

Stephanie continued through the document. "It also says what her funeral arrangements should be." She handed the document over for David to read for himself. As David read through the Will, Stephanie sifted through the rest of the pile. She got a chance to confirm what David's mother looked like from the passport, which matched the person in a picture on David's sideboard. There was a death certificate for Stephen Walker, which judging by the age must've been David's father. There was a bank book with Midland Bank containing five thousand two hundred pounds and a life assurance trust certificate for one hundred thousand. She handed them both over to David. Even though he was surprised, she could tell that it didn't make him feel better. He clearly wasn't the money-grabbing type. There was a sealed envelope with David's name hand written on the front. Stephanie passed it straight to David, who opened and read it carefully.

'Dear David,

If you are reading this letter then it means that I am no longer with the living. I wanted to let you know just how much I love you and have always loved you, ever since you were born. You came into our lives when the country was going through one of its most difficult times. Your father and I did our best to try and shield you from so much, but sometimes failed you when you needed our love and connections the most. Despite what you might think, your father spoke of you all the time to our friends and his colleagues. When visitors would comment to him on the lovely artwork or fixtures around the house, he'd always respond back proudly with 'My son did that'. He also used to sometimes watch you play football without you knowing. Strange, I know, but he did it anyway. I wish I'd told you this when he died, it would've been much easier. But we all think that time is endless and that we'll get round to whatever 'it' is.

So if I haven't said it to you in person, I wanted to say it here. Do what's in your heart, son. Work to live and find someone that loves you for who you are, not what you can provide... she's out there, somewhere.

All of my affairs should be in order. The house is yours if you want it and there's a life assurance policy that should make things easier financially. If you ever need any help, please contact Chief Inspector Tom Barnes; he'll know what to do.

I will love you always and forever.

Mum X

Stephanie watched for David's reaction. Even without reading it herself, she could tell it was from his mother. He stifled a tear and folded the letter back into the envelope. In some ways, he was lucky, she thought. Her father had never left anything for her mother. She picked up the last document which was the one that surprised her the most. It was the deeds to 7 Woodland Rise in Sevenoaks. She'd never actually seen deeds before – for most people, they were always something the bank seemed to have ownership of. But it wasn't the deeds that surprised her, it was the fact that they were already in David's name that amazed her.

She handed it over to David. "I think your mother really cared for you, David. She certainly knew how make sure you weren't robbed by the Inland Revenue!"

David looked, but didn't really pick up on the gravity of what the woman was saying.

"I'm no expert but from what I'm seeing here, the Inland Revenue can't tax you on assets you already own, which includes the house and the life assurance trust certificate."

David smiled to be polite, but his eyes just glazed. "It sounds wonderful, but it won't bring her back and could never make up for what she must've suffered before she died."

"You're right, David, I'm sorry for being so insensitive. I meant no offence, it's just rare to see a situation where someone's thought ahead so well. When my dad died, he left us in all sorts of problems; we ended up having to leave our home."

"It's alright, Stephanie. No offence taken. I'm not even sure what I'd do with the house anyway," he said.

"Can I make a suggestion? The police have finished their forensic work there, so the place will be empty. Why don't we go over to your mother's house and you can decide how you actually feel about the place?" David was a little reticent, but Stephanie felt that he needed a little nudge. "We've got to sort out the funeral arrangements anyway; why don't we drop by the place just for five minutes. I know you think I'm being pushy, but I think you'll know for sure once you're there. We can then go and speak to a funeral director. How does that sound?"

Stephanie *was* being pushy, but David realised that she was only doing these things for his own good. "OK, let me get some shoes on."

"I'll wash up the cups…tidy home!" she said with a smile.

Stephanie took on the driving duties whilst David gave directions. She'd insisted, given the alcohol he'd probably consumed the night before.

David couldn't help casting what he thought was the odd surreptitious sideways look over in Stephanie's direction. As she drove, the constant use of the pedals made her skirt ride up, showing her stocking tops.

Stephanie had sensed David's glances. She awkwardly tugged her skirt down the first time it happened, but it soon rode back up again

– and so she just left it. Besides, she didn't mind David looking at her legs; he was nice guy and she was proud of her form.

As they arrived at Woodland Rise, Stephanie was impressed by the private entrance and the size of all the houses, but chose not to say anything.

At the house, David took a little time to put his key in the front door. He really wasn't sure what to expect. He wondered if the remnants of the murder scene would still be there with blood pooled on the carpet and splattered up the walls.

"Do you want me to go in and take a quick look around first?" Stephanie asked, sensing David's reticence.

"I'm just not sure," he said. She held out her hand for the key, but David decided that he needed to show a little less weakness than he'd shown of late. He opened the door quicker than he would normally – almost as if he needed to force his weight over the threshold.

The first thing he noticed was that the hallway carpet was missing and there were a couple of holes on the wall. Apart from a little damage to the back door and a few things missing from the kitchen, which again included the carpet – everything seemed pretty normal. It was much the same story upstairs.

As they made their way through the rooms, Stephanie watched as David took in the details. "How are you feeling, David?" she asked.

"I thought we'd come into a gruesome disaster area, but I'm surprised how empty and... normal things are."

Stephanie was about to say why the carpets had been removed, but decided against it. "Is there anywhere else you want to look around?" she asked.

David ran his hand down one of his mother's satin blouses. "No I don't think so. I'm glad you brought me here... I'm not sure I would've ever come on my own."

"I think we sometimes exaggerate things ten-fold in our minds. I know I've done it in the past."

Back in the car, Stephanie drove them to the police station.

"How come we're here?" David asked.

"I don't know who the funeral director is, so I'm hoping one of my colleagues inside will know. Do you want to wait here? You can come inside if you like, but there isn't anywhere nice to sit and they won't let civilians past the front desk, I'm afraid."

"No, that's fine, I'll wait." David watched the way the detective sergeant got out and how her long blonde hair bounced as she walked in front of the car to the entrance of the station. A couple of carnal thoughts entered his mind until he caught himself. *This is your mother's funeral you're here for!*

Inside, Stephanie found a private office for herself and called Inspector Brand to update him on the situation. "I've been speaking with the son this morning, sir. He's currently in the car outside. He was a bit worse-for-wear, which is to be expected, I guess, but I've managed to get him in a better frame of mind now. We went through the documents and by all accounts, he's pretty set for life. The Will stipulated that she wanted a non-Christian cremation. Where do you want me to take him, sir, and what's the procedure to follow?"

"We have a funeral director we use near Camberwell police station in Southwark called Hayden's. I've arranged everything with them and we'll pick up the tab. See if you can get him over there today or tomorrow. Whichever day it is, make sure you're there. They'll also provide any coverage if he asks to see the body at any time. Be sure to call ahead to make sure you are dealt with by Patrick Hayden – he's an expert in these matters. If the son asks why the funeral directors are all the way in Southwark and not local, the party line is going to be that all personnel from the World War II Radar Research Establishment are to be looked after by the State."

Stephanie wrote all of this down, along with the address and telephone number he gave her for Hayden's.

"What do you think the son's state of mind is at the moment, Munroe?" Brand asked.

"If you mean how compliant is he likely to be, I'd say 75%. There's always a risk, but he's been pretty receptive to my help so far, sir."

"That's why we chose you, Munroe. The sooner there's a casket, the sooner you'll be back on a prime case. Keep me up to date whatever the time. Leave a message if you have to."

"Yes, sir." They both clicked off the call.

David woke up with a jolt when Stephanie opened the car door. The lack of sleep had caught up on him. "What did you find out?" he asked, rubbing his left eye.

"Quite a lot actually." Stephanie repeated the official line about the State paying for Nancy's funeral.

David looked away. Memories of his father's technical discussions at home filled his thoughts. He'd always been so preoccupied with work. But those memories were now confused after reading his mother's letter earlier.

"Are you alright?" Stephanie asked. David looked back at the woman and shrugged his shoulders. "So, the funeral director they use is a place called Hayden's, just about an hour away in Southwark. I took the liberty of ringing them and said we would head over – it seemed like the best thing to do today... Y'know; get the hard stuff out of the way, so-to-speak. Is that alright? Again, I hope I'm not overstepping boundaries here?"

David rubbed his eyes which were now a little red and sighed inevitably. "Sure, let's go."

From Munroe's mission perspective, the meeting between David and Patrick Hayden couldn't have gone any better. David relayed his mother's wishes for an intimate funeral and Patrick gave advice and guidance for every step of the process. Hayden's would deal with everything from acquiring the medical certificate and registering the death to the purchase of five death certificates; in order to wrap up his mother's affairs, companies would need original documents. All David had to do was choose the coffin, the urn for her ashes and any particular words or music he wanted for the service. Patrick suggested a short ceremony on Wednesday at 12 o'clock, which was fine with David.

* * *

CHAPTER 44

BAD NEWS TRAVELS

BURGLAR WHO MURDERED OAP IN HER HOME BURNS TO A CRISP IN CAR CRASH

On Wednesday 29th March, 28-year-old Austrian Lukas Mayer broke into a pensioner's home in Sevenoaks, Kent and brutally beat his victim, 65-year-old Nancy Walker, to death. Police believe the widow, who lived alone, disturbed a burglary when she came home from shopping in the early afternoon. Evidence showed that Mrs. Walker desperately tried to fend off her attacker, but Mayer used a cord in an attempt to strangle her. He then bludgeoned the woman's face, breaking her jaw and eye-socket, before shooting her three times in the chest. Mrs. Walker was pronounced dead at the scene. A Kent Police spokesman said that it was the most horrific murder they'd ever seen in the county.

Police officers were initially alerted when a silent alarm was tripped at the woman's home. They arrived as the killer was making his escape in a stolen carpet-cleaning van. Officers gave chase, but after five minutes the burglar lost control of the van and crashed into another stationary vehicle. Police say that Mayer hit the other car at such velocity that the entire front of the van was crushed on impact, immediately engulfing the vehicle in flames. Police were unable to get to Mayer and he died from his injuries before the arrival of the fire brigade.

It is not understood yet why Mayer, from West London, targeted this particular house in a private road in Kent, but he did manage to make his escape with cash and some jewellery from the house.

Nancy Walker had been a civil servant until her retirement, having played a vital role at the Radar Research Establishment which developed Britain's radar defences during the Second World War. Chief Inspector Tom Barnes of Kent Police said, "This was a despicable crime. The injuries inflicted on Mrs. Walker were brutal and horrific and our thoughts go out to her only son."

Local residents who knew the victim where in complete shock at barbarity of the murder, with one woman saying, "He got the justice he deserved."

The Sun

* * *

At Alexandra house, rather than retreat from her initial confrontation with Angela, Laura decided that the best form of defence was to attack in the only way she knew how; through mental dexterity and will power. At breakfast times before school, Laura made sure she sat as near as possible to Gordon, smiling and engaging him in conversation at any opportunity which always incurred Angela's wrath. She'd employed similar tactics before against Lee, by constantly staring at him across the table to make him react. After a few days of the treatment, Lee had indeed reacted, but not quite in the way she'd expected. Lee had tipped his entire bowl of porridge over her head. Whilst embarrassing and messy, the result had been exactly what she was aiming to achieve... another physical punishment for her younger brother.

Conversations with the other children in the home were never exactly high-brow. This was exemplified by the newspapers delivered each day – tabloids only. There was no *Times* or *Guardian* for Laura to extend her academic knowledge from, not even the *Mail* or *Express*. Instead, just titillation, gossip and sport were part of the morning routines. But if Laura wanted to be more popular with boys or people in general, she needed to put herself into the mindset of those that read the most popular papers by far in Britain. *The Sun* and *Mirror* had an initial circulation of seven million people in Great Britain, and you could treble that in secondary daily readership – which meant that over a third of the nation read one of these papers each day. Laura impressed the other kids with her ability to scan-read the articles in double-quick time. They would try and test her knowledge to the most obscure stories they could find. In most cases, Laura had the high-level view of each article's content. She refused to take questions on the sports or horse racing section though – they were just too boring.

On Monday 10th April, Laura wished she could travel backwards in time. This time last year, she'd received a new guitar for her birthday and had all the attention she needed from loving parents. But she would never forget this, her twelfth birthday. Fred had been kind enough to give her a birthday card before she sat down to eat breakfast and scan *The Sun* before school. But instead of continuously flicking through each page every thirty seconds, Laura got stuck on page 5. Her attention was initially drawn to the victim's name and then the pictures of Nancy and Mayer. She read the full story... slowly and twice. Laura's face lost what fine colour her pale complexion had. She barely touched her breakfast and folded the newspaper closed before handing it over for the other kids to look at.

Fred saw the look on her face before the girl got up to put her cold toast in the bin. "What's the matter, Laura?" she asked.

Laura paused before answering. "Oh nothing. Just sad about my birthday; that's all."

Fred didn't buy it, but chose not to dig any further. "I'll get you a birthday cake from the shops today for when you come home from school. It's something I do for everyone here. You're twelve now, right?" she said, attempting to lighten the mood.

Laura just nodded as if in her own world, finished washing her plate and collected her things for school.

After everyone had left the home that morning, Fred went back to the now stained and well-used newspaper. Nothing made sense that might upset the girl, until she got to page 5. As she read the article the penny dropped. The picture the newspaper had used wasn't the best, but there was definitely a likeness to the woman Lynn had brought with her after Lee ran away. The woman must've been about the same age and Lee had protested about his surname being King – he said it was Walker. She now knew why Laura had been stunned... her grandmother had just been murdered.

* * *

Over the weekend, Vivienne had still not seen any article or obituary in the papers she'd ordered each day. There'd been nothing in the broadsheets. Then she realised that she might be missing a trick, and expanded her reading to the bottom-feeding tabloids as well. Her hunch paid dividends when she finally got round to reading Monday's edition of *The Sun*. There he was in black and white, the man that ruined her life and sent her into hiding. As she read through, Vivienne tried to piece together what had been done behind the scenes. There'd been no mention of the man's real name or any potential links to the KGB or Stasi. There was also no mention of Theo or anyone being caught for espionage. She certainly didn't appreciate being called an OAP... even though they were technically right.

Vivienne slapped the paper down on her room table. The story was from the perspective of the provincial police who wouldn't have known any better, which meant Theo must've had something to bargain with... *unless The Chief needed to keep things quiet from the Americans?* These were questions that would be answered when she next made contact – which could wait until tomorrow. For now, she had her own plans to execute.

Dressed in ordinary clothes, Vivienne put her coat on and grabbed her handbag and stationery. At reception she gave instructions to cancel all but one of her daily papers. She walked to the nearest *WH Smith* newsagent and purchased a few copies of *The Sun* along with an Ordnance Survey road map, took her car from the hotel car park and drove north-east.

Four hours later, she was sat in a little tea room overlooking the beach at Skegness. Skegness seemed quite desolate out of season, which was just as well because in-season, the place was like most British seaside towns – rough around the edges and full of drunk tourists. The place held no real sentimental value to her and she'd never set foot in Lincolnshire before, but that was precisely why she'd come. Any call she made to The Chief would automatically be traced to a location and any letters she sent would also show a postmark.

The tea room was quiet enough to relax and enjoy a hot potato and write the notes she wanted to send. The first letter was to Lee, care of Caldicot School. Having seen the way the article had been worded, she couldn't be sure that The Chief would be able to keep his word when it came to being able to see her grandson. She also couldn't be sure that Lee had been given advanced warning of the story breaking. The note was short and included a page torn from one of the newspapers.

Dear Lee,

I hope you are getting on well with Mum and Dad and the school is working out for you. I have lots to tell you. I will be in touch when I can, but it may take some time. If it's not allowed through Mum and Dad, I will find some other means. Please keep this to yourself for now and remember, not everything in the papers is factually correct!

Love you lots,

N Vx

P.S. Please destroy this after reading.

The second note she wrote was to Lynn Franks at Hertfordshire Social Services. She wondered whether the woman had tried to get in touch as they'd discussed. It was only fair to let her know that Laura would not be forgotten.

Dear Lynn,

You may have tried to contact me without success. Since we spoke over lunch, a number of unfortunate events have occurred – one of which I have enclosed. As you will see, not everything in black and white can be counted on. I have not forgotten about any of our conversation, but in the current circumstances, the person of interest will have to remain in situ until other control measures can be put in place. I trust you will continue to do what's in their best interests of safety. I will be in contact again as soon as practicable.

Yours sincerely

N

P.S. Do not place this on file.

Before sending the letters, Vivienne retrieved a handful of coins from her purse and made a call from a telephone box into HQ to speak to The Chief.

"This is Empress for The Chief." The line went quiet for a minute or two. To some this would be disconcerting, but Vivienne knew that he was either swamped, not at his desk or arranging for the call to be recorded. Vivienne wouldn't be fazed, whatever the reason was; she needed answers.

"Empress, how are you holding up?" The Chief said, his voice that of genuine concern.

Over the past few days, Vivienne had thought about her situation and how much she'd lost because of Theo.

"I've always understood the risks, but it's difficult knowing what I've had to put my only son through – especially as he's barely had the chance to come to terms with the loss of his son," she said, letting the words hang momentarily.

"So, I guess you've read the article and you have questions?" he said knowingly.

"That would probably be an understatement in light of what I've just been through." Three familiar beeps in the earpiece warned Vivienne that she needed to put another coin into the money slot.

"It's not something to be discussed now, but you deserve an explanation. Shall we meet – just you and me?

"I'd like that. Would Liverpool Street station be alright, sometime this week? Vivienne didn't want to meet at any place where she needed her car. The Chief knew just the right time. As disciplined as she was, he couldn't risk whoever Nancy was now turning up at her own funeral.

"Wednesday lunchtime, 12 o'clock?"

"Agreed, at the entrance to platform ten?"

"Perfect," The Chief said. "Anything else?"

"Have you communicated with the guardians yet?"

"No, not yet. It's been a little busy here. But I'll be sure to do so by Wednesday."

"Thank you."

"Ciao for now, Empress."

Vivienne replaced the receiver and opened the Yellow Pages. The conversation with The Chief had sparked an idea. A few short calls later and having posted the two letters, Vivienne drove to an auto parts shop, where they were able to make up three different pairs of number plates on the premises. She was pretty sure they would come in handy at some point and stored them in the boot of the car with the necessary fixings inside the spare wheel compartment.

With her work for the day done, Vivienne drove back to Windsor, giving more thought to her future. Having to drive miles out of her way every time she wanted to do something was not the way she wanted to live the rest of her life.

* * *

It was The Chief's assistant who called Debbie. She suggested finding a copy of *The Sun* and reading page five; more would be revealed when Empress made contact.

It took visits to several newsagents before Debbie managed to buy the last copy in the local area. The article stunned her. Later, talking it through with Chris, it brought home the fragility of their situation. What on earth would they say to Lee?

They'd need to be more vigilant in everything they both did professionally and personally. Chris also wondered whether taking on the responsibility for Lee was now a liability for them both, but he kept that thought to himself.

* * *

CHAPTER 45

A SLICE OF POWER

déjà vu

[ˌdeɪʒɑː ˈvuː] noun

a feeling of having already experienced the present situation.

Laura ran all the way home after school without stopping, occasionally turning back to see if she'd been followed. *I can't believe I just did that!*

She'd had no pocket money from the home yet, but there were some things she needed… so that afternoon, she had talked herself into the school secretary's office and, whilst the woman had gone to find something, taken some stamps, envelopes and a pound note from the petty cash tin. Her heart pumped madly at the first feeling of the exhilaration of stealing something; and getting away with it. She now understood why Lee used to do it, but still wasn't sure whether she'd have the guts to do it again. It seemed to be so easy for Lee. She also surprised herself at being able to run the distance from school to home non-stop. Yes, she was out of breath, but she also felt that she could've run further without the satchel of books over her back; a big surprise considering she only did gymnastics once a week at school now.

Whilst the home was quiet, she went up to her room to take off her uniform. Instead of changing into her casual clothes, Laura just hung out in her room in a thin roll-neck and a pair of knickers. She grabbed a pen, paper and a hard-backed book to lean on, and lay propped up on her front on her bed to begin writing a letter.

Dear Mum,

I am so so sorry for what happened to you and dad the other week. I never meant to cause you all those problems – I was trying to protect you and little Jon Jr...

Laura's thoughts were disturbed by a knock, and the sound of her door opening. Initially shocked and ready to shout at whoever had invaded her privacy, she stayed where she was when she saw it was Gordon, Angela's man.

He stood one step inside the room, motionless, his eyes on stalks at the sight of Laura's slender, fit figure in white cotton knickers. Laura put the letter inside the book and turned over to reveal the tight-fitting roll-neck that contoured her breasts perfectly.

"Is there something you want, Gordon?" she said, not covering herself.

Gordon stuttered, slightly tongue-tied. "I – I just... wanted to say happy birthday."

She smiled nicely at him. "Thank you Gordon, that means a lot to me."

"I wanted to say something this morning, but y'know." He shrugged.

"Y'know what?" came Angela's loud voice behind him. She'd just come upstairs and there was Gordon standing in that bitch Laura's room. She burst in beside him to see Laura in her scantily clothed state.

Angela put herself between Gordon and Laura and started pushing him back out of the doorway. "She's twelve years old and you're nearly fifteen, you perv! You'll go to a young offender's prison if I tell on you."

Gordon hit back. "But you're only thirteen, what's the difference?"

Angela's face went red with anger. "I'm nearly fourteen, there's a big difference!" She pushed Gordon out of the room and tuned back to Laura. "And you can stay out of our business!" she spat.

Laura laughed. "It's not my fault he came into *my* room. Perhaps he prefers someone a little less... insecure?" she said loud enough for Gordon to hear. "Shut the door on your way out."

"Slag!" Angela said before abruptly walking out of the room, intentionally leaving the door wide open.

Laura got up from her bed and went over to shut her bedroom door again, but not without shouting down the hallway, so that everyone could hear. "You're welcome to come and pay me a visit whenever you like, Gordon... just leave the dog at home." She put on some clothes and went back to finishing her letter.

Dear Mum,

I am so so sorry for what happened to you and dad the other week. I never meant to cause you all those problems – I was trying to protect you and little Jon Jr. Please believe me, what I said about dad was all true – he really did do those things to me. I only said something to the journalist because you thought I was lying. But the man misled me; he said he wouldn't repeat anything about dad, and that he was just trying to find out about Lee.

The social worker forced me to give a statement to the police, but I can ask them to retract it if you want me to. She also wouldn't tell me where they were taking Jon Jr, even though I said that I'd take care of him for you. All I want to do is come home. I'm currently being held in a children's home at:

Alexandra House Children's Home

268 Risbygate Street,

Bury St. Edmunds,

Suffolk

Please can you come and get me. I love you all very much.

Laura xx

Laura addressed the envelope, affixed the stamp and put the letter in her bag for the next day.

At dinnertime, Fred presented her with a large pink birthday cake with twelve lit candles stuck to the top. The children all sang happy birthday except Angela and then Gordon, after he'd received a swift finger-jab to the ribs. Laura blew out the candles, her wish being that the letter would find her mother in a forgiving mood.

"It's entirely up to you, Laura, but the children usually cut their cake into pieces for everyone to share," Fred said. Everyone's eyes were either on Laura to see what she would decide, or the cake.

"I'm happy to share," she said, smiling. She counted round all the heads at the table and quickly calculated the fractions needed for the cake. She cut good sized pieces for everyone, and left Gordon and Angela till last.

"Here you go, Gordon – you can have some of my piece as well," she said, giving him a larger piece than anyone else.

He sat wide-eyed. "Thanks, Laura!"

"Oooooh!" the rest of the kids all sniggered, as Laura handed the last sliver to Angela.

"Here you go, Angela. Sorry it's so small, but it's all that's left. I must've miscalculated." Angela seemed lost for words. "Never mind," Laura continued, "it would probably just go to your thighs anyway. Us girls need to look out for each other, don't you think?"

Angela wanted to shove the minuscule piece of cake in Laura's face, but she just left the slice on the plate and walked out of the dining room.

Fred kept Laura back after everyone had finished at the table that evening. "That wasn't called for, Laura. I'm not sure what's going on with you two, but I don't want any grief at this home. Even though it's your birthday, you can do the dishes tonight."

Laura didn't care about the dishes. It wasn't like she had anything better to do anyway. It was worth it just to see the face of that 'madam' who'd had the temerity to threaten her on her first day. But, there was something she wanted to get off her chest to Fred.

"I don't know what I've done specifically to deserve it, but I was wondering why I don't get pocket money like the others? Angela said I'd have to pay her back for some money that Lee stole when he ran away, but I don't see why I should have to pay for his sins?"

"Well firstly, people don't just get pocket money. It's a privilege that's earned," Fred replied. "Most of the pocket money the children get here is from a fund set up by their parents or the people who can no longer look after them. The rest get a small amount for doing jobs around the house."

"I do jobs, so I should get something, shouldn't I?" Laura countered.

"Agreed, Laura. If and when you go from being a temporary stay to a permanent resident, you'll get pocket money because that'll all be sorted out with your parents."

"So why do I need to bother doing jobs now, then?" Laura said cockily.

Fred walked right up close and personal to her. "Because if you don't, Laura, I may not bother to do my jobs, like provide nice food for you, let you use the hot water, heating in your room and washing facilities for your clothes. Is that clear to you?"

Laura was angry and just wanted to slap the smelly woman in the face. She tried to stare Fred down into looking away first, but Fred was formidable for an old woman. Laura turned and walked towards the kitchen sink without saying anything. She might have lost this battle... she just had to think of a way to win the war.

* * *

On the morning of Wednesday 12th, Stephanie arrived to pick David up from his home at 10:15. He had made an effort by wearing dark navy trousers, crisp white shirt and a navy tie. His hair was freshly washed and he wore cologne that wasn't overpowering. *Scrubs up well*, Stephanie thought.

Despite his sombre mood, David couldn't help being bowled over by Stephanie's appearance. She wore a sleek, fitted pencil-dress that showed off her figure to a tee, with dark stockings. Patent black stilettos and matching clutch bag finished off the outfit. It wasn't just her clothes that knocked David for six; Stephanie had really gone to town on her make-up, her skin porcelain-perfect and her blonde hair flicked up at the ends.

"Should I come in or do you want to go now?" she asked softly.

"I'm sorry, please come in – I just need to put some shoes on. You look wonderful, by the way."

Stephanie allowed herself to blush slightly. She was used to compliments from the guys at work, but they always seemed to have a lurid undertone to them. David's had a simplistic innocence that made her feel like a woman again.

David laced up his polished shoes and swung the matching navy suit jacket on. "Chief Inspector Tom Barnes said he wanted to pay his respects at the funeral. I hope you don't mind, but I said it was OK?"

Stephanie winced inwardly, but replied, "Absolutely, whatever you feel is right."

Traffic was light and so the two stopped off and made conversation over a coffee before arriving at the crematorium chapel, fifteen minutes before their allocated appointment. Tom was already there and asked David how he was holding up. The truth was that if it hadn't been for Stephanie he really wasn't sure what state he would be in by now. There was sadness, yes, but really he just felt empty.

Patrick Hayden met them all and gave each of them a small sheet of card, handwritten in italics, which showed the short order of service. "Have you decided whether you'd like to say anything, David?" he asked.

"I'm not sure I can. Every time I think about her, I see the way she died."

Tom spoke up. "Would you mind if I said a few words? Then you can decide if you want to add anything afterwards."

David agreed. It took the immediate pressure out of the situation.

The pallbearers brought in the black-draped coffin, and Patrick gave a brief introduction to the ceremony, paying tribute to Nancy Walker's life. This was slickly followed by a quiet listening to one of the records David had brought with him – *Ev'ry Day I Love You (Just A Little Bit More)*, sung by Jo Stafford. Then Tom was invited to speak. He talked about when they first met and how she had always been there to help him whenever he needed it. He closed with a message to David to say that he would always be there for him in return. David couldn't bring himself to speak when Patrick signalled to ask if he wanted to say anything.

Patrick gave a closing word before the coffin was committed to the conveyor belt to Frank Sinatra's rendition of *Stella by Starlight*.

When it was all over, David walked outside and watched the oblivious traffic pass by. *Was that it? This life... was it that disposable? You come, you go and the world keeps on turning?*

"Shall I take you home now?" Stephanie asked.

Before David could reply, Tom appeared at her side. "I just need to speak to Stephanie for a moment, if that's OK."

Stephanie gave her keys to David who walked over to her car to let himself in.

"Are you off to see Brand?" she asked.

"Yes. Anything you want me to say on your behalf?"

"Just that I assume the mission is now over and I'll be ready for a new assignment tomorrow."

"Will do," Tom replied. "Try to let the boy down gently, won't you!"

Driving back to David's home, Stephanie pondered what she should do next. "We're only a few minutes from your place; would you like to go for a quick drink before I drop you off?" she asked.

David perked up a little, not necessarily for the drink, but more for the company. In the small saloon bar of his local, the conversation seemed to flow much better than when they were in the car, and they both began to open up to each other. David was surprised to find out that Steph (when she was off duty) was an athletics county champion in the 800 metres and pole vault of all things.

"Do you know what you're going to do with yourself and the house and everything?" she asked.

"I honestly haven't really thought about it; I guess there's no immediate concern. It's much nicer than my flat, but I don't know if I could actually live there now."

"Sounds sensible to let the dust settle a little bit first and see how you feel in a while. Can I give you some advice?"

"Sure."

"Just make sure to leave the heating on regularly. It's a lovely house; but it'll quickly fall into disrepair if it's left to the elements."

David acknowledged the advice as the barmaid rang the bell for last orders. He was mentally exhausted from the last five days, and declined Stephanie's offer of a second pint.

"Come on, I'll drop you back home," she said.

"Thanks, Steph... thanks for all you've helped me with. I wouldn't have been able to do this without you, but I'll walk home now... I just need some fresh air."

"You're a good guy, David, so I hope things turn out better." She reached into her handbag. "I don't usually do this, but here's my card." She took out a pen and wrote on the back. "And this is my home number."

David's heart lifted momentarily, as the faintest glimmer of light appeared at the end of the dark tunnel he'd been walking through the last three months. But as they parted and she drove into the distance, for the first time in his life he truly felt alone.

In the car, Stephanie wondered whether she'd done the right thing. Only time would tell.

* * *

Vivienne arrived at Liverpool Street an hour before she was due to meet with The Chief on Wednesday morning, wearing the dullest clothes she could find. She'd thought about buying a wig, but it didn't seem particularly necessary for this meeting. Besides, she didn't want to use up potential disguises in case she needed to go deeper undercover in the future.

Rather than initially occupy one place in the station, she took a circular route around the various platforms before finding an ideal spot in the corner of the only inside café, where she placed an order for two coffees. From her vantage point she could observe the comings and goings across five platforms, number ten being the nearest, whilst purportedly reading a copy of *The Times*. The Chief was always a potential target, so she knew that someone would be in amongst the people somewhere – she just needed to mark them.

At 11:37, two men walked into the station together and split up. One took a position near platform nine and the other not far from where she sat. What gave them away was their constant horizon-scanning. It was exactly what she was doing, although she managed it with more subtlety.

She knew that The Chief had arrived when the two men signalled to each other. 11:59 and there he was striding across the concourse, umbrella in hand. Vivienne got up and walked over to the nearest agent.

"You can tell The Chief that I have a nice spot to talk over here." The man tried to act nonchalant, but Vivienne knew she'd surprised him.

The agent at platform nine walked to The Chief and escorted him over to where she was sat.

He looked around before sitting down. "You can both give us some room," he said to the lead agent, and they both moved towards platform ten.

"How have you been... 'Empress'?" he asked, wondering if she'd divulge her new identity.

Vivienne didn't have any particular issue with this. She'd eventually have to anyway if she was to maintain any future involvement with The Service – but she just wanted to know what that involvement would be first.

"Well, I still have a couple of bruises. I guess we don't heal as quickly when we get older. I've been seriously inconvenienced, I have nowhere to live and I imagine that my son's life is a total wreck at the moment. So, "could be better" would be the honest answer," she replied.

"I'm sorry. I should be more sensitive about these things."

"No... I'm sorry. I shouldn't bite your head off about the situation; what happened wasn't your fault. I'm just annoyed that one of our own compromised me in the worst way." Vivienne looked away to emphasise the point. She looked back at The Chief. "Did you find out why Schäfer broke into my home?"

"The short answer is no, but we're going to do some digging on that one. We didn't get much from Theo, only that he knew the man was watching you when you met in London and that he'd given Schäfer your telephone number. The assumption is that he must've had access to someone at British Telecom who provided your address. I think that's something we need to get someone to look at across the entire network."

"What else did you find out from Theo?"

This was an interesting question for The Chief. Empress clearly knew something was up by the story that went to print. "Can I get a coffee first?" he said.

Vivienne looked over her shoulder to see the waitress already making her way towards them with two coffees on a tray.

The Chief smiled. It was the little things that made good agents exceptional and Nancy Walker was definitely that, even if she did go by a different name these days. "There's only so much I can say, but you deserve an explanation. What Schäfer told you was right, Theo does have a wife in Egypt and Turkey and that's how he was compromised; that and the promise of money to help him with his financial burden."

Vivienne nodded her understanding. It was something she had thought about ever since their meeting near St. Paul's. "Don't tell me, the Russians have a CIA mole and they're paying Theo to be an intermediary via Schäfer?"

"If it were that easy, we would've exposed him and faced the usual petty retaliations from Moscow." The Chief watched the Empress' face as the cogs began to turn.

"The mole isn't a mole and is passing disinformation via Theo?" she questioned.

The Chief shook his head. "Close but less straightforward. Theo was also being paid by the CIA to pass on genuine information to Schäfer."

Vivienne's head flinched backwards slightly. This didn't make sense and was not something she'd seen before.

The Chief recognised the look. "So you can see that exposing Theo isn't a good idea until we find out exactly what's going on," he said with a raised eyebrow, as he stirred and sipped his coffee.

"So, he's still in play?"

The Chief nodded. "For now."

Vivienne sighed. She'd been compromised all because of one man's greed. She'd seen it before. Money always talked. "What about Janet, does she know?"

"Yes, and I suspect that marriage may not last too long. But we'll smooth things over with her."

"Such a shame, she's a lovely lady." Her words were just meant to fill a gap in the air as Vivienne's mind momentarily zoomed back to the thoughts she'd about Theo whilst eating pizza. Janet hadn't seemed to matter much then. "So, what's your plan going forward?"

"Well you saw the article. We need to see where the chips fall on the Russian side when they come asking for Schäfer's body. Presumably, the intel will dry up for a while when the Americans get wind. Theo has been asked to continue as normal for now. We'll just have to see who makes the first move."

"Puts Theo in a precarious position; how do you think he'll react?"

The Chief didn't want to expose too much about the uncertainty of the situation. "I've asked MI5 to put him under close watch for now."

Vivienne nodded. She understood the message and backed off from that line of questioning by changing the subject. "Have you spoken with Chris and Debbie yet?" she asked.

"They're waiting for a call from 'Empress' and were signposted to Monday's article. Nothing else has been said, so you have the green light."

"Thank you; it means a lot."

"You're welcome...." The Chief paused, letting the last word hang for a second.

"I go by Vivienne now."

"You're welcome, Vivienne... it's a lovely name." The Chief smiled and glanced at his watch. "So, tell me more about the sister?"

Vivienne noticed the glance and logged it in the back of her mind. "Laura is different from Lee. They're both clever but Laura combines academic intelligence with long-term strategic thinking. Given her current situation, I think there's huge potential, but she'll need to be eased into the role. I just need to make sure her choices are limited."

"What sort of timeframe are you estimating to have her in the programme?" he asked.

"I'm not sure. Six months to a year?"

"You'll keep me updated?"

"Of course," Vivienne said.

The Chief looked at his watch again. "I'm sorry... Vivienne, but I'm going to have to run very soon."

Vivienne could see the man looked a little uncomfortable. "Just one more thing," she said. "What's happened with David?"

It was the question The Chief was dreading through the whole meeting, but there was no other choice; he had to bite the bullet. "Special Branch assigned a liaison officer to make sure the whole situation was properly handled with the right outcomes." He paused. "The funeral of Nancy Walker took place at 12 o'clock today in accordance with her final wishes."

Vivienne's mind went back to when they'd agreed the meeting. He must've known then. The Chief read her expression. "I'm sorry; I just couldn't risk anything – especially if the place was being observed. You understand don't you?"

With a hint of a smile she nodded a reluctant agreement. It was annoying but the man was right, it was just hard for her to relinquish control of her past life. At the merest of signals, the two agents reacted in readiness as The Chief stood, leaving Vivienne seated. "We'll speak when things progress?"

"Yes," she said.

"*Bon chance.*" The two agents escorted him away, covering front and rear.

Neither The Chief, his men nor Vivienne saw the man standing in a far corner of the station near platform two, who'd taken pictures of the meeting with a zoom lens.

* * *

PART 7

(April 1978 – July 1978)

CHAPTER 46

POISED

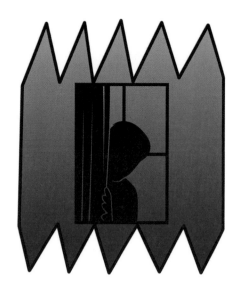

From the time of their arrests in March, Jon and Louvaine King had both maintained their innocence. The police knew they were guilty as hell, but trying to prove everything in court was never straightforward. The case had become high-profile and the leading investigative officer sought significant input from the Crown Prosecution Service to make sure they had enough evidence for everything to stick. They'd also tried to build a case for Louvaine being an accomplice but there were no laws that required her to report Jon's crime to the police. Even though the prosecution's case was solid, it was totally dependent on Laura's testimony to really make sure her parents got what they deserved.

Louvaine and Jon's lives after the arrests had been made unbearable. They'd been released on bail, subject to relinquishing any passports, not living at any other address, not contacting or attempting to contact Laura, Jon Jr. or Lynn – with Jon also having to report to the local police station twice a week. They'd arrived home to find their windows smashed and bright orange graffiti broadcast across the front of the house clearly marking them out as '*Rapists*'. The inside of their home hadn't fared much better after the police had completed their search. Louvaine was like a rabid dog to anyone who looked at her, but none of the neighbours cared and abused them both whenever they were out in public. They couldn't even get served in the local shops, having to travel out of town for shopping when they could – and when Jon's tyres weren't slashed or fuel lines cut. Jon had been sacked from his job at Marconi because the company couldn't afford the reputational damage, whether he was innocent or not. The news had spread and nobody else would touch him with a bargepole either. With no money coming in and little in the way of any benefits, they fell behind on their mortgage payments.

Louvaine was only interested in finding out where Jon Jr. had been taken and when Laura's letter arrived, she reacted in the only way she knew how. Ignoring the bail restriction, she wrote back.

Laura,

Who do you think you're kidding with your stupid little apology? You say that you're sorry but you still told the journalist about Lee and it was your fault we had to get rid of him. All you ever did was bully and tease him. Don't think I didn't see you trying to take Dad away from me – always on show like a little slut. He may have played with you, but it was me he always wanted. Thanks to you we were arrested and Jon Jr. was taken away from us. The house and car were vandalised and dad no longer has a job. Everyone calls us rapists now. Our lives have been ruined all because you couldn't keep your mouth shut – or your legs together. And after all we did to get you into the grammar school.

You've put us in a position where you can't come home, even if we did want you back. Don't ever write to us again because I won't read or reply back!

Louvaine

* * *

Lynn Franks maintained regular weekly contact with Fred regarding Laura. With the court date set for May, she needed to make sure the girl would still be there to give testimony. She updated Fred with what was happening at her end, listing out all of the charges Laura's parents would be facing and their bail conditions. The CPS Lawyer would need to visit the home to speak to Laura in preparation for the case.

In return, Fred spoke with Lynn about the story of Nancy Walker in the paper and that Laura had seen it. Not being a natural liar, Lynn let Fred do most of the talking about the situation. There was no way she could let on that the story was fake. She'd been pretty horrified and surprised at having received a letter from a dead woman and wondered how Nancy would eventually make contact with her.

Because Laura had not been given any mail privileges, Fred was surprised to receive the handwritten letter addressed to her two weeks later. As a matter of nosiness and precaution she opened the envelope and read the contents. She'd seen some bad things in the past relating to how children were treated by their parents when they arrived at the home, but this was borderline psychotic. When she called Lynn seeking advice on what to do, they both agreed that Laura should be allowed to read the letter. Because it violated the parents' bail conditions, Fred was to keep it in her possession until handing it over to the prosecution lawyer.

That evening after dinner and after Laura had finished her jobs, Fred went upstairs to her room and knocked on the door.

"Do you mind if I come in, Laura?" she said softly.

Laura was finishing off some maths homework that taxed a minute portion of her brain. She was a stubborn girl when she wanted to be and neither of them had spoken much since the birthday cake incident.

With only one chair in the room, Fred motioned for Laura to sit opposite her on the bed.

Laura saw the opened letter in Fred's hand and instantly knew there was going to be a problem. She recognised the handwriting as Fred handed her the envelope. "I think you should read this."

"It's been opened," Laura said sharply.

Fred maintained a warm tone. "I think you should read it and we can talk afterwards."

Laura warily took the one-page letter out of the envelope, sensing bad news from Fred's voice. As her eyes began their journey darting from left to right, her comprehension stumbled over and again. Not because she couldn't understand what was written – her mother had perfect handwriting – but because she couldn't understand how cold and untruthful she could be to her own daughter. How could her mother come down on the side of a rapist? Laura's eyes watered as her heart sank. She was trapped here in a children's home with no other avenues for release. She'd burned her bridges with her real dad, Nan was now dead and her mother had made it very clear that she didn't want her back.

Fred took the letter from Laura and offered her a shoulder to cry on, but she refused. Not out of any particular hostility towards the woman, it was simply that she just wanted to retreat emotionally.

"Can I ask what you said in the letter you wrote to your mum, Laura?" Fred asked. "I'm not sure anything warrants this type of response."

"I just said that I was sorry for the situation I'd put them in by talking to the journalist. He seemed more interested in finding out about Lee than anything else." Laura knew that this wasn't strictly correct, but the more she repeated the lie, the more it felt true.

"Was there anything else?"

"I promised her that everything about what Dad did to me was true and that I might be able to retract the statement if they could bring me home again."

"Whatever happened, Laura, there's no place for what your stepfather did to you. I can't believe your own mother wouldn't do anything about it." Laura had no answer for this; she couldn't believe it either. "I want you to know that I have no real interest invading your privacy like this, but at the moment I have a legal requirement. Your parents were both bailed by the police and one of the terms was that they were not allowed to contact you. For all I know, they could've been coercing you to tell lies in court when you testify or trying to get you not to testify at all."

Laura looked at Fred to see that what she was saying was true.

"Cross my heart, dear," Fred said.

"Can I keep the letter?"

Fred was somewhat surprised at the request. "I've got to keep it for now, because it has to be handed over to the prosecution as evidence. There's some pretty damning stuff in here. I'm sure the police can give it back to you once the case is closed if you still want it."

Laura's mind churned. Since giving her statement to the police, she'd wondered whether she really wanted to testify against her parents. But her mother had now made the decision for her. If they didn't want her back, she was going to make damn sure they paid the price for it. "Thank you, Fred. Sorry for going behind your back."

"I understand, Laura. I probably would've done the same thing and I suppose you had to try. But I have to ask you not to do anything like this again. The court date is just around the corner and hopefully it'll all be over soon."

Laura gave a polite smile which was Fred's cue to leave.

* * *

The last thing Lynn expected at 9:30 on a Monday morning was a call to say that she had a guest waiting for her in reception. Social Services could be manic sometimes, but she had nothing in her diary until 11 o'clock.

"Who is it?" she asked the receptionist.

"The lady's name is Vivienne Cooper." The name didn't sound familiar. "She's from Essex Social Services."

"OK, I'll be down in five minutes," Lynn said as she wrote the name on her notepad.

The receptionist indicated to Vivienne where she could sit and wait. A few minutes later Lynn walked out from a side door, immediately recognising the woman sat in front of her.

"Na... Vivienne?"

"You must be Lynn Franks?"

Lynn played along. "Yes, that's correct. How can I help?"

"Do you mind if we speak in private?"

"Of course, please follow me." Lynn took Vivienne into an empty side room where they sat opposite each other.

"So, you received my letter, then?" Vivienne said, having read Lynn's initial reaction.

"Yes, and I'm glad I did."

"Oh, why's that?" Vivienne enquired.

"Because if I hadn't seen the story myself, I'd have been pretty shocked when Fred read it through over the phone – especially given our last conversation. I tried calling, but there was no response; so I never called again as you instructed."

"I figured that would be the case, which is why I wrote."

"Do these sorts of things happen very often? You know, in the papers and everything?" Lynn asked.

"No, not often at all. It was in *The Sun* because we needed a wide coverage."

"Well, you should know that I catch up with Fred every week and Laura saw it too."

"Did you say anything?"

"No. I'd read your letter the day before. I think Laura was pretty shocked though," Lynn replied.

"This has been a bad situation all round, Lynn. Laura's real father and my only son had to bury his mother a couple of weeks ago. Imagine how devastating that was for him."

Lynn tried but really couldn't get close. Vivienne took out a notebook and pen from a large linen shopping bag she'd brought with her. "Are you still carrying the... gun?" Lynn said lowering her voice.

Vivienne smiled. "No. It's awkward being dead, I can assure you, but it also comes with certain freedoms too. I'm safer now that I'm dead than when I was alive."

"What's with the notebook?" Lynn asked.

"I was hoping you would give me a full update on everything... I was going to make some notes if that's alright?"

"It's probably best if I get the file, if you don't mind waiting. It's just one of six cases I'm working on at the moment and I wouldn't want to get the specifics confused." Lynn left Vivienne for a few minutes before she came back to the room with a thick folder. She updated Vivienne on the case against Mr. & Mrs. King, giving all the charges, copies of the correspondence between Laura and Mrs. King, the court hearing date and location as well as Laura's general progress and behaviour at the home.

"Do you think the reporter from the *Herts Advertiser* will be following the case to conclusion?" Vivienne asked.

"I would expect so, but I'll make sure he's at the hearing."

"How do you think the case will turn out?"

"Well, we have enough to convict Mrs. King on some of the minor stuff for sure," Lynn said, "and for Mr. King to be convicted of taking an indecent photograph and possession. I think the letter could also work in our favour, but the rest really hinges on Laura's statement and testimony standing up to the defence lawyer's scrutiny."

"Do you think she'll be reliable?"

Lynn wasn't so sure of this and intimated so to Vivienne. "I think Laura might be more resolute now, but the CPS aren't taking any chances and they're sending someone this week to prep her before the hearing."

Vivienne nodded. Lynn had done an excellent job with everything so far. "Shall we meet once the dust settles after the court case?"

"I think that would be fine. I just hope I'll have good news for you."

"Well, I have to say that what I've seen so far leads me to believe that you're capable of handling everything exceptionally well. My only concern is that Laura is beginning to stagnate in the children's home. Her mind isn't being stretched. To that end I would like Fred to encourage Laura to seek a tutor or tutors for what she's missing."

Lynn frowned. "How do you expect to her to do that? I'm not sure she's capable and where's the money going to come from?"

Vivienne put the notebook in her bag and pulled out a stack of twenty-pound notes. Lynn's eyes went out on stalks; she'd never seen that much cash before. "This is a thousand pounds," Vivienne said. "It should cover a lot of tuition. Laura needs to be given some responsibility for her life, so finding and learning more about the things she's interested in will be stimulating. I think it's crucial that she's given this opportunity before she testifies. There needs to be a light at the end of what is a very dark tunnel right now."

"That's very kind of you... Vivienne," Lynn responded. "I should count this and give you a receipt."

"Of course. Please also make sure the money is drip-fed to Fred and Laura. I'll also want Fred to make sure she keeps accurate records of how it's used!"

"When Fred asks, who should I say the money's from?"

Vivienne thought a little. "Just say it's part of Laura's inheritance."

Lynn looked surprised at the response, but chose not to pursue the matter further. With everything done, she looked at her watch. Her next meeting was due soon and she needed to prepare. "How will I contact you now?" she asked.

"I don't have my own number yet so I'll be in contact when I can, Lynn, and thank you for everything."

Both women stood and shook hands. Lynn was about to let Vivienne walk out of the room, but a question that had been bugging her needed to be answered. "One more thing, Vivienne, and I'm sorry to have to ask this, but if your death can be... faked, how do I know that you didn't do the same with Lee?"

Vivienne looked at Lynn and nodded. She set her bag down on the table and took out a manila file. "Your question is perfectly valid,

Lynn, but I have no reasons to lie to you. After Louvaine skipped town for the second time, David and I hired a private investigator." She handed the file over to Lynn. "This file contains all of her reports on the investigation. Although this report is private, parts of it may prove useful to the prosecution for questioning. Have a read through... you can make your mind up from there. But just so you know, I have no influence over the French police or newspapers. The only cover up I could detect was the over-zealous nature in which they approached Lee on the bridge and effectively forced him to his death."

Lynn thanked Vivienne and watched as she left the building. She took an envelope from reception for the cash which she then placed her file, and made her mind up to read the new file at home that night.

Before making the journey back, Vivienne stopped by a local newsagent. In exchange for ten pounds, the owner agreed to package and send a copy of the *Herts Advertiser* to her hotel in Windsor for the next three months.

* * *

CHAPTER 47

NO DEFENCE

On the day of the trial, Laura was understandably nervous, not knowing quite what to expect. The prosecution kept her out of the court room to protect her from onlookers, but it was precisely the fact that she couldn't see what was going on that created the tension. But the time did give her the opportunity to think about Fred's new idea to choose extra tuition.

The prosecution and defence gave their opening statements and testimony was given by Lynn and Fred; Lynn's was the key testimony once it was disclosed that the children's grandmother was recently deceased. Thanks to Lynn, the prosecution had also managed to summon Anne Dawkins from Kent Social services to give evidence relating to the early foundations of the case against Mrs. King. The scene was played out in front of the reporter from the *Herts Advertiser* and the packed public gallery upstairs.

By lunchtime the evidence was damning enough for the defence lawyer to seek a deal for his clients, but after conferring with Laura and Lynn, the prosecution refused any notion of a deal.

After a lunchtime adjournment, the judge ordered the public to be excluded from entry to the courtroom. The prosecution lawyer advised Laura to try and avoid eye contact with her parents as much as possible because they could still intimidate her with just a stare. But when the time came for her to be put on the witness stand, it was Laura whose stare intimidated the most. She meant business.

Through skilful and open questioning, using information provided by Lynn and the statement provided to the police, the prosecution allowed Laura to explain the entire two-year saga from her inside perspective, from the time when Lee caught Louvaine having an affair, all the way through to the arrests at their home. As instructed by the prosecution lawyer, Laura made sure to include information that the defence lawyer might ask about in order to blunt the man's weapons when the time came. It was compelling testimony for the jury, who lapped up everything Laura said, but it was the letter from Mrs. King to Laura that sealed their fate.

The defence lawyer was understandably hard on Laura, but she'd been well schooled and the judge came to her aid on a number of occasions – which kept the jury in her corner. She admitted that she felt partially to blame for the assaults on Lee, but that she'd only carried out her mother's orders... someone she was petrified of. Mrs. King had exemplified this precisely with multiple outbursts throughout the hearing. When she alleged that it was her daughter who had instigated the sexual advances towards Mr. King on a number of occasions, Laura countered tearfully, "I couldn't stop him! He's much bigger than me and threatened to have me removed from the home like my brother was. I didn't know how to stop the pain; especially after I told mum and she accused me of lying. He certainly wasn't playing."

Throughout most of Laura's testimony, Jon King had remained motionless, often with his head in his hands. When the defence had finished his questioning, the judge adjourned the hearing for the day – instructing the members of the jury not to discuss the case. But at least two of the jury members spoke with the local journalist afterwards.

The next day was set aside for the testimony from Mr. & Mrs. King. With so much weighing against them, their lawyer advised them to allow him to submit guilty pleas for the charges where there could be no contest. After much consternation and much to the disgust of Louvaine, Jon King gave the instruction for the lawyer to plead guilty on all the charges relating to him. But Louvaine agreed to nothing.

Louvaine King wanted her day in court – her opportunity to put the records straight. But this was foolhardy and only served to harden the resolve of a now irritated jury. In the end, the prosecution made such a compelling case based on the guilty pleas, that the jury really didn't have much choice but to throw the book at the wretched woman.

By the end of the day, Jon and Louvaine King were both remanded in custody pending a sentencing hearing, with the judge ordering a joint report from the police and social services with recommendations.

* * *

CHAPTER 48

RENTAGHOSTS

Laura was given the rest of the week off school to allow her time to recover after the ordeal of the trial against her parents. The prosecution and all of the other adults involved had all celebrated the victories, but the impact of what she'd done to her family hung over Laura like a spectre. She wondered how lenient the judge's sentencing might be after Jon's guilty pleas, and now that her mother had her address, whether she would be in danger of some form of retaliation.

The receipt of the money to fund her education was a welcome relief. Laura spent the money wisely. Rather than buying new books, she bought boxes of old books from the local charity shops covering all sorts of subjects. Finding quality tutors was going to be harder than she thought. She wanted to be tutored in English, Maths and languages, and with Fred's blessing, eventually sought advice by writing to one of her old teachers at the grammar school in St. Albans.

* * *

Three weeks after their meeting, Vivienne kept the promise she'd made and called Lynn from a hotel pay phone in Oxford. Even though she'd seen the closing article of the case in the *Herts Advertiser*, Lynn was able to provide detailed updates about Louvaine, Jon and the baby. Lynn told her of the problems Laura was having trying to find good quality tuition in the subjects she desired. Vivienne made notes and thanked Lynn again for everything she'd done to help her grandchildren.

As the pips sounded to warn that the call would end soon, Lynn asked what Vivienne wanted her to do with the private file she had. Vivienne was just able to provide the London PO Box address before the call ended.

* * *

Beep, beep, beep, beep.

"Hello?"

"This is Empress. I believe you've been expecting my call?"

Chris recognised the voice at the other end. He was glad they still hadn't said anything to Lee, having read her death article. "Yes, but that was a month ago!"

"I understand, but a number of loose ends needed to be tied up before making contact. I would like to visit the three of you; when would be the best time?"

"Saturday in a week's time is the best – that's our weekend with him."

"Shall we say lunchtime on the first then?" she suggested.

"I'll let everyone know," Chris said.

Vivienne thanked him and ended the call feeling the butterflies of excitement in her stomach. She'd really missed the young lad and wondered how he'd been adapting to all his life changes.

Before leaving the city, she purchased a batch of language books from the Oxford University Press bookshop and sent them in a parcel to Fred with strict instructions that they be given to Laura.

With nothing but time on her hands before being reunited with Lee, Vivienne began the long and arduous business of finding a new home. As a temporary measure she moved out of the hotel into a small and inexpensive rental cottage in Old Windsor until she found something to her liking.

* * *

On 1ˢᵗ July, Vivienne made the relatively short journey to Chris and Debbie's home in Taplow, arriving a little earlier than expected. This was habitual for her as a matter of caution, but she needn't have worried. Lee came scampering to the front door and nearly shattered the glass with the force at which he'd opened it. He immediately jumped up to his Nan and wrapped his arms around her shoulders.

"I've missed you, Nan," he said, almost tearfully, as the excitement coursed throughout his body – his emotions on a real high.

Vivienne hadn't been this happy for a long time and smiled the same way she had when David had been born. "Oh darling, I've missed you so much too."

Debbie and Chris now appeared in the hallway and smiled whilst inviting a 'dead lady' into their home. Lee could hardly let go and literally pulled her into the house by hand.

"Welcome back... Empress," Chris said.

Lee looked up at them both in slight confusion. Vivienne smiled. "It's good to see you both again, but I now go by the name of..." Lee wanted to interject with 'V' but remembered what his Nan had said in her letter about keeping quiet. "... Vivienne."

"Oh, Vivienne's such a nice name. That's the name I always wanted," Debbie said, which left Chris looking a little surprised. Lee also gave a confused look .

"I promise I'll explain in a bit," Vivienne said. She couldn't stop looking at the young boy before her. "You've changed so much since I last saw you, young man; you're taller and getting more handsome by the day." Lee beamed.

"Isn't he just," Debbie said, as she ruffled the boy's golden blonde hair.

"That's what good exercise will do for you. Helps you grow, doesn't it, mate?" Chris said manfully.

"And I'm eight years old now too," Lee said, as he took his Nan's coat before they all went into the living room.

Vivienne felt guilty. She wondered if Lee had mentioned this as a hint, but he just continued talking excitedly about everything he'd been up to since they last saw each other. She decided the present sitting in the car boot could wait for later, whilst Debbie went outside to the kitchen to make drinks for them all.

"I've been playing football again and I'm in the school team now. Dad's been teaching me electronics, photography and Ju-Jitsu... look!" Lee got up, swung a leg around Chris and followed up with a choke hold. Chris parried by standing up and tickling Lee on the back of one leg and slamming him back onto the sofa playfully, with an added elbow to the ribs for luck. Lee righted himself, as Debbie came back with a tray of hot drinks for the adults and a coke for Lee. "And I've been learning point-to-point navigation, even in the dark!"

Vivienne hadn't seen him so exuberant in years. She smiled and laughed with him as he cuddled up next to her. This was his true natural state and she was so thankful that Debbie and Chris had done such a wonderful job with him so far.

"Why don't you bring down some of your school work so that your Nan can see how well you're doing there too?" Debbie asked. Lee took a gulp of his coke and shot off upstairs to his room. Debbie knew she wouldn't get much time, so came straight out with what was on her mind. "We saw the story and were worried about whether Lee would see it," she said.

"Do you think he did? He looks in pretty good spirits." Vivienne was proud of how Lee had kept things to himself – assuming he'd received her note, of course.

"We haven't seen or been told of any abnormal behaviour from the school," said Chris.

"I'll have a little chat to put things straight with Lee in a little while. Obviously, drastic things have transpired that necessitated my perceived elimination. My one concession with The Chief was that I remain in touch with Lee and you both. I'm sure that you'll need to clarify any changes with HQ, but I see my role as passive and moral support for Lee as he grows up. I'm hoping that works for you too?"

Debbie was about to agree, but Chris was first to respond. "Is there any chance that you being here, now or in the future, could compromise us?" Debbie was a little surprised at the boldness of the question, but Chris wasn't playing games. He could see that Vivienne was understating her position, and any situation that required Nancy Walker's death to be reported in such a public and violent way could potentially have serious repercussions for them all.

Lee heard traces of the conversation as he came back downstairs, but chose to say nothing.

"I don't think so, Chris," Vivienne replied. "I was very careful before and will be even more vigilant now. But I appreciate why you're asking."

Chris wasn't wholly convinced but chose to leave things there.

Lee sat down again. He thumbed through some of his geography and maths books, as well as select English test results. Vivienne knew that he was covering up some of his less flattering works, but chose to ignore that for now. David used to do the same when he was young.

After they had eaten a lovely lunch that Debbie prepared, Vivienne asked if it was OK for her to pop out for a walk with Lee.

"You don't need to ask," Debbie said. "I'm sure you've both got lots to catch up on."

Lee took his books back upstairs and came back downstairs with his sneakers on, all ready to go. Once outside, he asked his Nan if she was alright to walk up the hill.

"Are you getting cheeky?" she said with a smile. "Come on, lead the way... we have much to talk about!"

As the two walked out from the driveway, Chris made a mental note of Vivienne's license plate – not realising it would be of no help at all.

* * *

Lee took his Nan by the hand as they headed up Berry Hill. Checking behind and with no one in the immediate vicinity, he asked Vivienne about the newspaper story.

Vivienne sighed – it was time the boy learned some truths about life as an agent. "It's a long story. I'll try to summarise things for both our sakes. I've been in The Service for a very long time. I used to recruit people from other countries as agents, information sources or mercenaries..."

"What's a mercenary, Nan?"

"They're soldiers who take on private missions for money." Lee nodded his understanding. "Anyway, I ended up marrying one of the people I recruited just before the war broke out. That was your granddad?" Lee nodded his understanding. "His real name was Stefan Winkler but it was changed to Stephen Walker when we married. I thought we were using him, but he was really using his position to spy for the Germans during the war. I actually caught him when I was pregnant with your dad."

Lee's heart momentarily skipped as the image of his father entered his mind. Life with his dad seemed like a lifetime ago.

"We both nearly died that night," Vivienne continued, "but as you can see, we survived. He promised not to do it again once he learned that he was going to be a father – but he lied. Fast forward seventeen years, and through a tip-off, I found that he was involved in a spy ring, but this time for the Russians. Stephen hadn't been exposed but it was only going to be a matter of time." She stopped and turned to face Lee directly. "This is a very nasty business, but if Stephen had been caught there would've been all sorts of repercussions for me, David, my entire network and the country. So... I killed Stephen, Lee – the KGB spy who called himself a husband and father."

Lee wasn't sure quite what to say, but he could see the steeliness in his Nan's eyes. "I don't get why that meant you had to fake your own death, Nan?"

They both looked side-to-side and began walking again.

"Well, it all started when I contacted one of our agents recently, who happens to be a reporter for the *Daily Mail*, to plant a story for me. When I met with him, I noticed that we were being followed. That man went by the name of Lukas Mayer... the man from the article about my death." Lee frowned. He still had no idea what the connection was. "Lukas Mayer's real name was Florian Schäfer and he and his family originate from Austria. Your grandfather was also from Austria and he had a sister called Lillian Winkler. The coincidence is that Lillian married a man by the name of Lukas Schäfer and that Florian was her son."

Lee had difficulty working out the connections in his head which showed on his face. Vivienne knew she needed to simplify what she was saying. "So the man who followed me was the son of granddad's sister in Austria. Granddad was secretly communicating with her and I think she blamed me for his death. I guess she was technically right, but none of that would've happened if he wasn't a traitor. I'm a true patriot, Lee, and I have served my country proudly my entire life."

Lee was finally getting to grips with the situation. "So did that man follow you home then, Nan?"

"That's a good leap of thought, Lee. He tried, but I gave him the slip. Unfortunately, it turns out that the reporter I went to see was being bribed by Schäfer and sold me out."

Lee was angry that someone would sell his Nan out. "What was the reporter's name, Nan?"

Vivienne looked at Lee and thought for a minute. Maybe Lee could be her insurance policy, like Lillian was for Stephen. "His name is Theo Greaves and he works on the foreign desk at the *Daily Mail*."

Lee repeated the name ten times over in his head to ensure it was memorised forever. "So what happened then?"

"Once I knew I'd been compromised, I set about putting things in place to try to ensure my safety. But as I'm retired, I was limited in what I could do. But my instincts were correct, and a few months ago,

Schäfer broke into my home whilst I was out. He triggered some traps
I'd set, and an emergency response squad arrived. Between us we made
a plan for me to look like I was entering the house as normal. But it
wasn't normal because I was armed."

Lee looked up at his Nan in surprise. "You had a gun?"

"Like I said, I needed to put things in place to ensure my safety. One
of which was carrying a gun."

Lee was fascinated. "Do you have it now?"

Vivienne smiled. "Not at the moment – Nancy Walker is dead.
Unfortunately Florian Schäfer underestimated this old lady and was
shot three times after he'd grabbed me and pushed me to the floor." Lee
squeezed his Nan's hand in admiration. "So everything you read in the
paper was put in place to take the spotlight away from me... which also
helps protect you."

"But what about Theo Greaves? You said he *still* works at the *Daily
Mail*? Shouldn't he be punished or killed for selling you out?"

"I thought the same thing, but it turns out that there's a lot more
in play that could affect whole countries or nations. That will always
trump one person as far as governments are concerned."

"It's not fair, Nan."

"There's a lot that's not fair in this life. Lots that I will teach you
about for as long as I can."

Lee didn't like the melancholy way in which his Nan just spoke and
held her hand tighter. He thought through what his Nan had said for
a while... *Dad!*

"If you're dead, what happened to Dad?" Lee said desperately. He
couldn't help calling the man 'Dad', even though he'd supposedly closed
that chapter of his life.

"That's the saddest part of all, Lee. I've lost my home and David believes me to be dead too; we're all having to start new lives. I can only hope that he's OK – I've not seen him since before the incident. He'll have plenty of money now, though, and the house of course, but I doubt he'd want to live there. I hate what I've had to put him through, but these are the sacrifices we make for our country." It was all Vivienne could do to justify the means to achieve the ends.

As they rounded the next bend of the hill, they both stopped. On the right was a cricket club and a stately home on the left. "Any preference?" she asked.

There was no way that Lee wanted to spend the day going round an old house, so he pointed to the cricket club and guided Vivienne in. "I sometimes come here. The players sometimes let me practise with them and I play with their bats and pads. If I'm really lucky they let me sneak a couple of jam sandwiches during tea."

"I haven't watched cricket in years. Do they sell teas or coffees here?"

"Yep, and cokes as well," Lee beamed.

After buying a bottle of coke and tea served in a proper cup, Vivienne and Lee made their way over to an empty bench and table not far from the clubhouse. The sun had come out and it was a perfect day to watch the match. Lee sat next to his Nan so that they could both see what was going on.

He could instantly tell from the scoreboard that the game was five overs in, with two of the opposition out already. He sucked the end wet on his paper straw, which in turn made his coke last longer.

"I'm sorry I wasn't able to be there for your birthday."

"I'm sure you were there in spirit, Nan."

Vivienne chuckled. "You know, apart from being a couple of Rentaghosts, I also came to give you some updates to our agreement," she said.

"How d'you know about *Rentaghost*?" Lee asked, surprised.

Vivienne smiled again. "I'm not just a breathtakingly pretty face you know!" she said, exaggeratedly flicking the locks of her hair with her fingers.

Lee laughed. He'd never seen his Nan like this before. Perhaps being dead had been a relief for both of them.

"So, do you remember what you asked me that time in The Chief's office?"

Lee knew this without thinking. It was emblazoned in his mind and in his heart forever, like the way cowboys branded their animals.

"I said, please don't let Dad forget me, and make sure the family is made to suffer."

"That's exactly how I remember it too. So, for the first part, I want you to know that I no longer have any control over David's actions. But what I can tell you is that he does keep your ashes in an urn on the mantelpiece where he lives. My only hope is that he's placed mine next to yours so that he remembers us both."

Lee nodded, but it seemed weird to be spoken about like a dead person.

"On the second point I have good news."

Lee's heart skipped in anticipation, wondering whether his Nan's version of good would measure up to the things he'd dreamed of.

Vivienne pulled a notebook from her bag and opened the page she had reserved with a bookmark. "Now remember what I told you – some of the most brutal punishments are psychological, yes?"

Lee acknowledged what his Nan said, but wasn't too optimistic at the news she was about to impart.

"After planting the story about your death in the *Daily Mail*, the reporter – Theo Greaves, if you remember – pursued the case further.

After interviewing Laura, he found out that not only had the family done awful things to you – but Jon King had done some bad things to Laura too. Remember when we talked about 'shaking the tree'?" Lee nodded again. "Well the tree was well and truly shaken. A case was built and eventually the police raided their home. The house was searched and Jon and Louvaine were arrested. Laura and Jon Jr. were also removed from the home at the same time, pending police investigations and a trial at court." Vivienne read from the notebook. "I am here to tell you that Louvaine was eventually convicted of child abuse relating to you, assaulting a police officer, causing actual bodily harm to a social worker and convicted of neglect in relation to Laura. She is now serving six months in Holloway prison, which is the worst women's prison in England." She didn't look up and Lee only gave half a smile. "After the search of the family home and testimony from Laura, Jon King pleaded guilty to child abuse relating to you, three counts of rape and unlawful sex with a girl under 13, sexual assault, taking an indecent photograph and possession of an indecent photograph of a child. He is now serving fourteen years for his crimes at Long Martin prison in Worcestershire."

Lee frowned at the list of sexual charges Vivienne had reeled off. He thought about asking his nan for more details, but she still remained head down – not allowing him to interject.

"After being removed from the home, Jon Jr. was given up for adoption. He will not be allowed to go back to Louvaine and she has also been pronounced as an unfit mother on her police record and with Social Services." Vivienne looked up at Lee and spoke without reading from the notebook. "As for Laura, she was also permanently removed from the home, and thanks to a nice lady called Lynn Franks, now resides at the Alexandra House Children's Home. She even has your old room and now goes to the local, very ordinary comprehensive school." The corner of Vivienne's mouth turned up into a half-smile as Lee began to giggle – slightly at first and then uncontrollably. "I hoped the irony would tickle you, young man. Time to finish up that coke... we're not done yet!"

END

ABOUT THE ALBUM

As with *Say Goodbye*, this book was always intended to accompany the album of music that was written for it. If you've read the book without having had the chance to listen to the album, I hope you'll take the opportunity to do so. If you have had the chance to listen and enjoy the album, I thank you, and have provided a brief guide to where each song fits into this story.

TRACK 1   LET ME GO

With her desire to test her new found confidence, Laura tries to manipulate her stepfather – which seriously backfires.

Whilst this was recorded with one artist, the song is arranged as a back & forth between Jon and Laura, and explores each of their perspectives after the bathroom scene.

TRACK 2   BE SOMEONE

As Lee's situation changes having met his new parents, he begins to come out of his shell and flourish. He's becoming his original character again and begins to see a future for himself.

Few people escape past difficulties. This song shows that with a little mental resilience, encouragement and love – we can all Be Someone.

TRACK 3   TELL THE WORLD ABOUT YOU

As Laura begins senior school she finds herself unpopular with the girls in her year group. She receives advice to watch and emulate what the popular girls do, which she heeds well. After flirting and seeking the attentions of boys two years her senior, she is intoxicated with her new found confidence and sexuality.

Isn't it thrilling when we become popular or needed for a reason? It's a potent drug that just makes you want to tell the world, fills you with purpose and makes you feel amazing – *while it lasts.*

TRACK 4   I'M A PSYCHO NOW

Nancy is only underestimated by those who truly don't know, or haven't worked for her in the past. Before, during and after World War II, she had learned to become the ruthless hammer her alter-ego represented.

This song represents the harder and vengeful side of humanity... the side we feel when we've been wronged by those closest to us!

TRACK 5   AND I WONDER

Laura has read the headline about the death of Lee King. Once her brother, the responsibility for his demise weighs heavy on her conscience as she walks to school – fearing for her soul.

Regret: a feeling of sadness, repentance, or disappointment over an occurrence or something that one has done or failed to do. Will Laura end up in heaven or hell?

TRACK 6   5:50 AM

The police, social workers and press prepare, getting into position to raid the home of the King family.

This sythwave instrumental serves as a backdrop as all hell breaks loose when Jon and Louvaine are arrested.

TRACK 7   ANOTHER LIGHT

Still grieving about the news of his son's death, David is now given the news of his mother's tortuous death – he is emotionally shattered.

This song reflects that sorrow one feels when losing that one person who means everything to you.

TRACK 8   GIVEN UP

Having ended up separated from her family and placed in care, Laura writes to her mother to ask for forgiveness.

When you've done everything you can do to seek forgiveness for a wrongdoing but are still rebuked, it is not wise to remain a beggar. This song is about cutting toxic ties in ones' life and moving on.

TRACK 9   IN FRONT OF ME

With news having travelled that Nancy has been murdered and Lee having some inside knowledge, he is overwhelmed to see his nan is truly alive when she arrives at Chris & Debs' home.

Take your mind back. Do you remember that heartfelt jolt when you were reunited with someone you truly missed?

ABOUT THE AUTHOR

Leveraging the resounding success of his debut masterpiece, '*Say Goodbye*', autolemy® has consistently enthralled readers with his enchanting storytelling prowess. The release of his eagerly awaited second novel, '*Assisting Fate*', has served as a powerful affirmation of his standing in the literary realm. This enthralling sequel not only met but greatly surpassed the lofty expectations set by his inaugural work. autolemy has unequivocally established himself as a maestro of narrative, adroitly crafting intricate plots and indelible characters that resonate with the harmonious notes of a musical symphony, etching vivid imagery into the hearts and minds of his avid readers and listeners alike.